J. M. Simpson

Beautiful Rienzi

the secret vendetta

J. M. Simpson

Beautiful Rienzi
the secret vendetta

ISBN/EAN: 9783743377073

Manufactured in Europe, USA, Canada, Australia, Japa

Cover: Foto ©Andreas Hilbeck / pixelio.de

Manufactured and distributed by brebook publishing software (www.brebook.com)

J. M. Simpson

Beautiful Rienzi

THE SELECT SERIES.

A WEEKLY PUBLICATION.

Devoted to Good Reading in American Fiction.

SUBSCRIPTION PRICE, $3.00 PER YEAR.   No. 11.—MAY 14, 1890.

Copyrighted, 1890, by Street & Smith.

Entered at the Post Office, New York, as Second-Class Matter.

BEAUTIFUL RIENZI;

OR,

THE SECRET VENDETTA.

BY

ANNIE ASHMORE

AUTHOR OF

"The Bride Elect," etc.

NEW YORK:

STREET & SMITH, Publishers,

31 Rose Street.

PREFACE.

If, in these records of a life which was held in the chains of rankling secrecy, there is too much of shadow, and too little of the smiling day, remember that the clouded life was dear to her who writes these pages; and if the pen lingers too fondly, too ardently, as oft it may, on her whose sorrows were sublime, because sublimely hidden from the eyes of love, remember with pity the Southern heart which drank deeply of icy woes, and had to learn the hard lesson of patience.

THE AUTHOR.

The Select Series.

A SEMI-MONTHLY PUBLICATION

DEVOTED TO GOOD READING IN AMERICAN FICTION.

PRICE 25 CENTS EACH.   *FULLY ILLUSTRATED.*

Latest Issues.

No. 37—IN LOVE'S CRUCIBLE, by Bertha M. Clay.
No. 36—THE GIPSY'S DAUGHTER, by Bertha M. Clay.
No. 35—CECILE'S MARRIAGE, by Lucy Randall Comfort.
No. 34—THE LITTLE WIDOW, by Julia Edwards.
No. 33—THE COUNTY FAIR, by Neil Burgess.
No. 32—LADY RYHOPE'S LOVER, by Emma Garrison Jones.
No. 31—MARRIED FOR GOLD, by Mrs. E. Burke Collins.
No. 30—PRETTIEST OF ALL, by Julia Edwards.
No. 29—THE HEIRESS OF EGREMONT, by Mrs. Harriet Lewis.
No. 28—A HEART'S IDOL, by Bertha M. Clay.
No. 27—WINIFRED, by Mary Kyle Dallas.
No. 26—FONTELROY, by Francis A. Durivage.
No. 25—THE KING'S TALISMAN, by Sylvanus Cobb, Jr.
No. 24—THAT DOWDY, by Mrs. Georgie Sheldon.
No. 23—DENMAN THOMPSON'S OLD HOMESTEAD.
No. 22—A HEART'S BITTERNESS, by Bertha M. Clay.
No. 21—THE LOST BRIDE, by Clara Augusta.
No. 20—INGOMAR, by Nathan D. Urner.
No. 19—A LATE REPENTANCE, by Mrs. Mary A. Denison.
No. 18—ROSAMOND, by Mrs. Alex. McVeigh Miller.
No. 17—THE HOUSE OF SECRETS, by Mrs. Harriet Lewis.
No. 16—SIBYL'S INFLUENCE, by Mrs. Georgie Sheldon.
No. 15—THE VIRGINIA HEIRESS, by May Agnes Fleming.
No. 14—FLORENCE FALKLAND, by Burke Brentford.
No. 13—THE BRIDE ELECT, by Annie Ashmore.
No. 12—THE PHANTOM WIFE, by Mrs. M. V. Victor.
No. 11—BADLY MATCHED, by H. ...

The above works are for sale by all ... O. McCORMICK, Gen. Pass. Agt.
address, postpaid, on receipt of p' ... ay

STRE

P. O. Box 2734.   York.

THE SECRET SERVICE SERIES,

(S. S. S.)

Comprises the Best Detective Stories by the Best Authors.

Issued Monthly.   PRICE, 25 CENTS EACH.   Fully Illustrated.

☞ This series is enjoying a larger sale than any similar series ever published. None but American Authors are represented on our list, and the Books are all **Copyrighted**, and can be had only in the SECRET SERVICE SERIES. **Bound in Handsome Lithograph Covers.**

For sale by all Newsdealers, or will be sent by mail, post-paid, on receipt of price, 25 cents each, by the Publishers, STREET & SMITH, 25-31 Rose Street, New York.

BEAUTIFUL RIENZI.

CHAPTER I.

WHAT I FIND IN MY NEW EXISTENCE.

> " At first it seemed a little speck,
> And then it seemed a mist;
> It moved, and moved, and took at last
> A certain shape, I wist."—COLERIDGE.

Since my earliest childhood, I, Ivanilla Rienzi, had lived with my grandmother, in Italy, who had claimed me because I bore her name. I was the second daughter of her younger son, and would inherit her property. My father early in life had left his native land, gone to America, and literally carved for himself a fortune as master sculptor and architect in New York. Here he had married a sweet, gentle wife, and made his home; here his two daughters had been born, and from here, fourteen years ago, I, the youngest, then a tiny imp of four years, little red eyes and blurred, had been trotted down to a great puffing steamer, by the side of a stately grandmamma, who called me *"Poverina mia,"* (my poor little one) and bade me kiss mamma good-by, for I was going away to a pretty home among grapes and oleanders. But I did not care for these visionary glories, but began to cry when I saw a pale, sad face which was the dearest on earth to me, and fastened my little fists like crabs in her beautiful hair, for then I was passionately pressed to her soft bosom, then borne, plunging wildly, to a certain cot, where I fell fast asleep, and so missed a last sight of the motherling.

Years of childhood were spent under the sunny skies of Italy. I had grown to love my grandparent with all the force of my heart. My studies were all under private tuition; my world lay in my grandparent and our lovely home by the Venetian waters. All fervor, romance, spontaneous passion, I awaited the hand which should open the page of life to me.

It came—the hand of death.

My beloved grandmamma slowly, calmly faded, and at the same time my mother, whom I could scarce remember, was sent from her bleak American home to revive in the milder Venice. She it was who stayed me in my great affliction, closed the aged one's eyes, and presided by the dying bed with gentle cheer. She it was who first directed my sick heart to the home across the sea, and to the unknown sister who waited to welcome me.

And so my good uncle, Signor Andrea Rienzi, who was a bachelor and a great man in Venice, took care of me, and brought me away from loved Italia and my invalid mother to Liverpool, where he put me on board a steamer, and under the care of a learned doctor of something, who was a philosopher and afraid of women, and so shipped me for my new home.

Behold me then at the wharf in New York, sitting very impatiently in the ladies' saloon of the steamship A————— waiting for some one to come and claim me.

Other ladies had put on their prettiest dresses, and donned their sweetest smiles, and had gone away with husbands, fathers, brothers, and guardians, only giving a hasty hand-shake to friends who had been made in the two weeks at sea, and who would be forgotten in two weeks more.

And as I frowned at Ivanilla in the mirror, a figure stood in the door-way of the saloon looking at me; and as the door swayed to and fro she held it open with one arched hand, while a smile half of doubt and wistfulness dawned on her lips.

And her face was beautiful as a dream, her eyes blue as the rippling waters of the Brenta far away in my sunny Venezia, her figure tall and regal like a Cleopatra's, and her charms in their affluence were scarce of this bat-like world, where dusky wrong clouds all things.

"Is this—yes, it must be Iva!" said the lady, tremulously.

"Heavens!" cried I, "are you my sister, Isolina?"

Her arms were round me by this time; she was embracing me; my head dropped on her bosom—she was mine. All this loveliness, this grace was mine; this yielding bosom was swelling for me, the tie of blood bound us together— *my sister!*"

I clung to the exquisite vision and wept with joy as I inwardly resolved to deserve the love of so peerless a being; and while I was looking up at my sister's perfect face, the father came in, grand as a Roman emperor—dark, kingly, soulful—and folded his swarthy, sun-ripened child in his arms, as the sweeter vision had done before; and we all laughed and wept together, though we were but strangers.

We gayly recovered Professor Eustacio from a trance of philosophy at the open hatchway of the luggage-hold, and took him home with us in a rattling carriage which passed through scenes strange to eyes accustomed to the creeping waters and gondolas of the water-city; and my happy father led me by the hand up through a square garden into the tall mansion, where the dark polished door was thrown open and I was ushered into a hall of lofty magnificence, where a low-toned waiter bowed and welcomed Miss Ivanilla "home."

And who so radiant and sprightly as this new companion of mine, when she had taken me up into her own pretty dressing-room, and ensconced me in a deep downy tipping-chair, which swayed me gently back and forth with a dream-like motion. How she laughed and fondled me when I made known at last the thoughts that were in my burning soul.

"Isolina," I murmured, timidly ; " you are the loveliest being I ever saw. You are so much fresher and fairer than grandmother Rienzi, though she was fair in my eyes—and even Signor Frinli, who was forty-eight, and very handsome, and a divine music-master, seems gross beside you. You must be the Queen of Beauty in this city, and have many to adore you. Will you care for my love too ? I am eighteen, you know, and not a child, and I think my heart never was so moved as it has been by you. Will you let me love you, my sister ?"

"Oh, you darling—yes!"

She was unlocking little golden trinkets to show me, but she came without them and knelt before me, with her bright eyes raised.

" We must be thorough sisters," she said, softly. " We must love and trust each other as we love and trust no one else ; we must let nothing come between our hearts."

"Beautiful one," I murmured, "each thought of my soul shall be yours—each wish of your heart, my prayer— and you to me the same. Is it not so ?"

And suddenly, with a richly carmine cheek, she clasped me close, and her heart thrilled with a nameless emotion, whose intensity was all unknown by me.

On the 6th of October, 1862, I arrived at my new home, and commenced life in New York.

I soon was introduced to my sister's gay friends, and I found she was the belle of her circle ; none so regal, none so lovely as she. At ball and concert, reunion or drive, she reigned supreme, by right of her intellectual powers and matchless loveliness.

They called her " The Beautiful Rienzi," and my head was almost turned with triumph. I worshiped her with the fanatical enthusiasm of a devotee, and more deeply as the days went on, and often my father laughed and said that Isolina was my first love. She may have been. With secret exultation I watched the uniform firmness with which she checked the devotion of her many admirers, the serene simplicity with which she passed through adulations, as if unconscious of them, and brought her deepest tenderness to me.

The shimmering dusk was mine to creep close to my sister and drink in her soft perfections, like fondest lover, and in these sweet thought hours I learned to ponder something.

Though her eyes were clear and open as an infant's, to my vivid glances, though her lips responded with the ready laughter or the gentle sigh to my varying moods, still sometimes I felt as if her heart were hidden from me, as if her thoughts were not always explained to me, or her moods translatable.

Why those flushes, sweet and strange, sweeping over her tender face when silence fell between us ? Why those wistful sighs, which lighted that bosom soft as cygnet-down, even in the midst of my merriest fantasies of talk ? My hands might clasp hers longingly—my eyes appeal, but those smiling lips spoke not but by caresses ; the fire glanced out and rouged the tender cheek and brought the amber hair into flame-like halos, and she looked like some gorgeous fire-spirit, and like the spirit, her soul was beyond my reach.

Yet I was loving her more and more; my heart of passion was surging to its depths. I shall love that bright vision with its fair face of supreme beauty and its halo of fire-bronzed hair, forever! These days with my beautiful sister were the happiest of my life.

*   *   *   *   *   *   *

On the last day of October we sat together at the window of the drawing-room, looking down into the busy street.

Her arm was around me, and I was leaning against her chair.

As gayly I spoke to her, the hand I toyed with closed vehemently; she bent forward, and her face was hidden from me, but her dainty ear flamed up a sudden scarlet.

"Ah, ha!" I cried, with sportive triumph, "who thus moves my beautiful lady's heart? Is the conqueror coming?"

She turned as I jested. I had thought her animated by joy, but this seemed no joy. Her blue eyes were dark and stern, her brow inflexible; the flush was not of pleasure, but of anger.

"My sweet one!" I exclaimed, "what has grieved you? Tell *me*, my sister."

She did not answer. She drew me forward and kissed my brow. It was a hasty, eager kiss; then she advanced to the door as if to fly, and shrank back when her hand was on the lock. The door opened; a name was announced by the servant, which I failed to catch, and a gentleman entered.

Dazzled by the glory of the clouds I had been watching, I could not discern at first the visitor's face. I saw him seize her hand and bend to kiss it. I saw her draw it from him, and tower before him a moment in inflexible silence; then she turned to me, and the golden sunlight fell on her face, which was troubled and distressed.

"I beg your pardon!" exclaimed the gentleman, in a

low, musical voice. "I was not aware of the presence of another lady."

"My sister Ivanilla—Mr. Cecil Beaumont," said Isolina.

On the instant a small, strong hand was clasping mine, a pair of fiery, red-brown eyes leaped into mine. I raised my eyes to a face which was pale, and fierce, and resolute, despite its boyish youthfulness. And as I read what was expressed in the restless face, I saw behind its mystic beauty a great sorrow in the past, or in the future, which threw a chill weight upon my soul.

"Is this the foreign sister? They say she is a goddess of romance; all heart, nerve, sympathies. What then will your sympathy do for me? Behold me, a poor wretch, who lives on his wits—ay, an author—and an exile, in a land of enmity, condemned to win bread from hands which helped to dig his father's grave. Behold me, a victim to the Queen of Beauty, kneeling to a heart of ice. Come now, do you pity me?"

"Mr. Beaumont!" broke in my sister's voice, so coldly and with such scorn that I scarce could believe I heard my mild-hearted Isolina.

He turned to her and took a quick step toward her with such hunger, wild and yearning, in his eyes that one could on the spot discern the reason of his being there.

"Shall I go away?" I whispered to my sister.

She bowed her head, though I hoped she would detain me.

It was he, the visitor, who caught my hand as I passed, and pressed it to his lips.

"Plead for me!" he whispered, once more transfixing me with those fiery, red-brown eyes.

I shivered and retreated, my heart throbbing with dismay. The deepening sunset smote my sister's face, and filled the room with glory. I turned softly to the door, glided out and stood in the hall alone.

Darkness filled that face and room when next I looked upon them; the shadow had slid within the portal, and our days of girlish happiness were over.

CHAPTER II.

I CHASE A PHANTOM, AND FAIL TO FIND IT.

" It speaks of storm and tempest;
Wild horror and despair;
And its numbers chill the life-blood,
For the dirge of DEATH is there!"—ANON.

I got my hat and paced up and down the gravel walk before the house. The evening was chilly, and the beds of purple petunias and black pansies were bathed in a white hoarfrost, the forerunner of that winter I could not remember.

I drew my scarf yet tighter round my shoulders, though I felt no cold; my blood was burning, my cheeks fevered with the strange prophetic dread which had come upon me; dismay was at my heart.

An hour passed by—to me a long and anxious one; the sun sank like a rocket, in an inflamed haze, behind the houses; I looked up fixedly now at the drawing-room windows where broad gleams of firelight spurted out between the curtains; I went to the stone parapet by the garden gate and looked longingly down the street for my father; I was lonely, thus shut out from my sister by a stranger. I was terrified, and crept back to the door.

At the foot of the steps I met Mr. Cecil Beaumont.

"Ah! the dark eyed lady!" he said, laying his hand lightly on mine. "Do you know that I have never heard your voice yet? Come—you are going to befriend me?"

"Signor, what can I do for you? I would willingly make you less wretched if I had the power."

"Why do you think I'm wretched, my little one?"

"Your eyes—alas! there is a tragedy of woe in them; I shudder with grief as I behold them."

"It has not come yet," he answered, with a hollow laugh; "but it is coming. She, 'The Beautiful Rienzi,' will share it—do you hear?—if this little hand of yours does not try to ward it back!"

His wild, desperate face became pale; I recoiled and looked at him in terror.

"What can *I* do, Mr. Beaumont?" I exclaimed.

"You can be my advocate; she loves you, and will listen. You can see that no interloper comes between us—and when they do, apprise me."

"Be a spy, sir?"

"Pshaw! a spy on your own sister, Miss Ivanilla? That is impossible—the sisters hide nothing from each other."

"Or from their lovers? Instruct me; I have not learned your American usages."

"You refuse, then, to plead for the hapless refugee? You laugh at the agony of a heart sensitive as your own, and writhing beneath sorrows of which scorned love is the crowning one. You turn from your countryman and refuse to help him?"

"My countryman? I never turn from an Italian, sir."

"My mother is an Italian, and I inherit all her fire—with but little of the bravery of my Virginian sire. I can bear poverty, exile, and toil, my friend, but I cannot bear to lose the heart I love so wildly."

"Perhaps she loves another, sir."

He flung away my hand; his face petrified with jealousy. He put his hand to his heart, as if I had stunned him, and eyed me desperately.

"I have no proof for such a supposition," I said, my heart aching for him; "I do not think my sister's affection is engaged to any one; but how else could one construe her coldness to you? Courage, my friend; I will sound the waters of my Isolina's soul, and if an image is painted there, you must be content to ride away, asking no questions, as a true knight should. If not, Iva shall paint thee there in brightest colors; I will be your friend, Mr. Beaumont."

He caught my hand and kissed it ardently. A wondrous change was in his face; its hard, desperate look was gone, and it spoke but of sweet tenderness; those melting eyes fixed upon me a wistful gratitude, too pure, too sincere for treachery.

"I will dare to cherish hope, then, with so resistless a pleader as you, lady," he murmured, gently. "Oh! be my friend, or I shall not answer for myself!"

Quickly he vanished down into the street, and I fled in the gathering gloom back to the house.

The ruby firelight alone filled the drawing-room with a somber light, funereal and uncertain; my sister's figure,

tall and slender, was sharply defined by the flickering jets
as she stood on the hearth with her back to me.   There was
something in her attitude which struck me with an unde-
fined feeling of disaster.   My heart began to flutter—I ran
in, and stood side by side with her, looking up into her
face.

That face, in which I gazed, was pale and perplexed;
wonder, or terror, or remorse, had contracted the arching
brows until they met in two depressed curves; her dark
eyes, questioning, affrighted, fixed themselves upon the
crumbling embers, as if to read a dreaded destiny; her
bosom heaved with coming tears, as yet restrained.

"What grieves you so?" I whispered ardently.   "My
darling, tell your sister everything."

She turned and clasped me to her heart with a long,
shuddering sigh.

"What shall I tell you, Ivanilla?" she murmured.

"Your whole heart—everything.   Why has the coming
of Cecil Beaumont affrighted you?   Who has stolen the
love away that the poor young Southerner covets?"

She listened to me in dread silence—she scarcely
breathed—her pulse seemed suspended.   Again that shuddering sigh rent her bosom; but she did not speak.   I threw
back my head and looked at her, and she turned her face
away.

"Alas! you hide your heart from Ivanilla!" I moaned.
"You have thoughts which you never told to me!   Tell
me—*tell me*, my beautiful—you have a lover?"

"No!" she cried, in a tone which startled me.   Her sadness had vanished—her face vibrated into an incontrollable
smile, sudden and strange; she met my gaze, flushed, and
vailed my eyes with her velvet palm a moment.   When she
released me, she was calm again; that rapture, or agitation,
had passed away, and I was shut out after all.

"Who is Cecil Beaumont?" I asked, after a long pause.

"He is a gentleman from Virginia—a clever author, they
say.   You appeared much delighted with that book,
"Veronico"—that was his."

"He has a grand genius, then.   Pity you could not love
such a soul!   And he *does* adore you!"

"I am very, very sorry to be forced to believe that!" said
my sister, gravely.

"But why?   His character is not——"

"His character is blameless, Iva, so far as human eye can judge. He is a most exemplary person, and a pattern of filial affection, they say. He supports his mother by his writings. Oh, me!"

This last exclamation seemed wrung from her in sudden distress; she sighed heavily and wearily.

"How long have you known the Southerner?" I asked.

"I made his acquaintance last summer—at Saratoga," she answered, in a sinking voice. "He had just been liberated from prison. He was captured with a company of Confederates some three months before and brought up North. He was the son of a wealthy Virginia planter, who put himself at the head of a regiment when the war commenced, and fell in one of the first battles. The plantation was burned, and the estate destroyed; Mrs. Beaumont forced to fly and hide with her slaves in the swamps, with Cecil as a protector. A small remnant of Colonel Beaumont's company gathered round his son, and Cecil became a noted guerrilla and a scourge to our men, whenever opportunity occurred. At length swamp-fever carried off a third of them, and the rest were captured in the Chickahominy Swamp, the skeletons of themselves. Most of them were exchanged; but there was no one to take interest in young Beaumont or his mother; they were sent North and at last liberated. Young Cecil came to Saratoga, an invalid, and there he met me, and without any design on my part—not the slightest, Iva—became too much attached to me. It is very false of him—he is treating very cruelly an amiable young lady who was very kind to him when he was sick and in prison. Her father was governor of the prison, and mainly by her influence the young soldier was liberated. He sought her hand, and was accepted—poor child! her disinterested love scarcely merits such returns."

"What! is he so false as that?" I exclaimed; "but who could help loving you, Isolina? You are so beautiful and grand!"

She smiled rather sadly, and resumed:

"Miss Meredith spent last winter at New York, and a sweeter creature I think I never met. She became a warm friend of mine; and you can understand how painful it is for me to be the cause of wrong to her. I have sent the inconstant young man back to her once already, and I fondly hoped that his sudden passion would pass away, and she would never be pained by knowing of it.

"And this is all the reason of your distress? You love no one else?" I exclaimed, with eager interest.

Again that flash of mysterious agitation crossed her face.

"Who put such a thought in your brain?" she returned, sadly. "I have no other love—you must believe me, Ivanilla."

I did believe her; a new thought occurred to me.

Perhaps she loved the poor young refugee in her secret heart, but sternly crushed the feeling for the sake of her friend. And if so, what a heart my beautiful sister had! Ah, what a grand soul!

I admired her more than ever—I contemplated her inflexible sense of honor—I glowed with enthusiasm.

But meantime she had told me nothing.

There was a masked ball that night, and our father would have us go—in character, too, as he was never tired of showing the contrast between his two daughters.

There moved "The Beautiful Rienzi," pale, serene as a star, in the velvet and diamonds, the lace ruffles and pointed diadem of Mary, the lovely Queen of Scots. Here skimmed the little swarthy Italian peasant, in her short petticoat, velvet bodice, and basket of grapes on her arm; a very Momus of laughter, as an Edinburgh fishwife, with a crab at her back, jostled her and shouted, "Caller-ou!" There were Turks and Dervishes, Chinese, Monks, Quakers, Indians, Sultans, Stars, Nights, Mornings, Peacocks. Birds of Paradise, Ravens, even Mount Vesuvius—which was represented by a lady in a pointed dress with flame-colored feathers in her head.

Minerva took me under her charge—a friend of my sister, and a great favorite of mine, because of her wit and sprightliness—one Miss Belle Cranstown, who shall hereafter be more fully set forth in this story; and under her wing I had a most exhaustive time, laughing at her sallies and being introduced to some fierce-looking Moors who were scouring the room for their Desdemonas.

Once the beauteous Mary Stuart passed me with a loving smile, and my merry friend Belle burst into a laugh at the Scottish queen's companion, a resolute-looking lady, with a furious ruff and long, stiff bodice.

"Brave Queen Bess!" she jibed, "twist the cousin round your finger. That's sister Lou, my dear, and I overheard a

Trappist telling the Pope in the corner there that the lady suited the character very well. Rather hard on either Lou or Queen Elizabeth—I sha'n't say which."

I was still looking with proud eyes at my lovely sister, whose calm perfections in her stately costume were absolutely dazzling, when suddenly she swung round from her lady-companion and gazed with a slowly deepening flush of wild emotion at a holly-wreathed pillar, beside which a figure was standing with folded arms. A mask shielded the face, and the nodding plume of Napoleon's hat cast a shadow across the mask, but the figure, clad *a la* the victorious conqueror, was tall and princely in its proportions, and there was a certain forlorn grandeur in the attitude that suggested aptly enough my lively friend's next remarks:

> " ' But one—a lone one 'mid the throng,
> Seemed reckless all of dance or song!'

as Mrs. Hemans says. What a gathering of the regal element! And what a coincidence! The Queen of Scots rushing to speak to poor Bony in the Island of St. Helena! But who is he? That envious mask hides all!"

Who was he? I could not tell. My sister had shimmered forward with eyes sparkling and hands outstretched, in eager, tremulous joy.

"It is—surely it must be my victor!" she murmured.

The figure shifted; my heart sank at the low, suppressed voice.

"Your majesty looked for a Bothwell, then? Your Bothwell tarries long, my queen, at his hermitage—better turn a thought to those who love your majesty faithfully."

"Sir," said my sister, shrinking back, "I thought you some one else. You speak in character, but I understand the taunt, and do not heed it. Mr. Cecil Beaumont forfeits even my respect, when he deals in taunts."

The exile bowed his head in silence; closer and closer I had advanced, leaving my companion in the midst of a group; I was now beside my sister, and I clasped her hand warmly. Napoleon bowed to the peasant.

"Have you forgotten—my little pleader?" he murmured in Italian, bending toward me.

"Come away!" said Isolina, coldly; she drew my hand closer.

"I beg one grape from the little peasant beauty's basket

—one smile to lighten my weary banishment," said the fallen conqueror, lightly. "Will my countrywoman refuse?" he added, in a lower tone.

I offered him my basket, and whispered with reproach:

"Signor, you did not tell me of your broken troth when you asked me to plead for you. Go back to your true love—leave her not for ambition or inconstancy."

Then I wheeled round and went away with Isolina. We did not stay long after that; the peerless face of the Scottish queen was grave, her eyes searching and weary; ere long we came to our father and asked him to take us home. Cavaliers unnumbered thronged round us in the vestibule; one small, strong hand caught mine and pressed it before the carriage door was shut, and I found a slip of paper in my palm, on which I quietly read:

"Be my friend, Ivanilla, or I cannot answer for my doom."

Once more the night came on; the storm shrieked fiercely.

"Heaven save the poor mariner!" said my father, who came home early to keep his lonely daughter company.

At five o'clock it was almost dark; you would have thought there were a thousand fairies in the air, had you dared to put your head out. The very house was rocking in the storm.

"Keep papa company while I dress for dinner," said Isolina, with her watch for the fiftieth time in her hand.

She left the drawing-room and went up stairs. I did not like her manner—it had startled me—it was so unnatural. I took up my harp and laid it away again. I could not play—I could not keep my father company. I slipped out and went up stairs.

My sister was standing at the window; Sophie, the maid, was taking hair brushes out of a dressing-case to commence her work.

"I would like to dress as usual with you; I couldn't wait with papa," I began.

She turned round and came toward me, and smoothed my cheek fondly with her hand.

"How—how pale you are, dearest! how cold your hand is! Why have you stood by that window so long? the storm has affrighted you!"

A tornado of rain and sleet drowned my voice; she

looked with an intent gaze toward the window, as if appalled.

"It is terrible!" she murmured. "But I've—I think I will go to my own room for a while; don't wait for me—I will join you at dinner. Sophie, dress Miss Ivanilla's hair."

"My darling, are you ill?" I cried.

"No," she turned her troubled face away; "I don't feel very well, that is true, but I shall be all right in an hour, if I am not disturbed."

"We shall not disturb you. Sophie, come into my room and dress me there; my sister is going to sleep."

The girl gathered up my dress and toilet requisites; we shut the dressing-room door behind us, and adjourned to my pretty bedroom, where our noise would not be heard.

My heart was chill and heavy; I felt shut out and held aloof, though my own hand had done it.

"Shall I do your hair now, miss?"

"Wait, we have an hour yet, and I can dress in ten minutes. Don't molest me."

The girl lingered about, waiting my mood; she took her sewing, and stirred up the fire.

"Shall I light the gas now, Miss Ivanilla?"

I had remonstrated with Isolina for standing at the window looking at the storm, but I was there myself, and weeping bitterly.

"Go away, Sophie!" I cried, sharply. "I told you not to molest me. I will ring if I want you."

I heard her go away, and the coal-fire burned drowsily, until the room was dark. My brow was on the window-pane, my eyes drearily fixed on the strip of garden beneath; the lamps on either side of the gate flickered like lanterns in a storm. I saw a woman gliding down between the black shrubs to the gate; the hail and the hurricane were beating her garments about; she battled resolutely against the blinding rain, but her figure was too slender and delicate for such rude warfare; she was caught up and whirled against the great stone parapet, and she held on there with her two clinging arms until there was a lull, while the storm-king regained his breath, then she opened the gate and drifted before the tempest down the street.

And this woman, out in the storm, defenseless in the

coming night, alone in the city streets! Great Heaven, this was Isolina!

I dropped the curtain and went to my sister's bedroom door; it was locked. I knocked once, twice. I thought there was a rustle within, and my breath thickened. No, it was but the hail rattling on her window.

I entered the dressing-room, it was empty and dark. I crept back to my room, shaking and sobbing, and threw myself on the floor to weep; the storm, without, was but a summer zephyr to the storm within my heart.

I now saw that she had a life apart from me—that I knew nothing of the girl I called my sister, and loved so fondly. She had her experiences which I must not share, which her father, who doted on her, must not know. Perhaps some mysterious ruin would come and swallow her up, and leave us bereft of her forever!

Then I pictured her purity, her goodness. Oh! we must not leave our loved one. I sprang up and hurried on a long cloak, resolved in my frenzy, to pierce the mystery. I locked my door, sped down stairs, slipped open the front door and ran out into the storm.

Ah! what a shrieking blast! These pitiless arrows of forked sleet, how would she survive them? In the heart of a resistless deluge of rain and wind, I was swept down the gravel walk to the gate; like her I clung to the stone parapet; as she had done, I waited for a lull, to open the gate and be whirled down the street. I would run with the speed of the wind and overtake her and bring her home, or weep until she let me go with her.

But when I turned my sad, half blinded eyes upon the home I was leaving, the clear ring of the first dinner-bell smote my ear. Was it possible? An hour gone by already? I could not overtake her now—she had been an hour in the storm. Were my eyes dazzled with the wind, or did I see a light pouring from the window of the locked bedroom? The heavy gate clanged from my passive hand—I gazed wildly up. A shadow was moving back and forward before the window, and now a blaze of light was visible from the dressing-room which I had left in darkness.

Was I in a miraculous dream?

I flew back to the house, stole up stairs, and gained my room. Sophie was knocking at my door and standing in the dark.

"Go, Sophie—I am here," I said in a sinking voice; the tempest had almost choked me.

"Oh, miss, I've been knocking, and knocking."

"Very well, I am here now. You can go away, Sophie. I intend to dress myself."

"Miss, there's not five minutes—the dressing-bell rang long ago."

"Go, Sophie."

I stood aside to let her pass, fearing she might touch my wet clothes. When she was half way down stairs I unlocked my door, flung off my dripping cloak, and lit the gas.

My hands were shaking with cold and terror. I could scarcely unbind my heavy black hair; sleet was among its coils, glistening and rippling down my neck. I stood before the mirror in a trance of bewilderment, looking at myself.

Heavens! was that wild vision Ivanilla? I scarcely knew that white, scared face, these horrid lurid eyes.

"Miss Iva, it's two minutes past six, and dinner is served," said Sophie from the door.

She came in, and I felt her looking at my back and all my dark rippling hair. I heard her gasp with wonder, but she made no remark. I turned round and she gasped again. She was looking at my face.

"Dress my hair, Sophie," I murmured; "and, my girl, you must see nothing—nothing, you understand? Sophie, be prudent!"

She set a chair for me before the fire, and put a footstool beneath my feet.

"Miss, let me get you a glass of wine!" she whispered.

I looked her scoffingly in the face and laughed.

"No, you silly child," I said; but my laugh was a ghastly deception.

All the while she was arranging my hair I was trying to frame a question, but in vain.

Then I heard the dressing-room door open, and a silken robe brush past my door, and I felt my cold face flame sudden scarlet.

"Is that Isolina?" I cried.

"Oh, yes, miss," answered Sophie, catching her breath at my abruptness.

She came toward me with my slippers in her hand, but I sprang to the door, and rushed down to join my sister.

The silken robe had vanished. I fell with force against the butler in the lower hall, and jingled all his glasses together.

"I beg your pardon, Marks. Is my sister in the diningroom?"

"Just gone in, missy. My! be you ill, Miss Ivanilla?"

He looked agape in my face, and I had to pass in, with the wild expression still unsubdued, to avoid him.

Isolina presided in our mother's place. Her head was turned from the door. She was speaking in a low, composed voice to my father. The hand which held the glass of wine toward my father was steady as ever, her tone serene and soft.

Could this be the mad phantom whom I saw fighting with the storm?

I slid into my place and watched her. I forgot to eat —to move. I was waiting for those blue eyes to show themselves.

"Iva—are you well, child?"

My father's voice gave me a great start. It seemed to come from a hundred miles away, and pierce my ear. The blue eyes were lifted at last with a quick alarm. My sister looked across at me in wonder. and those eyes were quite steady and tearless.

"See how excessively pale she is, Isolina—good gracious!"

Then they both rose with one accord. I saw them advancing. I shrieked and tried to evade the sudden blackness, and then—I knew no more!

<hr />

CHAPTER III.

IN WHICH I FIND THE DISADVANTAGE OF NOT BEING CLAIRVOYANT.

> "But there sings on a sudden a passionate cry,
> There is some one dying or dead!"—TENNYSON.

In the midst of my wonder I had fainted.

When I recovered I was in my sister's arms in my own bedroom, my father bending over me, with anxiety depicted in every lineament, and I was almost suffocated with the smell of *eau de cologne.*

"Poor little pet! Are you better now?" asked my father.

"What was it, dear?" said my father, tenderly.

"I don't know; I am not sick," I said, raising myself to see my sister.

She was holding my head on her arm, her countenance was calm and mild, but a curious flush was on one cheek, while the other was quite pale.

"Rest a while. You shall not go down stairs to-night," she murmured, kindly. "I am going to sit with you here."

Our father stood for a while looking at us in rueful silence, then went away and left us together.

"What have you been doing, Iva?" she whispered. "Sophie tells me your cloak, which she has hung in the wardrobe, is drenched. Those slight boots on your feet are wet and cold as lead. Where have you been, sister?"

To hear *her* ask that question I burst into a paroxysm of tears.

"How can you ask?" I sobbed. "You who were out in the storm too. Where were *you* on this wild night?"

"You must be mad, Iva," said my sister, huskily. "Who told you such a thing? You must get rid of the very idea of it."

"Isolina, I saw you from that window out in the street alone; and I—I went too, that I might share your danger. Oh, sister darling! I will be your slave, only tell me this dreadful secret."

"Share my danger!" she muttered more to herself than to me. "Oh, you poor little girl!"

"Tell me," I implored, vehemently, "why should you fear to impart your trials to one who loves you so devotedly? Am I not fit to be your trusted friend?"

She gently released herself from me and rose, and I rose too, though I was weak and dizzy in my anxiety to keep holding her before me.

"You must forget that you ever saw any one in the storm," she said, looking at me with a pale, set face. "You must utterly bury this night from your memory. As you value the peace of this family, Ivanilla, forget

your suspicions, until I bid them live. Will you promise
me?"

My head sank between my hands—my tears flowed from
a heart that was rent with disappointment as I said:

"I will promise what you wish."

Then she melted into love again—sweetly, tenderly she
nursed me; and as I lay on the sofa watching her slender,
willowy figure, I began to ask myself:

"Could it really have been she whom I saw?"

She was moving about like a person in a dream; that
fixed carmine stain had never gone out of her cheek;
otherwise she was alarmingly pale and apathetic; her
low, even tones might have been spoken by one who had
been mesmerized, for all the feeling that was betrayed in
them.

Such calmness could only be the result of some great nervous excitement.

I saw all this for some time with crawling horror; but
there was a something in her manner which kept me
dumb, and my own heavy head began to absorb my attention.

I thought that long evening would never end; my father
came up two or three times, Sophie hovered about with
anxious eyes, Isolina bent over me and bathed my temples,
and seemed to fill the wild chaos around me. They all were
full of cares for me, and no one looked at my sister, or saw
the ghastly composure that I saw between the spells of fitful
slumbers.

But when all the house had retired for the night and
absolute quiet was reigning, I then being intensely wakeful, a crisis came which showed mine had been no fever-
dream.

Suddenly in the sighing midnight rose a bitter cry, so
wild, so despairing—oh, so abandoned.

I dragged myself from my bed into the outer hall, my
limbs heavy as lead, and crawled to my sister's door.

These cries—these moaning sobs were Isolina's.

"Let me come to you—let me come, sister," I prayed, but
the door was locked. I feebly shook it, but strength failed
me and my head swam round."

"Oh, let me bear your grief with you, my darling," I
wailed; but these awful cries ceased not.

I sank in a heap on the cold, marble floor, and all power

left me for a while. When again I was able to rise, the sobs had died to an awful silence.

The crisis had come, was passed, and that torn heart had borne its grief alone.

I had an indisposition which confined me to my bed a fortnight, having contracted a heavy cold attended by a fever.

One day I was sitting by the dressing-room fire in a deep velvet rocking-chair a convalescent, with a shawl cosily pinned round me, and my empty medicine bottle on the coal-scuttle, the kindest of doctors having announced that it need not be refilled.

Two young ladies had just finished a morning call of congratulation, namely, Miss Cranstown. the quondam English sovereign, and her pretty sister Belle, the goddess; and Sophie was ushering them down stairs.

The elder lady, who, by the way, seemed of a very prying and gossiping disposition, had informed us that Mr. Beaumont had brought out a new novel, which was taking the fashionable circles by storm; that it evidently had modeled its heroine on a certain well-known beauty of our own circle. " Could we guess who now? It was ten times more weird and exciting even then ' Veronica,' and certainly threw a halo of romance over the heroine which might extend into real life. Was it possible we had not seen it? One would have thought the first eyes that looked on it would have been—never mind. Get it. Miss Ivanilla, and judge if you never saw people like Rediviva, and her love-crazed Fate, the Shadow."

As soon as the ladies had gone, I turned eagerly to Isolina expecting some indignant protest from her, on the subject of the new book; instead, however, she quietly ignored the subject by taking up a book of poems and beginning to read to me.

She was on her guard, for beyond the outward signs of care which the last fortnight's confinement might have brought, I saw nothing; her face was calm and placid, her left hand, long and arched, upheld the gilded book in a perfect curve of grace; it was little enough like the dusky hands which were idly clasped in my lap.

At last I missed what I had never noticed that hand divested of before, a curious double ring, with which I used to toy in the dusk evenings when we sat together in the drawing-room ; a broad, exquisitely chased band with two hands clasped to hide a ruby heart, which once I had played with until a spring suddenly was touched and a plain golden hoop was revealed from underneath.

This ring she had never explained to me ; she had once told me that it was not the gift of a lover, and I had asked no more.

The ring no longer sparkled on her hand ; the gift which was not from a lover was gone; I could not say that I had seen it since that night of the storm.

Had she given it back in that secret walk ? Was some tie broken which that double ring had represented? Had it anything to do with the man whose red-brown eyes were a prophecy of coming tragedy?

Oh, dull eyes of mortals! Why can they not pierce the vail of circumstances, and warn the heart from woe?

" This book is too sad for you, Iva. I will read another."

" Oh, let me share it—were it ten times as sad, let me suffer too."

I started at my own words and recalled myself ; she was speaking of the poem, I of the secret. She rose and put away the book. I saw that she understood me, by the sad and furtive look she cast upon me, and I blamed my inadvertence when she kissed me so mournfully.

Youth is the season of elasticity; I soon become strong and well again, and, with health, my spirits flung off much of their depression.

It was a considerable time before my blind eyes were opened to another change in my sister—a change which, like the rest, seemed invisible to all else.

She no longer beamed with loving affection toward our father; her sportive tenderness was all gone; she sat before him with downcast eyes—she watched him with furtive perplexity and sorrow in her sweet face. I have seen her shrink from his paternal caresses, with dismay unspeakable in her manner.

This change, of all, was most incomprehensible; a secret mildew seemed withering the very roots of our family love, and I alone was doomed to see the changes which to others were invisible—a gulf was widening between our bright Isolina and us—hands were dragging her into darkness, and I bound by a promise to keep silence, alone saw the threatening ruin.

About a week after my illness, Isolina came with a letter
which, with a very indignant face, she gave to me to read.
It was from Washington, written in a pretty, girlish hand
and signed "Lillia Meredith," and these were the contents:

"My Dear, Dearest Friend:—I have fallen into trouble, and don't
know any one whom I could fly to sooner than you. I was to have
been married last week to my dear Cecil, but to my alarm and mortification he has asked the time to be postponed, which I have accord-
ingly granted, until his pleasure. He is unaccountably changed of late —
indeed, I have reason to believe he has fallen in love with some lady
in New York, and tired of poor Lillia, from what he has let fall. I am
quite frightened about it, and come to you to know what I shall do.
Could you find out if my suspicions are correct and tell me? I would
go to her and beg her not to take my Cecil from me. Did you
read his last book? Hasn't he genius, eh? But his heroic Rediviva —I am so jealous of her—not one whit like poor little me. And
there's a queer little spirit flits in at the end of it, who, strange to
say, a gentleman who was here the other day, says, is exactly like your
foreign sister, Ivanilla. Such a mystic—so incomprehensible—an
emanation of fervor and fidelity, who brings Rediviva and her Shadow
together like a good fairy. I cried over the book and sat up three
nights to read it; I am so proud of my Cecil, but I hope his brain fancies will not turn him from his Lilly. Write immediately, my dear,
darling Isolina, and tell me what to think. Cecil is going to New
York next week; perhaps you will see him. If so will you put in a
good word for me?   Lovingly thy 'lily flower,'
                                        "Lillia Meredith."

This most girlish epistle being duly read, I handed it back
to Isolina with a curious look.

She was quite calm, if—as sometimes I imagined—she
really loved Cecil Beaumont, remarkably calm, if she really intended giving him up to his betrothed.

"What are you going to do?" I asked.

"I am going to invite Miss Meredith here to spend the
winter with us," she answered, with the same indignant
glitter in her eyes; "and I am going to see that Mr. Beaumont keeps his engagement with her. He cannot persecute me while she is here."

"But if he cannot love her any longer," I pleaded, faltering with dismay, as I remembered Cecil's desperate trust
in my advocacy, "if he loves you so much, you cannot
force back the heart torrents into a worn-out channel. Oh!
dear sister, take him to your love—tell Lillia Meredith the
truth."

"Impossible!"

She turned ashy pale; never had she looked on me so

sternly. I turned away in dismay and prayed that she would not spurn me.

"Don't look so distressed, dear!" she said. "You surely don't expect me to love him when I can't love him. Your anxiety on his account does your heart credit, but, my pet, it is ridiculous. He must marry Lillia Meredith."

"But if he will not?"

She laughed almost hysterically.

"Then he can keep on crying for the moon," was the reply; and she sat down resolutely to her writing-desk.

In a few minutes she had handed me the note she had rapidly penned, and bent over the desk to dash off an address, while I read it.

"DEAR LILY FLOWER:—Make your arrangements and come immediately to me. I wish you to be prepared to spend the winter with us. The change will be beneficial to your health—besides other reasons touching upon your happiness. The contents of your letter I shall discuss when we meet. Your sincere friend,
"I. RIENZI."

I gave back the letter with a deep sigh. I could not help my apprehensions from becoming visible; besides I sympathized with the poor soul who had loved my sister so passionately, and I did not feel half so much for the *fiancee.* Women never do.

"What if, after all, Miss Meredith fails to rebind him?" I asked.

She turned around with the sealed letter in her hand, and met my clouded looks. I cannot describe the sorrow, the remorse, the resolution in my sister's face. She pressed her hand hard upon her breast, and the very soul whose hidden face I longed to see, seemed trembling on her lips.

"Promise to have no secret plots against me in favor of any one!" she cried. "Promise to obey my directions in all that pertains to me!"

"I will obey you now and always!" I sobbed.

"Thanks!" she murmured, softly. Then she restrained herself, and went down stairs to dispatch her letter.

On that day, a gentleman who was the principal of a certain musical club which I shall designate as the "Cybelle Society," called upon my sister and me to prefer a petition.

The members of the society, which consisted of several of the most talented ladies and gentlemen in the city, were

about to hold an amateur concert on behalf of the soldiers
of the battle of——, who were crowded into the hospital at
Washington without the means to cling to their shattered
lives.   The concert would realize, it was hoped, enough to
build another hospital, and command the services of physicians and nurses.   Would the two young ladies, Miss
Isolina Rienzi and her sister, who, it was well known, were
both accomplished musicians, object to render their services at such a short notice, and sing some little piece on
the occasion?"

"What date have you fixed for the concert?" asked my
sister.

"The twenty-ninth of November."

"And this is the 19th.   We should have ten days for
preparation.   If my sister is agreed, we shall be most happy
to be of use, Professor Emerson."

"What does my sister say?" said the professor, turning his pleasant smile upon me; "is she Yankee enough at
heart to brave discomfort for the sake of the gallant fellows
who braved death?"

"She's courageous for anything, if she thinks it's right,"
said my sister, with a fond, proud smile.

The end of it was, that I slipped my hand into Isolina's
and said in a shy voice that I would do whatever she did;
and Professor Emerson went away delighted, promising
to send us our parts immediately, that we might commence
instant practice.

It arrived two hours later—a mammoth roll of music,
and a printed circular of directions, which informed us how
far from a sinecure our part was to be.

I declared it an imposition, when I found myself and
my harp introduced again and again, and declared that
I should fulfill but my promise, which was to sing "one
little song," thereby presenting an utter contrast to my
sister.

She plunged into her allotted part with almost fierce
avidity, and from the hour in which the music arrived,
devoted herself to mastering it.   For three days I scarcely
saw her.

On the fourth day a gentleman called with a note from
Professor Emerson, which laughingly he delivered.   Its
purport was that Mr. Ernest Lindhurst had been appointed as tenor in "La ci darem" (Op. Don Giovanni),

of which Miss Ivanilla had the air, and with her kind permission he would sing the duet with her once or twice before rehearsal.

"I have been introduced to Miss Ivanilla Rienzi before, under widely different auspices," said the gentleman with a smile of keen amusement at my embarrassed looks—"has the Italian peasant forgotten that she was presented to her spiritual father at Mrs. Lesmar's assembly?"

I lifted my eyes and looked at him attentively.

"Are you—were you the Pope?" I asked, with sudden recognition; "did Miss Cranstown introduce you to me as Pio Nono?"

"I consider myself deeply flattered to be again recognized in such different guise," replied the gentleman, in a low voice.

"I am afraid you will be shocked," I said, thrilling with a new and subtle ecstasy, which I feared my very voice would betray; "I am afraid you will wish you had to sing duets with some one else, when I confess that I was meditating a revolt against my part of the programme, and in consequence have not practiced a note."

He arched his handsome eyebrows in pathetic horror.

"You are not going to persist in this rebellion?" he exclaimed. with a ring of disappointment in his tones.

"Are you to be Don Giovanni?" I asked.

"I would have been, were you Zerlina."

"Then I shall be Zerlina. Come; here is the piece; you commence."

We turned to my harp, and began our first duet together.

By the time my new friend had taken his departure, I was almost as enthusiastic about the successs of the Cybelle Society's concert as Isolina.

CHAPTER IV.

TOO FOND BY HALF.

Demetrius—"Oh, why rebuke you him that loves you so? Lay breath so bitter to your bitter foe." MIDSUMMER-NIGHT'S DREAM.

The ten days of preparation passed quickly away, and the evening preceding the momentous 29th found us returning home from our first rehearsal, delighted with the promise of success which the manager had predicted.

A letter and a card were waiting on the dressing-table for us; the letter Sophie gave to Isolina, the card to me.

With some surprise I read the name, " Cecil Beaumont," and turned to the girl.

" Was this card left for me, Sophie?"

" Yes, Miss Iva, and he has been waiting down stairs for you to come back half an hour."

" Shall I go, Isolina?" I asked, timidly.

She looked up from her letter with a rather scornful laugh.

" Poor boy!" she exclaimed; "yes, go, Ivanilla, and prepare him for the bliss which to-morrow brings. Miss Meredith writes that she is coming on the 29th. Do your best to put him in a fitting frame of mind."

" I don't think I can," I cried, despairingly.

But I went down stairs, nevertheless, and reluctantly admitted myself into the drawing-room.

Indeed I was not glad to see Cecil Beaumont. Slowly I advanced until I stood close beside him before he noticed me, and, in a voice of cold constraint, I bade him good-evening."

He started, and turned toward me.

" I could almost despise myself for coming here, but you said you would be my friend, and I have been building upon your friendship," he said, in a low, husky tone.

" It is useless—oh, it is useless," I cried, with a sudden flood of tears. " I have tried and I have failed."

" What does that mean?" he exclaimed, catching my hand, and chafing it between his palms. "Does she love another?"

" I cannot tell," I sobbed; "but this I fear, my friend, my poor Cecil—that she does not love you."

" She does not love me—she does not love me!" he repeated, with a wild smile. " I feel quite stunned—quite stunned!"

How should I begin to prepare his mind for the coming of his betrothed? I felt it to be such a wretched farce that my manner was dry and almost contemptuous as I alluded to the subject.

" You betrothed yourself to a very amiable lady," I said, "you had better—your duty is to go back to her."

" I need not ask if this is the course *your* heart would suggest," he answered, keenly, "I only ask you if it is at all likely that any man who loved your sister would show sanity in forgetting her for another?"

"You should remember the claims of that other," I pursued, grimly. "I think you should put duty before inclination. I know Miss Meredith loves you."

He confronted me with a fierce determination in his eyes. His face seemed slowly hardening into stone.

"Begone with such heartless platitudes!" he hissed. "I come to you with a famished soul, and you feed me with husks that your own eyes mock at! Girl, I swear—I swear to win Isolina!"

"You are a madman!" I uttered, drawing away from him. "Tell me what you are going to do?" I continued, feeling it hard to resist throwing off my sister's colors, and joining him in an attempt to carry her heart in spite of herself.

"I am going to end this wretched game!" he said, vehemently, "and, my little friend, I have sworn to be the victor. I do not think you are displeased."

"No," I admitted, in a low, excited tone, completely carried away with his mystical power by this time; "I think —I am almost sure she must love you, and it is only Miss Meredith's claims which stand in the way——"

A cold hand touched mine and drew me backward. My sister came between us, her eyes full of reproach, her lips quivering.

"What! plotting against me after your promise?" she said, regarding me sadly. "Oh, sister! I thought I could trust you."

The gentle tone cut me to the heart. I could not say one word in self-defense.

She turned to Cecil Beaumont, and fixedly met his passionate gaze.

"You will have it then?" she breathed. "You are determined to drive me to extremity?"

"Yes, 'said Cecil Beaumont.

"Then you will have a final answer to-morrow."

"May I fix the hour, Isolina?"

"Pshaw! Well, as you please, sir."

"To-morrow night after the concert is over, then."

"Too late. Come here before we leave the house."

"I shall certainly come here as you have asked, but as you have given me permission to name an hour for our interview, it shall be after the concert."

" Very well, Mr. Beaumont."

It would be difficult to describe the tone in which this brief colloquy was conducted—the quiet scorn on my sister's part, the implacable defiance of the man. Both were determined, yet one must yield; and which should it be?

" I shall wish you good-evening, then, Miss Isolina," said the gentleman, bowing profoundly.

She inclined her head.

" Good-night, little friend."

He took my hand, and obeying an irresistible impulse, I went with him to the door.

" You think my case hopeless," he muttered rapidly, " but you need not. I have a hold on her which will force her to listen. She will be glad to cling to me—see now if she is not."

With these portentous words he wrung my hand, pressed it to his hot lips, and withdrew.

I came back to Isolina and flung my arms round her.

" You must reconsider the question," I cried, anxiously, "take him if you can—oh, do not rouse his desperate nature any further. He says he has a hold on you, which will force you to listen."

"A hold?" she repeated, incredulously, "what hold has *he* —poor infatuated boy? Less than the meanest soul that ever sued for my favor—and yet more than *you* have, my dear little sister—closely knit as you are to me, more than he dreams of, unhappy boy. Pshaw! what am I saying? Nonsense, I believe. To-morrow will rid me of Cecil Beaumont, I promise you."

" If Lillia Meredith comes to-morrow she will only heighten the storm, Isolina."

My sister sighed wearily and despondingly.

" Poor little Lilly," was all she said.

*   *   *   *   *   *

The twenty-ninth of November.

It came in through leaden banks of clouds, upon a white-draped earth. A white pall of snow had dropped slowly, through the night, upon the grim, iron-like streets ; the feathery morsels flitted down all through the pallid day, muffling the heavy noises and loading the gaunt trees with sheet-white garlands.

Gradually the rumbling car and carriage gave place to

jingling bells; all New York was out a-sleighing; Broadway
and Fifth avenue were flashing gay with bright equipages ;
the poorest streets assumed a holiday air.   At twelve o'clock
Mr. Lindhurst made his appearance in a fanciful looking
sleigh, shaped much like a nautilus shell, with a downy
heart of crimson velvet in which he kindly invited me to
nestle, and experience my first sleigh-ride.

Delightedly I consented, and sat in dumb enjoyment as
we dashed through the noiseless snow, and the myriad equipages; it was like a fairy scene to me, or a kaleidoscopic view
of St. Petersburg, and I felt grand as a Russian Czarina.

Yet perfect as was my pleasure, it received a check, when
on passing one of the principal hotels, I saw Cecil Beaumont
slowly descending the marble steps.   He saw me at the same
instant, and lifted his hat, with an ineffable smile of
triumph, or daring, which sent my thoughts trooping home
to my sister and her troubles.

"Take me home, Mr. Lindhurst," I said, gravely.

"What? and you have not been out an hour.   And see,
the sun is just melting his way through that bank of clouds
—the snow has stopped, and we are going to have a brilliant
day.   You will lose all the beauty of the scene if you go now,
dear Miss Ivanilla."

"There are other days with sunshine."

"Thanks for that gracious half-promise; I shall see that
you keep it with me.   But are you tired or cold?"

"I am not tired and I am not cold, Mr. Lindhurst, and I
never enjoyed anything half as much—but I would like to
go home now to Isolina, who is alone."

"How you two love each other."

He sped around a corner, and we went flying home.

As I went up stairs, Sophie met me with a piece of news
which did not tend to relieve my mind.

Miss Meredith had arrived.

When I entered the dressing-room, I found Isolina in
earnest conversation with a fair, blonde young lady
who had large blue eyes, a very pretty complexion, and a
mass of light glossy hair gathered in a mass of coquettish
tendrils upon her forehead. Further than these attractions,
she had no claim to superiority above the average fashionable lady, unless in the possession of a very winning, innocent manner, which made her appear even younger than
she was.

The first glance in Lillia Meredith's face assured me that she could never rival my peerless sister either in mind or attractions. I no longer blamed the inconstant lover.

"Ivanilla, this is your expected visitor, Miss Meredith," said my sister, turning to me.

Miss Meredith's eyes had been full of tears, in tribute to something Isolina had been saying, but now she sprang up and came to me, wiping them away with a sprightly air.

"Dear me, everything's hazy before me, I've been crying so. Now I can see you plainer, and what a romantic style you have! The nine muses look out of your eyes, Miss Ivanilla—oh! what would I not give to have a sister or a confidante like you! You are just exactly like his description!—oh, dear! Isolina has been telling me the most horrible tales of my poor wicked Cecil! Sha'n't we tell her all about it, Isolina?"

Isolina having gravely consented, Lillia, without permitting me to remove my wrappings, began instantly to confide.

"You see I nursed Cecil when he was a sick prisoner—my father was governor of the prison, you know—and I grew to adore him, though he was a Southern officer, and just as proud and fierce as they generally are; and for my sake, when he was liberated he settled himself in Washington and became an author; and though papa is very wealthy, he never said anything against my Cecil, just because he saw that my heart was set on having him. I am so glad I am papa's only child and can do as I like. But, oh! isn't it dreadful to think of—he has been cool to me these months past, and Isolina tells me that she is the lady for whom he has forsaken me. Poor Isolina! and wretched, wicked Cecil, to torture her when she does not like him. No wonder she is so distressed about it.

"He has been in New York here, dangling after Isolina who does not want him, and writing me the most horrible notes, half a dozen lines in length, but enough to put me in fits. Listen to this one, which came three days ago:

"'You shall ever be the sweet prison flower of my memory, which wooed me back to life—but no, no! You shall never wither in my chill keeping; I give you back your gentle love, my child of sunshine, and put the bridge of silence between us forevermore. Fate—remorseless terrible—urges me on to try the fatal chance once more, which gives me life or death.   C. B.'"

"Now. what in the world does he mean? I am frightened to death about it; in fact, that is what brought me here so suddenly. I think he is catching a fever—I am sure he must be sick, poor fellow!"

Here the young lady subsided into tears again, which she petulantly wiped away, and resumed.

"It it wasn't for this idea, I wouldn't have another word to say to him, not I, indeed! but I think it is just a sick whim he has got, and when he sees me he will forget it, and be fonder of me than ever, to make amends. So, when he comes here this evening, I am just going to be as kind as if nothing had happened, and I won't appear to know any-tking about his foolish penchant for Isolina."

Having thus arranged her plans to her satisfaction, Miss Meredith dried her tears and ran to open her boxes that we might see her last new dresses.

I could not but realize that this simple child was quite unfitted for such a man as Cecil Beaumont; his vehement depth of passions would annihilate her soft nature; she would never climb to his standard, she could not even look up to his moral height, without becoming confused and dizzy.

And yet, if ever giant soul required a strong, calm spirit to guide it into rectitude, his did.

Having displayed her wardrobe, and chattered herself into better spirits, Miss Meredith, finding Isolina too grave for conversation, turned her little flatteries and caresses to me, and finally conveyed me to her room. I sang for her and related bits of Italian romance, and had succeeded in amusing her, when the short afternoon drew to a close.

My pretty companion, tired with her journey, had fallen asleep, curled up in the end of the sofa, and I was free to seek my sister, who had been alone in her dressing-room all the afternoon—not practicing once, but quite silent. The door of the room was ajar as I crossed the hall from Miss Meredith's room, and the bright gas-light revealed my sister standing—a familiar attitude for her—with her back to the room, at the window. Her head was bent forward, and I feared she was grieving, so with an eager foot I approached her and fondly put my arm round her waist, intending to comfort her if I could.

She started violently, gasped, then turned her face to me,

and I saw affright written there, as plainly as if I had been a horrible vision from the other world.

"Darling, it is only Iva!" I murmured, soothingly.

She had a letter in her hand. I now divined the cause of her agitation; she did not wish me to see the letter, yet she would not wound my feelings by openly concealing it.

The brilliant gas-light was shining on the open page—my sister's eyes were jealously watching mine. I hid my face on her arm; my feelings of devotion and fidelity were quivering beneath the shock of her distrust; my cheeks were scarlet, and tingled on her arm.

"Put it away," I whispered; "I wish to know nothing, but I have seen a name."

She folded up the letter, steadily regarding me.

"What name did you see, Ivanilla?"

"Mrs. Victor Joselyn."

She turned her back to me, and looked out of the dark window again.

"Well——" she said, in a strange, unnatural tone, "would you like to ask anything about her?"

"I don't want to know anything about her that you are not inclined to tell," I rejoined, in a trembling voice.

"She is—or rather was—connected with a friend of mine, that is all," said Isolina, after a pause; "but it matters little now who she was—she is dead."

I did not know what to say; I was unaccountably shocked.

"Are you satisfied?" asked Isolina, turning an ashy white face to me again. Her expression was so despairing that I once more flung my arms round her, and burst into tears.

"Let me comfort you!" I sobbed; "oh, darling, let me!"

"Love me, Ivanilla—there's no one else to love me!" was the only answer.

Isolina roused herself from a trance of grief, and went to her desk. I saw now that she had been writing; a sealed envelope lay on the stand, which she proceeded to stamp, after which she lifted it irresolutely and looked at me.

"I would like this mailed to-night," she said, in an humble tone, "and I scarcely like to give it to Nelson myself, as his curiosity might be aroused. You are always sending letters to mamma, and it would be nothing unusual."

"Give it to me," I cried, eagerly.

"And you will not—will not——"

"*Look* at it? My darling, you may trust Iva."

She gave me the letter, with a sweet look of love, and I went away, eager to serve her.

Half-way down stairs I met Sophie.

"Go up and help Miss Meredith to dress for dinner; it is almost six o'clock."

"Yes, Miss Iva. There's the ge——"

"I cannot wait now, Sophie; I will be back in a moment to hear what you wish to say."

Why did I not listen?

In the second hall I encountered Cecil Beaumont laying his hat and gloves on the stand. He met me with a jaunty air. His eyes were glittering—his small sharp teeth were glittering also; there was a curious expression about him of being "girded for the fight."

"How do you do this evening, sir?" I uttered, hiding the letter in the folds of my dress as I approached him. "Will you walk into the drawing-room for one moment alone?"

"What does my little friend bring me to-night?" he returned, seizing my hand. The ill-omened envelope rustled against my silken skirt.

"Ha! does she send me a dismissal by letter?" he cried.

"Sir, this letter is not for you. Let me go."

"For whom then? For *whom?*"

His eyes blazed with sudden apprehension. In an instant he had drawn me into the drawing-room and shut the door.

"For whom?" he repeated, in the same tone.

"Sir, I decline to tell you. Let me pass."

"Did *she* write it, Isolina?"

I hesitated.

"This is most cowardly conduct," I retorted.

"She *did* write it then!"

By this time the letter was in his hand. The room being dim he deliberately drew me across to the fire, and bent over the address, his hand trembling too much with insane jealousy to allow him to read.

"Monster!" I cried, springing forward.

With superhuman quickness I snatched it from him and dashed it into the burning heart of the fire.

The ill-fated missive curled and broke into yellow flames in an instant.

When the last blue flame had given place to charred red rings, I turned haughtily to Cecil Beaumont.

"You have forfeited my esteem, sir. I wish you good evening, and go to inform my sister of the fate of her letter."

He paid no heed to me. His pale, dangerous face was full of scornful amusement.

"What does she write to *him* for? What has she to do writing to Dr. Pem——"

"Hush!" I hissed, putting my hands on my ears. "I shall listen no more. If you are a gentleman, forbear!"

He gazed at me incredulously, then burst into a loud, excited laugh.

"Does she make a tool of you, poor little girl? Does she tell you nothing for your fidelity?"

I stamped my foot with rage.

"Sir!" I exclaimed, "it would be well if I knew nothing when I fall into the unscrupulous hands of a desperado, who infringes the rules of honor!"

I rushed to Isolina's room.

"That madman—that Cecil Beaumont is down stairs, waiting to see you," I gasped. "He wrenched your letter from me and read the name—only the name, sister—do not look so dreadful. I did not hear it, and I burned the letter for fear he might open it. Oh! something dreadful is going to happen; he is half insane."

"Dreadful enough!" said Isolina.

She went down stairs with a face as cold and implacable as Nemesis herself, and the drawing-room door was shut.

I wrung my hands with terror, and felt half-possessed. But I had to calm myself and go to Lillia. Yet all the while she dressed and chattered I felt faint and sick from inward apprehension.

CHAPTER V.

'HEN AN IRRESISTIBLE BODY MEETS AN IMMOVABLE BODY, WHAT IS THE CONSEQUENCE?

" For she has tint her lover dear,
Her lover dear, the cause of sorrow."
BRAES OF YARROW.

I managed to convey Miss Meredith in safety down
) the dining-room where my father sat waiting. Some
ay badinage took place between him and the young
dy, during which I sat with my ear strained to catch the
ound of my sister's voice, almost oblivious to what was go-
ng on beside me.

And while my tortured fancy was picturing the scene of
despair and sorrow which was being enacted within the
room overhead, Isolina quietly tripped in and took her place
it the table.

"Who have you got up stairs, my dear?" asked papa.

" Mr. Cecil Beaumont is amusing himself until Miss Lillia
s ready to accompany him to the concert."

" What—me?"

The young lady's face beamed with delight, but she kept
her eyes demurely upon her plate, and papa was none the
wiser.

" Hadn't I better go and see him when dinner is over?"
whispered the girl, in a flutter of excitement.

" Better dress for the concert, and try the potency of that
rose silk and chatelaine," I responded, gayly.

" Oh, yes, indeed, I had better look my very best, when I
make my appearance. Poor, dear Cecil."

She could eat nothing, and laughed and talked almost
hysterically, until we were released from the table, when she
was in a fever of haste to get her evening toilet over.

She was, indeed, a lovely creature when thus equipped,
and as I looked at her, I began to think it quite possible
that her backsliding lover might prefer her smiles to my sister's scorn, and return to his allegiance, thus ending the
embryo tragedy.

" And what are you going to wear?" asked the young

lady, as I flung her white opera-cloak round her pearl shoulders.

"I? oh, anything! The saints defend me from attrac' ing anybody's attention. I shall get behind my harp whe my time comes to sing alone."

"Come, Lillia," said my sister, entering at that momen "it is time you were going down to your cavalier."

"Dressed so soon! Oh, and *what* a magnificent creatui you are, Isolina! Look, Miss Iva—are you not proud ('The Beautiful Rienzi?'"

I turned and looked at my dear sister; and I protest th; such loveliness struck through my heart with a keen, ye foreboding fondness.

I could not but feel convinced that Cecil Beaumont wou. never return to his homage—to the pretty *fiancee* while su(a star blazed before him.

Perhaps Lillia was thinking the same; a shadow crosse her soft brows, and tears stole into her eyes.

"No wonder everybody goes crazy about you!" she sighed "I declare, it must be rather a serious matter to have sucl attractions! Just think of the hearts you'll be forced t break, before you are gray-haired!"

A look of utter misery settled upon my sister's face; sh stood unrolling her music, absently, while her deep, ques tioning eyes fixed themselves upon the flickering coals, with an expression almost of fierce despair.

The stream of inward emotion was conquered in a mo- ment; she turned almost sadly to us, and began criticising Miss Meredith's dress, with anxious care.

"I am pleased with your appearance," she said. "I never saw you more becomingly attired. Now, go down to Mr. Beaumont, and try to make him forget his foolish in- constancy."

"What must I say?" responded the girl, helplessly. "If he should be in one of his darkest moods, I will be too frightened to say a word to him. Oh, do come with me."

"I? No; I have to look over this chorus," said Isolina, shrinking back. "Iva, do you go."

So Miss Meredith and I went down together, and I drew the little trembling creature into the drawing-room, where the loved of her heart was pacing back and forward with a deep, introverted light in his eyes.

"Oh, Cecil dear!—you have been ill; that was it," said he poor girl, bursting into tears at the first glance.

"Ah! shall I bear you to the play—the tableau?" he exclaimed, in an excited manner. "Shall you be witness, nd applaud the grand scene?"

"The concert—yes!" replied Lillia, relapsing into deeper larm; "I'll go anywhere with you, dear Cecil, that you wish."

A smile curled the lips of the lover, but an imperative glance from me checked the wild sally which was on his ips. He gazed at me strangely a moment, then took Miss Meredith's hand politely and seated her.

"I am glad to meet my lily-flower again," he murmured; 'will she breathe some of her innocent balm on the world-veary heart of her Cecil? I have not touched so tender a 1and, nor met so kind a gaze, since last I looked upon you."

She watched him half incredulously through her tears, ıs if such phrases were a new thing from him, but a some-thing strange and terrifying to her in his haggard face soon caused her to cower closer to him, and again exclaim:

"You have been ill, Cecil—oh! how terrible you are looking!"

He looked down at her, a calm, thoughtful glance, such as a brother might have bestowed, and began explaining to her the severity of his literary labor, and I, dubiously enough, slipped from the room and left them together.

"Well, are they reconciled in good faith?" inquired Isolina, anxiously, when I made my appearance.

I related the meeting, and eagerly asked how she had managed to bring him round to such a measure of submission.

"I informed him of a certain obstacle which debarred me from marrying him!" she replied, steadily, while she closed her piano and locked it. "Having become convinced that further hopes were impossible, he himself proposed to return to Lillia, and signify his intentions by accompanying her to the concert this evening."

"And is it possible that he has given you up so calmly?"

"He cannot—or I cannot—remove the obstacle; therefore he submitted to the inevitable."

At half-past seven we left the house with my father, who this night was radiant with pride and playful tenderness, as he drew the furs round us, and took his seat opposite. Mr Beaumont's sleigh had not yet arrived, so we left them still *tete-a-tete.*

How clearly I remember that November night!

Through the crisp night air and bright moonlight, we whisked cozily along to the clang of silver sleigh-bells; my father gayly chatting to me, my sister sitting quiet and motionless in the corner, I with my eyes intently fixed upon the passing objects. From the same hotel from which I had seen Beaumont descending in the evening, I noticed two gentlemen in loose British cloaks such as were then worn, stepping into a sleigh, drawn by a large white horse.

I watched the commonplace vehicle with no commonplace interest, from the mere fact of its proceeding from that hotel, and in the same direction as our own. The impatient steed which was certainly better fed than the generality of its class, ran abreast with us for some rods, then darted past and fell into line with a long stream of equipages just ahead of us, where the jingle of the bells mingled with our own.

Having watched this sleigh out of sight, I turned my attention to something else, and found by the increasing throng that we were slowly nearing the hall in which the Cybelle Society were to give the concert.

Long lines of vehicles were waiting to deposit their freight at the entrance doors, and a slow stream of those already emptied were moving onward to give place.

By an adroit movement our coachman succeeded in depositing us on the carpeted pavement much in advance of our turn.

But although I lingered on the marble top step, with a hundred eager eyes fastened on me, and my father already leading Isolina along the corridor; and although I kept them waiting some minutes while I gathered up my shawl on my arm and looked for my glove, I failed to see again those two muffled figures.

With an exclamation at my own foolishness, I joined the others, and before long we found ourselves among the performers, who, among much talking, greetings, laughter, and fluttering of robes, were receiving a few last instructions from the indefatigable Professor Emerson.

Isolina and I stood hand in hand together, hoping we would not be separated on the platform, and we were conscientiously listening to the professor, when a group of our friends discovered us, swooped around us, carried off my sister from my grasp to hear something better worth listening to than the professor's dry dissertation, and I was left almost alone with a pair of keen blue eyes beaming down upon me.

"Cheer up, Zerlina," said Mr. Lindhurst, extending his hand. "Do not look so forsaken Miss Rienzi. I will do my best to fill the vacuum, if you will allow me."

Just as the signal was given for the singers to make their appearance on the platform, a hand was laid on my shoulder, and a voice whispered in my ear:

"Where is Isolina? Quick!"

The breath scorched my ear. I turned in affright and beheld Cecil Beaumont.

"Why, sir, what are you doing here? Where is Miss Meredith?"

"Oh, I see her. In time after all," he muttered, turning from me and pushing through the crowd.

Isolina was in effect coming toward him with all haste; but she did not see him; her eyes were resting on me; she was anxious to reach me, that we might enter the hall and be together.

Not until she had almost touched him, was she aware of Mr. Beaumont's presence.

They met not five rods from me, and my ears, sharpened by extreme anxiety, drank in all that passed between them.

"Take my arm, Isolina."

"What—you? Where is Lillia?"

"Curse Lillia! I beg your pardon, but she's right enough. I implore you to take my arm—you can't crush in alone."

"I prefer to crush in alone. Go back to Miss Meredith."

"Isolina, look in my face and see if I can bear much more. Be wise and grant this trifling favor."

His red-brown eyes were flashing—his face dangerously white. No wonder she looked and gasped.

"Poor wretched boy," she exclaimed; "can I help it? I do not wish to give you pain, Heaven knows."

"Grant this favor then—such a mere rag of mercy to throw me—your hand on my arm sixty seconds. See, your

sister's hand is on Mr. Lindhurst's arm.   What difference
does it make to either of them?   Well, if you still refuse,
I will walk straight into Lillia Meredith's opera-box and renounce her forever."

That decided it.   Isolina, with angry, downcast eyes,
and flaming cheeks, stepped into the procession and walked
across the platform, her hand tightly linked to Cecil Beaumont's arm, and I followed closely, too much engrossed by
them even to lift my eyes to look around.

The instant we had taken our seats, the face of Beaumont
underwent a wonderful change.

I could not but suspect that he was trying to give the impression to all who chose to notice, that he was the favored
cavalier of "The Beautiful Rienzi."   I trembled for poor
Lillia Meredith, and raised my eyes to the reserved seats to
find her.   I soon detected the blush-rose dress in a seat very
near the platform, and met the large, wistful eyes of the
young girl fixed upon me with a timid, dazed expression;
then she turned them upon her lover, as if hoping to catch
a glance from him.

At length the business of the evening commenced,
and I had no more time for observation.   I have no intention of presenting to the reader the details of this concert,
which was conducted with perfect skill and taste.   I shall
merely touch here and there on those parts which immediately pertain to my history, and to myself.

As the moment approached that I was to sing my first
solo, Santa Cecelia! how my lips trembled! My hands grew
icy cold, my cheeks flamed, a suffocating weight of nervous
dread was on my heart.

At last my name was whispered by those around me, a
lady behind me gave me a gentle push which sent me to my
feet ; murmurs of "Don't be afraid," reached my quaking
ears, and Mr. Lindhurst's calm eyes rested on me with a reassuring smile which infused some courage into my half-
dead frame.   Without daring to look up, I took my place
beside a gayly bedizzened harp, swept the strings with wandering fingers which created an impromptu prelude, rather
out of the course as I saw by the professor's astonished looks,
and at length, with a desperate effort, plunged into my
song, quite unconscious of anything but the defects which
my nervousness caused.

This unique performance was gallantly applauded by the

great, kindly throng, and the gentlemen cried "encore," though I was now burning with remorse that I had not merited their kindness more, and thinking to myself how my gifted master in Venice, who had formed all my notes with artistic care, would have encored in a different mood ; but I swept a grateful courtesy and retired to my place.

I had now leisure to look about, and I used my eyes.

First they went a-trip to the dear father in the box, who was clapping his hands louder than any of them, his eyes sparkling with pride ; and we telegraphed a smile to each other. Then I looked at Miss Meredith, and my smile faded.

She was bent across the front of the seat, her ivory fan pressed against her bosom until it bent, her soft face cold and hard, her eyes fastened, her lips satirically smiling. Unutterably startled at such an expression, I directed my eyes also to the pair she watched so intently.

My sister sat some distance from me on her velvet chair near a piano, upon which shortly she was to perform. Her face was drooping, her face which was surely too bitterly reproachful to be turned to the public and Cecil Beaumont was bending his head close to hers, unchecked ; a music-sheet held up as a shield from other eyes, while he whispered ceaselessly. It was all interpreted but too well by wronged Lillia Meredith, mad now with jealousy and indignation.

The concert proceeded; there were more songs by ladies whose tones did not tremble as mine had done. The orchestra played through an opera while we rested ourselves. Isolina and the professor performed their piano duet, which was wonderfully admired. The time came at last for Isolina and me to sing a duet then much in vogue, though now somewhat antiquated, "Mira O Norma," from "Don Giovanni."

I stood with my sister in the empty area and watched her, while with a low, pathetic cadence, she fell into Bellini's sweet air, which strangely enough seemed to fall into a desolate chime with her life-opera. With what wistfulness she murmured the opening prayer; how her tones deepened into vehemence; how her vehemence intensified to passion as she sang:

"Ah! he shall feel, who caused thy anguish,
How deep hath been thy silent sorrow!"

I was carried away by her dramatic genius, and rendered my part with fearless enthusiasm, until my eyes fell on Cecil Beaumont, and then I knew not what I sang.

There he stood, or rather crouched behind a flag, watching my beautiful sister with a reckless and almost diabolical smile on his lips. Where was now the touching febrile pathos of that full-eyed Southern face? This was the bold abandon of a fiend.

I turned from this blasting vision to take up my part again. The orchestra hushed their notes to a gentle whisper, my voice, trembling as it was with other feelings, rose distinct with Norma's passionate rejoinder:

> "When the heart is cold that should have cherished
> Every hope of joy it falsely gave
> Wouldst thou have me live? Ah! no, thou wouldst not!
> My only haven, alas! is but the grave!"

I waited for Isolina's answering:

> "Hear me, Norma! hear me, I implore thee!"

I waited, and the echoes were dying.

What has smitten Isolina?

The wild eyes are fixed as if in a trance—her lips are whitening—her hands clasped. Doubt, sudden horror depict themselves upon the blanching face; she shrinks back, and with a soft Æolian-like brush of her heavy robe across the harp-strings, she sank at my feet.

The effect was electric.

There was a hush as of death, broken presently by the sound of hysterical weeping and cries of alarm. Confusion prevailed.

CHAPTER VI.

BAFFLED AFTER ALL.

> "O life as futile—then, as frail!
> O for thy voice to soothe and bless!
> What hope of answer or redress,
> Behind the vail! behind the vail!"—TENNYSON.

I stood there as still as my white-faced sister, powerless with dismay. I gazed with keen eyes into the heart of the throng where she had gazed, and nothing but faces of consternation met me; yet some face that she had seen in that throng had affected her thus. Many gentlemen left their places and approached the platform to offer assistance; over their heads I gazed at two figures hurrying in the opposite direction to the entrance door; gentlemen in loose cloaks; but what of that? My heart quaked, and—at what?

All this took but a moment; before any one could raise my sister, Cecil Beaumont had crouched over her and lifted her in his slight, strong arms, with such a visible air of the right to do so, that every one stood back and allowed him a free passage to the stage door, while I remained without the power to move, gazing after him at Isolina's pale face and closed eyes.

Some words broke on my benumbed senses. Mr. Lindhurst was leading me to a couch behind the piano.

"Compose yourself, my dear Miss Ivanilla—do not look so terrified. Your sister will soon recover — she only fainted with excitement. I think you are going to faint, too."

I roused myself from my stony stillness.

"No, I am not going to faint; I would like to go to Isolina."

He bent his head to catch my words; the singers had adroitly covered the accident by a full-voiced chorus and my words were lost in a sea of song.

I tore my hands from my friend and escaped by the door through which I had last seen my sister disappear. I was in the cold outer corridor leading by private passages to the dressing-rooms and main entrance. Whither should I direct my steps? I darted into the room behind the stage, and came out as quickly, two or three bandsmen were there repairing their bugles or cornopæns. I found the cloaking-room but it was also empty of those I sought. I wrung my hands and begun to wish my sweet sister had been gifted with the features of a Mongolian. I saw a flight of stairs leading into an upper hall, and I rushed up these as a last resource only to find myself in a wide, dark hall, evidently a school-room. But there was a door at my right hand which was locked, and at this I took my stand, knocking vigorously.

No one replied, so my heart went into my mouth with blood-curdling fears, as a stealthy step became audible.

"Monsters!" I cried, "I demand an entrance—I know you are here. Let me join my sister!"

I began imperiously. I passed through a descending scale until I was pleading and weeping for an entrance.

The door was suddenly opened and an old man with a tallow candle flashing in his hand, and a gray, stern face confronted me.

"Who are you, coming at this time of night, waking people out of their rest? What do you want?"

"I want my sister! O, misery! have I wasted the precious moments after all? Sir, I am looking for my sister, who was singing at the concert."

"What do I know about her then? Why come to my door for her? I have a wife in there, young woman, and you have wakened her up. Go away—I have nothing to do with the people who come into this building—I have only to lock them out at night—if they would ever go!"

"Sir, I beg your pardon——"

"All right—find your way down stairs again."

The door was snapped shut in my face; wringing my hands, I turned away.

I fell against Mr. Lindhurst in the lower corridor and he stopped my further search.

"Where have you been, Miss Ivanilla? Your father was very anxious to see you before he went home."

"Has my father gone home?"

"Yes, with Miss Meredith; they were anxious to be with Miss Rienzi."

"And where is she?" I burst forth passionately; "I cannot find her in all the building."

"Mr. Beaumont conveyed your sister home," said my friend, gently. "She was not able to sing again, so it was best for her to go home and rest."

"Mr. Beaumont!" I repeated—I felt myself grow pale under Mr. Lindhurst's anxious eyes. For her sake I commanded myself and concealed my emotions. "When did all this happen?" I demanded.

"Not three minutes ago. Your father left word with one of the stage-managers for you, that they had all gone home; and he did me the honor to say that I should take charge of you until your duties released you. I have just received this message, and was seeking for you."

"Oh, I must go now—I cannot stay here!" I cried.

Just then the professor came in from the platform, his countenance wearing an anxious expression. When he saw me it brightened.

"Oh! I am glad to see you here, Miss Rienzi. I was afraid you had both vanished, and my programme would sustain a severe abridgement. Come—everybody is looking down their list impatiently for 'La ci darem.'"

I saw that it would be selfish of me to go, so I consented to return to my place; but it was with a weary sigh that I encountered again the blazing lights and brilliant toilets.

Our duet of "La ci darem la mans," in which Mr. Lindhurst was Don Giovanni and I Zerlina, was a marvelous success; we were encored again and again, until I felt my silly head ring with triumph, and a spirited thrill ran to the ends of my fingers.

I stood with unfaltering mien once more alone with my harp, and swept the chords with a delicate touch as I sang "The Blind Girl's Song to Her Harp," which moved the ladies, in their jewels and satins, to weep, while the gentlemen dropped their opera-glasses and sat immovable.

And then, in my last, where as Dinorah I warbled forth "O, Tender Shadow!" lost in the enjoyment of the moment, charmed with so good-natured an audience, exhilarated by their looks of delight, I almost forgot the cares which had weighed down my spirits so long.

It was almost twelve o'clock before the warder of the Cybelle Hall locked the doors on the last of us. I was very weary, and lay back among the furs in Mr. Lindhurst's sleigh, looking at the radiant moonlight which bathed each silent roof with his blue-white tintings.

"Overworked, Queen of Song?" laughed my escort, bending down to look in my face.

"No; I am thinking of my success—I am proud of it."

He smiled as he regarded me.

"Am I vain to say so?" I asked. "I do not think my vanity has been fed. My master spent years in my tuition, and I at my best cannot do him credit. And then, to think that those who listened to us to-night—connoisseurs they certainly were—should be pleased with me! Yes, I am proud!"

"So am I," softly spoke my friend.

Then he sighed as he spoke again:

"So our little rehearsals are over," he said, pensively. "I

shall have no longer the delight of being taught how to
breath Italian by my little Zerlina! Don Giovanni's wooing
is over."

It was my delight to set those deep blue eyes sparkling,
and to call the grave, peculiarly sweet smile to the thoughtful lips by my daring words or glances. When I had stirred
his feelings until I thrilled in the presence of such fascina-
tion as I was unable to withstand, I would lightly change
my mood to hide my throbbing heart.

"What does that glance mean?" exclaimed Mr. Lind
hurst, meeting my alluring smile with flushing eagerness.
"Does my little queen retain her subject for some more
lessons?"

My queenly reply was a laughing nod.

"Nay," jested he, "that answer is more than royal—it
is god-like. Alexander affected the celestial nod of the
gods!"

"I cannot conquer the world," I replied, gayly, "but I
should much rather conquer——" My eyes finished the
sentence; I allowed him to press my fingers; I defiantly
lured him on. While thus I toyed with my awaking heart,
a deep sound awoke the sleeping silence of the vast city; a
slow clanging—one—two—three—up to twelve. It was midnight, as a solemn old bell in a church near was informing
us. As the last stroke died away, my smiling lips locked—
they chilled into colorless marble, and my heart sank with
a throe of deathly terror.

"Heavens!" I gasped, "something dreadful has happened!"

"What—what?" exclaimed my friend, growing pale as he
beheld my mysterious agitation.

He anxiously supported me and chafed my icy hands, but
I was not faint.

"Do you feel better now?" asked my friend.

The unaccountable terror was passing off, leaving, however, a strange impression on my mind that I did wrong to
stay at the hall; I was wild with anxiety to be at home.

"What has caused this hysteric paroxysm?" whispered my
friend, again chafing my hands.

Yes! that is what any practical person would call such a
mysterious visitation. "A hysteric paroxysm," and they
would account for it by preceding fatigue, excitement, and
anxiety.

"I am not hysterical," I said, very quietly; "but I am anxious about Isolina. Perhaps she is worse."

Mr. Lindhurst gave the driver a word, and in an instant we were dashing through the remaining streets which separated me from my home. Five minutes had not elapsed before I was bidding my escort good-night at my father's door. I thought the servant who admitted me looked very much bewildered; he held the door open after I had entered until I turned round and asked him the reason. "Oh, nothing, miss," he replied, solacing himself with a last glance down to the gate before he closed himself in. I proceeded steadily to my sister's dressing-room. It was empty. Well, it was late and she had been ill, of course she was in bed.

Sophie came out of my room, and looked at me with a surprised face, but said nothing while she removed my wrappings.

"Well, are you not going to speak?" I demanded, irritably. "Is Miss Rienzi well or ill; is she in bed?"

She dropped my muff and kept gazing at me. I made an impatient gesture, my fears growing clamorous.

"La, miss! isn't Miss Isolina with you?"

I hastily looked behind, and at each side. No, truly, Miss Isolina was not with me! My face whitened.

"What are you saying, Sophie? My sister came home an hour ago with my father, did she not?"

"Lawk alive, miss!" was all the response.

"Fool!" I raved; "have you nothing but gaping wonder for me? Where is she? Are you sure she is not down stairs with papa, or in Miss Meredith's room with her?"

"Indeed, Miss Iva, she's not in the house. White, he's waiting at the door to let her in; her and you, miss, together."

"And my father—good Heaven! has my father lost sight of her, too? Sophie, you will cease to gaze at me so! Am I an apparition? Who told you she was coming home with me?"

"The master, Miss Ivanilla. He said Miss Isolina had been sick and gone out to come home, but the air revived her, and she went back to the concert."

"Who told him that? It was false!" I cried, becoming distracted with consternation.

I ran to Miss Meredith's room without ceremony, and found that she had not retired.

"What can have happened to Isolina?" I burst forth. "I thought she was home two hours ago, and when I arrive, I find her absent still! Where can she be?"

"Where can she be?" repeated the girl, with a ringing laugh. "Don't you know? Can't you guess?"

"For the love of Heaven!" I said, gravely, "tell me if you have any idea where she is. Where did you see her last?"

"It is rather hard to ask me that question," she returned, with another taunting laugh; "but I will tell you. In the arms of my betrothed!"

"Explain," I said, swallowing my feelings.

"How am I to explain. Such treachery is beyond my power to explain. You, as well as I, saw him carry her away in his arms."

"And have you not seen her since?"

"Not I, my dear Miss Ivanilla; nor will you for a while, I fancy. Do not sit up to-night, I beg. They have given us all the slip—eloped!"

"Impossible!" I exclaimed, indignantly. "My sister did not love him. She would never elope with Cecil Beaumont."

"So she informed you and me, my dear," said Miss Meredith, bitterly; "but you see we have been duped. The deception worked very well, and she has got him safe!"

"Miss Meredith, I command you to cease these aspersions on my sister's integrity," I exclaimed. "You do not know a tithe of what she has suffered for you—ingrate. But I forbear to quarrel. You will not relieve my anxiety, so I will relieve you of my presence."

She came after me and clutched me passionately; her smothered rage broke out.

"Why did you not tell me how completely she had insnared him?" hissed the girl, shaking me. "Whether you say it is her fault or not—*she stole him* from me! Now, I tell you, her sister, as my message for her when she comes back, that I will never forgive her for the wrong and the humiliation she has made me bear. Let her beware. With all her beauty and her talent, the time may come when her beauty will be only a memory, and her talents turned to her own destruction. Then, perhaps, she'll be sorry for the trick she played me!"

She ceased with set teeth, and pushed me from the door; a furious, implacable foe, no more a gentle girl.

I went away without a word. I was stunned; blow after blow was descending on me; my heart was faint and sick. I went through the silent house as I should have done at first, to my father.

He was pacing up and down, a frown on his face such as I had never seen there before.

"Have you come home alone, then?" he asked, turning on me. "White says your sister was not with you."

I flung myself into his arms. The last straw broke the camel's back. The terror and grief which had so long been accumulating burst forth at last in a torrent of tears.

My father soothed and caressed me; his brief paternal sternness vanished before my distress; he implored me to explain what was grieving me.

"Tell me how it came that you lost sight of Isolina."

I sobbed after a while:

"I have not seen her since she was carried out of the hall insensible."

"What? Has she disappeared?"

"Father, did you trust her with that madman, Beaumont?"

"I can tell you nothing about her, my child, except that I hastened out of the hall as soon as she gave way; I would have got round to the dressing-room sooner, where I imagined young Beaumont had taken her, but Miss Meredith, who had been acting like a possessed creature before that, and had hissed in a most derisive and unseemly manner when the accident happened, delayed me by going into something that looked very like a convulsion fit. By the time I got her dragged out with me and wrapped up, a manager came to me and said that Beaumont had just driven off with your sister—if I hastened, I could overtake them, and put her in my sleigh, as Beaumont's was uncovered. I hurried Miss Meredith in and dashed off, but did not overtake them. When I came to our gate out there, a boy, who was waiting on the sidewalk, said he had been told to stand there and inform me that Miss Rienzi, feeling quite revived, had decided to go back to the hall and f·

her part. I asked him who spoke to him; he said a gentleman who was driving a lady in an open sleigh, and he had given him a quarter for the job. And that is all I can say on the matter, which is certainly a very extraordinary one for such a girl as Isolina to be embroiled in. Surely—surely she has not done anything clandestine?"

Here I told my father the exact case as it stood between Isolina and Beaumont, and related how earnestly she had tried to keep him true to her friend. The crisis had not come which was to force the whole of my strange story from me; I was resolved to keep my sister's secret history locked in my own bosom until she released my tongue.

"And do you leave me to infer that he has forcibly taken her away?" ejaculated my father, starting up; "By Heaven! this is an outrage that I will take good care to sift! Where's the young man's address? You don't know? There! there! don't cry, little one—go to bed and sleep— you are as white as a ghost. I'll see to this business—never you fear!"

He went with me up the long, desolate stairs, kissed me tenderly in my own little bedroom, and went away. I watching him from the window in the shining moonlight saw him with a servant by his side walk rapidly down the street.

Ah! that was a night! I watched by the window until my heavy eyes grew burning and blind. I flitted to and fro in my echoing room until my watch ticked me into a frenzy. I crept to Lillia's door, and, grown humble by misery, implored her to allow me to be with her, but the girl's mood was harder than mine, and she stoutly refused.

Weeping, I returned to my room, flung myself on my bed, and sank into a deep, dreamless sleep.

CHAPTER VII.

THERE IS NO GRIEF LIKE THE GRIEF THAT DOES NOT SPEAK.

" He is dead and gone, lady,
 He is dead and gone;
At his head a grass green turf,
 At his heels a stone."—HAMLET.

"Break, thou deep vase of chilling tears,
 That grief hath shaken into frost."—TENNYSON.

A presence was with me in my fathomless slumber; it brought me up from the circles of oblivion, until a sense of returning existence began to enter my dormant brain. Slowly though, for my weary head seemed clasped by bands of iron; but at last the Presence bending over me became a reality; I opened my eyes with a confused terror.

Was that my father's face? It was gray and distorted to my unsteady vision—surely ten years had passed since I fell asleep.

"Father!" I cried, springing up all at once; "what have you come to tell me?"

" Poor little girl," whispered he, compassionately, " I scarcely liked to waken you, you were sleeping so soundly. Oh, my daughter!"

He took me in his arms, and suddenly a great deep sob rent his frame. I said nothing, but I clung to him and waited.

" Something dreadful has happened," he gasped, after a while; "Cecil Beaumont was found—was found dead last night at twelve o'clock beneath a bridge, ten miles on the ——road!"

" *Dead,* father!"

" And they say——" Here he broke down and wept such tears as would kill a woman—tears that came with throes of agony and strong wrenches of the laboring chest while he rocked with me to and fro; "they say there has been foul play—that Isolina—my girl that could not harm a living thing—oh, my God! I cannot believe it!"

He was weeping—I could not.

"Where is she?" I asked, mechanically.

"She can't be found," this in a husky whisper; "the man who found the body says she must have escaped. I need not look for her, Iva!" he said, in a curiously helpless voice, "the officers of justice are after her—if she is alive, they will find her."

"Who told you this, father?"

"They were talking about it at the Exchange," he groaned. "I was here and there and everywhere, all night long, trying to trace them; young Lindhurst was with me until five o'clock. It was he who came to me an hour ago and said the merchants had a queer story among them on 'Change; some parties coming in from Greely's Mills where the accident occurred, brought the news. The young man's mother has applied to have her arrested; a band of detectives went out this morning to see Mrs. Beaumont and hear the particulars. Strange, isn't it, that the body was found not half a mile from Mrs Beaumont's house? What could your sister want there."

"Father, what are you going to do?" I whispered, helplessly.

"I will try to find my poor girl; I shall not leave her to be hunted down by the law. Oh, my child! my pride! I was happy when my eyes fell on her—never father loved child as I loved that girl. Oh, my darling, come back to your poor old father—don't be afraid of him!"

"Father," I said, reverently kissing his hand, "comfort yourself with the thought of her innocence. This misfortune is very heavy, but Heaven will bring it all right again, since poor Isolina was quite guiltless of any wrong, from beginning to end. Comfort yourself, dear father."

While I was speaking, I had been debating with myself whether I was justified in keeping silence longer on the subject of my sister's mysterious movements ever since the advent of Cecil Beaumont, and I reasoned that as long as there was a chance of this breach of confidence throwing a light upon the subsequent events, which might restore her to us, it was my duty to communicate what I knew to my father.

Inwardly praying, therefore, that the "happiness of this family" would not be destroyed by what I was about to relate—as she had declared it would—but would rather be restored, I poured into my father's ears the strange events which for some time had caused me so much anxiety.

He listened with fixed attention, and unutterable surprise, then rose in agitation and pain.

"I cannot understand one move in this extraordinary game," he cried, "but this I am convinced of—your sister has become the victim of some infernal conspiracy!"

I scarcely took in his words; he went away more ghastly pale than before, and trod heavily down stairs to his room, and left me alone again.

My watch had run down, so I could not tell the time; but I knew the day must be far advanced, and I changed my dress, and flitted to Miss Meredith's chamber-door with a passing wonder why I had not been visited by any of the servants yet. At my first tap the door was opened, and I beheld Miss Meredith in traveling costume, her hat on the dressing-table, and a tray, containing the remains of her breakfast, on a stand before the cheerfully blazing fire.

"Come in, Miss Rienzi," she said, politely; "I am glad to find you well enough to rise. I have been awaiting you some time."

She placed a chair for me, upon which I thankfully sat down, for a sort of vertigo had seized me while crossing the corridor, and I was quite dizzy.

"You see," she continued, sitting down and taking her coffee-cup in her hand; "I am on the eve of returning home. My visit to New York has been shorter than I anticipated, but I shall remember it with the deepest constancy. I am glad to have this opportunity of thanking you, Miss Ivanilla Rienzi, for your kindness, and bidding you farewell."

"You have not heard," I returned, in a husky, uncertain voice, "of the terrible calamity that has happened. When you know the extent of our trouble, you will feel for this stricken family, and accept my sympathy in your grief!"

"I have heard everything," said the young lady, laying down her empty cup. "Your housemaid told me what half the city knows by this time—that Cecil Beaumont's dead body had been found dashed to pieces at the bottom of a stream! I am sorry for you, Miss Rienzi—I am sorry that your sister turns out to be a *murderess!* It is even worse than if she had lured him from me for love——"

Here she grew white with passion, and wavered an instant; "but she only lured him on to destruction. I have no wish to keep you in ignorance of my intentions, Miss Rienzi; so I will frankly tell you that I intend to have your sister arrested for this murder. She shall be found and brought to justice, if my last dollar pays for it!"

"You are too late in putting your intentions into execution," I responded. "Mrs. Beaumont, his mother, has been before you. There is a warrant against her already."

"And is the very solace of revenge to be denied me?" cried the girl, almost furiously. Her hard cruelty had no effect on my frozen stupor; I even studied *her* in her vindictive mood, and wondered that my first impressions of her had been so false.

"I have nothing against you, Miss Rienzi," she said, glancing at me, as she rose to look out of the window; "but you must acknowledge that I have been basely treated by your sister; and I have a perfect right to join in the effort to avenge my dead lover. There—I see the cab is waiting to take me to the station. Good-by, Miss Rienzi; I am truly sorry for you—I don't think you could help it."

She reached out her cold hand to me, and I looked at her unfeeling countenance wistfully. I felt that it was not right to let her go thus; yet I had no strength to meet the emergency, or to oppose anything.

"You will not go away, my friend?" I appealed. "See how desolate I am. Stay and comfort me. She may be dead, too, dear one; and if she is, you would never forgive yourself for your hard feelings."

But she tore her hand away from me, and went down stairs where her boxes appeared to have preceded her, and in five minutes I heard the entrance door shut.

I crept spiritlessly to the dressing-room and sat down before the blazing fire. Sophie was there with a bit of sewing in her hands, and she ran for a footstool, and put my feet on it.

"Oh, my dear miss," cried the usually timid girl. "You should not have got up—no, indeed! You look dreadful."

"What is the time, Sophie?"

"About twelve, Miss Iva. I'll run for a bit of breakfast. You sha'n't go down to that great table all alone. Your pa's not home, and I'll bring it up nice and hot here."

"Yes," I assented; "I suppose I must eat."

Without preface or warning the girl flung herself on her knees beside me, and buried her face in her apron.

"I don't believe it," she sobbed violently. "I don't believe a word against dear, sweet Miss Isolina. Oh, Miss Iva, darling, don't look so terribly quiet—hasn't you cried any?"

"No," I sighed, "tears are denied to me; my heart is too stupefied yet. But I, too, know that my sister has done no wrong, and I thank you for your trust, my girl."

Sophie went out of the room with loud sobs, and I sat quietly looking into the fire and waiting for her return with my breakfast. But when it came, although I assured myself it was my duty to eat, I could not. My thirst was burning, and my throat seemed to crack whenever I attempted to speak, yet I could not force down Sophie's cup of tea, though fragrant as art could render it. I could not endure the girl's anxious eyes, so I left the tray and went down into the still drawing-room.

I restlessly wandered around the luxurious apartment; I read poetry and hummed an air which Isolina had often sung to me in the twilight hours. As the day wore to its close I grew wild with terror at my calmness and strove by every art to melt the fount of sorrow. Presently the door opened and Sophie came in through the gloom.

"Miss Iva, where are you?" she whispered; the master has come home and wants you downstairs to eat something. He's here waiting, miss."

I went out to the lighted hall and slipped my hot hand into his.

"Papa," I said, gently; "you have left me a long time alone. Did you hear of her?"

He did not answer but to draw my hand within his arm with a spasmodic grip; then he made me go down to the dining-room where dinner was laid as usual, only that my sister's chair was set to the wall, and her place empty. My father did not place me at the table; he put my chilled form into a great easy-chair beside the fire, and brought a glass of wine to me, which I drank obediently; then he made me eat, which I did with difficulty, for the ball in my throat almost choked me; but I was eager to give no trouble, so I managed it. After eating a brief meal himself, which I pityingly remarked was almost as small as mine, he left the table and took me up stairs again. The drawing-room was now brightly lit, the hearth swept, and blazing fire on.

He sat by this merry, crackling fire, and put my poor beating head upon his breast, and kissed me kindly.

"You have had a sad day of it, I fear, poor little girl," he said, "and indeed I am a little afraid for you—your head is like a furnace."

"I am very well, father—too well. Please tell me all you have been doing. You know while you have been working I have been waiting."

"I have very little to reward your waiting with," he sighed; "my work has been to little purpose. Your sister is still undiscovered, and all clews seem lost. I have been to Greely's Mills, and saw the—the body at Mrs. Beaumont's house; there was an inquest on it and a verdict was returned of 'Death by violent means.' I have been able to make nothing of that strange story you told me of your sister visiting some person at night, and writing to unknown people. If Heaven ever restores her to us, we may hear an explanation from her own mouth : but my belief is that she is embroiled in some wretched plot."

"And what more?" I cried, feverishly; "did you do nothing more? Is that all you have to tell?"

"I did nothing more, my poor darling, except to write to your mother. Keep up courage until she comes; you'll not be so lonely when there are two of you."

I raised my head and looked at him, and trembled from head to foot. I felt it coming, the long delayed storm of grief. I thought of my mother's anguish when that message should reach her; it seemed as if the fiat had gone forth with that message; that our grief was to be real; my eyes fell upon the pile of books and music, and pretty ornaments which her hands had worked, and which were to be put away now.

It came to me in a blinding flash, that my darling would come no more to me; that she was lost and dead to me, and dead to my family forever.

A wild shriek broke from me. I clasped my hands on my heart, and the pent-up tears poured forth in a torrent, my frame was racked and shaken with the tempest, grief and horror filled my heart, and seemed to find no bounds. At last my sorrow had begun.

CHAPTER VIII.

"I LOCK THE CASKET WHICH HELD THE GEM."

" Courage, poor heart of stone !
I will not ask thee why
Thou canst not understand
That thou art left forever alone."—TENNYSON.

The next day I, by my father's directions, searched her chamber for any possible clew of her late movements.

Carefully, though with ceaseless tears, I examined every paper which came in my way, and found nothing which could have the slightest bearing on the mysterious question. A few penciled sketches of woodland scenery were wrapped in silver paper, and hidden deep down in a drawer; a withered rose, once white, now sere and crumbling into faintly incensed dust, was clasped within a gold-enameled casket, in the same drawer, but what of these?

Her little rosewood desk was locked, with the key lying on top, and with a feeling of shrinking reluctance, I opened it. There were many letters, which I glanced at and replaced. Most of them had been written by my own hand before I joined my unknown sister; a good many were the peculiarly artless and innocent effusions of Miss Meredith ; there were several from Miss Belle Cranstown relating to benevolent projects in which she and my sister had been interested; finally there were several proposals of marriage from different gentlemen, some of whom I had already heard of, others with whose names I was unacquainted.

I wrote their names down on a slip of paper and resolved to ask my father about them.

Just as I was closing the desk I noticed a small gold knob, about the size of a pin's head, in one of the compartments. I applied myself to its examination, and presently succeeded in opening a secret drawer in which I found the missing double-ring. I held it in the palm of my hand, moving and twisting it until the slender hoop which lined it became detached. It was only a gold ring without chasing or ornament, but this very circumstance raised a curious train of speculations in my mind, which engrossed me for several minutes until I suddenly observed in the inside of the circlet the graven initials, "I. J., July 16th, 1862." Had I found some accurate foothold at last? Who and what was "I. J.," and where had my sister been on the sixteenth of July, last summer? Were these the initials of the giver of the double ring?

Long I stood revolving these slight proofs of some concealed events in my mind; vague speculation was the only result. I replaced the double-ring in its secret drawer and locked the desk.

All these dumb reminders of her overthrew my enforced calmness; I flung myself on the floor and wept until my very being seemed wept away.

Then I rose, drew down the blinds, closed the curtains, locked the door, and came away.

Henceforth no foot should cross the threshold, no eyes make common property of this deserted chamber, until the day that the shadow passed away from us, and my lost sister came home.

I related with minute care all that I had found to my father, and he listened attentively.

"The case amounts to this," he said, when I had finished:

"Isolina received a ring on the sixteenth of last July from some person whose initials are 'I. J.'—which she has worn since on her hand, until, as you believe, the night on which she went out in the rain-storm secretly. We can make very little of this, Iva, except that probably she formed some attachment last summer with a person whom she has not mentioned, and at the time she removed the ring, that attachment must have ended. I cannot see that either that circumstance or her strange absence from the house that stormy night are connected in any way with her present disappearance. None of the names which you have written down as applicants for her hand commence with the initials 'I. J.'—and I knew of them all. I do not think we can unravel the mystery—perhaps, my dear, we ought not to try until your poor sister is restored to us. I have perfect faith, and I know you have the same, in my kind, good Isolina's motives."

"But, father, her mysterious grief—what if she had enemies, who were wiling her away to destroy her?"

"I did think at first of secret conspiracies; but that is

hardly likely. We are in America, not in lawless Italy," replied my father, with a faint smile.

"This war—what if some parties, for political purposes, tore her from the bosom of her family, in order——"

"Isolina occupied too quiet a position, my dear. Who would ever dream of forcing away a private gentleman's daughter as a spy or anything else? Your surmises are wild, my child."

This was but the beginning of many such conversations. How often we sat together detailing the simple history of the lost girl, and trying vainly to dip beneath the transparent scanning of the past for deeper meaning!

Time slowly stretched between us and that tragic night. The dreadful death of young Beaumont gradually ceased out of men's mouths; the interest connected with it passed away, and the unhappy fugitive was forgotten. Even the bereaved lady, Mrs. Beaumont, had ceased her efforts to apprehend her, and had left the country.

Sad news came from Venice, which deepened the gloom of our lonely hearts. My mother had been so dangerously ill that the physicians had forbidden the disastrous letter to be showed her, until she was strong enough to bear it. She was now convalescent, but could not at present be burdened with any anxiety. The time of her return was postponed for an indefinite period.

There was one more sorrow which cast its shadow over us. Miss Meredith, as soon as Mrs. Beaumont had withdrawn her detectives from the search for the presumed murderess, had employed another staff, whose zeal and energy were quickened by many a secret gift and bribes to a large amount.

The cruelty, the heartlessness, and the injustice of this course was very hard to bear, but we bore it silently.

I had one friend whom Heaven sent me in my deep affliction, who came with generous sympathy, while others gazed from afar upon our sorrow; who identified himself with us when such connection shed no luster on his name; who was kind-hearted and true in our darkest days of humiliation, and this faithful friend was Ernest Lindhurst.

Ah! noble spirit that kept my sick heart from death, I kiss thy hands in love and gratitude!

And so the bat-like wings of time heavily flapped over me,

and bore us in the murky shadows onward, and months crept away into the past.

I leave these dim shades of Cimmerian darkness where the breath of the dead chills me—I come to the second act of the "Secret Vendetta," which was sped by unseen hands.

CHAPTER IX.

"I COMFORT OTHERS, AND GOD COMFORTS ME."

> "My life has crept so long on a broken wing
> Thro' cells of madness, haunts of horror and fear,
> That I come to be grateful at last for a little thing!"
> TENNYSON.

Four months passed away; my first remembered experience of frost and snow; also, my probation of great sorrow.

On the fifth of April, I, by the providence of Heaven, went to visit a district in Jersey City, which had been left in my charge by Miss Belle Cranstown, then absent for some weeks in the country. I may here explain that a society of young ladies had been formed for the purpose of visiting the families of the soldiers who had been disabled in the war, and supplying their wants as far as means would permit.

Miss Cranstown having been called away by the sickness of an aunt or cousin—I cannot remember which—I supplied her place, and as my own district required my presence only two days in the week, I went over on Wednesday by the Jersey City ferry, and found my way up Montgomery street to an obscure lane, where, close beside a large red brick building, with grated windows—as my memorandum, book informed me—I found the address of my first patient.

It was a tall, wooden tenement-house, with brawling families on every floor, and gradually deepening poverty the higher one climbed heavenward; but I was not afraid to pass the groups of rough-looking men, who were grimly enjoying the consternation of their employer at their strike for higher wages, and the gnawing of their own stomachs, as they leaned against the greasy walls, with their hairy arms bare and their feet unshod.

They learned to look for the "Soldiers' Friends" with tattered hats raised, and rough hands outstretched to clear the filthy way for the unaccustomed foot.

I ascended four flights of narrow wooden stairs and knocked at a door on the right hand. A young woman of very girlish aspect opened the door, whose sad face broke into a smile of joy when her eyes lit upon my badge.

"Come in—come in, miss," she said, eagerly; "I'm sure I'm so glad to see you. He'll be at rest now."

She placed a chair for me, and bent over a high bed in a corner, where a young man lay with his eyes closed.

"Charlie! Charlie!"

"I'm not, sleeping, Luce, my girl," said a quiet voice.

"Cheer up, then; here's a Soldiers' Friend come to see you."

The man raised himself slowly and looked at me. He had a thin, cadaverous face, which would have been delicately bleached if he were a gentleman, but was brown with winter's winds and exposure, for he was only a dying soldier. What strength he had—and it was very little now—seemed to flood into his eyes at sight of me; they were hollow and dim with sickness, but the added hope and joy made the face a brave and pleasant one, despite the coming conqueror.

"How kind of you! I was afraid I would have to go without seeing any of you; did No. 10 send you to me, miss, just in the nick of time as I was praying for ye?"

"No. 10 has had to go away to the country, but she sent one in her place; and as of course she knew you wouldn't care as much for a stranger as for her whom you learned to trust, she gave me a recommendation, which I will give you just as it came from her mouth. 'Tell Charlie Harrison that I send you in preference to twenty-seven ladies whom I might ask, because you know how to feel compassion.' There! will that do for a character?"

"Plenty—plenty for me," he responded, softly. His eyes looked wistfully at me as if to draw me nearer; he lifted his head to look at the other empty chair beside him, and I now saw that the poor fellow was utterly helpless, having lost both his arms. It was a log, with a soul in it.

I obeyed his unspoken wish, and seated myself close by his pillow, while tears of sympathy obscured for a moment his face.

"Now, ain't it kind in Heaven to send such deliverers to a poor chap like me, whose days of working are gone forever," he looked at himself apologetically, "and who can only live and eat, and spend money? I often think now that it would have been as well for that poor little girl there if I had died in the Washington Hospital, instead of making believe to mend, and coming here to fall into a decline and swallow all her poor little earnings, and take the roof off her head."

"Oh, Charlie!" cried the poor young creature, springing to his pillow and burying her face in his neck, with a fond, gasping sob; "oh, don't talk so—don't leave me, my own poor boy!"

"Hush! hush, wife dear! we've been very happy in this bit of a home, even though it was you that worked, and me that was the lazy grub in the leaf. I'll be happier when I'm commissioned to join the Blessed Army, Lucy love, that I spent my last furlough here with you. Hush, now, see, the lady, Heaven bless her, is distressed; and we are wasting her time. Run, now, my girl, while I speak to her."

When I could get back my composure, which in truth was somewhat shaken, I put the money which I had brought in the savings-bank I found on the mantel-piece, and drew off my gloves, as I asked if he would like any letters written.

I was not mistaken; the wife went back to the one window and to her slipper-binding; the sick man beckoned me to bend closer, that he might whisper to me.

"It's about her, Lucy, that I'm so anxious," he said; "who'll take care of her when I'm done for, Heaven knows! She's been used to comforts and kindness all her life, and how she'll manage to battle all alone I can't a-bear to think on't. She has a brother—or had—but though I've never said so to her, I'm afraid poor Len Rosecraft's knocked under. We've not heard from him since last year—he was a soldier of the Potomac, miss—when he wrote a letter which Luce got about the middle of November that he was slightly wounded, not lapped like me—only lamed with a gunshot, and as he wasn't no use till he was better he had got leave of absence and was coming to the New York Hospital to be nursed near us; and he had a good bit of money, he said, as he was going to share with Lucy, (she's his only sister, you know, and mighty kind he was to her); well, miss, he wrote that he'd be here by the last of the month, and, miss, by Heaven! we've never seen him yet! She thinks that maybe he changed his mind, and staid to be on hand when he got well, but I don't believe it. Len was a man of his word, and why wouldn't he write again if so? Now, miss, I want to tell you my ideas of this here business; bend down, miss, please—do you remember an awful railway accident that smashed the cars on the 29th of November?"

I shook my head, while a cold chill ran through me at mention of that fateful day to me and mine.

"Well there was, miss, not far from the city; and I can't help hoping poor Leander wasn't on that train, a-coming home wounded and helpless to his sister, to be killed at the last. I haven't said nothing about that to Lucy, of course; I wouldn't; she's got enough to drag her down, poor girl; but it worrits me. I want you to get Len Rosecraft hunted up when I'm taken off; for that girl's not in a state to be left without kith or kin in the world, and him and me was all she had. I'll tell you all I can about him, to guide you."

Here he entered into the description of the man's age, appearance, trade before he enlisted, and other details, all of which I carefully wrote down in my writing-case, to be laid before the society. Then he designated a small box on the mantel-piece, which I placed before him.

"Look over the things in it," he said, "and you'll find the letter; it's addressed to Mrs. C. Harrison, and his photograph is in the bottom of the box; a tall chap—yes, that's him, just as he looked, eleven months ago, standing up as Lucy's groomsman. Now, dear miss, if you'll take them two things away with you, and try to find Len, I'll die easier ; it's hard to have that poor little girl of mine all alone in the world, just when she should be looked after—oh, poor Luce!"

He turned his head away, and subdued the large tears before he proceeded further.

"She never had much hard work to do; she lived with her brother on his snug little farm a little out of Newark, and when I married her, it just turned out that I stole her away from comfort to sit down to starvation, for I was drafted off to the war, and three months after Len was drafted too, and the little farm was rented out, for Luce wouldn't go back to it alone. But as I was telling you, he was mighty fond of Luce, so he sold the bit of land, and it was half of the money he was bringing home to her, which would have been something for my poor mite, when sickness came. It's never come to hand, howsomever, and good, kind Leander is lost."

"You need not fear for her," I said, as soothingly as I could; "the 'Friends' look after the widows, and see that the pension comes to them. I will personally look after Mrs. Harrison until her brother can be found, and if we are unsuccessful in finding him, our society will provide for your wife according to her wants."

The poor fellow thanked me with his swimming eyes.

"It's a load gone from my mind then," he said, "and I'll not worry any more. Madam"—he dropped his voice to a whisper—"there's enough money in that savings bank to bury me; it has been kindly given from time to time by the Soldiers' Friends."

"Don't save that—it was for food and medicine," I replied, "and don't trouble about the other; it will all be attended to."

"Heaven bless your tender face, miss," was the grateful reply.

"I have nothing left to wish for. And will you be pleased to give Friend No. 10 my very best respects and grateful thanks for her great kindness to me and my wife ever since she found us out—if she don't come herself in time?"

I promised, and the wasted face sank back with a satisfied expression. Then I read some holy words of peace to him, and took down the illuminated text which Miss Cranstown had hung on the foot of his bed, replacing it by a new one; and after that I was ready to go.

"Madam, will you let me kiss your hand?" said the young soldier; "I haven't a grip left."

I bent over him with tear-bedewed eyes, and gave the poor boon. Then I went over to the window to give a few words of comfort to the wife. Poor young creature, slow tears were dropping one by one on her hands, as they deftly flew over the dainty satin slipper.

Lucy expressed her gratitude and thanks for the timely aid the Soldiers' Friends had supplied, but I no longer watched her flying fingers, or listened with undivided attention.

Looking down, through the high narrow windows, to see what view this family enjoyed from their elevated position, my eyes encountered the roofs and chimneys of gloomy houses, and far below a walled court, where women were walking back and forward, dressed in dark blue gowns.

"What are the women doing?" I asked, in the first pause.

"Oh, poor things! they're having their afternoon airing."

"What are they?"

"They belong to the big house just next door, miss; it's a private house for mad people, I believe."

"For mad people?"

"Yes, miss—for them as can afford to pay for being mad in private. There's many a person down there in that court, miss, I dare say, whose friends think they're having their seasons in Paris or London, or some o' them fashionable places."

"Are these all mad people, Mrs. Harrison?"

"Yes, miss; the ones in serge is mad—the ones in brown is the matrons. Poor souls! I often pities them, boxed up there."

I bade Charlie Harrison and his wife good-by, and found myself going down the long, steep flights of stairs.

The men, lounging in idle groups, saluted me as before; the women stopped their noisy chattering across entries, and dropped smiling courtesies. Miss Cranstown had other patients in this house, whose small rooms were reeking with soap and water and gay with sand, waiting her arrival, but I passed them unheeded and returned the expectant looks of their inmates with an unconscious stare.

Without, seemingly, the help of my physical powers, I found myself out upon the street and knocking at the door of the house with the grated windows.

A man in livery soon appeared.

"I wish to see the superintendent of this establishment."

"Which of them, ma'am?" hesitated the man.

I began to see that I must be cautious. I pondered an instant.

"Either," I answered; "I have no preference."

I was ushered into a comfortable apartment looking out upon the street, but close barred like the upper windows. I sat like a stone until the man came back.

"Dr. Oaks is engaged particularly, and Mr. Warrick is out. Will you be pleased to write your business at that desk, and leave an address?"

"Impossible—I must be attended to immediately. One

of the matrons will do; bring one to me without loss of time."

Once more I was alone, scarcely breathing—my consciousness all submerged in one thought.

In two minutes the man returned; there was an apologetic smile on his face.

"I am sorry to say that all the matrons are particularly engaged, too, madam. The fact is, it is against the rule for visitors to be received into this establishment; all business, however urgent, is conducted by letter. You had better write a note, madam, and I will carry it to the doctor."

"That won't do," I said, rising; "the matrons are walking with the patients in the court"—he gazed at me in surprise, and I returned a look of cool determination—"so without taking any of them from their duties, I will, if you please, be conducted to the court-yard where they are."

As he still hesitated, evidently taken by surprise, I advanced resolutely with the half-formed intention of passing him.

My wild expression in this instance stood my friend. Evidently thinking I was insane myself, he started back, closed the door, and rushed down a flight of stairs, probably to summon a keeper. I determined to risk all in one bold move, so I softly reopened the door, watched the man's hand on the iron balustrade until it had disappeared, then lightly followed him, keeping my garments out of sight.

He was unlocking a door at the end of a long corridor, with the upper half grated; I lurked behind an angle until he had passed through, then rushed after him. I was a second too late, however—the door closed with a spring and left me inside, gazing through the bars.

I saw what I came to see, however.

A file of women passed on the damp stone flags, not ten feet from me; round they came, some forty souls, in sad procession, two by two, with hands clasped before them in listless apathy. The women in brown kept an inner circle, marching round with watchful eyes and stern mien; and here and there a poor soul was sharply reprimanded, whose hands were pinioned and whose eyes glared from side to side, as her lips babbled with ceaseless energy.

But one among this Comus-like crew crept gently on, with head downcast and hards meekly folded together on her breast; and of them all her face was whitest and saddest.

'The rough serge gown was wrapped about a form once fairy-like with grace and health; but the coarse garment had dragged it into a stooping figure with a hollow chest; the brown hair was shorn, yet shone in flat rings like amber circlets round the pallid brow; the long, slender neck was bending meekly and bearing its yoke without demur; the little feet flitted wearily over the cold flagstones. Nearer it came —this apparition.

She lifted her eyes slowly—they filled with wonder and joy—then she glided out of the ranks and fell upon the ground outside the bars.

And this woman in the blue serge gown, whose companion waited for her with pointed finger and ghastly mirth— this woman, with the faded face and hollow, stooping form —great Heaven! *she was my sister!*

CHAPTER X.

TAKING UP THE DETECTIVE BUSINESS.

"Help, master—help! here's a fish hangs in the net, like
A poor man's right in the law; 'twill hardly come out!"

The man in livery, with a matron by his side, was hurrying toward us. I stretched my arms through the iron bars and seized my sister's hand. Come what would, I would hold her now.

"Why—what business have you here, madam?" cried the woman, angrily. "See, now, what you've done to this patient, and the rest will be as bad. Come—get up, and move along; no tricks, now!"

She put her firm hand on my sister's shoulder, and forcibly dragged her out of my reach; not before I had felt a sudden pressure upon my palm from my sister's fingers."

"Oh, be prudent," she breathed, almost inaudibly, with her eyes on the ground.

I gazed eagerly after her, as she feebly rose, assisted by the matron, and was allowed to sit on a wooden bench running along the high wall. I prayed God in my heart to grant me patience and wisdom to know what to do.

"Strangers are never allowed here," said the matron, opening the door with a key at her girdle. and dashing down an iron shutter over the bars. "And, Hobson, I can tell you, you'll hear about this, you stupid fool!" she continued, turning sharply to the man in livery, who was now beside us. "Come along, madam, and state your business above."

I was prudent, making no demonstration when my Isolina was again hidden from me, but followed silently the woman back to the room I had left.

"Now, ma'am," she said, grimly, "as brief as you can, if you please; my time is precious."

"I wish to understand what this establishment is, and what its rules are," I responded, in as quiet a tone as I could assume.

"This is a strictly private house, madam, for insane ladies whose families wish to conceal the calamity. As for the rules, one of the most stringent is that no visitor is allowed to see the patients, except by written order of the parties who placed them here. I'm sorry that you saw fit to break the rules, madam. I suppose you will not take advantage of the knowledge you have picked up to go and make mischief."

The half-cajoling, half-threatening manner of the woman aroused my particular attention. I began to understand that this establishment might not be always conducted on principles of the strictest honesty, and this knowledge made me doubly cautious.

"I shall take advantage of nothing, if my business is attended to in a satisfactory manner," I said. "I would like to know if a patient's family can come and reclaim her, when they think she has enjoyed the advantages of this house long enough?"

"Every patient is sent here for a certain term," returned the matron, warily; "for five, ten, or even twenty years; after which they are returned to the persons who sent them, unless the lease be renewed. We never change these rules."

"But supposing the person who sent them took the right upon themselves without consulting the family of the patient, what then?"

"We have no responsibility in the matter," said the matron, rising; "all business of sending or returning patients is done by letter. We never receive any personal communications, and no one ever recovers an inmate of this house who does not bring an order from the person who placed her here."

I thought carefully for a moment if I could go safely further, and decided to trust no longer to my own wisdom.

' "Thank you," I said, also rising, "I am satisfied with your report. I shall communicate with Doctor Oaks tomorrow."

It was five o'clock when I reached home. "Go," I said to Nelson, the coachman, "as fast as you can fly to my father's office, and tell him to come home." He sped with a will. I watched him run into the street, hail a passing cab, and rattle off in a cloud of dust out of sight. I did not indulge in my feelings, but sat still as a mouse, and calm as a stoic, in my father's room, thinking over the course we should pursue. Yet, by some means, all the servants seemed to know something had happened, and they whispered in the halls, and passed in and out on various pretenses, and gazed at me with eager, expectant glances.

In less than fifteen minutes the same cab drew up with a violent jerk at the gate, and my father hastily entered. At sight of him I felt my face growing hot with excitement; I was afraid my composure would give way, and so indeed it did, for I could not restrain myself from rushing out to the door and throwing myself trembling with the joyful tidings into his arms.

"What is it, dearest?" faltered my father. "I was afraid it was bad news—now I am almost afraid the news is too good. Come in here and tell me."

We re-entered my father's room and shut the door. I was calm again, although my voice was tremulous.

"I saw some one whom we both love, papa—some one who has been—who has been lost."

"Go on, Ivanilla."

"I would like you to go with me and fetch her home."

He ceased his rapid walk and faced me.

"Where is she?"

"She is well, father, quite well; but some one has put her into a place for insane people in Jersey City."

"Is she mad?"

"Heavens, no! that at least I am sure of. Whoever put her there did so very wickedly. But I will tell you the whole story."

I sat down, and in a few rapid words recounted my adventures. He listened anxiously.

"I am afraid we shall find it hard to get her out of their clutches," said my father. "It is clear to me from what you say that the whole concern is a swindle, where any one can be safely kept out of the way by paying well. The surest way of recovering her, would be to pay Dr. Oak visit this evening in company with a couple of detectives.

"But father!" I exclaimed, turning pale, "do you forget that a warrant is already issued for the murderer of young Beaumont? Are you willing to have our poor Isolina torn from us at the instant of our reunion, to undergo a public trial?"

We remained gazing at each other for some minutes. I cannot even faintly portray the repugnance and consternation which we both felt as we contemplated our poor Isolina's position; perfectly stanch in our convictions of her innocence, at that moment we both regarded the arm of the law with anything but friendly feelings.

"Ransom her, father," I said, "take any peaceable course to make them give her up quietly, and let us take her privately home, until we can go safely somewhere for the summer with her. She is not strong enough for any trouble just now."

"I will certainly keep her out of the reach of any rascally warrant," said my father, firmly, "until we have heard her own explanations, and gathered proofs of her innocence. We will go this very hour for her, and try, by either threats or bribery to get her out of their hands, before they have time to remove her out of our reach."

"They will not look for any communication before to-morrow," I said. "So we will take them unawares if we go to-night."

We conferred together some minutes longer, at the end of which Nelson was dispatched for a carriage, and I went to gather some needful articles of clothing for my sister, while my father filled his pocket-book with bills, in case of need.

It was a few minutes to six when we left the house and drove swiftly down to the Jersey City ferry.

"If all else fails," continued my father sadly, "I shall be obliged to put the matter in the hands of the police, even at the risk of seeing the poor girl conveyed from the mad-house to the prison."

"Do not fall back upon that," I urged, anxiously, "until we are satisfied that neither money nor threats have any effect. If, as you suspect, it is really a dishonest establishment, *I* may manage to give them some trouble; you know I saw most of their patients, and if any of them have been unlawfully concealed there like our Isolina, I can easily rouse the fears of the proprietors."

While we conferred, we had crossed the ferry, and were now entering the narrow lane from Montgomery street, when after a few directions to Nelson, we alighted, and leaving the carriage a few blocks off, threaded our way through the tortuous windings to the red brick building.

To my father's peremptory knock, the same man in livery appeared. He started back in consternation when he beheld me, and gave a quick glance at my father, which seemed rather to deepen his discomfort. Seen in the indistinct light of dusk, with his tall figure, and dark, stern face, he might be very properly taken for a person of authority—the Inspector of Police, at least; by a man, who had evidently often watched for such visitors before.

" I must see Doctor Oaks," said my father.

Away sped the man, with the alacrity of alarm, leaving us on the outer door step. After a protracted absence, during which a close cab drove up and stationed itself at the door, he came back.

" Come in," he said, trying to affect urbanity, and throwing wide the door; " Dr. Oaks will be most happy ——" here he caught sight of the cab, and remained wildly staring. " Walk in here," he said, recovering himself, and eagerly ushering us into the room that I had before entered. We did so, but no sooner had he withdrawn, than I followed him and stood at the entrance door within the shadow, listening with strained ears to his first words to the cabman. He ran out and now stood on the muddy pavement, telegraphing his arms excitedly.

"Drive on—drive on!" he exclaimed, angrily, "what makes you draw up here when you see persons at the door? Get off, out of this, and don't come back for half an hour, perhaps we sha'n't get the party moved to-night."

The cabman smote his lean horses into motion, and the servant slowly re-entered the hall where I waited.

" Take care, Hobson," I uttered, in a voice of warning, "that this house doesn't get itself into trouble. You had better send that cab home, when it comes here again. You hear?"

"Madam," said the man, who was in truth very much alarmed, "it's not my blame—I have got nothing to do but obey—and I hope nobody'll take the trouble to get me into a scrape."

"You need hope nothing of the kind," I returned, "unless you make yourself of service to us. See that no inmate of this house is removed without our knowledge, within the next hour."

The man promised with a profusion of assurances that he would do his best to warn us, and hearing steps, I slipped back to my father. I had just succeeded in whispering a few words to him, when the heavy tread approached us and a large, pompous individual entered, with a benignly bald head, a gold-rimmed double eye-glass astride his nose, and a half frightened expression on his broad, fleshy face. The instant, however, that his eyes lit on his visitors, the expression changed to severe grandeur and he seated himself with a portentous clearing of his throat.

"Doctor Oaks—at your service," he said, sonorously, while the stout chair creaked beneath his culminating weight; "there is some mistake here, I fancy—I was given to understand that a person—that a person, sir, who was entitled to gain admission, waited to see me. Who may you be, sir?"

"A person who has been sent here," said my father, looking at me, "to inquire into some circumstances connected with this house."

"Indeed—indeed!" repeated the doctor, tapping with his large fingers on the arm of his chair, and evidently puzzling himself as to the speaker's probable authority.

"To tell the truth," continued my father, in the same quiet tone, "a young lady who has for some time been missing from her friends has been traced to this establishment. I have no desire to bring this establishment at present under the surveillance of the law; but I would advise you, sir, to attend to this lady's request."

He looked at me in the same manner as before, and I turned boldly to the huge superintendent, whose rubicund face was now slightly streaked with fear or anger.

"The patient whom I saw walking in the court this afternoon is my sister who was abducted four months ago,"

I said, steadily. "I will claim her quietly, and say nothing of what I have become acquainted with in the house, if you deliver her to this gentleman and me immediately."

My listener's double eye-glass glared up and down my person with an air of awful majesty—anger prevailing over fear.

"This house is conducted on strictly honorable principles! I would have you know, madam, that no patient ever entered these walls who was not pronounced incurably insane by two physicians! We never admitted any one who was not made over to us by bond and seal of their natural or lawful guardians! Madam, I defy you to produce one proof that can impeach our integrity. *Others* may have made mistakes, or sought to defraud us by putting under our charge ladies over whom they had no legal authority. *We* have not the responsibility of that. We are not punishable for other people's frauds! *Abducted* indeed!"

He folded his arms magnificently and regarded me with virtuous indignation.

"Very good, doctor," said my father. "You have left a loop-hole of escape for yourself. We shall not look into your manifestations of integrity, but take the young lady who has been fraudulently pawned upon you and go."

"What is the name? I shall look in my books if she is here," said the superintendent, still puzzling himself over my father's real character, and half-dubiously coming to the point.

"Nay," said my father, smiling, "more than likely she has been entered here under a false name. Better ask nothing about it. The less you meddle in the circumstances the safer for you. You are not, as you say, punishable for other people's frauds."

"Then how am I to know which patient this lady claims as a sister?" queried the doctor.

"Any of the matrons will tell you which of the patients rushed to the grated door upon seeing me," I interposed.

"And now, before you produce the lady," remarked my father, "I would ask you a few questions. Who sent her here as a lunatic?"

"Sir, I am a man of honor!" exclaimed the doctor, flying into a passion, and betraying his knowledge of what patient we had come to claim; "and having given my promise to keep secret the names of my patrons, I claim the right, sir, to keep my word. No gentleman, sir, would ask me to break it!"

"I shall be sorry to extort the necessary information from Doctor Oaks by public measures!" said my father, quietly.

This threat had a very visible effect on the broad physiognomy of the superintendent. Its hanging cheeks became purple, and its ample lips pursued out with the dumb expression of feelings of the very liveliest order.

"I give you five minutes to remember the circumstances," added my father, sternly.

"Sir, I—I am ready to do my utmost to oblige," burst out the good doctor, retreating into his big shell with almost undignified haste; "but upon my honor, I know very little about it. The lady was sent here on the first day of December in a carriage with one servant, who delivered a letter, saying that Miss White would be made our charge until sent for; and meantime, her first year's payment accompanied her. We wrote out her indentures and returned them with the man, who drove away, and left her in our charge!"

"And why did you not demand proper proof of their right to deposit any lady with you?" exclaimed my father. "Was this honest dealing? And what guarantee have you that her fee for next year will be paid? And if not, what will become of her? She will be cherished here on the memory of her last year's fee, I suppose? Or perhaps her incurable insanity will about this time prove fatal!"

"Sir—sir!" cried the doctor, turning very pale, "I assure you that such a thing never occurred, and this is an altogether unprecedented case. Still, we have attended to the lady with the most devoted care, and loaded her with kindness on account of her very fragile health. She has had medical attendance of the highest order—yes, I may say the very highest, sir. I hope that will be taken into account."

"It shall certainly be taken into account, sir, and the character of the attendance most strictly examined into, if the lady's health is found to have been tampered with."

"My dear young lady!" exclaimed Dr. Oaks, turning anxiously to me, "your sister was in a state of settled melancholy when she reached us; I believe she is suffering from a softening of the brain, which will ultimately develop into hypochondria. We tried all that skill could do, but I confess in this case we have failed. Madam, I am only desirous of restoring her to her friends since she is beyond our skill; so I will give immediate orders that she be prepared to accompany you."

The doughty superintendent rose and violently rang a bell; suppressed fury and mortification had turned his obese face blue and convulsed. His double eye-glass covered my father with a suspicious and glassy scowl.

The man in livery appeared at the door.

"Order Matron No. 6 to gather Miss White's wardrobe together and prepare her for a journey immediately."

"She's all ready, sir, and the cab is at the door," said the man, with a side glance quick as light toward me.

"Fool!" muttered the man of honor, darting a malevolent scowl at his retainer. "You must be making a mistake," he added, for the general benefit; "I will see to this myself."

He hurried out, pushing his man like stubble from his path; but Mr. Hobson, whose eye was firmly fixed upon the main chance, soon crept back again.

"They've been waiting for you to get out of the way for the last twenty minutes," he said, in a rasping whisper; "Mr. Warrick has sat with his top-coat on till he is blistered with heat, and the patient—she won't be the better for his temper."

"Where did they intend to convey her?" asked my father.

"To a country institootion!" said the man, with a grin. "When the city gets too hot to hold any of the incurables, they prescribe country air for 'em, and when they get whisked off there, they're not found again, you better believe."

"You are a sensible fellow," said my father, tossing him a twenty-dollar bill "Take that, and if you see anything going on that doesn't strike your notions of propriety in connection with Miss White, come and tell me. Off now."

The man disappeared with a knowing nod, and in five minutes we heard the wheels of a carriage leave the door. We were becoming every instant more distrustful, when Doctor Oaks re-entered the room, his heavy brows bearing evidence of a recent explosion.

"I regret to say that Miss White is unfit to travel to-day," he said, with a succession of bows. "The excitement which she experienced to-day has left her in a very weak state. I will undertake to have her all ready for her friends to-morrow morning. Madam, for her sake, will you agree to this?"

"No!" answered my father for me, rising and looking resolutely at the doctor full in the face. "We shall either leave this house with the lady we demand, or I shall force you to answer for every dishonest dealing which has taken place since your private asylum was formed."

"Gently—gently, my dear sir!" exclaimed Doctor Oaks, turning yellow with alarm; "there's no necessity in the world for such violent measures—and of course I do not fear them, even if you put them into execution. However, it shall be as you wish—the young person shall be delivered up."

He departed with great alacrity, leaving us breathing more freely, in the hope that she was still within our reach.

The man in livery came and lit a small gasolier in the hall, and then pleasantly grinning, whispered a few remarks to us.

"There's been the greatest rumpus! Mr. Warrick is furious, and determined not to give in. He's for putting you off, and then making tracks, bag and baggage, through the night; but Oaks, who's the awfullest coward ever dared to be a rogue, won't have it so. I guess, though, the doctor will give you the girl all right now."

His head suddenly disappeared as a distant sound became audible, and we were left once more alone.

Some minutes expired in silent attention, when my ears caught the sound of feet approaching; not heavy and ponderous footsteps, but such as set my heart beating tumultuously. I gazed down the long stone corridor and saw two women approaching—one in a blue serge gown, the other in brown.

She came, white and eager-faced; her hands outstretched, her eyes straining, her heart out-leaping her haggard feet; she came at last, my lost sister, and fell upon my breast.

Oh, Heaven be thanked for this joy!

I wiped away her rushing tears, and with convulsive embraces whispered words of incoherent joy.

"My darling! my poor ne! have we got you at last? Have we got you at last?"

Then I remembered my father, but he was taking no notice of us, and listening to what the matron was saying in the hall.

"We couldn't get the lady's things gathered at such short notice," she was saying, "so Doctor Oaks says he will be happy to see you to-morrow, and answer to the best of his ability any questions you may wish to ask, and the wardrobe will be ready by that time. Also, Doctor Oaks hopes that the young lady and you will excuse him coming to you this evening, as a patient requires his particular care just at present."

"Tell Doctor Oaks to be ready to meet me by twelve o'clock to-morrow," answered my father, gravely; "and be so kind as to dispatch some one to the corner of the lane for a carriage which is waiting there."

Mr. Hobson made himself visible at this, and civilly offered to do us that service. While he was gone, my father suffered himself to look toward his child for the first time, though secretly, lest the curious matron might discover the emotions which rose to his face, and guess at his relationship to the patient. Ah! who could crush back the rising tear, who looked at that pallid, wasted creature, in her prison dress?

In a few minutes the carriage arrived, and in the next minute I had led Isolina out from under the roof of Doctor Oak's private asylum, and seen her safely seated in the back seat, with the wrappings we had brought placed upon her; and the bonnet and shawl which the asylum provided, thrown on the door step of that institution.

"My good fellow," said my father to Hobson, who officiously held the carriage door for him, "here's another testimonial to your worth," he handed him a twenty dollar bill, "and take my advice—don't let me catch you waiter here on my next descent upon the worthy establishment. Drive on, coachman."

Nelson, whose soft, melodious whistling had subsided into dead silence at the appearance of his lost mistress, now planted the hat, which in his surprise he had snatched off, back on his head, sprang to his seat, gave a triumphant chirp to his horses, and drove fleetly toward the ferry.

And at last my father was free to take his long-lost child in his arms, and bid her fear and grieve no more. She was his again, leaning on his heart as she had nestled, a happy, happy infant; she would creep into her place there, and tell him all the woeful story that had riven her from him, and never again should he suffer one shadow to come between his darling girl and him.

"Look up—look up, my precious one," he was whispering; "don't tremble any more, you are safe now, you are in your old father's arms, and he will keep you safe, my Lina."

But she only trembled the more, and clung with her cold, pale hands to me, never speaking, never lifting her hidden face.

"Give her time—let her feel that she is safe," I whispered.

So in silence we whirled through the crowded streets, and brought her home in the lamplight.

We led her up the garden path amid scented hyacinths, and, with our eyes filled with tears, bade her joyous welcome.

"You've come back to your father's roof, my darling, and Heaven grant that you may be safe and happy here!"

The servants gathered round with many a noisy exclamation of joy and consternation quickly following; Sophie spasmodically dropping torrents of tears hovered with longing eyes, and did what my father and I left undone, in our urgent affection; and at last the dear wanderer was left with us alone, and we were free to hear that hidden story of her woe.

And now it struck me how silent she had been since first we clasped her; how strangely passive and subdued, and now I saw that the proud, free spirit evermore had fled—that the fire, the vehemence of old was cold and lifeless, that the hidden soul was heavy with the horrors it had seen.

"Speak now, my beloved child," said my father, tenderly; "pour into our ears the strange events which have kept you from us, and placed you in that frightful place, and trust me to find the brutal offenders and punish them."

She turned as pallid as death; her teeth chattered; she eyed him with terror; she shrank back from him.

"Iva—Iva!" she moaned, casting herself into my arms; "tell him not to—not to make me speak!"

"There, my darling, there!" cried my poor father, with the tears upon his cheek, "don't eye me that way; I'll let you rest. my poor girl."

So we laid her down and soothed her fears, and she lay quiet, looking at me.

Well might I ask—was this our Isolina? Ah, now I felt how I had yearned for my Beautiful; how my heart had clung to her bright vision—how fond memory had painted me, my radiant sister; now that my eyes watched this wasted figure in the blue serge gown. And envious recollection cast up in pathetic contrast, a brilliant picture of "The Beautiful Rienzi" as last she stood in this room, robed in richness, her cheeks like the heart of a Languedoc rose, when the sunset gleams most redly through the leaves, her eyes filled with beauty's rays, her form replete with nature's rarest gifts.

Away with that fairy dream! Let it not touch the grief-stricken gray of this picture; gone is the tender grace of that day, vanished the brightness, the joy!

The shadow has spread dim wings above the sunny head and touched the bloom with death; the hand of Ruth has been busy; the unholy spell has been flung!

And yet—this dear wreck—she looks at me with silent, suffering tenderness; she will not speak, but her mute glance speaks for her and knits my sobbing heart to hers. Wrecked as she is, silent, mysterious, changed, I clasp her in my arms, and cry, with grateful soul uplifted:

" *Thank Heaven she is home again!*"

CHAPTER XI.

CONSPIRACY TO CHEAT THE GALLOWS.

> " Oh! breaking heart that will not break,
> Oh! pale, pale face, so sweet and meek,
> Thou smilest, but thou dost not speak,
> What wantest thou? whom dost thou seek?"
>   TENNYSON.

And now our duty lay plain before us.

Seeing that Isolina Rienzi was in her proper senses, though a little inclined to melancholy madness; furthermore, seeing that she either would not or could not throw any light on her share in the events which led to Cecil Beaumont's violent death, it behooved my father to mortify the weakness of his flesh, and display the same metal as that model of justice, who condemned his own son to death, and enjoyed the spectacle.

But my father was no Brutus; and had he been, I fear his kind soul would have been severely hampered by my outcries against this glutting of the sword of justice.

Therefore, in our mutual tender-heartedness, we determined as far and as long as circumstances would permit to keep the proscribed individual concealed in her own home, from the too hungry teeth of the law until she could gather up a measure of strength to survive its shaking.

We adjured our few servants to keep discreet silence on the subject of her return; and let me say here for the honor of American reticence and fidelity, that as far as I could judge, they never betrayed the confidence we reposed in them.

We had her apartment exclusively on the third story, and it consisted of her own bedroom and dressing-room, which were adjoining each other, and quite out of the way of casual visitors. These rooms were guardedly locked, and Sophie and I attended to her wants exclusively.

We thus hoped to be permitted to nurse our poor enfeebled girl for a time unharassed by the painful and harrowing steps which would inevitably be taken, as soon as she should be discovered by Miss Meredith's detectives.

For we found that she was shattered in health and in spirits to a pitiable degree. Her whole frame seemed to have been crushed by some jarring shock; her constitution was almost destroyed; and her nerves were so painfully weak that the slightest incident was sufficient to startle her almost into a frenzy of terror.

But while I proudly watched over my invalid sister, others had not been idle.

Upon my father repairing on the following day to Jersey City to keep the appointment he had made with Dr. Oaks, for the purpose of forcing the truth out of him concerning the person who had put Isolina into his charge, hey, presto! the scene was changed as completely as a juggler's trick. The large brick house was silent and empty; the brass knocker woke dismal echoes when he plied it; a large placard in the window announced that "This house to let,"

awaited any gentleman's pleasure who had a use for the
grated windows.

Dr. Oaks and his compeer with their prey and their
myrmidons had doubtless withdrawn into discreet retirement for a time, or flourished in some distant city safe from
the pursuit of inquisitive relatives and meddlesome detectives.

So, until my sister could tell us her story, all extraneous
knowledge seemed unattainable ; and we gathered in our
interests and centered them on her.

Oh! it was sad to mark the changes which these four
months had wrought in her.

Lovely she ever had been, and ever would be, even should
years creep one by one upon her and dull youth's freshness,
but now in her weakness, and gentle, uncomplaining
melancholy, there was almost a light and sweetness too holy
to be borne by eyes of love.

So engrossed was I with my poor sister, that I suffered a
week to pass before I resumed my visits to the soldiers'
families which had been so abruptly broken off.

Having carried the letter and photograph which had been
intrusted to me, to our superintendent, and held a consultation with my comrades on the matter, it was resolved
to send an agent to the Potomac, where the company in
which young Rosecraft had been, still was stationed, and
having gathered all available information from that point,
to trace him as faithfully as possible to his present quarters.

Having set in train the arrangements for carrying out
Harrison's wishes, I next directed my steps to the ferry, to
finish my visiting in Miss Cranstown's district. I found
abundant work awaiting me, and many objects of interest;
but none so sad as that which encountered my eyes, on running up at last to tell poor Charlie Harrison what I had
done.

There he lay dead, in his poor coffin of painted deal, his
kind face smoothed at last from lines of pain and white,
since the fever flush was gone forever. There he lay, calm
and moveless, though the girl for whom his last hours had
been so heavy, was weeping and moaning beside him; there
he lay with the fixed smile on his violet lips, with the fixed
eyelid sealed to the hollow cheek. The young soldier had
gone to join a host whose victories have crowned them each

a king; whose captain showed them how to fight, and how to die.

No more pain and weariness, no more care for Charlie Harrison. He has won his commission and gone away.

I took the young widow under my especial charge, and had her comfortably boarded in a safe family, where she could ply her trade and be under no fear that she would be homeless.

There I left her, until we should see if Leander Rosecraft could be found.

I took great care to go out as much as I had done before the event which had happened in our family; to frequent every scene which it might be supposed I would frequent; to be a constant and always to be depended upon visitor and servant in my society; and to keep up exactly the same demeanor of quiet grief, which I had observed before my sister was found. This was scarcely feigned; my grief was only one degree less now in the daily contemplation of my beloved one's sufferings.

Mr. Lindhurst came as usual, and in his kind, thoughtful way strove to fling rays of sunshine across my gloomy path. But, much as I learned to love him and depend upon him, I closed this page of my heart even from him, and locked the secret return within the limits of our own house.

I found her on the 5th day of April, and we nursed her quietly and without apparent danger for nearly four weeks, during which time we could not see that she gained much strength; and, what was even more painful, notwithstanding the ceaseless and tender love which we both lavished upon her; she still remained sunk in the profoundest melancholy.

Day after day found all our efforts futile to kindle a spark of light in that darkened heart. The father, whose deep, tender soul was yearning over his child, only seemed to throw additional shadow over her whenever he appeared. It became heart-rending to me to watch the sad, gentle face of my sister grow hard and despairing, whenever our father's foot sounded on the stairs. He would wait for me to unlock the door, and steal in with a basket of rarest fruit in his hand, and a smile on his dear, tender face; and it would be:

"Will my Lina taste these grapes? See, how large and luscious, and sweet as those grown on the sunny sides of

Vesuvius! Will my own darling tell her old father how she is to-day? Let me see those downcast eyes, if they are clear and bright!"

And, oh! to see her turn away in anguished coldness, while the tears dropped down her cheeks, and her quivering lips kept that stern and unending silence!

On the second of May a letter came from my long-absent mother which threw my father and me into such a transport of delight as we had not known in many a long day. It informed us that she had recovered from her long and obstinate malady; that she knew all the calamities which had fallen upon us, and had resolved to join us immediately and help us to bear our sorrows; that she trusted in Heaven that our Isolina's fate should be made known to us, and did not despair; that she would bring faith and hope with her, to cheer us, and that together we should trace to its source the plot which had driven one of our number from us.

This letter, so strong and healthful in its tone, infused new life into us; it spoke of hope, and bade us look beyond the present darkness; it seemed to prophesy a happier era.

"Run and tell your sister the joyful news," was my father's first thought. "Tell her that she'll soon have a mother to make her well—that will rouse her."

I hastened up stairs with the letter fluttering in my hand; my face was beaming with happiness; my whole being was transposed with joy; I was the impersonification of hope; I was the "bearer of good news from a far country."

In this state of mind I let myself into the sunless room, where alone my silent sister sat, a book unopened by her side, her dark, melancholy eyes resting on vacancy.

"My darling!" I exclaimed, placing myself before her, "I have such good news to tell you!"

She turned her spectral face and gazed at me in wonder, as if the light and life which I had brought with me were dazzling her dim sight.

"Papa sent me up with a message," I continued, in a tone of subdued eagerness. "He said 'tell her that her mother is coming to make her well,' and she is—she is, my darling; she will be here in a few weeks; she says so in her letter."

Strange, indeed, was the effect of my glad tidings.

My sister's face gradually became livid and almost distorted with a look of horror. She clasped her hands, and rose, looking at me wildly.

"My mother?" she gasped.

"Yes," I answered, abashed and affrighted; "our dear mother who has been desperately ill for months; she is coming home. Oh, sister, I thought this would make you glad!"

Her face relaxed and vibrated with a flood of emotion; she turned away and flung herself down, weeping bitterly. There was no joy in these tears; it was bitter, bitter grief.

"Isolina," I said, gently, "it is mamma. Surely you will not grieve when you understand that she is coming home to leave us no more. We shall all be home, then, dear, and you will be in the midst, safe from harm."

"No, no, no!" she moaned; "I shall go away!"

The last ray of pleasure vanished from my heart, leaving me pale and cold as she had been.

"Sister, what can you mean?" I cried; "go away? Where would you go away from mamma? Alas, poor sister, what are you saying? No one can love you like a mother!"

"Forbear!" she muttered, with a shudder—"let me forget, if I can. Yes!" she exclaimed, raising her face from her hands with a wild light flashing in her eye; "let me forget her, if I can—let memory die, if it will!"

Oh, what did these wild words mean? I dared not ask. The turbid veins were throbbing in her throat like dark cords; her breath was coming in short, choking gasps. I could only take her hands in mine, and hold them tenderly, until the sad paroxysm had lessened in violence, then I ventured to approach the subject by bringing in another. These words of hers about going away had alarmed me; I would show her how impossible it was, and instill it in her mind, so that if ever the crazy idea came to her again she would relinquish it.

"Isolina," I commenced, cautiously, "I am afraid you must feel very dull here in these two rooms, with the top of the house for exercise, do you not?"

Her attention was arrested, and she questioned me with her sweet sad eyes, mutely, as if to know what I was driving at.

"Have you noticed," I continued, "how we have kept

you hidden from strangers, and these doors locked ever since you came home?"

"Yes," she answered, in a rapid whisper, "but bolts and bars are nothing to her when she chooses to come."

"Who, sister, who?"

She pulled her hands from me, and covered her face.

"Never mind my ravings," she said, in a low voice; "I am insane, you know—a monomaniac."

"Nonsense! You are not to think so, Isolina; it is not true."

"Dr. Oaks and Mr. Warrick pronounced me so before they admitted me into their asylum."

"Two rogues. They were paid to conceal you from your family, Isolina, and I have no doubt they were paid by some wretch to pronounce you insane. Ah, I wish you could tell me who sent you there."

I allowed my excitement to carry me too far, and regretted the words as soon as they were said.

She recoiled from me, and fell to trembling.

"Have I said anything?" she whispered, brokenly.

"Oh, darling Isolina," I exclaimed, bursting into tears of distress, as I felt that her confidence was beyond my skill to win, "why do you hold aloof from us thus? You know that we would sacrifice anything to give you happiness or save you from danger. Oh, why will you not let us help you?"

She wrung her hands, and with large tears flowing down her pale cheeks, eyed me sorrowfully.

"I am breaking your heart, dearest," she said, bending toward me; "Let me go away, and forget me."

"No," I ejaculated, alarmed beyond measure to find that this insane fancy still clung to her. "If you go away from this house they will arrest you, and put you in prison.

"Why?"

Had I done wrong? I trembled at my own imprudence, but went on.

"No one can find out the cause of—of Mr. Beaumont's death, and they suspect—they have dared to suspect——"

It seemed to strike her in a flash.

"That *I* murdered him—*me*?" she cried. "Oh, poor Cecil; and I would have gladly died to save him."

I gazed at her vehemently. In my unskillful hands the secret indeed had slipped from my reach, but this I had heard from her own lips, this blessed assurance to set our hearts at rest—*she was innocent*.

Not that we required such an assertion from her, but perhaps when she was stronger, she might tell us sufficient to save her from the misguided grasp of the law.

I went down to my father, who was anxiously waiting the issue of my news, and told him all that had transpired.

CHAPTER XII.

TWO MESSENGERS AT THE DOOR.

"Softly! she is lying
With her lips apart;
Gently! she is dying
Of a broken heart."—Anon.

I was sitting alone in my father's room, anxiously waiting his appearance. At this moment he was with my sister, venturing to probe her memory gently; and I, chafing and trembling, misdoubted the result more and more as the minutes flew by.

It was almost an hour before he returned to me, and I saw by his face that he had failed.

"I have no influence with her," he sighed, throwing himself upon a sofa in an attitude of deep dejection; "she recoils from the subject, and from us all, I think. And, unfortunately, I have thrown her into a state of dangerous excitement."

"Shall I go to her?" I exclaimed, rising.

"No; she does not wish to see you; she told me to send her up Sophie, and not to allow Iva to go—she wished rest. To prefer a servant to you, her little sister, who should share each thought of her breast! It hurts me, little Iva, for you've been faithful to her.

"I don't feel it, father," I said, with would-be calmness. "You know she is sick, and has strange fancies."

"Oh, my girls!" he burst out, laying his quivering hand on my shoulder, "you whom I have encircled in one arm, and covered with my handkerchief when you were little birdlings together; what tears you so wide apart now? And to think—to think that she could cry scorn on her father's love."

He drew me close and groaned on my shoulder. He saw at last that icy wall which had risen up and shut him out; nothing but his blind unsuspicion could have made him blind so long. Grieving mutely for him, with nothing but silence for comfort, I softly kissed his brow.

"I will tell you the substance of our interview," he said, mastering his emotion after a time. "As you may suppose, it was a long time before I saw my way clear to come to the point. At last, when she appeared to be quite calm and reasonable, I asked her if she would answer a few questions which it was necessary for me to ask her. She instantly got up with much alarm in her manner, and cried that she would answer nothing. I tenderly asked her the reason, and got no answer. But dearest, I said, it is absolutely necessary that you explain what led to young Beaumont's death. Your life is in danger, unless you confide to some one the circumstances, so that they may be used for your benefit."

"'I cannot tell you anything,' she said, huskily.

"'You must,' I repeated, with firmness, 'I cannot leave this room until I understand your position.'

"She turned as pale as death, and eyed me strangely.

"'Who killed Cecil Beaumont?' I proceeded.

"'No one,' was the answer.

"'What?—was it an accident?' I cried, 'were you with him, and was it an accident?'

"She began to weep and moan, 'poor Cecil! poor Cecil?'

"'But answer me,' I urged.

"'What?—you demand an explanation?' she exclaimed, turning with sudden excitement on me.

"'I wished to know for your own sake, my child,' I answered, soothingly.

"This colloquy lasted for some time, but in spite of her feebleness, her excitement, and her weakness, I gained nothing from her. At last I relinquished that question, and took up another.

"'Tell me what secret you have, which you hide from me, and receive my counsel.'

"A strange, bitter smile crossed her lips, but she was speechless. I attempted to draw her to my arms, in order to win, by love and pity, her confessions, but she recoiled from me with a shriek.

"'Go away!' she cried, 'don't touch me!'

He stopped, overcome by his own recital, and bowed his face in his hands; silver hairs were glistening among his dark locks, and these added dignity to his sorrow. I drew near and knelt beside him, and we mingled our tears together.

"She repulsed me completely," he continued, sternly conquering his emotion, and retired to her chamber to avoid me. "I could not believe that she actually shunned me, and I followed to the door, for one more appeal. "'Lina, my darling girl,' I said, scarcely able to keep these tears from unmanning me, 'come to your old father's arms, and tell him who has tampered with your happiness.'

"She fixed on me a look of sudden and wild reproach.

"'*It was you*,' she exclaimed, 'and this is retribution!'

"'What do you mean, dearest?' I asked, gently.

"She became as white as a slab of marble, and clasped her hands together.

"'I cannot speak,' she whispered, 'and if you command me, I will go away and never return.'

"I saw that she was in earnest, and I urged her no longer. She threw herself on the bed and turned her head from me as a signal that she wished to be alone. I yearned for one word from her to show that her heart was not alienated from me, as her words implied, and I bent fondly over her.

"'I have been guilty of many errors,' I said, 'but never one which could bring woe to wife or child. Kiss me in token that love is not lost between us.' She only buried her face in the pillow and waved me away, while a fit of trembling seized her.

"'You are ill,' I exclaimed, 'shall I send for your sister?'

"'No—I want rest,' she said, choking with her emotions; 'let Sophie come to me!'

"I was forced to go, worse than unsuccessful, and that is all."

"Oh, father, what dreadful plot against her life and our happiness this must be!" I sighed.

We had not conferred five minutes longer, when Sophie's pallid face looked in at the door.

"I wish you would come up-stairs." she said, looking at me, "there's something the matter with Miss Rienzi."

"What?" cried my father, starting to his feet; "is she ill?"

"Sir, I wish—I'm afraid we must have the doctor," she said.

He asked no more questions but dashed into the hall, found his hat, and left the house, while with flying speed I reached my sister's chamber.

She was still lying on her bed, and her eyes were closed, with a strange filmy appearance, and her whole face was a faded white. There was something bound across her mouth which looked like a scarlet handkerchief, and Sophie came and pushed me away, and approached the bed with a white one in her hand.

"What's that?" I whispered, my scared eyes fixing on some scarlet stains on the snow of the pillows, "and oh, what's that?"

The scarlet handkerchief was ensanguined with my sister's blood; it oozed in a dark fringe upon the towel which lay upon her bosom; it trickled in little pools upon the sheets.

"A blood vessel burst!" said Sophie, attempting concealment no longer; "put your hand upon her breast here—see if it beats; I am afraid she is going. She kept her face buried in the pillows and I was here a good while before I knew she was choking in her heart's blood."

"Sophie, what shall we do? Tear away that crimson cloth, it will suffocate her. Oh, Sophie, she will die, before anybody comes, and I don't know what to do!"

I was quite useless; I fell on the floor, shaking with terror, and the faithful girl who was collected through it all, did what she could alone.

Before I dared to lift my face again, hasty feet approached, and my father came in, followed impetuously by our family doctor, who with one stride was at the bedside, with hands and eyes busy, while a stream of rapid directions issued from his mouth. And my father, with one rapt look at his Lina, came and lifted me up and held me in his arms.

"Don't sink, little daughter," he muttered, hoarsely, "oh, Heaven! don't leave me alone. Look at her, she's gone!"

In a few hours Dr. Graves was ready to depart; the effusion of blood had been stopped, the swoon overcome, and his patient was in a slumber. With the devotion of a lover my father waited on him in the outer chamber, and listened to his opinion, as the voice of an oracle.

"She's in a most extraordinary condition," he said, looking gravely at my anxious father, "some deep, mental disorder has occasioned this final rupture, and the state of emaciation which she is in, confirms the idea of mental rather than bodily distress having brought her so low. Wherever she has been, Mr. Rienzi, she has been most cruelly tampered with. It is a wonder her mind is not gone. I find in her a predisposition to mania, and under the present pressure she will succumb to it."

"What can we do to lighten the pressure, doctor? She can or will give us no clew to her sufferings."

"There's little can be done in that case, but do what you can. Keep her quiet, cheer and animate her mind; avoid every distressing theme; when she can be moved, have her out of this to some quiet spot in the country for change of air and scene; give her what she wants—anything, if you know of it, and then, perhaps, she may live for years. But I tell you honestly, Mr. Rienzi, don't hope too much, she may be spared long or short, but mark you—she's got her death blow. Now confide to me the circumstances under which you found her, that I may have some insight to the malady of her mind."

My father immediately complied with his request, he led him down stairs, and acquainted him with everything, and received in return the most cordial sympathy from the good old doctor who had been a family friend for years.

Then he went away—one more repository of our strange secret.

Quietly we put the house in order for its new misfortune; we made our preparations to wait for the victory of life or death in that secret chamber; we calmly prepared to take the burden of nursing upon ourselves, my father, Sophie and I, and still to meet the world's watchful eyes, revealing nothing. My father and I were to sit up each alternate night; Sophie to take the charge through the day, so that we might follow our usual duties, and divert suspicion. We had indeed little hope of bringing her through, but we resolved with Heaven's mercy and Dr. Grave's skill to do our best.

Under these arrangements, my father commenced the first night at ten o'clock, the door locked as usual, the windows carefully closed with shutters, the night-lamp burning low. I retired early that I might be ready to take my turn at three o'clock, and after starting awake feverishly two or three times to listen for a signal that "something" had occurred, I at length fell into a heavy slumber which lasted until the daylight began to struggle in, when I rose in haste and found I had overslept my watch an hour.

I flitted to the locked door and let myself in, and there my father sat by the dim night-lamp, pale of cheek and heavy-eyed, but vigilant as ever, as he counted his drops of medicine, and bent over the letter of minute instructions. The fall of gossamer could not be lighter than his touch on her pulse; nor the softest whisper of a woman, than the breathed caress as he poured the diluted drops through her parted lips and fanned her brow.

"How is she?" I whispered.

"The same," was the answer.

I approached and found her still sunk in her dream-like apathy.

"Why did you allow me to oversleep myself?" I asked. "You look very worn and tired, my father, while I have been stealing an hour of your rest!"

"I am not fatigued," he said, looking tenderly at my sister. "I do not know how the night sped; it seemed short."

"Go now," I urged; "you must be ready to attend your office at the usual hour, you know."

He fain would have lingered, but at last he yielded to me and prepared to depart.

"Study these directions well; I have found them of the very greatest use," he said; "why, I followed its dictates to the moment, and I really think such punctuality is a very great step in the right direction!" My dear father, he mentioned with pride his skill as a sick-nurse!

"What bottle is this?" I asked, lifting a large one up; "it was not here last night."

"That is one the doctor brought—he was here at midnight, and said she was not worse; he staid nearly an hour."

"He is very kind to us, papa."

"Yes, dear, he sympathizes with us in our sad position. Now I shall go. One charge I would vehemently impress upon your mind; let no imprudent noises disturb her—quiet is her life."

He went away and I commenced my watch.

I scarcely dared to move, lest some unforeseen sound might startle the sleeper, and spoil all; I read good Dr. Graves' cramped characters until I could repeat the directions from end to end, and my eyes wandered with all the restlessness of my impatient nature from object to object in the room.

There was a portfolio, of rather large size, leaning against the wainscot, behind a chair, out of which were exposed the corners of several sheets of Bristol board. It had fallen forward against the chair; one of the crimson ribbons which tied it was broken off, and the contents had slipped toward one end. Again and again my eyes returned to this object, with a pertinacity which became each time more disagreeable. I knew it was an old portfolio of my sister's, whose contents I had often carelessly looked over, and I suppose she had been looking at it lately, and left it there.

At last the sight of it became a sort of nervous torture. I turned my back upon it, and looked at something else; but malicious fancy reproduced it behind every chair in the room. I sprang up and cautiously lifted the chair aside, determined to push my enemy out of sight. As I lifted it, one picture from the many which made the portfolio so heavy rustled out and fell at my feet.

I put the portfolio behind a curtain, picked up the painting and sat down with a grotesque feeling as if fate had persisted in having her way, to look at what she had thrust upon me. It was but a tiny bit of painting in the center of a broad sheet of paper. No tyro's hand had rested on this page; my sister's brush, fine though it was, had never thrown these cold, sharp lights and glooms so vividly upon a simple scene.

A shadowy shape in the distance, like that of a cottage leaf-mantled; a heap of muffling foliage running down to the foreground and breaking off in the center, where one broad lane of straightly lancing moonlight streamed down; and in the pale flash of the heavens, half-encircled by somber frontage—two figures. *She* standing erect, her hands clasped together; her countenance raised, with a glad, exultant, tender fearlessness to his and this face, which was thus touched and glorified with love's conquest, was Isolina's! And who was the conqueror? A tall man who bent over her with an arm supporting her, and one strong white hand holding her clasped and smaller hands in the palm; a face whose like I had never seen was fixed by her upward glancing eyes, into solemn, almost wondering joy; and I studied it, even as it was studying my sister's.

It was a pale, high-bred, rather spare face, whose broad forehead caught the silver intensity of the moonbeam, leaving the bending eyes and mouth in shadow; those down-dropped eyes just touched the eyes of the woman, and seemed to pour the depth of a thousand souls into the glance; they expressed melancholy, yet pride, and the firm mouth had something of a haughty curve, though now joy had swept away every other feeling. For the rest, a slightly aquiline nose, whose tense nostrils denoted more than all the rest, that sensitive pride, which lived though vailed in every feature; dark clustering hair, and a small, jetty mustache, which did not disguise the beauty of the short curved lip.

Such was the picture which fate (so we call Providence) persisted in showing to me.

Was it a portion of my sister's past life that I had seen? that hidden life which was sealed in a book of mystery from us? Then *who* was this man who had told the "old, old tale," and with such success? Was this "I. J?" I should know that face, if ever my eyes encountered it; and I should look to meet that gracious, strong and true face, to the day of my death.

Had this man won her love, then left the flower to wither?

I put away the painting, for my father to see it, and returned to my patient, my thoughts full of this important discovery. But when I looked at that white, moveless face on the pillow, I felt how vain my plans and dreams were like to be for her.

The hours crept on with me, I scarce knew how; the utter silence gradually gave way to sounds in the street, soon followed by those in the house; steps fell on the stairs and halls, and the usual cleansing operations were guardedly gone through. With a curious intuition of what each sound betokened, I judged of the hours by the voices, without looking at the watch. Thus I inferred that it must be eight o'clock when I heard a startling peal of the door-bell, and the postman was at the door; but sounds followed which puzzled me, and caused me to hover anxiously over Isolina, lest she should be rudely wakened; strange voices and steps, and shutting of doors, with the most wanton disregard for the sick girl, for whom quiet was life. At last they ceased, and the house was quiet again, and more than an hour passed away. Then Sophie came slipping in with her master's key and locked the door behind her, and without coming to look at the invalid, busied herself in the dressing-room arranging the furniture.

"Sophie," I whispered, "come and see if you notice any change."

"Yes, Miss Iva," said the girl, hurriedly.

But still she staid, and when I rose and looked through the door-way, I saw her folding up some dresses and weeping violently though without sound.

"What is the matter, my girl?" I exclaimed.

"Oh, don't—don't say nothing, miss!" she gasped; "if I was to say one word, I'd scream out and kill that poor saint."

"Is my father all right, Sophie?"

"Oh, yes, Miss Iva, dear, and he's up this hour, and breakfast will soon be ready, and then I'm to take your place."

It was nine o'clock when I unlocked the door to go down stairs. I closed it again with a start, and turned to Sophie, my face whitening with a disagreeable shock which I had got.

"There is a strange man standing at the door," I whispered.

"Hush!—oh, Miss Ivanilla, don't!" returned the girl, wringing her hands; "don't ask me a word—I can't speak of it; and if she heard you she'd die. Oh, Miss Iva darling, run down to your father—run straight down to him!"

I braced my nerves and reopened the door, leaving Sophie to lock it on the inside. With downcast eyes I passed a tall, muscular man, clad in a dark-blue coat, who gazed keenly and silently at me. I went step by step down stairs, and, to my intense amazement, found two other men sitting on chairs on each side of the entrance door, who leered and nodded their heads at me. I passed them with an affrighted rush and gained the dining room, where my father was standing on the hearth-rug.

"Father, who are these men in the passage and at my sister's door? What does it mean?" I cried.

"They are waiting to take your sister away, to answer for the murder of Cecil Beaumont!" was the stern reply.

CHAPTER XIII.

AT OPEN DOORS DOGS COME IN.

"I was cut off from hope in that sad place,
 Which yet to name my spirit loathes and fears;
My father held his hand upon his face,
 I, blinded with my tears,
Still strove to speak; my voice was thick with sighs
 As in a dream."—TENNYSON.

My pen trembles, as I write these things. The black memory of that time rushes ever me and fills my eyes with unavailing tears. Pity that woman's heart could ever breed such vengeance, and pour it out so ruthlessly.

These officers were employed by Miss Meredith, and had been searching for five months for Miss Meredith's hapless friend. They had been paid to watch the house which had extended a hospitable roof over Miss Meredith's head; and these spies had at last discovered the fugitive.

For some time they had suspected that something unusual was going on in the house, and had set all their vigilance to the work of discovering what it was. They soon assured themselves that we had a concealed visitor; but not until last night could they determine who the visitor was. They set spies to watch Miss Rienzi's windows, and discovered the gleam of a lamp through the crack of the shutters, burning all night. They had seen Doctor Graves enter the house at midnight, and leave again at half-past one, and boldly intercepting him, they had asked who was ill in Mr. Rienzi's house. The doctor wavered an instant, but almost immediately recovered his wits.

"No one," he answered; "I have been having a rubber there, and staid later than I intended; 'twas long whist."

"Mr. Rienzi, Miss Ivanilla Rienzi, Doctor Graves, and—who?" queried the detective.

"Dummy!" was the prompt reply.

"But you went there at twelve o'clock; does Mr. Rienzi commence long whist at twelve o'clock?"

"No, but he finishes it," said the good doctor, cudgeling

his brains meanwhile; "and—if you had used your eyes as well as your curiosity, you would have seen something."

"Well, sir?"

"You would have seen me go there before dinner—this was the hour of my first visit—and be called away almost immediately to attend a case, which did not release me until barely in time for my supper at Mr. Rienzi's house."

They were staggered, but not convinced; however, the doctor was impenetrable, and they let him go with an apology.

At six o'clock in the morning, a young man, neatly dressed like a druggist's clerk, with a bottle sealed up in white paper sticking out of his pocket, accosted the parlor-maid as she was down at the gate, cleaning the brasses.

"Here is the medicine for the young lady," he said, handing her the bottle. She took it immediately and went with it to the house.

"Doctor Graves told me to ask how she was?" called out the young man; "he said I was to take back an exact account."

"Her pa sat up with her till four o'clock, and she was the same way then. Miss Ivanilla is watching now, and was to ring if any change happened; but she hasn't rung yet."

Having obtained the information he was in quest of, the young man, who was in truth employed by the detectives, hastened away, and Hester carried the bottle up stairs and delivered it to Sophie. She, seeing written upon it, "To be taken at 8 P. M.," and all unaware of the grim joke which the *double entendre* implied, carefully laid it on the hall table, to be carried in at 8 o'clock.

In half an hour three detectives entered the house, armed with a warrant for Miss Rienzi's arrest.

Unfortunately for that prompt obedience which ought ever to wait upon the mandates of the law, another warrant was just now in waiting for the accused, and so a short time was required to decide which power might arrest her first.

For until Azrael, the Angel of Death should roll up his parchment writ and cry her acquitted, none might enter the circle which His shadow cast over her, to lay hand of human vengeance upon her.

A declaration was written by Doctor Graves, and signed

by another physician who was called in, to the effect that Miss Rienzi could not without loss of life be removed from her room at present; and since nothing else could be done, the writ was served upon her where she lay, and men were stationed in the house to take charge of the prisoner until she could be examined.

A constable kept guard at my sister's door, and watched that no weapons or means of escape were carried in to the accused; two more kept watch at the entrance door and the area gate, lest the family or the domestics should attempt some desperate treason, and they paced up and down the little garden, peering at every window, staring in the faces of those who passed to and from the house; prying into the household arrangements, bullying the servants, joking over the gate with their passing comrades, smoking their nauseous tobacco, and making the best of their grim job.

Three days passed before my sister summoned strength enough to speak; each feeble breath indrawn seemed destined as a last; a film as frail as the night-fleece of a frost which melts in the morning sun, was between her soul and its home, a whisper in her ear might turn the balance trembling down into eternity.

On the fourth day she rallied; the feeble life threw up a brighter flame, and hope looked in at our shadowy door.

She was able to murmur our names, to lift her hollow eyes to mine in love, to faintly press the hand which gently pressed the lissome palm. She might live!

I welcomed my dear Isolina from the trance of death, with anxious fears and sorrow.

One evening, my friend, Miss Belle Cranstown came in, pale with sympathy and horror.

She had just arrived from the country, and heard of our misfortunes, and her tender heart was bursting with indignation at our sufferings.

"My poor dear," she sobbed, "it is too dreadful! can't these brutal men be sent away? Shame on the people that they don't mob them! It's too shameful this, for a Christian city!"

"We don't feel it so much now," I said, gently; "and they can't hurt us—yet."

She only wept the more violently at my resignation, and wrung her hands.

"Don't say so!" she cried; "how dare they suspect our good, pure Isolina Rienzi? Oh, I could swear to her innocence before a hundred courts."

I was melted to tears by my friend's generous distress, and I poured out my crushed and sorrowful heart to her in a relation of all that led me to find my sister, and the subsequent events. Then remembering my desire to win from her some information concerning Isolina's life at Saratoga the preceding summer, I asked her if she would answer a few questions. She readily complied.

"You were with my sister at Saratoga all the time she was there?"

"Yes."

"Are you aware of any gentleman meeting her there whose name had the initials 'I. J.?'"

After a protracted pause, Miss Cranstown shook her head.

"Can you remember where my sister was, and what she did on the sixteenth day of July? Oh, try to remember!"

Again my friend pondered deeply, and at last looked up.

"Yes, I can tell you exactly," she said; "poor Isolina was taken with a very severe headache, and I nursed her all day at the cottage, while mamma and the other girls went down to the city shopping. She was on the sofa in Mrs. Halcombe's front parlor all day, and she slept with me at night."

"Strange!" I mused; "what signification has the date on that ring then?

"Will you allow me to show you a picture?" I continued, rising; "I wish to know if you ever saw a certain face and scene."

I went to my father's room, and procured the painting from his cabinet, which, returning, I handed to my friend.

"Victor Joselyn!" she cried, in a tone of astonishment; "and what a miraculous likeness!"

I removed the picture from her hands, and placed it face downward on the table.

"You will easily understand," I said, gravely, "hat anxious we are to find out every step of her past life, tl" we may save her from this last, worst danger. So ho, then, my friend is *Victor Joselyn?*"

"I will answer you carefully," said Belle Cranstown; "but I cannot tell you much. Mr. Joselyn is an English gentleman, who came to Saratoga about the time we did, accompanied by an elderly physician of the name of Dr. Pemberton. These gentlemen were introduced to our party, and became the most intimate friends we had; but if Isolina was a particular favorite of either of them it was of the doctor, who was an old bachelor. Young Mr. Joselyn, as far as I can judge, paid no attention to any of our party. After some time they left Saratoga, and we all remarked that Isolina wore a ring which she had not worn before. My sister Louisa rallied her on the subject, and this was her answer: 'Mr. Joselyn has a wife already—I hope you don't expect him to be looking for another?' This answer surprised none of us, as Mr. Joselyn's conduct had not been such as to warrant any remarks. Judge then of my surprise to see that picture! It is a spot in the field behind Mrs. Halcombe's cottage, where a path ran down to a beautiful stream, and undoubtedly the man who acts the part of a *lover* is Mr. Victor Joselyn, as undoubtedly the lady's face is Isolina's! There is some mystery, Iva, which, trust me, I do not think will reflect upon either your sister's or the gentleman's honor. Believe that, Iva!"

"Thank you," I murmured; "you knew my sister well."

We both were silent, thinking.

"Dr. Pemberton!" I mused; "where have I heard that name before?" Then memory took up the chain of thought and slowly traced it back to that fatal night on which Cecil Beaumont had snatched my sister's letter out of my hand and read the address, of which I had heard the syllables, *"Dr. Pem——"*

Was this the secret correspondent to whom Isolina sent her letters when in distress? Then memory went backward again and reproduced that letter on which the bright gaslight had rested, showing me a lady's name.

"Mrs. Victor Joselyn!"

Then I recalled my sister's words—her tears, and her agony, with a strange chill pervading my heart.

"She was connected with a friend of mine. She is dead!"

Oh!, what dark thoughts were rising in my heart! Do you know the Satan-born pangs of the first doubt in one

you love? That painted story of given and accepted love—
a wife in another land—that wife's death?

Away with this ungenerous fear! She was pure, my own
sweet, darling sister! *This* could not be the secret curse!

I told all to my friend; and she solemnly declared her belief in Isolina's perfect innocence, whatever appearance went
against her. Such faith kept my heart from sinking utterly.

When my friend went away, I wrote down all that she had
told me, and then—with what poor success!—I tried to map
out my sister's life. It was an ellipsis—wild, incoherent; a
riddle; a paradox; it seemed to give the lie to her pure character!

Loathing my involuntary thought I flung it away, and
preferred impenetrable mystery, until Heaven should send
us light.

At last the authorities announced that Miss Rienzi must
be ready for them, by a certain day; and good Dr. Graves
applied all his skill to strengthen her for the approaching
ordeal; and so well did he succeed that she was able to leave
her bed, and sit—poor shadow!—in an invalid chair, two
days before the time specified. Then the doctor—I do not
know how—prepared her mind for what was coming; and so
well and delicately did he fulfill the task that when I was
permitted to join her she looked as calm and serene as ever,
and even uplifted, if one could dare to trace such earthly
emotions in a face which seemed etherealized until it was
like a spirit's.

But the day arrived in which she passed from her chamber doors, leaning on the doctor's arm, and half carried by
my father, to where a carriage waited at the gate, surrounded by a curious crowd, all anxious to see a woman
accused of murder take her first march on the road to the
gallows.

I see her patient eyes raised to my father, and then aloft,
to a stronger Father, whose arms cannot tremble as his
does! She smile a pale, pure smile, like that brave Minerva
who ever leans upon a spear, and she meekly meets the
eager, gloating eyes of the mob. Then the carriage is
whirled away, and I stand alone with my grief and my dark,
questioning heart.

About evening my father came home alone! She had
been indicted to stand her trial for murder, and now was
lodged in prison, where she must take her chance of life in

a close, cramped cell, whose iron bars were even stronger than Doctor Oaks'. Change of scene and air had been deemed necessary for her recovery. Here was change of scene and air! Here were quiet and rest and soothing companionship!

The trial was appointed to take place on the last day of May, and for the limited time before us my father strained every nerve to help the counsel who had been employed to defend his daughter in gathering what facts they could relating to the murder. It was a discouraging task, from the utter absence of friendly witnesses, or even an explanation from the prisoner as data to go upon. They had to work on, almost without a foothold for defense, and with the most telling testimony against them. And through it all, my sister kept inpenetrable silence on the subject, nor committed herself in the slightest to the astute and searching lawyer, who daily visited her. The firmness which she displayed, united to extreme bodily weakness, was amazing.

I need hardly say that I was with my sister every available hour in her cell to comfort and cheer her. She was very quiet and gentle, and seemed to like me to be there; but that peculiar look of resignation, touched with thankfulness, which I had seen in her face when first she heard she was arrested, still lingered there, as if she wanted to be sacrificed.

Once only she spoke of what was coming—one day when we were alone, and I had been wistfully seeking her confidence.

"Better for us all if I perish," she said. "I would rather die; but, little Ivaniila, if I go—remember, I shall tell *you* why!"

Her weak hand pressing mine, her hollow eyes shedding looks of love upon me, made this promise strangely solemn to me.

It was while affairs were at this crisis that we received a telegram from my mother, announcing that she was at Halifax, and would be home in two days.

CHAPTER XIV.

WHAT I SAW, OR SEEMED TO SEE.

"Are ye aware that he who comes behind
Moves what he touches?   The feet of the dead
Are not so wont!"—DANTE.

Three days before the trial, the English steamer arrived, with my mother on board.

She came sweeping up through the evening mists of the river and under the myriad stars. There was no moon, and the night was dark, as my father and I drove down to meet her at the wharf. I heard the loud snorting of the escaping steam and the rattling of the chains, as we drove down behind a stream of cabs and hacks thither bound for bewildered travelers. We stepped a little to one side, under a great fiery signal lamp, and my father went on board among the throng, leaving me sitting in the carriage waiting.

This scene is indelibly impressed upon my memory.

At first I regarded all this shifting panorama in the mass; then individually; gradually with concentrated interest. At first my eyes swept round the area, watching general effects, and ending off with the object nearest me—a man who leaned against the lamp-post. Anon, with a leap of the startled heart, I confined my distended eyes to the figure nearest me, standing, as I have said, beneath the signal lamp, and consequently in the very deepest shadow.

A cab, with flashing lights had rumbled past with its occupants—a happy, reunited family to judge by the babel of happy voices, and looking incidentally at the somber lounger, one gleam of yellow light from the passing cab had fallen on a face well known.

Heavens! how I had thrilled at the prophetic woe of these red-brown eyes. Had I not pictured that protean face, white and set? Ah, had I not mourned on a grave which held those shattered limbs?

A wild prayer rose in my heart; a blazing light shot up like a rocket in my veins; I steadily eyed the figure, now in the murky shadow once more. I shook the windows and beckoned, but had no voice to call; then I sank back, and leaning my head on my hands gazed wildly forth again.

It was dressed in a military cloak, a cap with a golden band on its head, a sword trailing. Its hand, which was gloveless and seemed bones, covered with glistening skin, hung down listlessly, its head drooped forward on its breast.

"Cecil!" I called, huskily, as in a dream; the sound reached him, for he raised his head, and I knew that the face in the dark was looking at me.

Suddenly the carriage moved off; I was dashed back on the seat, and Nelson drove rapidly down to the first gang-way.

I clenched my hands together. Why had Fate stepped in and dashed so strange a sight from my eyes? And then, almost instantly, incredulity attacked me. Could this indeed have been the murdered man? Surely fancy had tricked me with a grotesque coincidence. I tore my thoughts from so mad a fantasy and shook off the delirious impression.

My mother was approaching the carriage door, leaning on her happy husband's arm, and her eyes were directed in an eager gaze toward me, and the joy of seeing her swept away every other feeling, as I sprang into her arms.

"My child!" muttered the sweet, low voice of my infancy; "thank Heaven that you are still left to us."

"Welcome, dearest mother," I sobbed; "welcome to our hearts!"

I clung to her sheltering bosom, and wept my lonely, tired heart light; for, ah, it was so sweet to see, after these long months of pain, the dear mother herself.

But I quickly recovered myself, and, ashamed of my self-abandonment, hurried her into the carriage, where we could pour forth our mental emotions.

It was a sweet, tender face, my mother's, with no regularity of outline, but great delicacy of complexion, and that peculiar attractiveness and self-possession of style which makes the American woman second to the women of no other land in expression; her brows level and slight, but gracious; her lips fine in contour, though expressive of quiet firmness, and her eyes—ah, these were the beauties of her face, and bright as in her fresher years; they were large, blue eyes, clear as a transparent stream, and very like my sister's—though, thank Heaven, there were no tragedy-depths in them as yet, in the mother's.

My father and Nelson had been securing the luggage; now all was arranged, and we set off.

"Home at last!" said my father, holding my mother's hand in a close clasp, "and though there are many changes, we may all be happy under the same roof yet!"

"This is all one little family," responded my mother, drawing me to her bosom with a quick sob; "oh, Guiseppe, this is a cruel change!"

She had not heard yet that Isolina had been brought back to her home; or that she lay now in the Tombs charged with murder. Poor mother, she was coming home to sorrow!

But even in her fond, encircling arms, I raised my head from her bosom as we passed the signal-lamp, and gazed out with straining eyes. No muffled figure lurked there now; whatever it was, it had vanished, and my vision, true or false, was past.

Farther up the wharf I saw a group of men in military cloaks, and they also looked mysterious in the semi-gloom.

"Father," I asked, breaking in upon his conversation, "what are these?"

"Our brave soldiers, child; a detachment, I heard, was to leave the city to-night. Hah! there's young Ansehn, who commands the company. There's more than one will be missed from our circle this summer, I fancy."

I looked attentively at Ansehn; his face was pale, and his hand, which daintily held a cigar, was long and white, and his gold-banded cap and trailing sword were not unlike.

Pshaw, had I suffered such agitations for him?

Probably Mr. Ansehn, who was quite a petit-maitre in his way, tired of smoking cigars (no, he was not tired of that yet), tired of staring at the arrivals, had been much diverted at the young lady's attempts to improvise a flirtation.

"Fortunately," I thought, "he could not have recognized me under my silken vail; I might have thought of my vail before."

I flung myself back upon my mother's bosom, and thought only of her.

"You are looking pale and thin, my child," said she, scanning my face tenderly; "our child looks ill, Guiseppe; I miss the dusky roses, and the merrily glancing eyes of little Zingarella; I am afraid——"

She stopped and looked at my father in turn with mournful, terrified gaze:

"Oh, husband!" she cried, bursting into tears, "you are more changed than she. There was not a white hair on your head when I left you a year ago, and now you're an old man! Oh, Guiseppe, my dear love, why did you let them keep me from you so long?"

And there was the greatest change of all to come. Oh, poor mother-heart, keep strong for love of us!

As soon as we had brought her home, and waited on all her wants like fond, devoted slaves, my father led her to a private room, and told her all. What she suffered, I never knew; courageous, brave, and unselfish, she kept her anguish to herself and comforted him; her sweet face was pale, but not mournful, when they joined me and she infused a warmth of sunshine into my heart, sweet to feel, whatever she suffered herself.

Hope decks the pillow with lotus-wreaths and for the first night in months I slumbered sweetly. The dark cloud was vast as ever, but I seemed to see an edge of golden brightness curling the gloomy scroll.

But while I dressed in the sunny morning's rays with the realistic sense of things as they are, and not as they appeared to be—which a calm night's rest and broad daylight are sure to bring, the mysterious apparition of the past evening presented itself to my imagination with a sudden and overpowering vividness, which smote me into stillness in the midst of my dressing, that I might revise once more that brief moment of recognition.

Could it indeed have been a trick of fancy?

"No," whispered intuition vehemently; "be cheated by no unbelief. You saw him!"

So powerful was this conviction that I no longer felt ashamed of my credulity, but determined to mention the circumstance to my father, that he might sift the matter.

In this state of mind I went down stairs. It was early, but my mother was already up, and sitting by her open window.

Her hand was supporting her cheek, she was in deep reverie and did not hear me enter. I was grieved to see that her beautiful eyes were dark and iris-circled, as if she had slept but little.

"Mother dear," I murmured, crouching by her knee.

She fondly kissed me, and surveyed me with a long, loving scrutiny.

"You are a winsome sight to a mother's eyes," she said; "keep that smile, and these bright, brave eyes, and I'll always love to look at Ivanilla."

It was to my mother that first I confided the strange appearance which I beheld on the wharf.

She listened—and she might well be excused for it—as if I were crazed; but she did not attempt to combat my improbable belief. She pondered over the incident a long time, then she rose with a sigh, and stood looking at me with troubled eyes.

"I scarcely like to speak of what may have no existence," she said; "but I have a strong impression that some strange plot has been formed to ruin the happiness of the family, beginning, first of all, by ruining Isolina. If young Beaumont were really alive, it seems very much like a concerted plot to cheat the authorities into condemning your sister as a criminal. This shall certainly be told your father and Mr. Speingle, and the affair sifted to the bottom. And meantime, my child, lay down the case which has been on your shoulders, and leave it to us who are able to cope with it—be it your duty to soothe the unknown sorrows of your hapless sister, and we will do the rest.

"Mamma, what enemy have we—who would seek to harm us?"

"I do not know, Ivanilla."

CHAPTER XV.

ON TRIAL.

> " Are you called forth from out a world of men
> To slay the innocent? What is my offense?
> Where is the evidence that does accuse me?"
> KING RICHARD III.

Carefully as my mother had been prepared, it was a serious shock to her to meet Isolina. The ravages of grief and illness were great to me—they were stupefying to one who had not seen her since the days of her girlish loveliness and exuberant charms. Yet she betrayed little of her feelings to the weak invalid, but concealed them with the heroism which a mother can exhibit so nobly, and chose to act the part of comforter and nurse to the world-weary girl whose heart ached with a load which—ah, Heaven only estimated at its true weight! My attention was strongly arrested by the eager, intense look with which Isolina watched my mother during the first day of her arrival.

I could not trace that strange constraint with which she treated my father in her bearing toward mamma; but yet her manner was unaccountable. There was a gentle submissiveness and an humble affection, which blended with every look and feeble tone, as if an unforgiven wrong toward that gentle mother was burdening her soul.

But after a time all lesser interests were forgotten, and the day of her trial approached. It was extremely doubtful if she would stand the ordeal. Dr. Graves looked every letter of his name, but did his duty unceasingly, and visited the prison twice a day. My mother staid in the cell until the latest hour that visitors were allowed; my father almost lived in Mr. Speingle's law office. From his anxious face, when he came home to his hasty meals, I feared that the case was getting on slowly. As for me, these three days were alternations between despair and hope, and I was in a state of intermittent anxiety, painful to myself, and, I fear, intolerable to others.

On the evening before the dreaded day, Miss Cranstown came running in to see me, and to comfort me if she could.

She brought news which at another period would have caused me much sincere regret; but in my present mood, scarcely attracted my attention at the time.

"The fate of poor young Rosecraft has been ascertained almost to a certainty," she said. "He was traced on board the cars which ran off the track ten miles from New York on the twenty-ninth of November, and though the body never was found, undoubtedly he perished in the debris, as he was in a weak and disabled state. Mrs. Harrison must be cared for. She has a beautiful little child, two weeks old, and we must keep the melancholy news from her until she is stronger."

These tidings did not impress me at the time; but after my friend left they occurred to me, and, I know not how, aroused my keen interest. I contemplated the affair in all its bearings, and all things considered, determined to tell my father that night.

I did so, and was not surprised to find that the incidents connected with the disappearance aroused his most intense interest. He questioned me closely; and, late as it was, it being then about nine o'clock, hurried off to catch Mr. Speingle before he should leave his office.

The last of May dawned softly, with rose-clouds of filmy transparency; and as I, with restless soul, watched at my casements, I hoped that even as this day had risen, so might the innocent be raised from her night of sorrow.

My mother and I were early at the prison, and with tender care I arrayed my poor sister for her first appearance as "prisoner at the bar." She was very quiet and passionless and seemed to look forward with no terror to her danger.

Doctor Graves arrived at ten o'clock and carefully examined his patient's capabilities. He said that she was stronger to-day, and "If she is kept quiet she will stand a trial, but if it goes against her—she's gone!"

Rather a doubtful situation for an invalid to be in!

At eleven o'clock, a cab arrived to convey the prisoner to the court, and almost at the same moment my father dashed up to the prison and entered the cell.

There was an expression almost of exultation on his face, which was nevertheless looking very care-worn with the recent labor he had been undergoing; and after fondly embracing Isolina and whispering a word or two of encouragement, he turned to me and drew me into a corner.

"Remember," he said, "to answer plainly whatever questions may be put to you by Isolina's counsel. You will be called as a witness; keep all your presence of mind about you."

He gave me a few more instructions, which I anxiously listened to, and did my best to profit by.

The court was crammed; there was a dull hum of whispering voices, which subsided all at once as the judge and the jurymen entered and took their seats with all the "pomp and circumstance" of office.

The trial of Isolina Rienzi was the first case called.

There was a movement among the crowd, a straining of eyes, and rising from their seats as the accused walked slowly up between the officers, Doctor Graves closely following, with a grim, professional face, which expressed volumes of disapprobation.

With a meek glance upon the ground, and secret hectic tinging all her veins, my sister, too lovely for the eye of scorn, was led up through the throng, and given a seat beside her counsel.

The trial commenced. The counsel for the prisoner and on behalf of the State, unrolled their briefs, with glances of quiet antagonism at each other. Anxiously, I read the face of the opposing lawyer, and strove to make an estimation of his capabilities. Mr. Speingle was an eminent lawyer, and had thrown the whole of his talent and interest into my sister's case.

The indictment was read, proceedings were speedily under way, and I sat with my hand tight clasped in my mother's, a breathless and anxious spectator.

At last witness number one, for the prosecution, was called, and a lady clothed in black came forward from a conspicuous seat, and placed herself in the witness-box, bowing with the air of an empress to the officer who held open the door.

She raised her crape vail, erected herself, and glanced haughtily round, and I looked with wonder on the face of Lillia Meredith, yet so different from the simple and timid girl I had seen her, that I could not at first assure myself it was she. Her figure seemed expanded and was taller, fuller, and more assertive; her face, which had been responsive to every simple emotion, was hardened into a scornful look of determination; her large blue eyes seemed unpleasantly bright, and too much like the cold, glittering sparkles of a glacier. There was plenty of health, with headstrong spirit, to support all this show of resolution; care had not blanched or thinned her cheek; sorrow had not crept into her eyes. It was a heartless, selfish soul that looked out of those bold, handsome eyes upon my sister, drooping behind the prisoners bar.

She deposed that Isolina Rienzi had left the hall of the Cybelle Society at ten o'clock on the night of the twentyninth of November, in company with Mr. Cecil Beaumont, and left a message for Mr. Rienzi that she had gone home in a sleigh. That she had not gone home, but had driven straight on with Mr. Beaumont, and had not been heard of since, until her friends found her in a private asylum for

insane females. That Miss Rienzi was not insane, and
would give no reason why she was there. That the fact was
proved that Miss Rienzi had been with Cecil Beaumont at
the moment of his death, as they had been seen together by
a witness who was present, five minutes or so before the accident. That she, the deponent, had reason to believe
there was an *animus* in the prisoner's mind against Cecil
Beaumont as he had displeased her on the evening of his
death."

As she left the witness box, my unhappy sister turned
and looked on her with such a long, sorrowful gaze, that
the hard girl flushed to the brows, and quailed, despite her
bold arrogance.

Mr. Bently, the counsel for the State, then went on with
the facts of the case where Miss Meredith left off.

He said that on the night of the 29th of November, the
body of Cecil Beaumont had been found, partly in and partly
out of a half-frozen brook, just beneath a wooden bridge
over which he had been pushed, as had been proved by the
appearance of the bridge. The railing had been partly
broken down, and being old and decayed, had given way before the weight of the body which had been dashed against
it; furthermore, one panel of said railing had been found
beneath the body of the deceased, thus proving clearly that
he had been pushed over advisably, and with intent to kill
him. A lady's lace sleeve had been found clenched in the
hand of the deceased; also, drifted down some distance from
the body, a lady's handkerchief, on which was written Miss
Rienzi's name.

Both the sleeve and the handkerchief were produced.
The handkerchief I recognized—the bare sleeve I had never
seen; it was not like what my sister had worn on the
night of the concert; I rapidly whispered to my father;
he communicated to Mr. Speingle, who nodded two or three
times.

"The body," resumed Mr. Bently, "was discovered by
an itinerant salesman, who was now present, and would be
shortly called upon to give his testimony—who, upon discovering it, instantly ran to the nearest house for aid, and
brought back with him a man, who assisted him to carry the
body up to the house. This house happened to be Mrs.
Beaumont's, the mother of the unfortunate young man,
who dispatched him at once to the nearest magistrate for a

warrant to search for the person who had caused her son's death.

Here Obed Walsh was called, and duly-sworn.

Obed Walsh was a short, muscular fellow, with profusely tanned cheeks, restless, light-colored eyes, and lank hair, which fell like whithered grass over his forehead and ears. Those ears, disdaining the hirsute covering, cropped out like two leathery bat wings, large, upright, and eager, joining a strangely alert expression to the rough, shock head.

Being launched by the judicious promptings of Bently, he deposed that, on the night of the 29th of November, he was walking on the —— Road, about nine miles from the city, trying to reach Greely's Mills before the public-house folks would all be in bed. At a few minutes before twelve he was overtaken by a sleigh, which, as he stood aside to allow it to pass, he saw contained a lady and gentleman. They were talking so closely that they did not notice him, and the horse was rushing on of itself, for the reins were loosely slung over the gentleman's arm. Just as they passed him, the lady threw up her arms and cried, "Yes! I was born to be your curse, and this night will prove it!" The gentleman caught her hands, but she snatched them away and cried more fiercely, "Wait—wait! You won't seek to touch me in half an hour!"

With these ominous words the pair got beyond hearing. The peddler walked on for some fifteen minutes until he came to the top of the hill leading down to Greely's Mills, when he heard a strange rumbling noise, coming from the wooden bridge, in the bottom of the valley, as he thought; it was like the rattling of stones and the crashing of wood, then there was a dull explosion that shook the ground. He began to run down the hill, for he did not know whether it was before or after him, and he wanted to get straight into Hanover's public house, out of harm's way.

It took him a good while to get to the bridge, which he was just crossing, when he noticed part of the rail broken away, and the snow disturbed in a very curious manner, as if there had been a struggle. He looked over the brink, and was sure he saw something like a man lying among the rocks and water in the brook. He ran down, and found that the gentleman whom he had seen twenty minutes before, still warm. He dragged the body out of the water, and ran across the fields to a house which he saw half a mile or less, distant. When he was about fifty rods from the house, he saw a man running toward him whom he stopped, and told what he had seen.

"Where?" said the man.

"Come on, and I'll show you," said the peddler; "and the young girl as did it, I'm afraid, has cleared."

"Was there a young girl?" he asked, startled like.

Then the peddler told him what he had heard as the sleigh passed him. They ran on, until they reached the place, and scrambled down the rocks together. No sooner had the new-comer looked at the face of the body, than he cried:

"By Heaven! it's just as I thought. It's young Master Cecil!"

Then he said that he was a servant that belonged to the young gentleman's mother, and she lived in the house across the field. So they made a bier of hurdles, and carried the body up to the doorstep, where the servant left it, while he went to prepare the mother. Pretty soon he came out and helped the peddler in with the body, to a parlor where it was put on a sofa, and a lady came in and flung herself on the floor beside it.

The peddler went into the kitchen with the servant and they staid there about an hour, until Mrs. Beaumont came out and called the servant, and they talked together a long time, and then the servant came back, and asked the peddler if he would go to a magistrate who was about two miles distant, and make his deposition, and get men set on the tracks of the murderess. He got a sovereign from the servant, and set off though it was about one o'clock then.

Cross-examined by Mr. Speingle:

"You heard a strange rumbling noise, like the rattling of stones and the crashing of wood, followed by a dull explosion that shook the ground. Was this noise, in your opinion, caused by the young lady pushing the deceased over the bridge?"

The witness looked at the counsel for the State.

"Look at me, if you please, and answer my questions honestly."

"I'm not sure that it was."

" Did you hear of any other cause for such a peculiar sound?"

" Yes, sir; the night train from——ran off the track on account of the snow, just above Greely's Mills, and the engine boiler burst. I heard all about it, and saw it on my way to the magistrate's."

" Very good. Now Mr. Walsh describe in what manner the body of the deceased was injured."

" I couldn't exactly say. It were dead enough though, for the face was as white as cotton, and the breath gone."

" The face, Walsh? the face, did you say?" repeated Mr. Speingle, slowly.

There was an audible murmur in the breathless crowd; two or three men half rose up and sat down again.

" The face was as white as cotton," persisted Walsh, stolidly, having tried to catch Mr. Bently's eyes and failed; that gentleman keeping an impenetrable and contemptuous neutrality during what he appeared to consider Mr. Speingle's trifling. " Except," added Walsh, " where a lot of blood crossed it from one temple."

" Stand down for the present, Mr. Walsh," said the counsel for the prisoner. " If any of the jurymen who viewed the body of Cecil Beaumont are in this court, let them come forward," he uttered in a loud voice.

Three men elbowed themselves eagerly forward. Mr. Speingle pointed to one of them.

" I want that man to describe the appearance of the body upon which the inquest was held at Mrs. Beaumont's house."

The man was sworn.

" You viewed the body of course before you gave a verdict. Describe the face if you please."

" There weren't no face at all," said the man, a bluff countryman; " he were smashed to pieces he were, and the clothes was all that held him together."

Here a slight interruption occurred. Doctor Graves who sat close behind the prisoner raised his hand and enjoined silence: he then sent an officer to whisper something to the judge, and the prisoner was supported out of the court in a half-fainting condition.

" My mother rose and quietly followed her to a small antechamber, and the proceedings went on.

" What sort of clothes were on the body?"

"An evening dress such as the swells wear."

"Were they much saturated with blood?"

"Not so much as you would think, considering the mangling it had got; and I'm sure it's wonderful how a man could have been turned, and twisted, and battered the way he was, by falling over a gully like Crag's Brook, and so said we all—which showed clearly——"

"Stick to the subject," said Mr. Bently, impatiently.

"Which showed clearly," repeated the ex-juryman, "that she must have pushed him mighty hard, and thrown rocks or something after him."

Mr. Bently smiled maliciously.

"Then there were loose rocks on the bridge and round the body?" questioned Mr. Speingle with much interest.

"Not as I saw!" said the countryman, scratching his head. "I was there the next day too, and looked all around."

It was Mr. Speingle's time to smile enjoyably.

"Then that supposition is improbable, and we dismiss it with the natural question—'How could a young lady excavate rocks out of frozen ground to hurl over a bridge, and leave no trace?' Witness, you may go. Now, gentlemen of the jury, bear in mind, the body which Walsh helped to pick up from under the bridge had a white face, streaked with blood; the body upon which was held an inquest next day, 'had no face at all,' was held together by the clothes, yet these clothes were not stained with blood to the extent that so many wounds warranted. Miss Ivanilla Rienzi, come forward."

Some one led me to the witness-stand; for one instant my senses whirled, until my father came forward and stood near me; then I was calm, and recovered from my terror.

With a feeling of deep solemnity, I took the oath.

"Are you a Soldiers' Friend?" began Mr. Speingle, gently.

"I am."

"Did you on the fifth of April visit a sick soldier in Jersey City, by name Charles Harrison?"

"I did."

"Relate the subject of your interview."

"He was very anxious to see his brother-in-law, a young man named Leander Rosecraft, who had disappeared since the end of November; and Harrison gave me a letter which he had written and his photograph, to assist our society in finding him."

"Did your society search for him?"

"Yes."

"With what success?"

"He was traced to the cars which left for New York on the 29th of November, and ran off the track at Greely's Mills. Undoubtedly he perished in the explosion."

"Is this the photograph Charles Harrison gave you?"

A photograph was handed to me which I examined.

"This is the same photograph."

"Is this the letter?"

I scanned it carefully.

"Yes," I said again.

"Now," said Mr. Speingle, producing his pocket-book, while the most thrilling silence prevailed, "is this a photograph of the same person, and is this strip of paper written by the same hand that wrote that letter? Look carefully, madam."

Again a photograph was put in my hands; it was much defaced and twisted, but it was a fac-simile of the original one; then a strip of paper was submitted to my inspection. It was quite clean, though the ink was somewhat dim, and these were the words:

"Leander Rosecraft, Private, Newark Road, Jersey City."

On the other side was printed:

"C. C., No. 4827. To be worn round the neck over the shirt. In battle, under. Fight the good fight of faith."

It was an "identifier," given by a certain benevolent association of Christian men, to enable them to trace dead soldiers, and send their effects to their friends. In bewildered surprise I deposed to the genuineness of both these articles, and returned them.

"This photograph, and this 'identifier,'" said Mr. Speingle, and his voice rose clear and loud in the breathless silence, "was found in a lead box hung around the neck, and under the shirt of the body which is buried in Cecil Beaumont's grave. Considering all that has transpired concerning this strange body, which one says was mutilated and another says was not, may we not venture to say that Leander Rosecraft, the missing soldier, has been found——"

But here he was compelled to pause, while the excited

audience gave vent to their consternation. Lillia Meredith rose to her feet and sat down again, pale and electrified ; my father reached forward and wrung my hand ; the counsel for the State looked thunderstruck ; the judge sat forward with his hands on his knees ; the jurymen conferred in rasping and hasty whispers; Mr. Speingle waited phlegmatically for silence though there was a deep excitement in his eyes.

" Silence!" shouted the clerk.

A rapid hush fell on the convulsed throng—they were afraid to lose one word.

" May we not venture to say that the missing soldier has been found where Cecil Beaumont, *if dead*, should be found? Witness, stand up."

I rose again and came forward.

" This lace sleeve was found in the dead man's hand, upon whom the inquest was held in Mrs. Beaumont's house. Do you recognize this sleeve as belonging to the prisoner?"

I took it in my hands; it was much soiled and torn; also there was a considerable portion of it covered with soot, or smoke grime.

" This is not the sleeve my sister wore that night," I said.

Mr. Speingle took it from me and handed it to the jurymen on the bench.

" Gentlemen, examine it minutely," he remarked. "Now, my man," turning to Mr. Walsh, who had taken refuge near Bently; " how was it you did not see that sleeve in the hand of the gentleman you picked it up from beneath the bridge?"

" I didn't look for anything," he said, sullenly.

" You remarked on the appearance of the place, I suppose?"

" Yes, sir."

" Confess now—wasn't there plenty of soot and scum about the place, the remains of a gipsy fire, burnt sticks, ashes, and so on?"

" Nary a thing but clean snow and clean water," said the peddler, grimly.

Bently sat with a saturnine smile, eying his boots.

" Then," said Mr. Speingle, addressing the jury, "that sleeve cannot have been Miss Rienzi's, cannot have been at

Crag's Brook, cannot have been caught by Cecil Beaumont's hand in his fall over the bridge, as it is covered with smoke, oily dirt, and blood. On the contrary, that sleeve must have been in the midst of the railway accident, where the explosion of the engine took place. I have no doubt that Leander Rosecraft, when the catastrophe occurred, grasped the arm of the lady nearest him in the carriage, and brought with him a part of the dress which remained in the death-clutch of the poor, battered, mutilated body. I think we have proved, gentlemen of the jury, that Miss Rienzi did not commit murder on the body which was buried under the name of Cecil Beaumont. I propose now to show forth that she did not commit murder at all; that the body of the real Cecil Beaumont was not dead, and that Miss Rienzi has been foully conspired against, with intent to make the law punish her for a crime she did not commit. I have to ask a few more questions of this witness. Madam, relate what you saw three nights ago on the wharf, as you were waiting the arrival of a passenger in the English steamer."

"And remember, madam, you are upon your oath," interposed Mr. Bently, getting up and facing me.

This interruption confused me; I commenced, but so tremulously that a murmur rose from all parts of the house, as :

"Speak out! Can't hear!"

"Take time—don't be afraid," said the judge, mildly.

"You were sitting alone in your father's carriage?" began Mr. Speingle.

"And while I waited a few minutes for papa and mamma——"

"Stop, stop!" cried Mr. Bently, in an irritating manner, "at what hour? It seems to me that you and Brother Speingle are making it up between you."

The lawyer's insolence brought back my courage.

"It was half-past eight when we drew up beneath the signal lamp," I said, steadily, "and my father alighted and went on board the steamer, leaving me sitting in the carriage, while the driver occupied the box."

"Ah! but I thought your friend, Speingle, said you were alone!"

"Sir !" I exclaimed, flushing haughtily, " how often

am I to be thus rudely interrupted? Is this American courtesy?"

Cries of "No, no!" and murmurs of applause answered me.

"Order!" screamed the clerk.

"I was alone in the carriage, the coachman outside on the box, when from the window I saw a man standing beneath the signal-lamp I have before mentioned; a cab passed, throwing a bright light on his face, and I distinctly recognized Mr. Beaumont."

Dead silence followed this announcement, and even Lawyer Bently gazed into my face, speechless with surprise and incredulity.

"I was too much startled at first to accost him," I continued in the unbroken hush, my voice low and even; "and while I was shaking the carriage window, to lower it and attract his attention, the coachman, who of course, was not cognizant of my wishes, saw his master and mistress at a little distance, and drove down to them, and thus I lost sight of him."

"And you," Mr. Bently laughed satirically, "you tell this story on your oath—your irrevocable, sacred oath, before Heaven and on that most Holy Bible?"

"I do."

"So improbable! Why did you not put the person in custody?"

"I did not even think of what I could do. I was too agitated to do anything; I could not raise my voice to speak."

"As men of common sense," interposed Mr. Speingle, quietly, I ask the gentlemen of the jury if it would be natural for a young lady to descend from her carriage and look about for a constable on a crowded wharf, upon suddenly beholding the bodily apparition of a man whom she believed to be dead?"

"I think not," said a voice in the crowd.

"And after you recovered from your agitation did you make no attempt to discover your ghost? Make no inquiries—no fuss whatever?" pursued the undaunted Bently.

At this moment a messenger came in and handed a letter to the judge. He opened it, raised his eyebrows, read it rapidly, looked at the jurors, and handed it to the nearest. It passed from hand to hand, and seemed to occasion unbounded amazement ; the gentlemen on the bench were so engrossed they scarcely listened to the remainder of Bently's cross-examination.

"The emotions which occupied me on meeting my mother, who had been absent a year, banished for the first few minutes the impression which had been made upon me by seeing Cecil Beaumont, but while we repassed the signal-lamp, and indeed all the way up the wharf, I looked out of the window, hoping to see him."

"And saw nothing at all like him?"

"I did see a gentleman in the same costume whom at first I thought I might have mistaken for him; but my father, who knows him, sent a note to him, asking if he was beneath the lamp beside our carriage that night, and an answer was returned in the negative."

"Come, now—what's the name of this gentleman?"

"Captain Ruthven Ansehn."

"I would like very much if the learned gentlemen of the jury could see that letter."

"I have the honor of gratifying the counsel for the prosecution," said Mr. Speingle, blandly, taking a note from my father.

Smiling, the judge rose and spoke :

"This trial has come to a very unexpected conclusion. A letter has been handed to me, which at once acquits Miss Rienzi of murder or of intent to murder, in so far as it is written by the supposed victim himself. I shall read the few words :

"Sir:—I heard this hour that Miss Isolina Rienzi is on trial for the murder of Cecil Beaumont. At once acquit her; she is perfectly innocent of any wrong toward him. He was not killed in his own mad leap into Crag's Brook. If this is insufficient to clear her name, the writer can give further proofs of the truth of his statement. Along with evidence that Ivanilla Rienzi can give, concerning what she saw at the Atlantic wharf, I think it is sufficient. CECIL BEAUMONT."

A ringing cheer drowned the judge's voice; Bently rolled up his brief and threw it into his hat; the jurymen stamped their feet like boys hearing of a holiday.

"Order!" bawled the ushers, and the trial ended in confusion.

My sister was now summoned to appear. She came in this time leaning on our kind physician's arm, and a subdued sigh of sympathy swayed the multitude as she stood once more before them, her pale face so sorrow-worn and meek, lifted with its saintly patience to that of the judge. You could have heard a fly buzzing in the most gossamer of cabinets, while the judge addressed the prisoner :

"Inasmuch as it has been found that you were perfectly innocent of intent to injure Cecil Beaumont, and that he attempted self-destruction of his own free will, and failed ; and since it has been proved that he is alive and well this day and desirous of your acquittal, we do, without formal consideration of the question, honorably and utterly acquit you of the crime laid to your charge."

The ecstasy trembling in the hearts of a thousand burst upon the air; one moment my sister's white, seraphic face beamed on me a tide of joy and wonder, then she fell back with a low sob, into the arms of the doctor.

And with feet which trod on air, I followed her to the carriage and thanked Heaven that she was saved.

CHAPTER XVI.

MY PHANTOM.

"Is it gone? my pulses beat—
What was it? a lying trick of the brain?
Yet I thought I saw *her* stand
A shadow there at my feet!"—TENNYSON.

The house was noiseless; the crescent moon smiled in at my half-closed window-blind, low down in the mellow sky; the musky, dreamy perfume of the night-blooming cereus filled my room from a vase on the mantel; my sister's faint cough sounded from the west room, where she peacefully slumbered, Sophie keeping watch; no disturbing thoughts harassed me; I was full of gratitude for the mercies of the past day; exhaustion had prepared me well for my pillow; the night was wearing slowly on.

And yet I could not sleep.

My flights of thought consumed hours, and came back to find me wakeful as ever.

What had come over me?

No sound caught my senses; not a ripple of the waves

of air disturbed me; yet my ears began to beat and strain themselves to catch some movement, and they seemed to enlarge until my nervous system was one immense tympanum.

It came like the fall of gossamer—a murky shadow, nothing more, and it grew toward the middle of my silent chamber. A gentle rush of a new atmosphere enveloped me, which told me that my door was open.

But how could human hand have opened it and make no noise? My mind reasoned distinctly, and my body lay in a torpor of horror.

It came on, slowly, patiently, impalpably as an evening shadow creeping over sunny grass; it stole with a foot which might step on the golden lilies without bending their pensile stems, closer, closer; it loomed like a column of smoke before me, and stopped beside my bed.

What horror! I lay defenseless—my heart ceased to beat —I closed my eyes for the assassin's blow.

It came not, the stifling terror lifted, and I dared to look again.

The warning lunar ray shone upon the face of a woman standing beside my table, with a long, colorless flask in her hand, which flashed like a bar of crystal. A tumbler of water, thinly diluted with sour wine, stood on the table; my night drink.

It was an Italian custom, which the sultry nights now coming in caused me to resume.

She raised the tumbler in her other hand, and poured from the flask into it a hair-like stream of liquid which fell soundless, then slipped the vial into her bosom, and bending low, replaced the tumbler on the marble table, where the liquid it contained writhed and foamed into white for some moments. When the hissing sound was over she lifted her face to the shadowy sky, and the dreadful features stamped themselves into my heart; a face beautiful and vengeful, whitened and corpse-like with passion's scorching flame. A face to remember.

"My oath is fulfilled!" she said, in words without a voice. Had she spoken? or had the words passed from her soul to mine? She loomed once more toward me between me and the light, a vapor gray and deadly. She swooped close, and shot that terrible face into mine; I felt the lurid eyes fixed upon me—all feeling left the surface of my skin—I felt no breath, though her breath was close to mine. I gasped and tried to lift my spell-bound eyes, and she melted into the darkest shadow of the room.

A life-time of horror was compressed into the next hour. I lay moveless in my bed, chained hand and foot by terror, watching the gradual receding of the woman.

She flitted from the room by invisible degrees, a long, ghastly hand reached forward and grasped the door, and held it immovable while the shrouded figure grew into the outer shadow. Inch by inch it closed, and I thought time would not last to see it touch the lock.

In the midst of my watching, impenetrable darkness filled the room; the moon had gone down and the black hour before dawn had commenced. A double terror fell on me that she would return and destroy me in the dark. A cold moisture oozed from my brow, my limbs became paralyzed, my torpor deepened into insensibility.

When I revived the darkness had given way to bright, dancing sunshine; the horse-flies were noisily buzzing on the window.

I raised myself and looked round. All was as I had left it, even to a silk vail which I had thrown upon the back of a chair near the door. Would not a passing form have brushed the light thing to the floor? My tumbler was exactly where I had placed it, within the very ring of moisture which had fallen from it last night. Could mortal hand have replaced it thus, with no light to guide? I began to feel my pulse to see if I were not in some fever dream.

The soothing sounds of human life were ushering in the morning; my mind became calm. partly because of the exhaustion of my system; I insensibly fell into a deep sleep which was not disturbed until late in the forenoon.

"Dear heart alive!" said Sophie, who was bustling about my room, and who greeted my first stare with a courtesy, "but you have been sleeping soundly, Miss Iva, dear. I have been here fixing round for half an hour, and you never woke up. Do you know what time it is, miss?"

"No," I replied, slowly calling back my scattered senses.

"Half-past ten, miss. You're late for breakfast by a long spell, but your ma said you wasn't to be awakened on no account until you slept off your weariness."

"Sophie, did you sit up with my sister last night?"

" Yes, miss."

" All night? Had she a good night?"

" Yes, miss, she slept very nice and quiet, though she's weak and spent like, which isn't to be wondered at after yesterday. Yes, miss Iva, I sat up until six o'clock with Miss Isolina."

" Did nothing—did anything disturb you?"

" No, miss; was anything——"

" Oh, I don't know," I murmured, passing my hand over my confused brain. "Is my father quite well?"

" Yes, Miss Iva, I think so."

"And mamma—why don't you mention her? Is anything the matter with mamma? Speak, Sophie!"

"No, miss," said the girl, in a distressed tone. "I hope nothing's the matter with you, Miss Iva—now I look, you don't seem well or right like."

" I hope not!" I exclaimed, glancing mechanically at the tumbler upon the table. "Did I drink the water out of that glass?"

I could scarcely speak from alarm; the tumbler was empty.

" I don't know, Miss Iva," said Sophie, looking anxiously at me. "What is the matter?"

" Was it you that emptied that tumbler, or I?"

" The water looked clouded and warm—I threw it away, miss."

" Thank Heaven!" I exclaimed, in the first impulse of gratitude. But second thoughts came immediately. "I wish you had kept it, Sophie—it was valuable," I cried.

" I am very sorry, indeed, miss, if I did wrong; was it medicine?"

" Yes," I said, with a hysterical laugh; "it was medicine. Help me to dress, Sophie; I have a headache."

" Miss Ivanilla! My goodness! are you sick? Let me run down for your ma, or the doctor; he is with your pa in the library."

With a strong effort I mastered the weakness, and sat down trembling for a few minutes.

" It's nothing; it is passing away," I said; "finish my dressing and I shall go down myself; I want Dr. Graves before he goes away."

I regretted exceedingly that the tumbler had been emptied. What had I to prove that my midnight visitor was more

than a creation of nightmare?   I lifted the tumbler and
scanned it anxiously.   There was but one drop in the bottom, which ran round the crystal circle with the dry, bead-
like rapidity of quick-silver.   I asked the girl if she had
washed it.

"No," she answered; "I'll get you a clean tumbler,
miss."

"Never mind," I responded, "I want this glass."

I carried it down stairs, but I was so weak and tremulous
that I rested three times on the way.   It was with difficulty that I could open the library door and lean against the
wall.

My father and Dr. Graves were in close discussion; Mr.
Speingle, the lawyer, was also there, attentively listening to
the colloquy of the other gentlemen.

"Heavens!" ejaculated my father, catching sight of me;
"here's little Iva, as white as a ghost!   What has happened,
child?"

He came to me and took my hand; I was so awed and
solemnized by the horror I had experienced, that the sight
of so many friendly faces almost made me break down; but
I overcame my feelings, and came forward to the table,
where I put the tumbler down, and held my shaking hand
out to each of the gentlemen.

"What's the matter?" said Dr. Graves, putting on his
glasses and drawing me closer.   "You've got a nervous
headache, child, and your hand is as dry and hot as an
ember.   Eh! What's this?"   He bent his head and sniffed
loudly two or three times in my face.   "Who's been giving you chloroform, eh?   Now what—what does this
mean?   The child's nearly killed—she's drenched with
chloroform!"

"Impossible!" I exclaimed.   "I am not conscious of
having inhaled chloroform, but I am—oh, I am dreadfully
sick."

"Exactly," he said, seating me on a sofa, where I was
glad to sink my head on the cushions.   "Anæsthetics are
opposed to your constitution, and you opposed the chloroform until a sufficient quantity was inhaled to over-
power you, and you feel the effects this morning; nau-
sea, sea-sickness, headache, etc.   Now, don't you?   Come,
my dear, confess now—haven't you been tampering with
the chloroform bottle, for the toothache or something?"

"No, indeed," I answered, in a tremulous voice; "but there is perhaps truth in your surmise for all that. Papa, a very strange thing happened last night. May I tell it to you and these gentlemen just now?"

My father came near and sat beside me, and supported me with his arm.

"Go on, my daughter," he said, not a little anxiously.

I related the whole of last night's experiences as faithfully and minutely as my stammering tongue and burning thirst would allow me. The three gentlemen listened in blank amazement.

"What—what in Heaven's name would you call that?" exclaimed my father, when I had finished. "An attempt to poison a young girl in her own room?"

The lawyer seized a pen, and proceeded to commit my story to paper, with many interspersed questions. The doctor seized the tumbler and retired to the window with it.

"Now," said Mr. Speingle, throwing down his pen, "my opinion is that you've got some wretched enemy or conspirator, and he or she is at the bottom of all your troubles. The attempt at——"

"Poison!" interposed Dr. Graves, turning round.

"At poison," repeated Mr. Speingle, "which was made last night on the person of your daughter, proves that the animus is not directed against one member of your family, but against both. My advice to you, sir, is to send your family out of the city, to some safe place and put the whole of this affair into the hands of the authorities. Your lives are not safe at this rate."

"Safe!" responded the doctor, "safe"—they're not worth an hour's purchase! That girl has been nearly stifled with chloroform, and plied with poison to boot—rank poison! This tumbler is lined with it—the very smell is deadly. Get them out of this, sir, away to the country with them, where nobody'll know anything about them; the other one will die on your hands if you don't."

While thus my unhappy father was being conjured on either side, my mother, with somewhat of an anxious face, entered the room.

The instant her eyes lit on me, she clasped her hands with an involuntary gasp of alarm.

"How ill you look!" she cried. "Indeed Sophie was right. Good-morning, Mr. Speingle. Ah, doctor, I am glad you have not gone yet. I fear this is another patient for you."

"Be seated, madam," said the lawyer, ceremoniously placing a chair. "If you have an hour to spare, I should feel deeply indebted if you would bestow it upon me. The doctor is attending to the lady—she is not dangerously indisposed, for which we thank Heaven, madam. May I claim your attention?"

"Certainly," said my mother, seating herself, with a slightly paler cheek.

Dr. Graves very deliberately poured out a glass of wine from a decanter on the buffet and made me drink it.

"Cast back your memory, madam," began the lawyer, impressively, "and review each lady friend you ever had, and tell me if you are conscious of ever giving them cause of enmity against you. Any jealousy," he glanced with a faint smile at my father, "or wrong? In short, do you know of any soul who could bear you hatred?"

My mother sat reviewing her past life with an astounded face, and then she shook her head decidedly.

"Always bearing this in mind," continued the lawyer," "listen to the facts your daughter has just made known to us."

He snatched up the sheet of paper on which he had been writing, and read nearly word for word the story as I had related it.

Paler than ever grew my mother's face; her eyes darkened and turned toward my father in anxious appeal; when the words which the woman had used were repeated to her, she clasped her hands and bent forward with a sudden revelation on her face which caused the lawyer to pause, and fix his keen eyes upon her.

"My oath is fulfilled!

"What does that bring to your memory, madam? You remember something?"

"A mere surmise," she answered; "go on to the end. Perhaps my husband," she looked again at him, "may be able to recall some one who might have an oath to fulfill. Go on, Mr. Speingle."

The lawyer went on to the end, folded up the paper, and twisted it round and round in his fingers.

"My poor child," was my mother's first exclamation, while she bent over me and kissed me. "Oh, what an escape! Guiseppe," she lowered her voice to a whisper, "remember Gemma Lancinetto. Could it be she?"

My father started; the arm on which I leaned was withdrawn, and he turned an incredulous, half-amused face on my mother.

"Would she defer her revenge for twenty—yes, twenty-two years? No, no, my Maud, she has doubtless forgotten my name long before this time, if she lives."

"Well?" broke in the lawyer's business-like voice.

"It is not worth explaining," said my father, flushing, and looking proudly at my mother. "This foolish wife of mine was recalling a certain lady who intended to have stood in her place at my wedding, but for a reason, failed."

"Perhaps my good friend, Dr. Graves, would like his little patient there to go and lie down, and get a nice quiet little nap," said Mr. Speingle, looking significantly at the doctor.

"Let her stay," said my father, compressing his arm round me, in a close embrace. "I have nothing that I need hide from my little daughter. My wife was merely referring to a lady that I, while a very young man, in Florence, at the School of Arts, got engaged to. She was possessed of both wealth and beauty, but was unsuitable for me; and, therefore, as soon as I became aware of this, I released her from her engagement, and in the subsequent years of choosing a profession and coming to America, I confess I forgot Signorina Lancinetto's existence. Five years after we parted we met on our wedding day, when I was leading my wife here into the carriage for our tour, and the lady used some very hard expressions against me, which caused Mrs. Rienzi a great deal of alarm for a while, particularly one threat which she made, in very passionate Italian, that ' She would give me cause to remember Gemma Lancinetto to the day of my death.' In an evil hour I translated the Christian-like promise to my young wife, and cost her many a wakeful night afterward, but the lady, not being as good as her promise for twenty-two years, I confess I have long ago lost faith in her word."

"Gemma Lancinetto," said Mr. Speingle, opening his sheet of notes, and scribbling on the back. "Describe the lady as she was twenty-two years ago, Mr. Rienzi. This is important testimony."

"Describe her? Oh, beautiful of course, as an angel!"

said my father half-jocularly; "brown eyes, large, flashing, effective (especially when the lady was in a rage, as in her last I had the pleasure of beholding her), regular features, with enough *diablerie* in them to upset all classic calms and Grecian coldness; clear, brunette complexion, waving black hair, which just then was plentifully disheveled and maltreated by ten very spiteful fingers; medium height, exuberantly full; age about—age just twenty-one."

"If she lives she is forty-three now. Miss Ivanilla describe the woman you saw in your bedroom last night."

"I cannot," I said, with a shudder. "It was a very pale face, with great hollow caverns for eyes, and level, black brows, with an expression of strong vengeance; and a dark mantle muffled it all round, and hid the figure and all, but a long white hand, which—ugh!" I broke off, and hid my face on my father's shoulder with a prolonged shudder.

"Very good, very good," said the lawyer, writing down my words with gusto; "more than one might have expected from you, my dear, under such circumstances. Now, sir, we must find this woman. That is move the first."

"But such a chimerical idea," said my father, still half laughing. "I don't believe it's the same woman at all. Pshaw, as if a woman could keep true to one idea for twenty-two years, before she puts it into execution! Pshaw!"

"Guiseppe, do not laugh," breathed my mother earnestly.

"Such a woman as she would *never* forget."

"Whether it is Mrs. Lensetts, or whatever you call her, or not," remarked Mr. Speingle, doggedly, "it behooves us to find the person who broke into the house last night, and convict her of an attempted murder. I am sure you agree with me there?"

"Most assuredly;" responded my father, "we shall at once lay some plan to discover her—if we can even call her by name."

"Humph!" muttered Speingle, "I think we'll be able to call her by name by and by. I think we met her in the course of your daughter's trial, once or twice. Suppose that for the present we call her Mrs. Beaumont?"

"What nonsense."

"Not a bit of it, my dear sir. It's a well-known fact that young Beaumont had Italian blood in his veins; his father was not Italian—he was a Virginian—then his mother must have been Italian."

"But why fasten upon her at all?"

"Because she did one fraud that we know of. She substituted Leander Rosecraft's body for that of her own son, at the inquest, and concealed the fact that he was not killed."

"If you are finished with this young lady," interrupted the doctor, feeling my pulse; "I'll take the liberty of sending her off to get some food; and with your permission, Mr. Rienzi, I will take this precious tumbler home with me and analyse it properly. Cheer up, Miss Ivanilla. Nearly dead never filled the church-yard. You'll live to be as old as I am yet, never fear."

He hurried me rather unceremoniously up stairs, and sent Sophie for my breakfast; then he asked my permission to examine my bedroom for a few moments.

When he came back he was more abrupt than ever.

"That girl of yours is stupid, and you're all stupid together!" he exclaimed. "What's in your nose—" here he turned to Sophie, who was just entering with the luncheon tray, "not to smell the most overpowering scent of chloroform in Miss Ivanilla's bedroom? It's been poured on the very pillow she slept on!"

Sophie stood the picture of consternation

"I did smell something very queer," she said at last; "but Miss Iva said there was medicine in the tumbler of water which I poured away, and I thought maybe it was it."

"Child, I cannot understand how you didn't detect it," said Doctor Graves, resuming the reproaches which were addressed to me. "You should always keep your senses about you. You did very well about *seeing*, but if you had *smelt* as well, it would have saved you all the pain you have endured since she made off, besides, perhaps, assisting you to prevent her escape. Girl, go and throw all the windows up in your mistress' room, and change the bed-linen."

I could not understand either, how the pungent smell which now hung so heavily about me, and loaded every breath, had not attracted my attention when it was first administered.

But different as are the perfumes, I shall never, to the day of my death, approach the night-blooming cereus, without a return of all the horrors of that awful night, and a faintness chill as death, stealing over me, to remind me of one of the most blood-curdling episodes of **my** existence.

CHAPTER XVII.

THERE ARE FRIENDS, AND FRIENDS—WITH A DIFFERENCE.

"I bless thee, for thy lips are bland,
  And bright the friendship of thine eye;
And in my thoughts with scarce a sigh,
  I take the pressure of thine hand."—TENNYSON.

I shall pass over two days with a somewhat hasty review, for, in truth, I was not competent for much, for that time, as I was more than half an invalid and the doctor strictly forbade me to take any part in the arrangements of the family, or to excite myself in the slightest.

So I spent most of the time in my sister's room, where my slight illness had the effect of rousing her wonderfully into kind and loving cares for me.

To tell the truth, I had been frightened almost to death, and could not, for some time after the occurrence, raise my spirits from the depression that weighed upon them.

I was happy with my dear Isolina, however, and since neither of us was capable of bearing much excitement, we never alluded to subjects which were not of a calm and cheerful nature; and I was happy to see that my presence was a source of deep pleasure to her, and that she clung to me more closely than ever.

I heard little of the plans which were being made by my parents and our friends for our future movements. From this time the burden of anxiety was taken from my shoulders and borne by other hands, and I sank into the place which was best suited to me—that of nurse or companion to my beloved sister.

I was given to understand, however, by my mother, who had sustained almost as severe a shock as I in hearing of my adventure, that a vigorous search had been commenced for the would-be assassin, under the directions of Mr. Speingle. Mr. Lindhurst, with whom my father consulted about a suitably retired country place for us to resort to, recommended a certain obscure village on the Atlantic shore, whose charms of scenery, bracing air and retirement, he said, would fulfill our wishes admirably.

This place, which was designated Ranelagh, and which was so very obscure that my father said he had never heard of it, was the destination for which we purposed starting immediately.

On the morning of the day in which we intended to leave the city I went out to arrange my business as "Soldiers' Friend," and to leave my poor people in charge of No. 10, if she would undertake them. But Miss Cranstown not being at home when I called, I left a message with the lady president for her, and went to see the poor young widow, Mrs. Harrison, who had now set up a milliner's shop in a quiet little street, and seemed to be prospering tolerably well.

I carried to her the photographs, letter, and identifier of her unfortunate brother, which she received with sad thankfulness. She had now sustained the double loss of husband and brother, all who protected her. No wonder that her eyes streamed with tears as she bent over her orphaned boy!

"And he reminds me of them both!" she sobbed. "He has poor Leander's pretty curly head, and it sets so jaunty on his shoulders—just like him! But oh! he has his father's very eyes! My wee babe, you never saw your father —oh, no—no!"

Mrs. Harrison told me that Mr. Speingle had come two days and talked with her for hours about her brother, asking the strangest questions. She also showed me two golden dollars, which the kind old gentleman had put in baby's hand, and, with tears of gratitude, said he had promised to see that the child got a good education if he lived.

As I walked home (having some purchases to make I did not ride), I saw a handsome carriage at the door of a hotel, and at the moment in which I passed, a lady tripped down the marble flight of steps, and for the time blocked my further progress by her trailing skirts.

I drew back with flushing cheeks, when the lady, turning her head, disclosed the haughty face of Lillia Meredith.

"I am surprised," she said, looking at me from head to

foot; "I am more than surprised, that the sister of the celebrated Rienzi walks unprotected through the streets!"

The wickedness with which she sneered these words raised my slumbering passion like a spark to touch-wood.

"My scorn on the woman who proves a false friend!" I returned, gazing steadily in her face.

"Scorn Miss Isolina Rienzi, then!" she said, with a laugh, "and between your scorn and my vengeance, which I mean to pursue, perhaps justice may be satisfied."

"Miss Meredith," I said, turning pale with the effort to command myself, "circumstances have proved my sister innocent. Withdraw your persecution or this whole city will execrate your name."

"And do I care?" was the defiant retort, while her blue eyes scintillated with sparks of rage. "*She* was the cause of my being deserted this day, and for that I will be avenged. 'A blow for a blow'—that is my creed."

"'Tis a dog's creed that—a savage religion. I pity you."

"Reserve your pity for those who suffer by it."

"Beware!" I exclaimed, stung to the heart by her cruelty; "beware how you mingle gall in my innocent sister's cup. She is broken-hearted and dying with the weight of other people's crimes; no mean vengeance of yours is needed to hasten her doom."

"It has come already, then?" she cried, exultingly; "the time which I prophesied would come, when her beauty would be a memory and her talents turned to her own destruction! *Dying* is she? Come—I'm sorry for you, and will prove it. I will prove it. I will drive you home, lest some of the little urchins on the street recognize you and prove troublesome; and you shall tell your sister that Lillia Meredith is still human, though she has a dog's creed. Come in."

She turned the silver handle of the carriage-door and pointed to a seat, with a half-touched expression struggling with the harder lines upon her face.

I might have seized the momentary softening in its faint birth, and strengthened it into permanent contrition, by my own gentleness, but I was trembling with indignation and let the opportunity pass which might have saved so much sorrow.

"When you remember your enmity against **my** sister, I shall accept your benefits," I replied, coldly.

"Good! a long adieu then!" she returned, shutting herself in. "Drive to the station, coachman."

The carriage whirled away, and I walked on, still trembling with apprehension and anger. I knew she had just the character to cling stubbornly and pertinaciously to an idea until it was accomplished. Having chosen to consider Isolina as her enemy, no earthly power would turn the bitter prejudice from its channel. Your women who "never forget" are invariably patient, implacable, and tireless in their pursuit of vengeance.

When I reached home I found my friend, Miss Belle Cranstown, in the drawing-room, seated before the piano, in a most extraordinary flow of spirits, alternately rattling off waltzes and sallies of wit to mamma, who was listening with pleased enjoyment; and there also, to my astonishment, sat my poor sister in a deep easy chair near the window, also listening to the alla podrida which emanated from my lively friend, with a sweet, gentle smile on her face; which last was so great a stranger there that I stood in the door-way watching it with quivering lip.

"Ah, there you are!" cried Miss Belle, whirling round, "and pray what are you looking so surprised at? Ha! ha! don't you see we are giving the invalid a change of air to prepare her for Ranelagh?"

She skimmed over and gayly shook my hands, whispering the while:

"Met Doctor Graves in the city this morning—told me you were going away to-day—polite enough to tell me to chatter like a magpie, if I came up, and cheer you all up. Sure you need it, even *you*, poor little white ghost! Be gay, my little gipsy—laugh, and be gay—the worst is over!"

Thus finishing, with an additional shake of my hands, she brightly nodded her head and resumed the piano-stool.

"And what is this I hear?" said the young lady, beginning to fly through the intricacies of an arpeggio opera in C. by Beethoven, which wafted me on the wings of fondest memory to my Venetian home, where my dear old grandmother and I used to sit in the evenings upon the balcony listening to the lutes of the passing cavaliers under the awnings of their gondolettes—oh, these evenings, in the old-fashioned house above Rialto!—— What is this I hear? Hydra-head was out to tea last night, and came home and told me that the Queen of Hearts had vanquished one and was about to celebrate the victory!"

"Hydra-head?"

"Sister Lu, then," explained the mad-cap, turning round in the middle of her piece; "she said that Miss Iva was about to be united to—'one—a lone one 'mid the throng'— Mr. Lindhurst."

"And so she is!" said Isolina, holding my hand fondly; "and she will be as happy as a little queen, I am sure, with him."

"Bravo!" cried Miss Belle, catching my other hand in delight; "I'm glad Mrs. Grundy was right for once! My two ideals—you little gipsy, don't blush so charmingly. Look, Isolina! oh, kiss her—the pet, and may I kiss you, too—for congratulations?"

This half-absurd, half-touching embrace being over, Miss Belle seated herself at my mother's feet, leaving me still fondly held by Isolina.

"And so I have come to bid you good-by," resumed the young lady, with a sigh, "you dear old friend whom I have scarcely seen yet. Do you know Iva, that I know Mrs. Rienzi far better than her youngest daughter does?"

"Indeed!"

"Ah, you may look jealous! I have enjoyed her friendship ever since I was an unfortunate little wretch of six, staggering along every morning to school with a load of books as high as myself—ah, happy childhood! Your dear mamma scraped up a street acquaintance with me on the happy occasion of my running against her carriage in a hurry, and breaking my nose against the front wheel, while my books flew in at the carriage windows, for which I was treated to a ride home, a week of holidays, and a beautiful wax doll from my new friend."

"I don't think you enjoyed your first ride with me, much," observed my mother, laughing.

"I can't say that it was bliss unalloyed," admitted Belle. "I believe I was a little terrified by the shadow of my swelled nose on the carriage curtain, and shed more tears than smiles. Ah, me,

'My dreams come o'er me like a spell,
I think I am again a child.'

"I say, Ivanilla, what shall we do to bring back the light

to this pale shade? She looks as if she had bidden farewell
to this world, and the spirit was gazing an adieu upon the
mortal it loved before it

'Faded back like a sunbeam
Into the realms of light.'

"Shall we call her Heaven's chastened?"

She folded my sister's hand within her own, and gazed
with that tender, pleading look, until Isolina, gazing back
with brimming eyes, suddenly smiled a brilliant answer, and
burst into tears.

"Oh, thanks, my friend," she murmured, "that comforts
me. I will be Heaven's chastened."

Lower drooped the lovely girl, and whispered of a balm
which sometimes comes to broken hearts, until the world-
weary invalid gazed raptly and almost joyfully upon her.
Hope, long fled, stole back to her eyes; the despairing look
gave way to the new tide of heavenly comfort which was
shown to her; an eager, entranced expression was on her
face all the time these whispered words of Christian comfort fell from the lips of our gentle friend.

Why had I never tried such means of cheer? What had
my eager, worldly striving done for her?

Oh, sweet Belle Cranstown—gentle messenger, smooth be
thy pathway to the Life which is for thee beyond.

"Stay with us until we start this afternoon," said my
mother, when Miss Cranstown once more turned to us, her
eyes brighter than diamonds after their gentle tears.

"Wish I could, but alas!" she responded, with her usual
vivacity; "seven pairs of eyes watch for me elsewhere."

"Disappoint them," I suggested.

"And bring my unlucky faults to the tips of seven volu-
able tongues? Impossible! I go to guard my character."

"Don't go," pleaded my sister, earnestly.

Belle was pulling on her gloves in a great hurry, but
when she heard the mild remonstrance, she paused irresolutely.

"Well, I don't care!" she cried, throwing down her hat.
"Belle, I devote thy name to the tongues of the mighty
seven—a sacrifice to friendship. I left Louisa on Mrs. Lesmar's steps where we both were booked to spend the day,
and where I suppose they anxiously await my presence
in their gossips—I to supply the facts—they to embellish

and weave into tissues of—ahem! as Mrs. Lesmar, Hortensia, Georgiana, Leonora, Mary and Betty Lesmar, assisted by my sister, Lu, can weave such webs as endless as Penelope's, if you give them time.   I sha'n't aid them; I'll stay here."

Having thus expressed herself, Miss Belle picked up her little hat from the floor, fished her parasol, vail, and card-case from under the piano, and followed me up stairs.

After having pulled off her gloves and shawl, Miss Belle, in dead silence, dived into her pocket, and, after unfolding two or three circulars and charitable cards of various kinds, at last handed me a cut-out paragraph of a newspaper, which she bade me read.

"The *London Post* says that a party of gentlemen, who had penetrated into the deserts of Persia for scientific purposes, after undergoing several strange adventures, which are minutely described, left Astrabad with a caravan of Calaite merchants, and reached the frontier in safety; from whence they made all haste to return to their insular brethren, quite reconciled to pursue their experiments at home in future.   The plague they report as raging through Astrabad; and they were amazed to meet a young English gentleman there, who was working heart and hand among the smitten wretches as a physician.   This adventurous Englishman is called Victor Joselyn, and is the only representative of an old English family, whose estates are in Somersetshire."

"Do you know what I thought when I read that, this morning?" said Belle, when I had finished.   "I thought, 'All will be well with Isolina if she loves so noble a man!' Why should we fear anything, Iva, my darling!   Dry your tears.   If Heaven spares Victor Joselyn, we may trust him with our dear Isolina's happiness.   Let us never grieve our hearts with a question which we do not understand.   Incomprehensible as their friendship appears to us, I know that it is right.   So true a man—so brave and compassionate—must be the soul of honor."

Her enthusiasm infected me.   I dashed away the tears of dismay and grief, which first had sprung to my eyes, and looked almost with adoring regards at the name of my unknown hero.

"Oh, may Heaven spare his life!" I aspirated.

Miss Cranstown echoed my prayer with an embrace, and told me to keep the scrap of paper.

"I knew that strange picture vexed and puzzled you,"

said the dear girl; "and I brought you this to comfort you."

Then we had a confidential little chat on subjects which lay particularly near my heart; and I listened with a happy, glowing face to praises of a certain friend of mine, in whose excellence I took a very warm interest.

I believe my heart was almost recovered from the sick depression which I had felt for two days, when we went down stairs to lunch.

Miss Cranstown, with a flow of spirits which never flagged, and clever jokes innumerable, made herself wonderfully useful, assisted in the final packing of the various trunks, which were to be ready for the cabman at four o'clock.

Yet, when the final moment came, and my sister, fragile, pale, and lovely as a lily, stood in the door-way, where the smoky, city-grown foliage clambered up to touch her, and the languid flowers breathed faint incense, Belle broke down at last, and her sunny face grew pale with suppressed grief, while she bade my sister farewell; but her rushing tears were hidden from us all, as the dear, unselfish girl tied on her little hat, and quietly turned away, to trip modestly down the street and out of sight.

Mr. Ernest Lindhurst met us at the railway station, and lingered as long as he might within the car; then, with a shriek and a jolt, our train got into motion. My friend sprang upon the platform, and stood, with hat uplifted, and earnest regards, until we had glided away; then, with a quicker motion, like a racer when the blood pulsates through his veins and he leaps to the sweep of the first heat, we were borne onward to the new scenes, and left the old behind us.

CHAPTER XVIII.

SILVERLEA.

" So thick the boughis and the leavis green
  Beshaded all the alleys that there were.

    *   *   *   *   *   *

Growing so fair with branches here and there,
That as it seemed to a lyf without
The boughis spread the arbour all about." |
                        JAMES 1ST, SCOTLAND.

Our journey was soon over; my eagerly recurring query—
" Is this Ranelagh?"—was at last answered by my father in
the affirmative (who must have dislocated his neck to satisfy
my curiosity), and the train rushed with a savage whoop
into a small covered station; the guard shouted in at the
door, " Ranelagh!" and we rose from our seats.

In five minutes we were huddled together on a wooden
platform, my mother supporting Isolina on her arm; Sophie
mounted guard over a muffled cage containing my little
hoopoes from the Valley of Arno; a whimpering Neapolitan
pup in her arms, of undoubted breed but stupid disposition—also mine; a valise on either side of her, and an umbrella dangling from her little finger; while my father res-
cued our baggage from the incredulous vanguards, and I
looked about in vain for signs of the village.   At last we
were ushered out of the station by one of a group of boys,
whose straw hat was like the poet's dream:

" I had a hat, which was not all a hat,
  Part of the rim was gone;"

and after mounting a slight hill, the hotel of Ranelagh was
designated to us and I beheld the village.

There was a broad, grass-grown street, fenced off appro-
priately by what might pass for " broken lines " in geom-
etry, but to the general eye looked like zig-zag fencing;
infringed on, farther on, by some half a dozen houses on
either side, squatted cozily behind tall poplars or Balm of
Gilead trees.

On the horizon a deep, blue belt of ocean wavered with

many a heaving, comb-crested sparkle; to the right a scattered settlement of brown farm-houses cozily nestled in the valley; to the left a pyramid of wooded hills rose up, crowned with blue ether, and shut out the east winds.

A pretty spot was the Ranelagh village—surely peace and safety reigned here!

The hotel, by far the most pretentious edifice in the valley, was the nearest house to the station, and was enlivened by a flaming sign covering the whole of the second flat, which informed us that "Old Sol" was going to entertain us. Three young men who were shoveling earth into a cart at the side of the road suddenly disappeared behind the house, and were immediately after transformed into three waiters in white aprons, who lounged out to the front balcony and watched us approaching.

The landlord, with a broad, red, beaming face, and in a great hurry, came across a hay-field, and ushered us with a flourish into the house, where a young woman pounced upon us, and led the ladies of us into a very small bedroom.

Sophie, after depositing my little company of pets on a table in the outer room, took off her things, tied on an apron from out of her pocket, and grimly beating out a large cat before her, whose yellow eyes were glaring with greed at the birds, found her way to the kitchen to see about some food for Isolina.

We immediately divested our invalid of her clothes, and made her lie down in the soft, downy bed, which smelled of sweet clover and thyme, and was white as pure bleaching on grass which never was besmoked, could make it.

She was too exhausted even to speak; the journey had been great for her small stock of strength; but she looked and smiled so placidly, that I could not but hope this sweet place would restore her in time, and we were much comforted to see the wonderful appetite with which she ate the dainty little supper which Sophie brought in. Ten minutes afterward she was in a profound slumber.

The sun was just dipping behind the hills when we entered the eating-room where our dinner waited us, and where my father was seated, in conversation with the landlord.

"Yes, sir," the man was saying, "I think it would just suit you if it's a house to hire for the summer, you're after;

just exactly, sir. A quiet, healthy place you want, ma'am? Well, there's not a quieter nor a healthier place 'twixt this and New York, nor that same place; nor a prettier or more genteel, I make bold to say, miss."

"To whom does it belong?"

"Well, sir, it did belong (though it doesn't now—he's dead this three year), to Squire Granville; but now a brother of his owns it, in Connecticut, and as he don't want to come and live in it himself, he lets it out, do you see? So it's just waiting for you, sir."

"Very good. And to whom shall I apply?"

"The house-agent lives just across the street, sir. Do you see that house with the green shutters? that's Mr. Fernley's, and he'll show you over Silverlea, whenever you like."

"Silverlea?"

"Yes, miss, that's the name old Squire Granville, poor man, called the place. Oh, you'll like it, missy, it's quite a villar like, with lots of courts and courting places around, ha, ha! Parding me, miss, I like a joke with the young folks. You see there's lots of them white-barked trees on the place, and the sea comes in at the back quite beautiful miss; on a calm day, you could count most a hundred ships at once, way out on the Atlantic."

"Hush!" I ejaculated, laying down my knife and fork. "Your description is so charming that I will make my papa take the house, whatever disadvantages there are and he will blame you."

At which the jolly landlord laughed, deep down in his capacious thorax, and departed.

As soon as we had dined, my father hurried across the street to find the house agent, and my mother and I prepared ourselves to accompany them to Silverlea.

It was scarcely yet sunset, when my father returned with a dry, good-humored looking little man by his side, in whose company we started for our walk of half a mile, through the village and out to the shore.

Pretty indeed, was the road to Silverlea, with alternate fields of wheat and rye, and sometimes wastes of alderbushes, and downy, deep-green stretches of samphires, and here and and there a prairie-like roll of meadows, where herds of sheep lifted their white heads at our approach, and bounced away to the nearest clump of pine-wood.

Presently we reached the shore road, and ascended a sudden bluff, where fir-trees lined either side of the road, and the broad, lazy waves of the Atlantic rolled in upon the yellow sand.

"This is Silverlea."

I saw a white cottage with three pointed gables, a piazza running along one side and upheld by pillars of Corinthian simplicity, a veranda on top of the piazza, with a delicate tracery of carved wood by way of parapet, and many a quaint panel of Gothic ornament interspersed.

A pointed bay-window in front, with Gothic pendants, imitated by the long, narrow windows down the sides, which looked out on all sides to green retreats and shady terraces. A more delightfully incomprehensible, romantic little villa could scarcely be conceived; it looked at one point like a Spanish casino, with its verdant jalousies and trellised balconies, and I almost listened for the lute of the troubadour, and looked for the lovely Andalusian to appear, after her seclusion from the scorching sobano, to drop her bouquet of orange blossoms into the bosom of her serenader.

"Oh, father!" I exclaimed, "take this paradise."

"You will find it very nicely furnished," said Mr. Fernley, knocking smartly at the door. "Mr. Granville was a gentleman of taste, though a bachelor, and his brother not caring for these things, left the furniture just as it was for the use of the tenants. The housekeeper, who is a fixture here, keeps everything in exact order, as you will see, and is as peaceable a woman as ever breathed."

At this moment the door was opened by an old woman in a white muslin cap and stiff gown, who dropped a low courtesy to Mr. Fernley and another to us.

"How de do, Mrs. Haller? Some visitors I've brought over to see the house; all the way from the city, too. The housekeeper, sir, I was telling you about."

"Glad to see you, Mrs. Haller," said my father, walking in. "I think we shall be old friends pretty soon. Nice little place, eh, Maud?"

We all marched successively into the various rooms, which were certainly furnished very prettily and tastefully, and kept in admirable order by the housekeeper.

We wandered about until the silver moonbeams were stealing through the moveless trees; and to my unbounded delight my father decided to rent Silverlea for the summer.

We returned in the fairy-like beauty of the summer night to the hotel.

CHAPTER XIX.

WAS IT " CIRCUMSTANCE?"

> For a raven ever croaks at my side,
> " Keep watch and ward—keep watch and ward!"
> —Tennyson.

The next morning all arrangements were satisfactorily completed with Mr. Fernley for renting Silverlea, and we were transported in Mr. Stanton's best wagon from the hotel to our new abode, which proved to be quite as lovely by daylight as it had appeared by night.

My sister turned her wistful eyes from side to side, and her wasted cheeks flushed faintly with pleasure. She drank in the exhilarating sea-breeze and murmured softly, " I shall rest here!" at which my silly, credulous heart bounded with joy.

With considerable pride, I conveyed Isolina up stairs to the chamber which had been allotted to us, and which was glistening with pristine freshness from Mrs. Haller's careful hands. Daintily papered walls of white and silver; pure fleecy drapery, looped back from the windows by light silver tassels, a dark-green carpet with clusters of white water-lilies scattered over-it; a low French bed with a canopy of fleecy lace; an emerald-green vase with a silver adder twined round it, and filled with odorous fresh-plucked water-lilies on the mantel; a cheval-glass in one corner, which reflected again the pretty combination of colors. Such was the little chamber assigned to Isolina and me.

I saw that she liked it, and I was pleased; so I threw open the window and drew her to look at the same view which had enchanted me at night.

"Yes," repeated my sister, turning softly to me; "I shall find rest in this lovely spot, for awhile!"

But at present she was so exhausted by the short drive from the village in Mr. Stanton's wagon that she had to lie down and rest.

Being naturally of a very impatient nature, I determined to acquaint myself with all the points of interest about

Silverlea without loss of time, and so with this end in view,
I repaired to the kitchen to make the more intimate acquaintance of the housekeeper; leaving my mother gently
swaying herself in a rocking-chair in the pretty parlor before the window, and my father enjoying himself luxuri-
ously in an arm-chair on the piazza, his eyes fixed compla-
cently on his wife, his panama hat on the floor beside him,
and his back against a leafy pillow—the picture of calm
enjoyment.

I found the kitchen, a low, wide, yellow-painted room,
with three little square windows, looking out upon a court,
or hen-yard, as I supposed, from the quantity of feathered
creatures croaking and cackling in noisy enjoyment of some
scattered grain.   A brisk fire made of wood crackled upon
the stone hearth, and from the stone-oven alongside a
savory steam was issuing through the corners of the iron
door, which assailed my hungry nostrils irresistibly.

"Ah, Mrs. Haller, what a quaint-looking place!" I
cried, taking a delighted survey; "and how strange and
nice everything is!"

She was busy brightening sundry dish-covers to add to
the already long row on the yellow wall, and she laid one
down to look round and laugh.

"I guess, miss, there's plenty of life in you and never a
taste of the blues!   So you like my kitchen?"

"I am enchanted with it, Mrs. Haller. Is that the
bench that the young farmers sit on when they come courting in the evening?"

She laughed softly.

"Little miss," said she, "they ain't many come a-court-
ing to Silverlea nowadays.   I don't know what they might
have done if I was young and frolicsome, but age makes a
difference, as I believe. No, indeed, miss. There's not
been a young man inside this kitchen since old master died,
except one young gentleman—and he thought little enough
of courting."

"Didn't he?   Well, I'm going to establish a new *regime.*
I am going to fill these halls with youth and jollity—these
pegs with wide-awakes—that bench with rustic beaus!"

"I'm thinking our chaps round Ranelagh would feel
rather shy of such a city miss as you—from foreign parts to
boot—so I've heard."

"I should hit the heels of my Achilles. Get another

bench for the other side of the porch, Mrs. Haller. We shall hold our conference there. How hungry I am!"

"Dear heart alive! What would you like, miss? Some bread and nice sweet-milk fresh from butter-cups?"

"Infusion of butter-cups?"

"Lor! there ain't many butter-cups like my big black cow!"

"Oh!—bliss itself, signora! Better than the richest goblet of wine expressed from grapes grown on the sunniest plank of Vesuvius!"

"Did you say 'yes,' miss?"

"Most decidedly, my friend. And may I have a tumbler for my sister? Ah, thank you! you are kind. But I shall explore a little longer before I awake her. Where does this lead to?"

"Into the back yard, where the kitchen-stuff is; and yonder's the stable; and this court is for everything—chopping, feeding fowls, cleaning vegetables, and all."

"Is kitchen-stuff fish, flesh, or fowl—mineral, vegetable, or nondescript, my dear Mrs. Haller?"

"Law sakes, I don't know! only it's the grass and stuff, and the apple-sass, and such-like. Would you like to see the chickens? Just open the door of that log-house and look into a half-barrel at them."

"Shades of Diogenes! juvenile philosophers! What little fuzzy things! Oh, you pet! You are the king of them, with your little broad bill and twinkling eyes!"

"That's the only chicking out of a brood of thirteen. Do you like hop-beer, miss?"

"Very likely I do. I never saw any."

"Not! You shall have a drink of it this very day. Why, where was you raised, I wonder?"

"Not on hop-yeast, you may be sure, my friend. Oh! there is the well! What a heavy, moss-grown bucket; and how cool the air is when I put my head down!"

"Goodness gracious! Don't fall in. See—are you fond of posies? Would you like to make a tisty-tosty of cowslips? There's lots back there in the old orchard."

To the old woman's evident relief, I left the vicinity of the well, and ran through a wicket-gate into a little forest of old gnarled apple and peach trees.

All at once I came upon an old man who was rolling down the grass with a heavy stone roller, and so intently employed that he did not see me, though I stood close by him.

"All alike—all alike!" he muttered, driving at a stone which lay in his way. "Get over, will ye! Yes—will help herself in spite of me, and run into devil knows what scrapes, while I grub, grub, grub here—heh! This is rough ground."

"Is that hard work?" I asked, wishing to apprise him of my presence.

He turned round and stared in surprise at me.

"'Morning, miss. How long have you been here? Well, not very hard, when it's not up hill. I didn't see you, miss, before this minute, and you gave me a bit of a start."

It was a queer old face into which I was looking, and I could not help feeling mysteriously impressed.

"I'm sorry if I startled you," I said, wrenching myself from a reverie; "I was looking over this pretty Silverlea, and did not expect to see anybody."

"You are one of the new tenants then, miss?"

"Yes; we arrived from New York yesterday."

"You're not an American, miss."

"How do you know that?" I asked, laughing.

He folded his arms on top of his roller, and gazed at me, with his chin down on his sleeves, with a kindly intentness.

"Your tongue betrays you, miss. Ain't you Italian?"

"Yes, from Venice. I came last autumn."

The man raised himself suddenly.

"What's your name, young lady?" he exclaimed.

"Rienzi—Ivanilla Rienzi; my father is Guiseppe Rienzi, the architect."

The dark, wild face grew dingy white; it showed such consternation and heavy anger, that I stood transfixed with surprise; a thousand fears, banished for a season by the peaceful scenes in which we had taken refuge, rushed back into my heart.

"Who are you, sir," I demanded.

"The gardener at Silverlea, miss," he answered, in a stifled voice.

"Your name?" I continued, anxiously.

He affected not to hear me; picked up his roller and walked on.

"What is your name?" I repeated, more imperatively, slowly keeping step with him.

"Ralph Morecombe," he threw the name at me, as a dog emits a snarl at losing a bone.

"And have you ever heard of us before?"

"What makes you think such a thing, Miss Ivanilla Rienzi?"

"No one ever greeted a stranger, or a friend, as you have greeted me. You are an enemy—and why?"

I steadily escorted him along the grassy sweep, secretly trembling with sick consternation, but outwardly firm.

He trudged on, dumb as a stone, until the last of the grass was pressed down; then he turned on me, a cold fury in his eyes which well might make me tremble.

"Look here, miss," he said between his teeth; "I don't advise you to run your neck into any noose that you can't run it out of again—it's dangerous. Better see nothing, and say less!"

"I do not understand you, sir," I responded, "but I shall find means to understand you, and have your position here looked into; sir, you will have to explain your threats."

"Ha, ha! a fool's colt is soon shot! By-by, missy!"

I retreated hastily through the orchard, making no answer to his taunting words; in fact, too terrified to speak.

"Who is that man in the orchard?" I asked impetuously of the housekeeper, as I entered the kitchen.

"A man in the orchard? Oh, I suppose you mean old Ralph the gardener."

"Who is he?"

"Well, he's just—he's just old Ralph, the gardener," said Mrs. Haller, with a puzzled look.

"Where does he come from?"

"I can't rightly tell you, miss; from everywheres, I do believe; he's more like the Wandering Jew than anything else, I'm sure."

"What is his other name?"

"Morton—Motley—no, Morecombe, I believe. He's a surly old chap. Hope he didn't frighten you, miss?"

"How long has he been here, Mrs. Haller?"

"He came with the last tenant; let me see. All last winter he was here off and on."

"Oh, Mrs. Haller, who was the last tenant?"

"Mrs. Ringwood, miss, from Vermont, if I recollect right; a pious, good lady, if ever there was one; and yet a queer one."

"Tell me how."

"Well, miss, I'll tell you all about it——"

"Mrs. Haller!"

I sprang aside with a scream. Ralph was at my elbow looking at the housekeeper with a lurid scowl.

"I have cut my hand—come and bind it up."

"Good lack!" muttered the old woman; "whatever set the man to chopping up his hands—jist when there's some use for them!"

She hurried to a drawer and picked out some linen rags, while the gardener started out again, and waited in the court-yard, leaning against the well.

"I hope it ain't bad," said Mrs. Haller; "for I do hate idle men around, like pison."

I stood beside the sputtering oven and gazed intently through the window, as she followed the man out.

Ralph still kept his hand thrust into his bosom, and impatiently elbowed her away when she extended her bandage; then he began to speak with angry, threatening gestures, and from astonishment, Mrs. Haller's face changed to something very like anger, and she gave her muslin frills an indignant toss and turned to enter the kitchen; but the man clutched her by the shoulder, and with the sudden glare of a wild beast at the window, dragged her out of sight, and I ceased to hear even their voices.

I stood alone in the cheery kitchen, a cowering, discomfited pain in my heart, which robbed me of all courage.

In ten minutes Mrs. Haller came in, and very, very quietly slipped about her work for some minutes, saying nothing. Her kindly old face was grave and pale; her hands trembled a little in spite of her.

"Was the cut very deep?" I asked in covert scorn.

"Oh, no, miss—oh, no," she answered, with unnecessary earnestness.

"Will you please tell me the rest about Mrs. Ringwood, now?" I remarked, not daring to look up.

A low sigh heaved Mrs. Haller's bosom.

"There's nothing to tell; I hadn't ought to have said anything, my dear," she said, very quietly.

"Perhaps it is something which concerns us?" I persisted.

"No, nothing, miss. Please don't ask me nothing; that's

a dreadful man! There's a pitcher of milk for you and the sick young lady, and tumblers. Shall I carry it in?"

"I will carry them myself, Mrs. Haller. Thank you."

Obeying the hint, I betook myself to the parlor.

The sun glimmered in through the hanging wreaths, as before; my father lounged on the piazza with the same contented ease; my sweet sister reclined on the little sofa between them, gazing with satisfied eyes into the heart of the vernal glades; I only carried gloom and fear in my bosom, for the serpent had stolen into my paradise.

"What's the matter with our little gipsy?" cried my father, peeping in at me, "has she got a fright cow milking?"

"If I did, I secured the milk;" I answered with an attempt at gayety. "See, my sister, this is a specimen of true milk—warranted pure from chalk and water."

"You look weary, sister," said Isolina, looking up into my pale, depressed face, "let me fan you awhile, and lie on this sofa—the heat has been too much for you."

"Bah!" I answered, laughing, "the heat never makes me ill. I never suffered heat when the sirocco blew most burningly in Italy."

"But there *is* something the matter," said my mother, seeing me clearly for the first time.

"A raven croaked at me in the orchard," I answered, meeting her anxious regards with a smiling look.

Very soon I found myself out on the piazza, behind my father's chair.

"Come with me until I tell you something," I murmured.

We slowly paced together to the end of the piazza, and leaned over the pretty railing.

"Papa, we are not safe even at Silverlea," I began; "the only two people who are here are in league against us."

"Nonsense, child! Why, you poor little girl, you are getting so nervous and fanciful that I shall soon be alarmed about you. That fright you got at home was bad for you, Iva."

"Papa, listen to me," I repeated, with tearful earnestness. "We are not safe here. There is a gardener here whom you must see—he is connected with—with our enemies. There was a Mrs. Ringwood living in this house last winter; I am sure she was connected with our enemies; there is a photograph of grandmamma's house in Venice, in the basket of one of the statues within that drawing-room; does that look like mere accident?"

"My dear child, you perfectly astonish me! You seem to have plunged into the midst of conspiracies."

I told him the different causes of my alarm.

"You are not alarmed without cause apparently," he said, when I had finished; "still there may be some misapprehension. Perhaps the surly dog meant nothing; perhaps Mrs. Haller, who really seems a most respectable woman, was silent on the subject of Mrs. Ringwood from other causes than those your terrors suggest. This matter can be quickly sifted."

He went back for his hat and let himself out to the garden, with the determination of at once confronting the gardener.

Disconsolately I drooped over the little gate, my face buried in my hands. This haunting terror had come back to me like Faust's Evil One, and was dragging me into horrors from which my fainting heart crawled loathingly. All the brightness of Silverlea was hateful to me; that dread face, with the passionate eyes for blood seemed lurking under every tree; it danced before me with mocking sneers on the pale, curled lips, and a voiceless whisper rushed like a molten stream of lead into my brain which chanted:

"*My oath is fulfilled!*"

A hand rested on my shoulder; I cowered down with a shriek of agony, and my excited brain almost turned.

"My dear child, are you afraid of me?"

It was my father, back again; grave enough by this time, but gazing pitifully down at me, and evidently amazed at my agitation.

"Be more calm, Ivanilla," he said raising me and tenderly pressing me to his bosom; "there is really no cause for such mortal terror; we may have enemies, but Heaven has saved us hitherto; ask Him to save us still, my daughter."

"You are back very soon, papa."

"He has gone to the village to get something mended at the blacksmith's, Mrs. Haller tells me. Dear, I don't think we are authorized in molesting the housekeeper; she is a very conscientious person, and I am sure would not wrong us. She has given me to understand that Morecombe warned her not to speak of Mrs. Ringwood, because the lady was in some political intrigue. The truth is, I believe in my own heart she is a rebel spy, or some such thing, and we have nothing to do with her intrigues. I shall sound your bugbear Morecombe when he returns."

But Ralph Morecombe did not return; day after day passed on, and the gardener's place was still unoccupied. Our servants came down from the city, and located themselves; a boy was hired, at first by the day, to do the gardener's work, then for a month, and no one came to displace him.

After a week my father had to go to the city, summoned thence by Mr. Speingle, and we were left alone at Silverlea.

Alone and unmolested, the most perfect peace and security reigned here. Time stole on, and touched my disturbed heart with balm; I began to breathe more freely as the days went on; my dark fears had proved groundless.

I became in a measure happy in our charming Silverlea with my beloved mother and sister. It was joy itself to me to lead Isolina daily to some farther point of interest in our sylvan retreat, and to comfort her shadowed life through Nature's loveliness.

CHAPTER XX.

I CRY " WOLF" ONCE MORE.

" In your eye there is death,
  There is frost in your breath,

    *   *   *   *   *

So keep where you are; you are foul with sin;
  She would shrink to the earth if you came in."
                    TENNYSON.

Strangely intermingled with the tender life I lived with my sister, was the weary life I hid from her.

I had a restless spirit which could not be laid wholly, however secure we seemed to be ; I was forever watching, sometimes placidly, sometimes feverishly, always vigilantly.

Every evening, when the heat of the day was over, I rode out on horseback, accompanied by Nelson. Dr. Graves had been to see Isolina, and Dr. Graves had ordered that it should be so, after studying me sharply for some time.

This exercise formed in me a habit which no one could wholly account for, nor could I account for it myself. No matter how fair the scenery was in the direction of Shirley Sands or the Cat's Head hills, I always shaped my course round the village road in time to meet the evening train from New York.

I watched every arrival with jealous eyes, and became as regular a visitor to the Ranelagh Station as the urchins who loafed under the butternut tree at the corner, with a persistence which seemed half insane.

Sometimes I was ashamed of this habit, when strangers stared curiously at me, but notwithstanding this, and owing to some inward promptings, I never broke my tryst with the evening train.

One evening, to my unutterable confusion, my eager watching was rewarded by seeing my lover alight from the car. The urchins all grouped and gazed congratulatingly at me, when the handsome gentleman handed his valise to Nelson, to ride home with, and walked slowly by my side, his hand on my saddle-bow.

It was very gratifying to have all the youths in Ranelagh rejoice that my long waiting was at last successful.

Mr. Lindhurst had come down to spend a day with us, having left his business with his clever young clerk "to take a trip to Eden," as he flatteringly declared.

"But I do not find my little Iva looking well," he said, regarding me with far too close a scrutiny for my nervous face to bear unmoved; "darling, how weary—how feverish you are! Why, love?"

I hid my groundless, womanish fears, for I was ashamed of them ; and I told him, gayly, he had brought the medicine. So we walked home by the beach, and the moon sailed up to smile blandly upon us, and my imprisoned heart swelled more freely for a space, in the love of the man who was dearest to me.

His visit passed so quickly; the hours fled on winged feet, while he soothed and comforted us all, and ministered to my sister with the tenderness of a brother; I forgot to tremble with sick fears at every sudden sound, and clung to him with almost childish dependence.

Once more the sun sank behind the hills; that mystic hour which oft has marked the dark events of this history; that hour whose approach called me from the most engrossing employment to the watch.

I had been playing to my sister and Ernest on the little

piano; but glancing at the clock I started up, as affrighted as Cinderella when the enchanted hour was striking.

"I must go," I exclaimed.

"Out to-night?" said Isolina; "oh, need you go to-night? Take a double gallop to-morrow when Ernest is not here."

"Sister," I muttered, almost tragically, "let me go."

"But you are weary with walking so long on the beach this afternoon. Dear Ivanilla, I am sure you should not go out to-night. If Dr. Graves saw you how he would make you lie down."

I stood the picture of dumb obstinacy, gazing from face to face.

"You are determined to go?" said Ernest, in a low voice.

"Must!" I whispered.

"Will you walk? It would be half an hour before the horses were ready."

"Yes, yes; I will walk."

"A walk in the cool sea-breeze may do her good," said Ernest, turning quietly to Isolina. "I think with you, that riding is too violent an exercise after her fatigue—she shall walk with me."

I darted from the room and flung on my hat and scarf, and casting one fond, remorseful look on Isolina's wistful face, I turned away from the door, my escort by my side. I led my lover the shortest way over the sands to Ranelagh Village; the tide had crawled in and was full; I did not care; in my blind hurry I scrambled over rocks and clung to crumbling banks, which, were this not the charmed hour, would have been impassable barriers to me. Ernest followed, sometimes catching me back from a whirling wave. sometimes swinging me over the slippery rocks. Conversation under such circumstances was impossible.

At last we reached the road which led straight into the village, and, panting with our wild scramble, I was glad to lean on my companion's arm.

"Now, tell me what all this means," said Mr. Lindhurst.

"All what? Hist! I hear the shriek of the coming train."

"You cannot walk so fast. I feel your heart like a sledge-hammer against my arm. Ivanilla, what is this excitement for?"

"Hush! They are coming round the curve of the hill—

now they cross the wooden bridge—in one-half minute they will be here."

" How can you tell so well?"

" Have I not watched? Come, come! We shall be late."

" Whom do you expect?"

" No one—any one. Come!"

I was wild with excitement. I dragged him close within the station, and hung gasping on his arm.

" My darling, what can be the matter?" murmured Ernest. " I don't like to feel you tremble like this. I am sure you are ill."

The boys under the butternut-tree ceased imitating the shriek of the coming engine with their fingers to their mouths, and began to chatter in would-be whispers.

" She's got another chap with her to-night."

" Wonder where the horses have gone to?"

" Grass, likely. Who do you think she watches for?"

"Don't know; she's as regular here as old Jobson, the carrier, is at the post-office."

These remarks were intensely audible to me. Whether my lover heard them or not, I could not tell; he was looking anxiously down at me, and not at all interested in anything else.

The evening train stopped; the few passengers stepped upon the platform and ran about clamoring for their luggage.

Few, indeed, there were to reward my curiosity.

Two farmers' wives and a little girl dressed in calico, who were each saddled with a blue-spotted handkerchief bundle, and a hand-basket, and all seemed glad to see their native hills again. A city exquisite, of blasé appearance, cigar in teeth, cane in hand, with colored gloves, the accurate shade of two dogs which slouched at his heels—who honored us with a profound stare, as he sauntered up to " Old Sol."

" There is no one else," said I, in a depressed voice. " Come away."

" Yes, my love, the dew is falling, and my little girl is too long under it."

He gladly led me off the platform for, perhaps, twenty rods. Like Lot's wife, I looked back, and became transfixed.

" What has happened?" cried Ernest, seeing my rigid face.

A woman had flitted cautiously out from the station. She stumbled over the ill-laid platform and dashed aside her thick crape vail. One moment the colorless face was turned to me, with a red glow of the vanished sun painting an unearthly scarlet upon, and streaming into two flaring, red-brown orbs.

I have said I should know that face among a thousand; I looked upon it now.

"Good Heaven!" muttered Ernest, throwing his arm around me, "how ghostly you are! Lean on me, and I will take you home."

"Oh, don't let her see me," I moaned with chattering teeth; "keep between us—oh, come away."

"What, that lady? She cannot harm you! Don't be afraid."

We hastened on a few paces, I clinging to his arm, and scarcely able to pick my steps. Oh, what cruel fate had sent me here to face my enemy?

But I rallied my senses with a mighty effort.

"Where is she, Ernest?" I asked.

"The lady who came out of the station? She is ascending the steps of the hotel, and a man has just carried some luggage into the house."

I turned quickly. The woman was facing on the top steps of the balcony, a white hand shielding her eyes from the western light; again that female form struck horror to my heart; again I gasped convulsively, and my face grew white and hard.

When we gained the beach-road which led up to Silverlea, and when the village was quite hidden behind the fir-trees, Ernest seated me on a stone by the road-side, and stood before me with my hands gathered firmly in his.

"My love," he said, gravely, "I cannot tell how your strange conduct through all this walk has alarmed me. Will you not explain it?"

"Oh, Heaven! what shall I say?" I cried, bursting into hysterical tears; "where shall I begin this dreadful story? It bristles with horror. That woman has found us. Alas, she is our enemy."

"My beloved girl, what is this?" said my lover, pressing me fondly in his arms. "You cannot mean that that person is Mrs. Beaumont, whom your father is in search of?"

I hung on his breast speechless for a while; my self-mastery was all gone; prolonged anxiety had made me weak as a child. I was worn out with watching for danger.

When I could speak I told him all; his face was pale and quiet when I had finished. He caught me to his heart again and strained me tightly there.

"You will not leave to-night?" I moaned, piteously.

"No, my darling; no, no!" exclaimed my lover. "I could not leave you now."

"And you will not leave us until she is arrested—don't protest. She will come, when the night is blackest, to poison us; she will come to-night!" I almost shrieked.

"Hush, hush!" he whispered, "I will guard you, my girl. Nothing shall enter Silverlea unchallenged to-night."

He hurried me home, and confusion arose at my coming. I was ill, and could not hide it, and the eyes of love divined my powerlessness. There were hurried consultations between my mother and Mr. Lindhurst, and messengers were sent to the village; but I was too ill to notice much.

I watched my sister with insane terror lest she should leave the room and fall into danger as the night advanced, and I implored her not to leave my side.

"Hush, my darling!" whispered Ernest, "see, your words terrify her—oh, take care!"

Then I became as urgent that Isolina should retire to bed as before I had been that she should remain; for I felt the effort to restrain my breath killing me, and I knew that alarm for her might be fatal. Sophie came and took my sister away, and I beckoned the girl back to me and whispered, with streaming tears:

"Lock her door, Sophie; oh, lock the door and sleep beside her!" And then I hid my face in my hands with a shudder of renewed panic, for words my sister had used once in a thrill of terror came back to me like a spell:

"Bolts and bars are nothing to her when she chooses to come."

This was the woman whom she feared; the woman who had slid like a vapor into my chamber, through bolts and bars. I felt it; I saw with a flash of conviction that the crisis which was to destroy us had come.

"She comes to fulfill her vow!" I exclaimed, writhing in my lover's arms. I shrieked as if a hyena were rending my vitals, and for the third time in my life I fainted.

After a strange inward experience I revived, and found

my mother's face bending over me. Hours had passed; it was midnight, and I was on my mother's bed, she alone beside me.

The unnatural strain on my feelings had passed away; I was able to hope for the best, instead of dwelling on the worst.

"Mamma, I have been a child," I murmured; "forgive me."

"Thank Heaven that you have recovered!" whispered my mother, tremulously. "I did not know the strain which has been on your mind all these weeks."

"Listen! What is that?" I exclaimed, sitting up.

"Mr. Lindhurst, my love. He is pacing the hall to-night. Shall I open the door and tell him that his Iva is scared by his footsteps? Fye, child! love must be very deaf, as well as blind!"

"No, no. I shall have to listen to it. Mamma, what has been done? The woman——"

Even while I spoke profound exhaustion closed my mouth; I sank gently back against my mother's arm and fell asleep.

CHAPTER XXI.

A TRIP IN THE RAIN.

"A miser, seeing a mouse in his house, said: 'What art thou doing, dearest mouse, in my house?' And the mouse, secretly smiling, replied: 'Fear nothing, my friend; we do not want food from you, only lodging.'"—Greek Anthology.

When I awoke I was lying alone in my mother's bed, the broad daylight shining on my face, and the sounds of Mrs. Haller's kitchen, which was near, reminding me cheerfully of the neighborhood of human beings.

It was nine o'clock; what a bridge of time stretched between me and the startling events of last night!

I hurried on my clothes and opened the door.

Sophie was busily sweeping down the steps with a hand-broom.

"How is my sister?" I asked.

"Oh, are you up, miss, and better? Yes, you look bright, Miss Iva, dear. Miss Isolina is sleeping yet; she didn't have a very good night, I'm afraid. She was anxious about you, and my nose would snore, though I tried my very best not to let it."

" I am sorry for that, Sophie, but I don't think you can help it. Did you keep the door locked and sleep on the sofa?"

" Yes, Miss Iva; and Mr. Lindhurst he came twice to the door and asked me if all was safe. Sure, miss, I don't know what the panic was for. Be there burglars round?"

"I hope not, Sophie. Where is Mr. Lindhurst?"

" In his room, now; he staid up all night, and your ma has made him go now and sleep."

" Where is mamma?"

" In the kitchen, I think, speaking to Mrs. Haller."

I went into the breakfast-room, and sat waiting for my mother to come in.

After all, what had I to fear? This was home, and who could invade these sacred walls unseen? Surely I had turned a Machiavelli, to question with dark suspicion the good faith of every living creature.

While these thoughts were occupying me, my mother entered and greeted me tenderly. There was a puzzled expression on her face which I did not fail to notice.

" Mamma!" I cried, "tell me what has happened."

" My dear, I am at a loss what to think; you must have made some curious mistake last night. The truth is, the only lady who arrived at Stanton's last night is Mrs. Ringwood, the widow lady who staid here last winter. Nelson has made as many inquiries as he could in a private way, and it seems perfectly preposterous to molest such a person. She is an elderly, quiet, invalid lady, with gray hair, and she has quite a reputation for her charity. Mr. Stanton's people spoke of her almost with veneration. She has been traveling for her health, and came here hoping to re-occupy Silverlea for the summer, quite unaware that it had been let to any one else. She is undecided yet whether to go away or try to find some house round Ranelagh which would suit her. The probability is that she will stay at the hotel some days. Now, my dear, does it not seem ridiculous for us to proceed in any way against a lady of Mrs. Ringwood's reputed character?"

" All this sounds very plausible, mamma," I responded, gravely, "and I confess that my convictions are staggered. One cannot be sure that a face seen once by the faintest of moonlight, and amidst the most abject terrors, would be recognizable again; still, I adhere to my suspicions that the face I saw last night is the same. And now, to shake the apparently strong position of this Mrs. Ringwood. Why has our housekeeper been forbidden to speak to us of her? How should an irreproachable widow lady fear the gossip of an old woman? You see, at the very outset, this lady conceals something, which proves she is not what she seems."

"You reason acutely; but I have been speaking to Mrs. Haller of this, and from what she says, I think the poor lady is not to blame. Mrs. Haller is a well-meaning woman, and will not break a promise she made to Ralph Morecombe, but she gave me to understand that Mrs. Ringwood's secret relates to some disgrace in the family—a son who, perhaps, is eluding the law—and she wished to keep the circumstances from the boy's friends. My dear, we have no right to pry into any one's private affairs without good proof of their identity."

"How probable it is that the son is Cecil Beaumont," I sneered, still suspicious. "Oh, mamma, do not deceive yourself.

"I shall not," she answered; "but we must not be imprudent. We can do nothing without proof; what a mad course it would be to arrest a lady like Mrs. Ringwood on your single accusation. No, no; we must send for your father and his lawyer, and consult them; perhaps at this very moment they have discovered the real culprit who attempted to poison you."

"We shall go and call on this woman, then, mamma?"

"If you wish. You can then judge more calmly if your suspicions have any foundation; and I will surely be able to detect any hidden treachery, if she is, as you say, 'not what she seems.'"

Mamma wrote a note to my father which Mr. Lindhurst promised to deliver, and which we expected would bring him down by the morrow, with Mr. Speingle, to examine into the cause of our panic.

We agreed to drive Mr. Lindhurst to the station to catch the midday train, and from thence mamma and I were to call at the hotel and see the widow lady.

We left my sister in her chamber in company with Sophie, who was charged to allow no one to see her mistress until our return, and at half-past eleven we drove away from Silverlea.

It was a dismal day; white sheets of drizzle were skurrifying landward over the black and leaden waves; sullen clouds lowered over the dripping trees, and sudden gusts swept the small chill rain-drops upon the carriage windows.

My spirits sank in unison with the atmosphere, when the station was reached, and Ernest held my hand, bidding me farewell. I burst into tears.

"I will go back with you—I shall not leave you!" he exclaimed, impulsively.

"No, no!" I answered, restraining myself; "I am foolish. Farewell! I am not afraid. Adieu, my love."

Tears dropping fast hid his beloved face from me. I turned my head to the carriage cushion, and my mother shut the door. In two minutes Mr. Lindhurst was rattling over the wooden bridge, and round the curve of the hill, and we were once more alone.

"Now, shall we visit Mrs. Ringwood?" said my mother, gently breaking in upon my grief. "Do you feel capable?"

Indeed I did not; my courage had all oozed away with the vanishing train.

"We cannot go alone," I said, imploringly. "Let us get Mr. Fernley to go with us. He can introduce us, you know."

And so it was decided. Nelson drove up the street and stopped at Mr. Fernley's cottage, which was directly opposite "Old Sol," and while he knocked at the door I gazed at each window in turn which the hotel afforded, in hopes that the noise of the carriage might have attracted my *incognito* to the window.

But either the lady was deaf, or exempt from the weakness of her sex; I gazed in vain.

Presently a woman appeared at the door with a gravy spoon in her hand, and a half-peeled onion in the other.

"Is Mr. Fernley within?" asked mamma from her seat.

"Not jest yet, ma'am." She cautiously poked her head out between two intermittent roof-torrents, and looked up and down street. "I am looking for him every minute, ma'am."

"What shall we do?" said my mother, turning to me. "Had we not better introduce ourselves at the hotel?"

"Oh, no!" I exclaimed, shrinking from the idea of an

encounter without a protection; "let us wait for the house-agent."

"Guess you'd better come in, ma'am," said the woman from the door. I still urged my mother, and we alighted.

"Take the horses down under cover of the station," said mamma to the coachman; "we may not want you for half an hour. We can walk across the street to the hotel."

We followed the woman into Mr. Fernley's bachelor parlor.

"Have you any idea how long your master may be absent," asked mamma.

"No, ma'am. I was in the kitchen when he went out more'n an hour ago, and I wouldn't have know'd, only I hear the door slam after him, and seen his legs passing my window. 'Now,' thinks I, 'where are you off to?' But he'll be back to dinner sure, ma'am—he never misses; and it's always punctual at half-past twelve. It's—twenty-five minutes past twelve by our clock. Sit down, miss; I must go turn my beefsteak."

The woman bustled away, leaving us standing in attitudes of impatience and indecision.

"We may as well be patient," said my mother, seating herself; "there is nothing hurrying us."

I placed a chair close by the window and sat down. Some minutes of silence passed by, during which time my eyes reverted from window to window of the opposite building, but I found nothing to rivet my attention.

"Listen!" I hissed, with upraised finger. "What is that?"

My mother sprang to my side and looked out.

"You can see nothing, mother—the window is rushing with water, and a bank of fog has rolled between us; but hist! Do you hear the creaking—that grit of wheels—a sound of feet on their wooden balcony? Heaven! why did we come here? Ah! I see an outline through the volume of obscurity; a carriage is at the door of the hotel."

"Heaven grant it may not be for Mrs. Ringwood!" ejaculated my mother, with real alarm.

"Mamma, a man is drawing the horse close to the foot of the steps. Now he is spreading a shawl over the seat. I cannot see more; the glass is dense with steam and rain. Ah! I have wiped the pane; now we can see better. Mother,

mother! the lady is mounting into the carriage. The woman
—mine. Oh, mother, they have dashed off—we have lost
her."

"Call Nelson," said my mother, turning white.

I rushed to the door and looked down the street; already
had the carriage passed the station; it was flying up the
road to Silverlea. I flew out heedless of the heavy rain,
and almost knocked a man down, who was stepping across
the wide ditch in front of the house.

"Hallo!" cried Mr. Fernley. "What's all the hurry for,
madam?"

"Oh, sir, who is that? What lady was that who drove
away?"

"What lady? Mrs. Ringwood, who has kept me with
her all——"

I darted away, leaving him staring with astonishment.

The station was full of loungers, to whom Nelson was
displaying the perfection of his bays.

"Out with the carriage, and dash up to Fernley's," I
muttered at his elbow, then sprang in.

Without a word he mounted, whirled round the vehicle,
and obeyed me to the letter. Mr. Fernley had just gained
his own door step; and he turned with a concerned expression of face to look at the arrival. At the same moment
the door opened from within and my mother appeared.

"Good morning, Mr. Fernley," she said, calmly, shaking
hands. "I was about to call on Mrs. Ringwood—has she
gone?"

"How unfortunate. She had important business at
Shirley and had to go in spite of the weather. Can't
I——"

"Probably she will call at Silverlea during our absence,"
cried my mother in an agitation which she could not conceal. "We shall follow her. Good-morning again, sir."

She took her seat, and Nelson slammed-shut the door.

"Home!" she said, flinging herself back, and the carriage moved off, leaving the bewildered house agent standing under the double stream of roof-drops, expostulating.

As soon as we had cleared the village, Nelson drove on at
a rate which made the carriage windows rattle in their
frames, and the trees rotate like dancing dervishes.

In two minutes we were at the gate of Silverlea, and

Nelson opened the door. His face was glowing, and his voice animated; our excitement had infected him.

"Shall I drive home, or straight on? The little buggy is just ahead down in the next hollow. I could catch up in ten minutes, ma'am."

"Straight on, then," said my mother, without a moment's hesitation. "We must see the lady in the carriage."

He sprang to his seat, and Silverlea vanished from my eyes.

CHAPTER XXII.

A WILD GOOSE CHASE.

"God gave you that tongue of yours, and set it between your teeth to make known your true meaning, not to be rattled like a muffin-man's bell."—CARLYLE.

A train left Shirley Sands, at half-past one, and from the haste in which the carriage was flying it seemed as if the lady intended to elude us by catching the train; we had six miles to go, from the gate of Silverlea; it was a quarter to one, now.

On, on! down into a hollow, where the surly blast suddenly missed us, and howled over our heads in the upper current; then out on the long sand beach, and through the crawling foam by a short cut, and up a long hill before we came in sight again of the pursued.

"What are they doing?" cried my mother, dropping the front window; "do they seem to see us, Nelson?"

"Don't know, ma'am; they keep too snug. Can't see nothing, ma'am, but a big, black umbrella, and the little horse a-spanking it!"

He urged on the already excited bays, and slowly, imperceptibly, we gained upon the buggy.

"She is without doubt trying to escape us!" ejaculated my mother, after watching speechlessly; "and oh, horrors! she may be successful! We are but a mile from Shirley Sands; and it is twenty minutes past one. She has but to rush into the station, secure a ticket, and be away before our very eyes!"

I wrung my hands and gazed forth.

The piercing shriek of the coming train broke through

the dense air in close proximity; not half a mile stretched between us and the station at Shirley Sands.

"Quick, Nelson! *Fate, fate!*" I shrieked, tapping on the window.

Again he lashed the now infuriated horses, and we plunged madly through the deep, shifting sand.

Still we gained upon them, but slowly—too slowly. One long hill to climb—the buggy was at the top; one long descent to the next valley, and Shirley would be reached.

The dripping horses broke into a reckless canter up the hill, and the fitful sheets of rain swept down—a dreary, desperate picture. We gained the summit; but our will-o'-the-wisp had disappeared.

Down in the valley nestled a small, confused cluster of houses, some maple trees, an arch of in-coming ocean, a long station house, with a grimy engine protruding, which emitted black volumes of smoke and puffs of shrieking steam.

Down we rushed recklessly, with a crunching of our wheels, like thunder on the rocky hill-side. Nelson's sharp eye marked the fresh wheel-tracks, and, without hesitation, he dashed into the station, where a confused mass of vehicles were wedged together upon the narrow platform.

"No time to lose," he cried, banging open the door, "train off in one minute. There's your man behind that load of hay—don't see lady nowhere."

We alighted and followed Nelson through a throng of shouting guards, grumbling farmers, and backing vehicles, in safety to the other end of the open building, where the buggy stood, and the little brown horse, with his nostrils dilated and foam-flecked, hung his head and snorted at his feet.

Beside the carriage stood a man, clad in a rough dreadnaught, and slouch hat. His hands were thrust into his pockets; his head was slightly bent forward, with a singularly crafty air; his eyes were peering from underneath the shadow of his hat, luminous and startling; he was softly whistling, and watching our difficult approach with calm triumph.

Not until we were confronting him did I recognize Ralph Morecombe, the runaway gardener.

"What, did you drive her here?" I exclaimed, starting back. "Renegade, where is your mistress?"

"Hush!" murmured my mother, "who is this person?"

"The man who absconded from Silverlea—Ralph Morecombe."

"Be kind enough to direct me where to find Mrs. Ringwood," said my mother, temperately. "I should like to see her before the train leaves Shirley Sands."

The man slowly shifted his regards from my face, and honored her with a slight wave of the hand toward his dripping hat.

"Madam, if it's Mrs. Ringwood you want, she's——"

"Quick—out with it!" I hissed, impetuously.

"Not here," he concluded, turning to me with an unpleasant sparkle in his coal-black orbs.

"I implore you, patience, Ivanilla!" whispered my mother, drawing me back. "Do you mean that she is not at Shirley Sands?" this to the sneering villain himself.

"I said that, ma'am," he responded.

"It's false, then!" I stormed; "she left Stantons Hotel with you, and we have not lost sight of you since."

"Miss Rienzi is mistaken. Mrs. Ringwood did leave Stanton's Hotel with me, but—" here he made a long, deliberate pause and stroked his long, grizzled beard, and eyed us with a gradually deepening smile, as the engine gave one last shriek and suddenly moved out of the station with its train of carriages. "But," he resumed, "Mrs. Ringwood did not come all the way with me; I left her on the road. Sorry to give you such a drive for nothing."

He moved off and began to mount into his buggy, but Nelson stepped to the horse's head and grasped the reins.

"Not yet, mister," he growled; "my mistress hasn't given you leave yet, as I've heard. Step out, old chap."

And step out he did, for Nelson had the best of it with the excitable animal rearing in his grasp and ready to dash down upon the railway track, carriage and all, whenever liberty should come.

"All right," said Morecombe, with a sinister satisfaction, as he settled himself against the wall and folded his arms; "I'll wait as long as the ladies like."

"Where is Mrs. Ringwood?" asked my mother, firmly controlling her feelings of indignation; "tell me, if you please, if she went off in the cars which have just left?"

"No, madam."

"You wretch, tell me the truth!" cried I, trembling between anger and the fear that we had in some way been out-witted.

He stared at me with a smile of detestable insolence, but said nothing.

"My child, you will have to leave me with this man a few minutes," said my mother, entreatingly. "Your feelings are carrying you beyond prudence."

"What does he mean, then?" I exclaimed, choking with apprehension. "Where has he put Mrs. Ringwood?"

The man stood immovable and unconcerned, with that intolerable smile on his face, and his features fixed. My anger rose beyond all barriers of prudence; I darted close to him and shook his arm, in the intensity of my indignation.

"Villain!" I ejaculated, "you shall answer for the crimes of your mistress, if she escapes—remember that!"

His face slowly changed, and became absorbed.

"What crimes?" he asked, drawing back.

"Oh, you will ruin all!" breathed my mother, drawing me away.

My passion cooled, and I saw my own imprudence.

"Mr. Morecombe, I ask you once more where your mistress is?" said my mother.

"You passed her on the road, madam."

"Explain yourself," said my mother, patiently.

"Mrs. Ringwood is at Silverlea."

"At Silverlea!" she grew whiter than the dank mist outside.

I felt my flaming heart grow cold as the winter wind.

"How can that be?" I asked, in a low voice; "did we not see you all the way from Ranelagh to this place?"

"Not all the way, Miss Rienzi; not when my mistress alighted at the Silverlea gate and walked up to see Mrs. Rienzi and her daughters, who unfortunately are not all at home. Oh, not all the way!"

This allusion to the state of affairs at Silverlea almost frenzied us with consternation.

"Why did you not tell us this when you saw us pass the house?"

"A servant, madam, only obeys orders."

"But apparently you have no business to do at Shirley."

"I have done the business," said the crafty villain, moving off; "and now ma'am, if there's nothing else you would like to know about Mrs. Ringwood, I'll go back to her."

"You shall wait until we have preceded you," I cried.

He did not heed me; with a sudden spring forward he wrenched the reins out of Nelson's hands and led the horse out of the building, muttering, as he did so, words which I could not hear.

Just as his foot was on the step he was laid flat on the sandy road by one blow from our lusty coachman's fist.

"Lie there, ye old scoundrel!" he said, coolly securing the horse to an iron ring. Then he led out our carriage, and held the door open for us.

"Oh, Nelson!" exclaimed my mother, in deep distress, "I wish you had not touched him."

"Couldn't help it, ma'am," said Nelson, respectfully touching his hat; "he called our Miss Ivanilla a viperous little cuss and be hanged to him; he may be thankful I didn't twist his old whirlbones into splinters."

"Go and see if he is hurt, Nelson."

"Couldn't see it, nohow, mistress. Sorry to disobey ye, but it's not for them varmin to be coddled. Humph! the old coon is getting up, bad luck to him, and I must drive on."

He clambered into his seat and passed close by the prostrate man; he was now on his knees, his hat a crushed mass under one knee; his long grizzled hair flowing down each cheek; his lips white and working with rage; his eyes glaring with the terrible passion of a wolf before the spring. He waved his arms wildly as we passed, and shook his clutched fist.

"Ah, accursed vipers! wretches! I will be revenged!" he shrieked, shrilly as a maniac, in Italian.

Ralph Morecombe was an Italian.

We were now dashing up the hill, from 'Shirley Sands, and we sat side by side grasping each other's hands and writhing with a sense of a disastrous defeat.

I marked the slow recurring milestones in an agony of dread presentiment; misery reduced us to silence.

Nelson made good progress, though the horses were somewhat blown by the heavy roads; we soon became aware by the increased speed that we were taking our turn in being pursued. The grit of the light wheels came closer and closer; if Morecombe could dash past us he was determined to do it.

We had reached a high part of the road, built up from

the encroaching sea, with a high water-bar of rocks on either side; and here while I watched breathlessly from the window, I saw more than once the beautiful head of the little brown horse, whose fiery nostrils were distended, and his eyes glowing with ambition to head us. Just where the road was narrowest, Nelson drew up square in the middle of it and stood up.

" Look here, old chap," he cried, brandishing his whip, " this here stick's well loaded, and whenever the nose of that beast comes near enough I'll drop it like a stun between his eyes—so do as ye like."

Down he sat again and drove on deliberately; but though the road became wide enough to admit two abreast, Mrs. Ringwood's man kept well to the rear for the rest of the way.

The rain slowly abated, the wind moaned over the surging tide and slowly veered to the west; at last the white walls of pretty Silverlea gleamed through its leafy covering, and the spent horses trotted up to the door.

The shallow steps which led up from terrace to hanging garden, and every grand walk was rushing down its little stream of rain drops, like the silver tinkle of bells in a fairy revel; the flowers, fresh washed, and perfumed, raised themselves stiff and tall, with painted petals blooming joyously in the struggling sunlight.

Never had Silverlea looked more lovely, more innocent and happy; it was the garden of Eden before the serpent blighted its glory. And now for the home we had left so sacred.

A strange hush pervaded the cottage, and this listening hush struck terror to my heart.

Sophie came down the stairs; and there was that in her face which seemed to be asking forgiveness for a wrong committed.

" Where is Miss Isolina?" asked my mother.

" Indeed, ma'am and I couldn't help it!" said the girl with a courtesy; " there's a lady in the drawing-room, and Miss Isolina she *would* go to see her, and she's been there an hour and more!"

My mother instantly turned to the room designated, and entered. I could not follow yet; profound terror nailed me to the spot, while I listened for some outcry from that fateful room. None came; the low murmur of voices caught my car; Sophie quietly drew off my hat and cloak; my gloves remained on my hands, and I did not dream of removing them.

"Miss Iva, I hope you're not angry," said the girl; "I couldn't keep her when she *would* go down!"

I saw Ralph Morecombe fastening his horse before the door, and the dread of meeting him aroused me from my indecision.

With a scarlet flush mounting to my cheeks, I entered the room.

CHAPTER XXIII.

MRS. RINGWOOD.

Fly, O my child, fly!! * * *
Instant death threatens thee, and swift as light
Will the stroke fall; the traitor's toils are laid;
The poison in its gay glass sparkles bright!—TASSO.

"And this is your youngest daughter?"

It was a small, sinewy hand, which held mine, a hand with long, clinging fingers which stealthily seemed to wreathe round mine with a sudden pressure, which, despite my glove, sent a thousand shafts of mysterious flame through my system, as if fire had been struck between us; it was a tall figure in black which stood before me, with a face bending downward in a gaze which I could not meet. I bowed silently, and turned away. My mother was stationed near the window; Isolina sat within the arm of the sofa, and by her side I placed myself.

Now I could lift my eyes to Mrs. Ringwood's face; she was not looking at me. Could such a face accompany such a hand?

It was mild and elderly; with some benign wrinkles on the forehead, and around the mouth; the lips were pale; the hair banded low on either cheek, and as white as if India's clime had bleached it; the eyes which could have told perhaps what all the rest denied, were protected by blue optic-glasses, and whether they were gray, blue, or lurid brown like those of the midnight murderess I could not tell.

In all points this lady upon whom I was gazing seemed

so quiet, orderly, and timid a woman as any to be met within the holy pale of church membership. In fine, though my whole being was thrilling with one of those preternatural fits of shuddering to which I am subject, I could not even to myself say—This is she!

My obsorbing study was broken upon by my sister's strange caressing of my hand; she had drawn off my glove, and was now pressing my fingers in her own with almost insane eagerness.

I turned and looked at her.

What horror—what fear was this? What strong repression on the rigid lips? What death-like pallor over the whole face? '

Could that bland widow lady cause such dire emotions? Dark distrust blazed up in my heart in spite of all her seeming.

"Who is that woman?" I whispered, passionately; "tell me—fear nothing!" She only carried my hand to her lips, and gazed with furtive entreaty toward the sweetly smiling visitor, who at every movement, turned her face toward the cause, with a quickness which reminded me oddly of a bird of prey.

She had been speaking ever since I came in, but it was only the commonplace of ceremony which she uttered; nothing could have been more polite, proper, or amiable than the phrases which she was mildly wading through. My mother answered by signs.

Did my ears deceive me, or did I indeed detect the slightest accent of a foreign language on the lady's tongue? Do ladies from Vermont pronounce with an Italian accent?

"I have spent a very pleasant afternoon with Miss Rienzi," said Mrs. Ringwood, turning her blue glasses toward the sofa; "I am charmed with such an acquaintanceship."

My sister started, and fixed her eyes on the face of the widow lady as if she was fascinated, then rose to her feet, and as suddenly sank back again, taking my hand and convulsively pressing it.

"I am astonished to see how the time has slipped past," continued Mrs. Ringwood, with a shade more of decision in her voice than there seemed occasion for; "and that it is almost three o'clock. Why! how the time has flown!"

"I am sorry we have kept you waiting so long," said my mother; "it is a long drive to Shirley Sands."

The lady bowed and turned with a peculiarly determined manner to Isolina, as if she were silently demanding something. The agitated girl again half rose, and with sudden malice I directed a deliberate stare at the optic glasses, and pulled her back.

"Pardon me," said my mother, suddenly breaking the silence, "but have we not met before, Mrs. Ringwood?"

A short pause followed this abrupt question; then came the lady's reply, in a mild, bland voice.

"I do not know, I am sure, dear Mrs. Rienzi. Perhaps you have been in Vermont?"

"No, I have never been in Vermont?"

"I have lived all my life there until within the last few months. My dear husband died——" this with a deep sigh, "and home was home for me no more."

A delicate handkerchief with a deep black border was carried to the pale lips, and received the sigh. The rest of the face looked for a subtle instant, as if a sneer had distorted it.

"Do you remember where we met before?"

I said it in Italian, and walked slowly up to the lady, until my foot was on the very hem of her dress. No human being can conceive the secret terror with which I approached her, and forced myself to speak to her; but I stood my ground with clenched hands before her.

For one instant her head was raised with a startled look; her features changed to dull gray, then a flash of dusky red; I could have sworn those benign wrinkles were cunningly simulated with a pencil dipped in sepia; they belied so much the tigerish grit of those white teeth; but the next moment her regards were turned to my mother with an air of gentle appeal.

"What did the young lady say?" she murmured; "I think she seems distressed."

My mother would have answered, but at that moment a bell rang, and a sudden thought seemed to strike her.

"There is the bell for luncheon; allow me to remove your bonnet, Mrs. Ringwood; you have fasted, I dare say, as long as we have."

I gazed in astonishment at my mother. What! ask her to break the bread of friendship under our roof?"

"I will be glad to take a little refreshment with you," said Mrs. Ringwood, frankly; "but I cannot remove my bonnet; I have overstaid my time beyond the most extended call. I see my faithful creature out there waiting me."

My mother rang the bell and directed the luncheon tray to be brought in.

"Your servant, Morecombe, is an Italian?" she asked, quietly.

"Yes—yes, I believe so," minced the lady pleasantly; "poor creature, he is everything I believe, but a most devoted soul!"

It was evident this lady did not intend to be unmasked; she was perfectly able to hold her own against two such foes.

Mrs. Haller came in, carrying a tray, which she set on the center-table; then turned with a respectful courtesy, to leave the room.

"Stay," cried Mrs. Ringwood, rising, and holding the old woman's wrinkled hand lightly with the fingers of her left hand; "I did not ask you when I saw you before, how my poor people are?"

I confess my suspicions seemed somewhat ridiculous as I listened to Mrs. Haller's account of old Jobson, the carrier's, rheumatism, which had never come back since that bottle of opodeldoc, and of Mrs. Dawson's white swelling; and how the Hopper family all went to Sunday-school, now, in the clothes she made for them; and how the Widow Reynolds missed her tracts and tea, with sundry other bits of charitable gossip which contrasted as incongruously with the desperate character which I assigned to this woman. Meantime my mother busied herself in pouring wine into four glasses and bearing them on the tray, while she removed a dish of cold fowl to a smaller table in the window, and leisurely commenced to carve it.

As she did so she leveled one intense glance at me, then almost turned her back to the visitor and went on carving.

That glance said as plain as eyes could express it—

"*Watch!*"

Then, indeed, I began to understand, and to admire my mother's sagacity. Mrs. Haller at last left the room; Mrs. Ringwood drew near the table and sat down. As she did so her long vail fell forward between me and the glasses of wine. In an instant it was swept gracefully to one side, and the lady was sitting back in her chair with her hands folded in her lap.

Had she done it?

My cheeks blanched white ; my eyes glittered with excitement. Now to manage my part.

I rose and lifted the tray with the four glasses upon it, and offered it to Mrs. Ringwood.

"Nothing but a glass of wine!" she said, smiling pleasantly.

She engaged my eyes, but I was not unconscious that she had lifted one glass and slightly designated another, by striking it with the glass she was lifting, while she turned those mystically hidden orbs toward the sofa.

At that my sister clasped her hands and fell back gasping.

I resolved to see the meaning of this signal. I carried the tray to my sister. She shook her head and waved me away wildly.

I lifted the marked glass and placed it on the mantelpiece; the other two I carried to my mother.

She lifted one and set it beside her; I came back with the tray, and took the last glass in my hands.

Now, all my suspicions were centered in the marked glass, which I had placed on the mantel-piece. I was thinking how nicely we had her in our power, if I could succeed in saving that glass. While thus I pondered, I raised my wine to my lips.

A sudden shriek broke from my sister. She sprang with the swiftness of light to my side, and dashed the vessel from my hands.

"Oh, mother, mother ! too much !" she cried, and fell at my feet among the fragments of broken glass, and wave of ruby wine.

CHAPTER XXIV.

A NEW FACE AT THE DOOR.

"Be near me when my light is low—
When the blood creeps, and the nerves prick
And tingle; and the heart is sick,
And all the wheels of being slow."—TENNYSON.

"Lock the door, mother!" I cried.

She had already sprang to do so, but the woman was as quick as she.

With a flash of her long hand, she swept my mother's glass of wine off the table. The next instant her lithe fingers were pressing down my mother's upon the door handle.

Even in this supreme moment she was hiding behind her mask.

"Are you mad?" she exclaimed, regarding my mother steadily. "Your daughter requires your aid. Go to her, I will send for a doctor; would you seek to detain me?"

"The hand she pressed upon sank and released. My mother swayed aside, and the visitor vanished from the room.

"Mamma, are you mad?" I, too, cried. "Detain her! Will you let the assassin go?"

Why did she not move?

My sister's heavy head was in my arms; but I laid it on the wine-drenched floor, and darted after the woman.

What folly! Could my girl's hand and infant cunning hope to conquer the bold plotter? They were swooping down to the gates of Silverlea, the man and his mistress, and no wild commands of mine could reach them now.

Almost frenzied, I returned to those I had left.

What! both senseless—both smitten down!

My mother was sitting on a chair, with her hands helplessly pendant; a bewildered expression on her face, which was fast changing to unconsciousness.

"Mother!" I shrieked, "do not give way. We must raise poor Isolina from the floor. She will die here!"

I might as well have invoked the helpless Flora at her side. Her eyes turned upon me with unconscious, mournful gaze; a weird flame began to burn in her cheeks.

That unnatural look informed me of the last calamity.

I now remembered the peculiar manner in which the woman had pressed down my mother's hand; also a jewel which I had seen on her right hand, which she often adjusted. I remembered the horror of my sister as she tore off my wet glove, after one of the stranger's hand-grasps, and gazed at my fingers.

Were they *both* poisoned, and was I all that was left to father of his dearly loved family? *Two* victims—and I escaped?

Oh, Heaven, have pity on the wretch who escaped!

I went to my mother, and lifted her heavy hands.

"Which hand did she touch?" I said, in trembling tones. Her mournful eyes lifted themselves to me with a mighty effort. Her head fell back as the lethargy attacked her. She, too, was unconscious.

I fell on my knees beside her and seized her hands again. My eyes were dim with horror; but I dashed them clear of tears and ferocity. Now I could discern a tiny puncture on the back of the middle finger, with a faint-blue ring round it. I wildly sucked it.

Clammy drops began to bedew her brow. The lethargy developed itself. My mother slumbered heavily.

Also the room was in death-like silence. I alone seemed living. Heaven has given me life to save the others. I must try to do so.

I went out and called the servants.

"Go away and send Nelson for a doctor!" I cried, when the housekeeper appeared.

She gasped, and stood with her eyes fixed.

"Away!" I exclaimed; "and come back again instantly."

She went, and Sophie rushed down stairs.

"What's the matter, miss? My good gracious—your voice is just dreadful; and your face—Lord!"

"Wheel in a sofa from the parlor—I will help."

"But do tell me, dear Miss Iva, who is sick?"

"You shall see, my girl—you shall see."

All this time I was making her wheel out the sofa. I pulled recklessly at it; and almost lifted it bodily into the room. Mrs. Haller hurried in, and the two women broke out in chorus at the sight they saw.

"Yes," I assented, almost smiling in my bitterness—"it *is* rather dreadful, is it not. Both poisoned, Mrs. Haller— both poisoned by the lady you call Mrs. Ringwood. Come, Sophie—my mother first. Lay her on this couch; unfasten that collar. Now, Mrs. Haller, my sister! Yes, I shall hold her head—I am quite strong for anything. So—now go and get what you can to prevent the effects of the poison; *what* poison I cannot say."

The old woman began in a quavering voice to pour out various recipes for counteracting poison, and I listened to her list of antidotes such as chalk and oil, milk, iron-rust, vinegar, starch, white of egg, etc., with patient helplessness.

"Go and bring some one of these many nostrums, then," I said. "You may blindly hit on the right one. Has Nelson gone?"

"Yes," whispered she, in an awe-struck voice.

"Can he easily find the village doctor?"

"I told him where to go—a mile up the Cat's Head hill, on t'other side of Ranelagh. He went on horseback."

"He will not be back in time," I said, relinquishing my last hope with bitter fortitude; "they will be dead long before help can come to them, if my sister is not dead already!"

Mrs. Haller began to weep, and hurried away for some of her medicine; Sophie, terrified into perfect silence, was beating my sister's cold hands, in the manner approved for a swoon.

Her bodice was unlaced, and her beautiful bosom lay still as a bank of snow, frozen by a north wind; she was not sleeping like my mother, and I thought she was already dead.

I came away without a word, and something turned my body cold like lead; my heart grew so stony that I no longer felt the pangs of sorrow. I secretly rose against that Creator who seemed to have devoted us to destruction; I no longer strove against what seemed His merciless will; let these victims die. Fate had marked them. With cold fury in my heart, I left the house, and stepped out into the garden.

I fled from Silverlea, and found myself on the road to

the village. My wild thoughts began to shape themselves. I would have the murderess arrested before she could leave Ranelagh. I would have revenge, and it should be sweeping.

Faster and faster I walked; my hands clenched, my eyes hot and tearless. The afternoon sun was glimmering through the rows of trees, and on every spear of grass hung a string of diamonds. All down the sandy road to Ranelagh were banks of purple violets and primroses, with a tear in every heart, but they breathed no comfort to me. A group of happy-eyed children passed me on their way from the village school, and every voice sank to silence as I passed.

"Look at her! look at her!" they cried, huddling together.

"She's lost her bonnet and shawl! She's one of the ladies from Silverlea—let's go and help find 'em."

But I soon outstripped them in the search, and forgot to look behind at them.

The village street was quiet and deserted as usual; but a group of strangers were standing at the foot of the hotel steps, and they all gazed at me with faces of concern or surprise, and said something to each other like what the children had said; but I was impervious to external expressions, and walked through the midst of them, only seeing before me my great purpose of vengeance.

Mr. Stanton was standing on the balcony talking to a gentleman; I caught him by the arm and pulled him aside in the middle of a sentence.

"Where is Mrs. Ringwood?"

"My gracious, Miss Rienzi! what's up?"

"Where is Mrs. Ringwood, sir?"

"I—I'm amazed; do you know there's nothing on your head? Where did you come from, for Heaven's sake?"

I shook his arm until he grew red with the violent motion.

"For the third time, I ask you, sir—where is Mrs. Ringwood?"

"Miss Rienzi, if it's a matter of importance, I'm sorry for you," he exclaimed, with considerable feeling; "she's gone half an hour ago."

"Where?"

"Indeed I can't tell you. I wish for your sake I had asked. It was quite a sudden thing; she hired two of my rooms for a week, then went to Shirley this forenoon and took her baggage off with her, without even an apology, which was strange for a lady like Mrs. Ringwood. She took the three o'clock up-train to New York, and I suppose will be in the city by six."

" Did her man go too?"

" Yes; her man, their horse and wagon. My goodness! if I had only known Miss Rienzi it was so important——"

" Is there any means of sending a telegram to New York?"

" Well, now, none nearer than an office at Shirley Sands."

" Ha! six miles and a half from here. Too late, probably. Well, I must try. Give me a man to send to Shirley Sands."

" Anything in the world to oblige. Sammy! here Sam!"

He went away vociferating, and I was left alone to wait. Oh, impossible task! I paced about in smothered frenzy.

A gentleman on the balcony was eying me curiously; I went out to him and caught hold of his sleeve.

" Sir, are you a doctor?"

" No, I am not a doctor. I belong to the —— Bank."

" Are any of these persons physicians?"

The persons designated were some dozen young men, habited in fishing and shooting blouses, still standing at the foot of the steps, and all gazing breathlessly at me.

" This lady wishes to know if any of you gentlemen are physicians?"

" Sorry to say I am not," answered some; they all shook their heads.

I turned my back on them, and re-entered the house.

Mr. Stanton was looking about in perturbation of mind for me.

" Oh, here you are. Sammy'll be ready in two minutes —he's saddling the dapple mare, and anybody can tell you how she can put through it."

" A pen and paper, then, my friend."

He ushered me into a small room and placed the materials before me. My two hands trembled as with ague; I clutched the pen, and dashed off in almost indistinguishable words the following:

" Meet the six o'clock train from Ranelagh with an officer, and arrest Mrs. Ringwood; dressed in black; white hair, blue spectacles; turquois ring either on right hand, or secreted about person. Attendant: man with long, grizzled hair; dark eyes; slouch hat; name Ralph Morecombe. Brown horse, white feet; dark green buggy, brown hinges. A murder has been attempted; results unknown."

"IVANILLA RIENZI."

This I addressed to my father and sealed. I thrust my hand into my pocket, but found I had not my purse.

"I have no money, Mr. Stanton; lend me some?"

"Certainly, Miss Rienzi."

Again he hurried off, and soon came back with a couple of notes, just as one of the servants rode round to the front on a tall, sinewy roadster.

"It is four o'clock now; tell him he will win twenty dollars if he sends off the message before three-quarters of an hour."

Stanton flung himself down stairs, and in one minute the messenger was cantering off at his best pace.

"Now do tell me what's up," said the good-natured landlord, puffing up to me again. "Something extra must have happened, for your coachman rode past here like the mischief a spell ago."

"He was going for the doctor."

"Lord love you, how unfortunate! I could have told him, if he stopped when I hollered to him, that Dr. Whitney had gone on his Thursday's circuit to Briarville, and won't be back to-night; he never is."

"Where is Briarville?"

"Full twelve miles off, t'other side of Cat's Head, miss."

"They are lost, then! If there was a chance, they have lost it!"

"My dear Miss Rienzi, who is ill?"

"All I have at home—and they must die like dogs, without help! Oh—oh!"

I darted out, determined to fly back to them.

"My dear young lady, wait till Mrs. Stanton gets a bonnet for you," cried the landlord, entreatingly.

I did not heed him, but advanced to the knot of youths at the gate; they parted in two groups, and left a passage for me; I walked through the midst of them, my mind unconscious of them.

There was a light carriage before Mr. Fernley's door; a tall, white horse was pawing the hollow in the ground, and turning his arching neck every moment to whinny impatiently at the closed door.

I might have invoked Mr. Fernley's help in this hour of extremity, but evidently he was engaged with a visitor.

Fast, fast I sped down the gravelly road, the busy devil in my heart tempting me to blaspheme. I was going to that desolated home, which no prayers had sufficed to save from destruction.

"Miss Rienzi! Miss Rienzi!"

I quickened my speed. I could not face mortal in this dark mood. Let me fly the presence of man.

Footsteps gained upon me; I suddenly dropped my pace, and stood, determined to suffer this interruption also.

A hand was laid on my shoulder.

"What in the world is this?" panted Mr. Fernley; "what brought you out in this guise?"

He had had a long chase, and was almost spent.

"What guise?"

"Good Heaven! something dreadful has happened, by the look of your face! And you have no shawl nor hat on, do you know that?"

His words had some impression on me; I began to understand why I had attracted such universal attention.

"I forgot a hat," I stammered. "I will go home now."

"No, you won't. Come up to my house, and get a glass of wine, and a bonnet; you are as pale as death."

He drew my hand upon his arm.

"No," I muttered, peevishly; "I shall go home as I am. My mother and sister are dangerously ill—perhaps dead. I hoped to get a doctor, but have failed."

He stared at me for some time, confounded at my communication. Suddenly he dropped my hand and began running up the hill toward his own house again, as fast as he had come down.

I stood looking after him, almost as confounded as he had been, and saw an incomprehensible scene transacted.

The carriage which I had seen at Fernley's door was just appearing on the brow of the hill when the stout form of Mr. Stanton loomed in sight, passing it excitedly, and waving a large, dark shawl. The driver of the carriage looked round, and drew up, when a hurried consultation appeared to take place. While they parleyed, Mr. Fernley joined them; and the conference became general, all being highly excited, and pointing repeatedly down the hill. Presently the white horse began to move down the hill too, and Fernley came running ahead, and waving both his arms at me.

"Stop—stop!" were the words which eventually reached me. "Here's a gentleman—a gentleman who'll drive you ho—home!"

The procession bore down upon me; the stout vanguard was left far up the hill, and was fain to seat himself upon a bank, and witness the proceedings. Mr. Fernley flung the shawl round my shoulders, and stuck a very large pin in front.

"All right," he gasped; "here's a doctor."

"Hand her up here!" cried the stranger.

I was half-lifted, half-dragged, over the high wheel of a slender, two-wheeled spider, and drawn across the driver's knees; and instantly the light vehicle was dashing toward Silverlea, at a rate which made the air swish across my face in a fierce gust.

Never a word spoke the gentleman; but one arm was passed tightly round my waist, to prevent me from being tilted over the wheels; and all his attention seemed absorbed in guiding his horse clear of the stones, the least one of which might have sent the slender thing which we rode in, spinning over the bank.

"Where's the gate? That white one? Soh! soh, Hassan!"

The stranger gently seated me on his narrow seat, vaulted out, and opened the gate. Now I had an opportunity of looking at the doctor, whom Fate or Heaven had sent me.

It was a grand face that; with eyes as keen as an eagle's, and hair like combed jet and silver. Was this a village doctor?

"Are you Doctor Whitney?" I asked, as he led the horse through.

"No. Who's Doctor Whitney?"

He came and took my hand in his. Standing beside me, he was as tall even then as I, perched on the high seat; his gray eyes, with the iris clear and black as a bird's, read my features intently.

"Now, listen, little girl," he said, gravely. "I am not such a stranger as you think. I have come thousands of miles to serve this family—your family; your closest interests are interwoven with mine. Now, trust me as you would a friend; tell me what calamity has befallen you; tell me in a word."

A thrill of hope ran through my chilled heart; convulsively I pressed my lips to the hand which held mine in such kindly keeping; my woeful eyes gathered comfort in his face.

"Oh, will you indeed, befriend us?" I cried.

" Prove me, little girl; only prove me."

" We have an enemy," I breathed, with abated breath, "a woman who has brought us nothing but ruin. She came here to-day under a false name, and poisoned my mother and my sister. I alone escaped."

" Isolina?" The stranger's eyes darkened with apprehension.

" Yes, Isolina. They were both insensible when I left the house."

" This woman's name?"

" Mrs. Ringwood."

" Hah! I thought so! Viper!"

His face was hard and bitter; he clenched his hand as often as I had done, when this viper's sting was sharpened.

" What were you doing down in the village bare-headed?" he demanded, leading his horse up the lane.

" I hoped at first to arrest her before she should leave the village, but she had escaped. I sent a telegram to my father, that she might be intercepted at the New York station."

" Right! you have your father's spirit, girl."

He stopped at the door; Sophie rushed out, her eyes swollen with weeping, and flung her arms about me.

" Oh, Miss Iva, darling, where have you been?" she cried; "I thought you had run and drowned yourself!"

" How are they, Sophie?"

" Misses is sleeping so heavily! and Mrs. Haller says it's no use——"

" And my sister?"

" Oh, Miss Iva, don't ask! I believe she's dead!"

" That's enough of news," interrupted the stranger's decisive voice; "run, now, girl, and carry in the medicine-chest which you will find under the seat. Young lady, show me in."

He almost dragged me into the hall, flung his hat and

gloves on the stand, and went into the room which I pointed out.

"There's no one here," he said, reappearing.

Mrs. Haller opened my mother's bedroom door and looked along the hall; he instantly approached her.

"Where are the patients, ma'am?"

"Here, sir—both in one bed," moaned the old woman, raising her hands.

He entered, and, like a spiritless child, I kept by his side.

My mother's deep breathing filled the room; her face had become very pale, and somewhat drawn. My sister lay beside her as stiff and moveless as a figure shaped in clay.

The doctor went first to her, and bent over her for a full moment. An expression of profound dismay was on his countenance when he looked up again.

"Is this Isolina?" he exclaimed. I assented.

"I should not have known her," he muttered, almost sternly. "Oh, poor girl!"

He examined her pulse, laid his ear on her heart, and felt her temples; then he bent down until his face almost touched her breathless lips. After this he went round to my mother.

In an instant he had seized her hand and was poring over it; it was now swollen and almost livid.

"How long has she been asleep?" he asked.

"Nearly an hour and a half."

"Humph! What's this? poultice? stuff! That's right, my girl; put the medicine-chest down here, and be legs for me. Now, Miss Ivanilla," he took my hand and led me to the door. "You are to get out of this and go to your own room, wherever that is, and do exactly what you're told, and nothing else. Don't look so despairing, child; I'll tell you a bit of news to take away with you. I can't find any traces of poison about your sister, and it's not too late to save your mother, though the danger is great. There! I knew that would fill these dry little eyes with tears; go away now and cry, and then lie down and rest yourself a long while."

He pushed me away with gentle firmness, but still I clung to him in my newborn faith and trust.

"Oh, sir," I sobbed, "tell me who it is that has come

thousand of miles to befriend our poor doomed family? tell me, that I may bless his name!"

"Reserve your blessings, child," he responded, gravely, "until I have earned them by Heaven's help. Meantime, believe in the fidelity of one who has long known your sister —Dr. Pemberton."

CHAPTER XXV.

MY FRIEND.

> "Rise, happy morn! rise holy morn!
>   Draw forth the cheerful day from night;
> O Father! touch the east and light
>   The light that shone when Hope was born!"
>
> TENNYSON.

I fell on my knees in my own room and prayed as I had never prayed before to that God who had sent me my heart's desire—a friend in need.

My dark cloud of unbelief fell from my soul in that ardent prayer of thanks and contrition. My spirit, chastened by long trial, turned to the sun at last, and all my life of vain struggling passed in review before me. I laid myself and my sorrows at the feet of the Christ who was caring for my loved ones; I resolved to devote my life to Him. Sweet hope and trust filled my being then; I wept with pure love; my soul, which had been a rebellious and shuddering immortal, exulted in its Saviour and feared no more.

As thus I crouched by my bed, trembling with excess of ecstasy, Sophie came in, and to her I turned my rapture-shining face, eager to impart my feast of consolation.

"Sophie," I whispered; "weep no more. They are in God's hands; that takes away the bitterness. I am ready to give them up if Providence wills it, or I will take one back, and bless the Giver. Sophie, be resigned, and give cheerfully."

"Dear miss," said the girl, wiping her tears away, "I've prayed and prayed, but I don't see as my prayers can help 'em much now. Howsomever, that strange doctor has sent me up, Miss Iva, to see if you are in your bed; he says you've got to take a rest after what you suffered."

"We shall obey whatever he says," I answered, rising with

meekness; "and, Sophie. I leave you to attend to Dr. Pemberton's directions, and to charge Nelson to do so too whenever he comes home. Dr. Pemberton has our interests at his very heart."

While the girl unlaced my slight boots, which were soaked through with the rain-water, into which I had heedlessly walked, and through which my long garments had trailed, she told me what had happened when we left the house in the morning with Mr. Lindhurst.

"You hadn't been gone an hour," said Sophie; "and I think the rain was driving hardest when a very gentle knock comes to the front door. Miss Isolina was sitting in the window there looking out at the storm on the sea, and I was sitting alongside of her sewing, and keeping as good care of her as I could, as your poor, dear ma said, when of a sudden Mrs. Haller comes up the stairs and says that Mrs. Ringwood was in the drawing-room, called to see your ma, and since she wasn't at home, she'd like to see the young lady. At that I spoke up, and said I knew that your ma, or you either, wouldn't like for Miss Isolina to trouble herself with strangers in their absence, and Mrs. Ringwood would just have to wait, for I had given my bounden word that out of this room she should not go; and Miss Isolina says in her sweet way, which was always thinking for other people: 'Tell Mrs. Ringwood just how it is with me; but assure her that I would like very much to see her; and if she will wait a few minutes mamma will certainly be home; she only went to the station.'

"Mrs. Haller said that ought to do, and went down to the lady, but by and by she comes up again with a card in her hand which had some words written on to it; and as soon as my dear young lady read them she just got as white as that curtain and got up and said, 'I must go.'

"Then I cried out again that my word was passed to take care of her, and out of this she should not go; but she didn't even answer, and the shimmering little hands of hers trembled so bad she could scarcely hold on to the door-handle. Howsomever, she managed to go down stairs with the card in her hand, and wouldn't take none of us for help.

"I was so mad at Mrs. Haller for carrying up the second message, that I up and told her the doctor had specially forbid Miss Isolina to have any worry, for her life, and that your ma would be crazy when she come to know; and Mrs.

Haller she looked as vexed as could be, and said Mrs. Ring-wood was a fidgety old woman, always follering up other people about her charities, which was a hobby she rode to death last winter; and I asked her what was on the card, which wasn't very polite of me, I am sure; but I couldn't see how anything about sick beggars could have moved your sweet sister so; and Mrs. Haller said she couldn't make out a word of what was written down; that it looked like gibberish in a foreign language, but she expected Mrs. Ring-wood wanted money to clothe somebody's brats. And there they sat and sat, with the door shut tight on them, till I couldn't sit nor stand with the fidgets. And then you come home."

When the girl had concluded this relation, she drew down the window blinds and left me to take the prescribed rest, which the doctor seemed to consider necessary.

She left me, with a brain intensely busy and my heart stirred to its depths; and predisposed for anything but rest, though my limbs ached and I was faint from exhaustion.

I had been perhaps half an hour thus, burying my head in the pillow and forcing my eyes to remain shut, when the door was slowly opened and a stately form, which was not Sophie's, appeared on the threshold.

"Humph!" said Dr. Pemberton, coming to my bedside; "you are a good, obedient little girl—trying hard to lie still, which under present circumstances is an act of heroism; but, of course, failing. Just what's to be expected—pulse rapid—head hot; *would* fly through the village like another Godiva. We'll set you up in a few hours, though; glad to see that you've tucked yourself honestly into bed, and no shams" (glancing at the pile of garments on a chair). "What's this?" lifting it up; "a dripping wet boot! Oh, you wicked child! Here—be good enough to swallow this, and go to sleep."

He poured some drops out of a small bottle into a glass of water, which I drank obediently, then caught his sleeve just as he was going away.

"Tell me one thing, doctor—have you come too late?"

"No, thank Heaven!" was the fervent response; "not too late for either, I hope. I think that Providence is going to give me the lives of both. There, go to sleep, my child."

And with these blessed tidings he went away, gently locking the door behind him.

When I awoke, the moonlight was streaming in through the interstices of the blind; I was a long time lying there before I could recall all that had happened; my memory had been too deeply swallowed up in the dreamless slumber. But I heard the clock in the hall strike one, and at the same time a foot approached my door and it was unlocked by Sophie, who glided to my bedside.

" You're not asleep, Miss Iva?"

" No, I have just awoke. What news, Sophie?"

" Oh, miss, we've much to be thankful for! That wonderful man has saved them, dear heart. Miss Isolina, poor lamb, is sleeping in the room next here; your ma is sleeping or resting, I don't know which, in her own bed. Miss, it's all right."

My soul seemed too small to hold the joy which these words brought me; I could not speak, but my heart could speak to Heaven.

" The doctor has sent me up to desire your presence," continued Sophie, who was softly weeping with thankfulness. " Dr. Whitney is there, and they want you."

So I rose and dressed myself in the brilliant moonlight with light fingers, which often clasped each other as my thoughts shaped heavenward.

The two gentlemen were in the drawing-room, talking in low, animated tones, and they both rose and approached me with outstretched hands, and both gazed with deep attention at me.

" Let me feel your pulse," said Dr. Pemberton, seizing my wrist between his thumb and finger.

" Put out your tongue," said the village doctor, who was an undersized, thin, anxious-looking individual, buttoned into a white linen coat with black buttons.

" Pish! nothing the matter with her but hunger!" said my friend, good humoredly ; " needn't examine her tongue for that. All right again, hey ?"

" I think so, sir."

" Feel clear-headed? your eyes are as bright as diamonds; how is the head?"

" Quite clear, I think sir," I replied.

" And hungry?"

" Yes, indeed!" I responded earnestly ; indeed I was

famishing; nothing had crossed my lips, since a slight breakfast the day before, with my mother.

The doctor went to a tray which seemed to have been in waiting, and selected some viands which he brought and ordered me to eat.

"You have got an hour's business," said Dr. Pemberton, "and you must prepare yourself for it."

He watched me with great relish, while I ate, and rubbed his hands with satisfaction.

"Upon my word, young lady," he exclaimed, "I wish all patients were as obedient as you. Eat away, you poor little dear—they've famished you."

When I had announced myself somewhat appeased, they gave me a note which was waiting on the table.

"Feed the body first—then the mind;" observed my friend in his usual half-serious way; "so there's no chance of this robbing you of that fine appetite. A boy brought it from Shirley Sands, or some such place, at ten o'clock of the night."

It was a return telegram from my father, and it ran thus:

"Met the six o'clock train, but saw no Mrs. Ringwood. Traces lost. Will join you first train.   G. RIENZI."

My face fell when I read these tidings; she had again escaped; she had another chance to commit her crime.

Without a word I handed it to Dr. Pemberton.

"Missed her, has he?" cried the doctor, reading. "Humph! traces lost! No, thank Heaven, not while I'm here, I hope. Cheer up, my little friend; I think I know where she is."

He folded up the dispatch and returned it to me.

"Miss Rienzi," said Dr. Whitney, nervously, "I have waited—that is, my professional brother here has desired me to wait, so that we may hear from you the particulars of the incidents which happened yesterday. Here are a number of fragments of glass which your housekeeper collected from this carpet (which I see is unfortunately stained with wine), and here is a glass of wine which I am told was on the mantel-piece untouched, and which on analysis, my professional brother and I find to be quite pure. The fragments of glass are coated with strychnine —the glass of wine is pure; now my dear lady, as perhaps your explanations may be of very great importance I shall have much pleasure in writing them down, and keeping the notes, if so required."

The ceremonious little man here displayed before my shrinking eyes, the proofs of Mrs. Ringwood's foul attempt.

"It will soon be over;" said my friend, encouragingly. "Just detail all that took place during the woman's presence, so that Doctor Whitney's report, being by an uninterested party, may have some weight."

I told the circumstances as minutely as possible; the gentlemen both agreed that she had dropped the poison into the two wine glasses at the moment when her vail fell forward, and that the third glass which she had indicated, was unpoisoned, and intended for Isolina. *Why* this division was made was an impenetrable mystery; it defied us all apparently. My friend Doctor Pemberton hazarded no solution.

Doctor Whitney related all that he knew of the lady during her stay at Silverlea; she had been from some time in December until April an inmate of the very house which an inscrutable Providence had led us to take refuge in; and for some time a young gentleman had been with her, who was rarely seen, and whose retirement it was whispered was in consequence of some State crime, which had driven him out of society. Who he was no one could rightly ascertain. The housekeeper suspected him to be Mrs. Ringwood's son, and a Southern spy, but she was never encouraged by the widow lady to ask any questions.

At this point of the village doctor's story, I cried hastily: "Did you ever see the young man?"

"I did, but only once, and under rather peculiar circumstances," he replied. "About six weeks after the arrival of Mrs. Ringwood I was passing the gate, when the man Morecombe intercepted me and asked me if I could see a patient without alarming the village. I asked him what he meant, and he said:

"'There is some one up there badly in want of a doctor who knows how to hold his tongue and use his brains.'

"'If there is any one ill at Silverlea, I shall be happy to be of use,' I answered, turning my horse's head; 'and as I am not in the habit of violating the confidence of my patients, you have nothing to fear.'

"I was not prepared, I confess, for the kind of patient to which I was introduced. The room was darkened, and

Mrs. Ringwood, whom I had seen sometimes in church was sitting by the bed. My patient turned out to be a young man in the last stages of weakness, who had just reached the crisis of a brain fever, and, though conscious, was so prostrated that recovery seemed impossible. Some intense emotion had evidently seized upon him with the return of memory, and produced a hemorrhage from the lungs, and he was fast bleeding to death. The circumstances were so imminent that no questions could be asked, and it was only by the most extreme measures that I reduced the bleeding and alleviated his sufferings. No sooner was the danger passed than Mrs. Ringwood dismissed me, paying me handsomely, and promising to summon me if required. I was not summoned, however, and after the caution I had received I was careful to keep my own counsel about the widow lady's visitor.

"Describe the young man," I exclaimed.

"My dear young lady, it would be impossible for you to have recognized your own father after such an illness. I daresay you never saw a young fellow with a shaved head, and skin as white and bleached as a piece of dressed kid? The only objects in the face which looked like life were a pair of restless, large brown eyes, which flashed now and then with a very curious reddish glare, the like of which I never observed before. Can't account for it, sir—can you? Could it be the effect of repeated light on the retina, or some unusual property contained in the figment or coloring matter? Very extraordinary eyes they were, from whatever cause."

"Stay!" I cried, with upraised hand and breath coming thick and short; "Doctor Pemberton, he has described Cecil Beaumont's eyes! This woman—beyond the possibility of doubt—this Mrs. Ringwood is Mrs. Beaumont!"

"I may add one thing more," said Doctor Whitney, commencing to button his coat; "the young man had a deep scar on his left temple, which was scarcely healed, and one arm was in splinters, and bandaged up. The widow lady gave me no explanation of these wounds; I was allowed to believe that he had been a soldier—probably a Southern soldier.

"And now I must be off and catch the fag-end of my night's sleep, for indeed I am a little shaken by the rate at which that zealous young man Nelson made my old mare

canter all the way from Briarsville. I hope anything I
have told you may be of use, and that this strange business
may be satisfactorily settled. Pray command me, Miss
Rienzi; ask your father to make use of me for any information he may deem me in possession of. Sir, I leave the
ladies under able and skillful hands; I have no fears for
their ultimate recovery, when the eminent Pemberton is
their physician. I shall send the medicine from my labora-
tory in the morning, doctor. My dear young lady, good-
night. I cannot help complimenting you highly on the
address and presence of mind which you have displayed
under the late trying circumstances. Your conduct does
your heart and intellect credit. Good-night."

The ceremonious old gentleman here bowed himself out
of the room, and softly shut himself out of the house.

"Good fellow that," said Doctor Pemberton, senten-
tiously; "is always ready to help another across the stream.
Now, Ivanilla——" I quite started at the sudden change
of manner, and at my own name on his lips; his calm, gray
eyes were fixed with the intensity of deep thought on my
face. "Now, Ivanilla, we have a conference before us, in
which we must use our memories and reasoning powers to
the utmost. You must tell me *all* that has happened in
connection with your sister, since you came from Italy, and I
shall compare it with the facts in my possession. But first
you would like to know exactly how my two patients are,
would you not?"

"I have been longing to ask," I said.

"Knew it very well, and admired the first patient little
girl that I ever saw, with black eyes. Be comforted, my
child; your mother is safe and in a healthful sleep. From
the symptoms of her seizure, Whitney and I incline to the
opinion that the poison administered by the pressure of the
ring must have been a deadly extract of the Egyptian
papaver, which must have been prepared with the most
infernal skill for the purpose. I should like to get that
turquois ring; I rather think it will prove to be a curiosity.
As to Isolina, the insensibility which alarmed you so much
was only a protracted fainting fit, approaching to catalepsy
in its strength, occasioned by the dreadful horror which has
been in her mind, allied to the extreme weakness of her
body. Poor girl! I wish I knew all that is in that tortured
heart. I'll warrant there's been black sinning against her!

But, thanks be to a merciful Providence which sent me here at the right time, she's better, and will be quite revived in a few days.

"My little friend, I have relieved your anxiety to the best of my ability; now sit you there, and relieve mine. Tell me your side of Isolina's history."

I began from the day on which I first beheld my sister in her matchless loveliness holding back the door of the saloon and looking at me; I recounted every link of the dreary record, from gloom to gloom, of the slowly gathering sorrow; and with my heart kindled by his evident sympathy and deep emotion into burning vehemence, I recounted with passion and tears the wrongs of me and mine unto the bitter end.

Then my friend clasped me to his breast in a sudden and uncontrollable burst of tenderness.

"Noble, heroic girl!" he cried; "you have been faithful indeed to the sister you profess to love. But you have suf- too much for that loyal little heart to remain unbroken. In the name of those whose lives are bound up in Isolina Rienzi, I thank you."

"Now tell me who you are, and what you have to do with my sister's life?—a benefactor you must be!" I breathed, resting trustingly upon the arm which was still thrown around me.

But he smoothed my hair with thoughtful hand and shook his head slowly.

"Be content with what you know of me," he said; "you know enough for the heart to bear. When I can help you, you shall know what knit Alphonse Pemberton's heart to you."

When the dawn was stealing in, and the lamp burned with a wild and haggard gleam, our conference was ended.

CHAPTER XXVI.

MY DARLING — ADIEU.

"The bloom hath fled thy cheek, sister,
  As Spring's earth blossoms die,
And sadness hath o'ershadowed now
  Thy once bright eye;
But, look, on me the prints of grief
  Still deeper lie.
Farewell!"—Scottish Song.

Later in the morning I was standing on the piazza, drinking in the sweet, cool breeze, and leaning against a pillar, all draped in multiflora vines, whose odorous roses swung toward me on the zephyr, filling my soul with delight.

I had been watching my mother slumber since dawn, while the doctor and our faithful Sophie refreshed themselves with a rest; and now Mrs. Haller was in her chamber, while I stole out for a few minutes into the golden sunshine.

I became aware of a presence near me; I turned my head from side to side, and beheld a figure standing midway on the piazza, between the door and the steps.

"Isolina! What imprudence!"

Yes, it was she. Her hands were clasped together; her eyes were fixed upon me wildly; she seemed about to fly, but her feet remained rooted in an attitude to depart. A broad sun-hat was on her head and tied under her chin; a black silk scarf was round her shoulders, a satchel hanging on her arm.

"Oh, my dear sister, where are you going? Go back to your bed; you should not be up. Come!"

I advanced and seized her arm; the sentences came in faltering gasps; a sickening premonition was in my heart.

"I am going away," she said, turning her pale face from me. "I would not willingly have pained you by this scene, Ivanilla; I thought you were not here."

"Going away? Where—where, my own darling?"

"It is my duty to go—and my lips are sealed. It would

have been better if you had not met me; it is so cruel to us both—this."

"No, no, no!" I cried, throwing my arms around her. "You shall not go! Not another word! Come in this very instant, my dear, and never harbor so mad a thought again. Where will you go, sister? Could you leave father and mother and sister, to break their hearts for you?"

"Forbear!" she said, in a low, agonized voice: "my cross will kill me if you add another stab to my heart. Iva, farewell!"

She strove to free herself, but I held her with both hands, and would not be shaken off.

"Never!" I muttered; "I will make the place resound with my shrieks first; I will not let you go!"

"I implore you to have mercy on me, Ivanilla!" she breathed, tremblingly; "I am not strong, and I prayed Heaven to give me enough strength to do this sacred duty. As you love me, let me go."

"Will you see Dr. Pemberton first?" I sobbed.

"No, no! He does not know!" she answered, piteously.

"Can you leave our dear mamma, unwelcomed back to life?" was my next appeal; "that wretch poisoned her, Isolina!"

"I know—I know. My life shall be between this family and danger in future. Fear that wretch no longer; she and hers have wronged you cruelly; all is past now."

Her face was frightfully pale, her breath struggled on her lip, her hands grasped wildly at the air.

"If ever you loved poor hapless Isolina," she gasped once more, "let her go and do her duty."

Ah, hour of sorrow! my arms dropped from about her; I ceased to importune. Her duty! who was I, to interpose?

"Let us meet in heaven," she whispered; "tell our saintly mother that I loved her truly, Ivanilla—little sister I cannot thank you for what you have done for me. Sweet darling—a long good-by. Oh, my own little Iva, good-by."

She pressed me in her arms, her tears broke forth; her bosom swelled tumultuously; bitter was the parting there.

"And our father—what for him?" I said, remembering how dear these words would be to each heart.

"A prayer—and my forgiveness!" was the answer. She

pushed me from her, wildly, and turned away, down the shallow steps.

In a dream I watched her let herself out at the gate; in a miserable dream I saw the distance widen between us; her white hat sometimes shone between the trees—she vanished from my view. The lovely scene was quiet and serene and lifeless!

I could not move hand or foot while this war of conflicting feelings was going on, then suddenly, like the death-knell of the condemned, came a long, chill whistle from the railway station. She would go away in the cars, and be lost to us forever. If I would, I could not recall her now.

I rushed like a maniac among the whispering aspens, and flung myself upon the dewy ground.

But this paroxysm of despair passed away at last, and softer thoughts succeeded. Could I not trust the Hand which supported me better than that? Would He allow our dearest and our best to come to harm?

Hours had passed over my head of which I was unconscious, and when I rose from my hiding-place I was astonished at the height of the sun; it could not have been less than nine o'clock.

My mind was in a strange whirl of ecstasy and unnatural elevation; I had soared beyond the touch of earthly sorrows; I could almost exult at the magnitude of any sacrifices.

In this mood I returned to the house, and found that my absence had caused great anxiety.

"Oh, Miss Iva dear!" said Sophie, who as usual was weeping bitterly, "you hadn't ought to go away this way! And your clothes are wet with dew, and your hands so hot! Missy darling, I don't know how you'll bear it—Dr. Pemberton says there's news for you. Go in there."

I went into the parlor, and there, to my surprise, I found my mother. She was sitting in an easy-chair, her head leaning against the cushion, her face wan and sorrowful, her eyes red with weeping. She looked so frail and pitiful, with her muslin wrapper flowing round her small, elegant figure, and one hand smoothed in bandages, that I could have wept over the grief she suffered, when I was above feeling my own.

Dr. Pemberton was swallowing a hasty and solitary breakfast, with a hat on a chair by his side.

"Yes, it's just what I thought, madam," exclaimed he, when I appeared; "she's been at some frenzy work. See that face! Have you been flying after your sister, Ivanilla? Come here!"

But I did not go to the good doctor; I flew to my mother and laid my strange, light head upon her bosom.

"Mother, why should you mourn?" I exclaimed. "God is taking care of her. Give Him whatever He asks for—He is welcome—welcome—welcome! I would give you, mother sweet, and father, and Ernest, if He said it, and live alone, and be happy."

But my rapture only inspired her with terror; she turned to the doctor her beautiful, appealing eyes, and burst into tears.

"Unnatural excitation of the nervous system," said the doctor, who by this time had my hand in his; "pulse flying. My little girl, why must you always be at a crisis of feeling? You're too sensitive, and too ethereal; the wild Southern blood which is rushing through these veins will wear you out if you don't learn our Northern philosophy. You must learn that this life is made up of disappointments, and expect them. Lay another fold of philosophy on your heart, child—it's not callous enough."

He dropped my hand and turned suddenly away; his last words had sounded husky and forced; his philosophy seemed to fail him him just where it should hold out best.

"Do not be alarmed for me," I breathed, again, throwing my arms about my mother; "I am resigned; our beloved Isolina has gone because it was her duty to go, and Heaven will comfort her, for she left her heart with us."

"Duty!" howled the doctor, in a rage, "the sorceress has bewitched her, and you. I think. Duty!"

But nothing could disturb my enraptured mood. I recounted to my mother every word which had passed between my sister and me, the doctor listening most attentively.

"There!' he said, throwing me a note, "that's what she left us."

"You whom I have known and loved as mother, blot me out of your memory now. I go to guard you from the vengeance of one whom misery has maddened. I cannot tell you what I have sworn to keep secret—darling mother; respect my vow. Do not pursue me;

give me up to what I swear to be my duty, and though this parting may be to all time, meet me in eternity! Cherish my Ivanilla; oh, love, how can I break your loyal little heart! Heaven's blessing on those who made my whole life happy; their prayers for the heavy days that come upon me. Farewell mother. Isolina."

These incoherent, wild words bedewed my eyes with tears; I laid my head upon my mother's lap, and wept, but not bitterly; it was for the grief of others; not for my own.

"Yes, cry — cry, it'll do you good," said the doctor, "it'll cool your brain, poor girl. I don't like these ecstasies, when one's friends are snatched away—not natural—there must be a terrible rebound some time. Madam, don't check her; she requires it."

But I dried my tears and looked up. The doctor had finished his breakfast, and was preparing to depart.

"Where are you going, Dr. Pemberton?" I asked, wistfully.

"To get Gemma Lancinetto arrested!" was the startling reply.

"You will not—please do not attempt to pursue my sister; she is doing a sacred duty, and we have no right to tamper with her conscience."

"Good Heaven, child!" he cried, "can you be so credulous? She has gone to sacrifice her l'fe, I'll lay my hand on it, to save yours. Conscience! You don't know the woman you have to deal with—you never saw the Lancinetto."

"An interruption here occurred to the good doctor's indignation; a gentleman on horseback appeared coming up the lane.

In an instant Dr. Pemberton was on the piazza waving his hat with every demonstration of joy, which increased as the rider approached, until he dashed down his hat and ran out with his head uncovered, and received the horseman in his arms, as he dismounted.

"Guiseppe! met at last!"

"What, who is this?" said my father, whose pale and anxious face was seamed with haggard care.

"Not know Alphonse? Little Alphonse, your old comrade?" cried the doctor, impetuously, and yet we paddled in the same brook, and loved the same sonnets in Virgil for the first twenty years of our lives? And so you have forgotten your Damon?"

" What? Alphonse Pemberton—my college friend?"

A look of joy lighted up my father's face; he grasped the doctor's hand, and wrung it with a joyous laugh, and leaned on his shoulder fondly. "Surely I'm dreaming, are *you* my little Alphonse—the visionary and the genius— you a son of Anak?"

" And yet I knew my Guiseppe," responded the other, "though his hair is as white as flax and his face thin and old. Come, I'm not here for nothing, my friend; I have something to tell you, which I have known for a year, about your daughter; and if I had dreamed then that she was a child of my Guiseppe, perhaps her fortune this day might have been brighter."

And the mother and I, who were the beings of a later life, and had no part in the love of that far off time, held each other's hands and looked on with wondering eyes.

But very soon my father remembered his dear ones, and embraced us with solemn affection.

"I met Nelson going down to the village, and he has told me all," he said, "and again I have to thank my friend," and he held the doctor's hand warmly, "for saving my wife from a cruel death. Dear Maud! from what have you been delivered, Maud? Doctor Pemberton was the closest friend of my boyhood—you have often heard me mention Alphonse? This is he, give him a welcome, wife."

"Not only a welcome, but my deepest gratitude for what he has already done for us!" she answered, offering her hand with a warm smile.

When we had all become somewhat calmer, the doctor told my father all that had happened, and they retired to another room to arrange their plans together.

What his mission was, precisely, I did not then know.

The interview between the two old friends lasted for more than an hour, then they issued forth in a fever to depart.

"Speingle has managed to get the most of Mrs. Beaumont's history," said my father, hurriedly, and kissed us; "and my good friend, Alphonse, can supply what he has failed to obtain. It is pretty clear the whole life of Gemma Lancinetto, all but *one point*. The precise nature of her power over Isolina. If we manage to arrest her, as,

Heaven be praised, I have every assurance that we will—that secret link will be forced from her, I hope."

"Hope for the best," chimed in the doctor, who was in fully recovered spirits. "I don't intend to come back to you—no, not I—without the runaway Isolina! I'll cage her, never you fear! And Iva—if anybody comes here in my absence asking for me, give a spare corner to the old doctor's guest until he returns; will you?"

And they each sprang to their places, and dashed off with waving adieus to the anxious ones they left behind.

CHAPTER XXVII.

THE MAN I MET ON THE SANDS.

> "A happy lover who has come
>   To look on her that loves him well,
>   Who lights and rings the gateway bell,
>   And learns her gone and far from home."—TENNYSON.

That was a long, sacred day, which my mother and I spent together when we were left alone. We communed with very full hearts after the terrible dangers from which we had escaped; and I poured some of the wonderful comfort with which I was supported into her willing ears, until even she smiled in renewed hope, and began to lift her head, which had so sorely drooped in sorrow.

In the quiet evening I loitered through the dewy walks of lovely Silverlea down to the bit of sand which girt it in.

At first I thought only of my darling, who so often had walked these summer paths with me; my arm felt empty without the touch of her hand; my ear was desolate without the rustle of her dress over the withered scrolls which fell from beech and aspen; and I wept when I stood on the bed of white sand where she used to love to linger. And as I gazed over the chastened waters which glided softly in and seemed to walk warily after the storm of yesterday, I felt it hard for awhile to say, "Thy will be done!"

Oh, it was hard; the old wounds bled afresh; my heart pleaded sore; but I did not move until I could say, "I give her up to Thee," and once more calmness came to me.

Slowly I paced along, farther round the little cape

which held my home, drinking in the peace of earth and ocean.

Then the sound of a step on the shell-strewn beach made me start and prepare to retreat.

Some one came round a sudden angle of rocks and faced me, and all at once I stood still and gazed with deep attention. The moon came out with radiance from the golden haze, and shone on a face bronzed with oriental climes and grave with life's shadows, which seemed to have been manly, though the years were indeed but few; but withal a face God·gifted with lion-like bravery and physical perfection, and likeness gifted with the beauty of the soul.

The pedestrian bowed low, and removed his hat, upon thus suddenly encountering a lady, and gravely stood aside to let me pass, supposing by my abrupt halt that he blocked the way; but instead of passing on, I still eyed him eagerly, with doubt and joy thrilling me into silence.

With a second reverence lower than the first, the stranger took a few steps onward.

"Can you pass me by?" I cried, impulsively; "you are Victor Joselyn."

He turned again, and his bright, falcon-like glance swept my face in eager scrutiny.

"I shall be happy to greet a friend, if this is one," he said, very softly.

Both my hands reached out to him, and locked themselves upon his arm in joyful welcome.

"And you don't know who the friend is?" I exclaimed, ardently; "does your heart tell you nothing—does it feel no warmth?"

"It feels wondering gratitude at this sweet welcome from a very lovely lady."

"There is only one can welcome you more warmly. I am Ivanilla Rienzi."

"What! the little sister? her sister?"

"And your friend, Victor Joselyn, and this is my hand to prove it. Ten thousand welcomes to Silverlea!"

He took the hand and the whole body in his arms, and I wept with joy upon his breast, whom for the first time I met this summer night.

I give no solution of this subtle chord which drew us heart to heart, and overthrew all the obstacles which etiquette and lack of sympathy set up. This man was the keeper of my sister's heart; he was hers; I loved her so deeply that I fell at once into my place, as the sister of her he loved, and my affection swept into this channel, and ever afterward remained there.

So much for the man who stood by the chiming sea, holding me clasped to his breast.

"Now," I murmured; "come home to Silverlea."

"Not yet," said the stranger, tenderly; "we must understand each other first; will you confer with me a while?"

"Yes," I answered, with a serene smile; "I know so little of Victor Joselyn that it is meet that he should explain himself a little, after so extraordinary a greeting," and I looked with fond and glistening eyes into his face.

We slowly paced over the rippled sand, and with one accord turned aside to a quiet nook, where some quartz rocks were strewn upon a flat sea rock.

Here he flung his ample cloak, and spread it daintily for a carpet, upon which he seated me; then he flung himself down beside, and raised to me a face whereon was depicted every noble though chastened attribute of beauty.

"Who shall begin?" I asked, with playful fondness; "we are two strangers who know one mutual friend—shall we talk of that friend? No!" I added, with a sudden sigh; "not yet, the subject is a sad one."

"Not yet," echoed Victor Joselyn, mournfully; "let us make each other's acquaintance first."

"May I ask you a few questions then? I know so little——"

"Ask me anything, dear child, as if you were my sister."

"And you will not deem me impertinent? I shall be very personal I fear, but I know so little. Ah, well. I am not afraid of being misunderstood by you, Victor Joselyn. In the first place, then, I wish to understand the precise friendship which has existed between my sister and you? You have been married, signor? Pardon me."

"Yes," said the stranger, with a face of doubt and pain; "but I thought no one knew it. Did she tell you?"

"She told me—once," said I, rather puzzled, "and I think others knew it well. Now, will you pardon me for what comes next? Your wife died?"

There was a slight silence; my companion looked at me

as if Medusa's head had grown upon my shoulders, and was petrifying him with horror.

"My wife died!" he repeated, incredulously. "Oh! Miss Ivanilla, can you tell me that so calmly? My wife dead?"

I could not understand him; I began to feel embarrassed; my cheeks glowed a little; what mistake was I making?"

"Let us begin again," I said, forcing a laugh; "I was asking you that question, and you retort by asking me one. We will be patient and wade throught his labyrinth of misconceptions. I shall tell you all that I heard of Victor Joselyn. I came from Italy nearly a year ago, and made my sister's acquaintance for the first time since infancy. I soon suspected that her heart was pledged to some one, but she never spoke on the subject. She wore a ring—should I tell you this, I wonder? Yes, I should tell Victor Joselyn everything!—she wore a double ring, and engraven on the inner hoop were the letters 'I. J.' Have you two names, signor? Is Victor the only one?"

"My name is Victor Joselyn, nothing else. Go on."

"I once found a water color painting of a scene near Saratoga, where *you*, sir, were holding my sister's hands, with a look which betokened love. I found out that the face was that of a Victor Joselyn, who had made the acquaintance of some young ladies at Saratoga, my sister among the rest."

"Yes, I painted it," interposed my listener, with a sad smile; "it was a sportive gift to my poor girl. Go on."

"My sister once had a letter in her hands, in which by accident I read the name, 'Mrs. Victor Joselyn.' I told my sister what I had seen, and she said that Mrs. Victor Joselyn had been a friend of hers, but was dead."

"Did she say that?" he cried, with increasing agitation. "Oh, false Isolina!"

"I do not understand! It is a Sphinx's riddle!" I ejaculated, almost weeping. "Are you not a widower, then?"

"I never heard until to-night that I was."

"And you have been married! Then—then, sir, was my sister in truth any friend of yours? Have I misconstrued?"

"You have not misconstrued," he answered. "Isolina was my friend; my closest friend; I married once, and Isolina was the woman whom I married."

He caught me once more to his heart, and bent his head

upon my shoulder with a sudden sob of grief. His strong frame quivered, his heart throbbed in quick muffled beats; the memory of that blissful day was rending him; the sacred curtain had been drawn too suddenly from that long vailed mystery.

"Brother," I breathed solmnly; "whom God hath joined, let no man put asunder! You have a right to claim her from every other duty; she is yours. Ah, Victor, let me welcome you to a loyal sister's heart."

My blood glowed with sudden joy, though his strange announcement had almost stunned me. Strange that I had not deemed that possible before.

"She never told us—why was it a secret?" I whispered presently. My friend resumed his place, and went on.

"It was me—all my fault!" he responded, sadly, "I bound her to silence for a silly scruple, and I have been justly punished in losing her love. Never since the day of our union has she suffered me to meet her; oh, Ivanilla she implored that we might never meet again!"

"Why—why?" I exclaimed vehemently.

"Alas! I cannot tell, I have been led to believe she was false to me, and loved another."

"It was false!" I responded. "Oh, Victor, what wrongs are we about to unvail?"

"I see there is a world of explanations to be made on both sides," he said. "Let me tell my story, dear Ivanilla, then you shall tell me yours; we shall then have a better chance of understanding how my darling wife was led to cast me off, whom she so sweetly and solemnly vowed to cling to as her husband."

CHAPTER XXVIII.

"FOR O, 'TIS LOVE! 'TIS LOVE!"

"She half inclosed me in her arms,
   She pressed me with a meek embrace,
And bending back her head, looked up
   And gazed upon my face.

"I calmed her fears, and she was calm,
   And told her love with virgin pride,
And so I won my Genevieve,
   My bright and beauteous bride."—COLERIDGE

The waters rolled in softly and the moon cast her silvery rays around us; and in our cozy nook, where perfect silence reigned, Victor Joselyn told his story.

"My father was the only representative of a very old family in Somerset, and had an estate which from generation to generation had been added to and improved, until it was one of the finest to be seen between the Mendip and Quantock hills. I believe my father was the first Joselyn for centuries who had not been a prize farmer, sportsman, and jockey. He was an Oxford man, of high talents, a refined taste, and a passion for the fine arts. He traveled for years through the classic scenes of Greece and Italy, and made pilgrimages to Palestine, in which he feasted his inordinate love of beauty, on everything which was rare and priceless.

"The mansion of his ancestors was torn down, and a stately palace rose in its place, which soon became filled with costly and beautiful mementoes of every land he had visited.

"So much for my father's character.

"I remember little of him; he died when I was ten years of age, leaving myself and a sister, two years my junior, completely orphaned. My mother I could never remember; and her name had always been shunned in our house ever since I could recollect. My sister and I had been placed under the guardianship of a faithful friend of my father's named Dr. Alphonse Pemberton, who proved almost more than a father to us both until I became of age, and took possession of my fortune.

"On that day, my guardian, obeying a secret codicil of my father's will, put me in possession of the strangely hidden history of my mother; and I found that the house, which I had always considered untarnished, had its escutcheon blackened by a stain, which blurred my life forever.

"During one of his visits to Italy, my father had seen in one of the principal theaters of Rome a beautiful actress, whose attractions were so extraordinary that he, obeying his natural passion for obtaining. what pleased his eye, almost without knowing who she was, laid his brilliant fortune at her feet, and to his joy was graciously accepted. 'Stella' forsook the stage, married her English adorer, and to the lasting envy of some half a dozen others, was borne to the ancient palace on the Lower Avon, in old Somerset. Upon more minutely studying his prize, my father found her to be the daughter of a patrician family of Florence, who in some moment of ill temper had fled from them and gone upon the stage. She had a ferocious temper, was an infidel of the most daring type, and soon evinced the most perfect indifference to her husband, and the children which she bore him.

"Before long my unfortunate father was glad to rove in distant countries more than ever; during which time his wife, as the fit seized her, would suddenly leave home and her two infant children to travel likewise to various places on mysterious missions. In this way, my father once met her hurrying through the streets of one of the cities of the United States, quite alone and unprotected, as he was bringing to a close a long tour which he had made through North America. She never made the slightest explanation, but went home with my father, and remained a year, during which time he did not venture to leave her alone, as her moods seemed more desperate than before. A third child was born, a daughter, and when it was three weeks old, my wretched mother disappeared with it, and mother or child was never heard of since, despite the most careful search. I was four years old when this happened; my sister Alicia not more than two.

"Such was the birthright that became mine with my fortune. It changed me from a gay, careless youth, into a humiliated brooder, forever chafing over my disgrace. I became morbidly alive to every whisper that my galled pride

could construe into pity for my misfortune. My beautiful
estate and palace halls grew terrible to me; every priceless
gem of art reminded me of my father's fatal love of the
beautiful, which had ruined the honor of his name. My
gentle and lovely sister trembled in my presence; I cast a
chill gloom over her, for which I loathed myself; yet when
I tried to be my old self the semblance was so unnatural
that she grew more terrified than ever. At last I fell into
ill health, and my dearest friend, Doctor Pemberton, ordered me to travel. I went the grand tour, treading in the
very footsteps of my father, and came back as unhappy as
ever. More so; I was growing fast into a misanthrope.
I became almost a monomaniac on the subject of my humiliation. I questioned everything. I began to doubt my
own right to the name I bore. Doctor Pemberton became
alarmed and once more ordered me away from a scene
which only plunged me in misery, this time announcing his
determination to accompany me. We came to America,
four years after my unhappy grief had come to me, and
after wandering through every State, North and South, just
as fancy led us, I at last found what I was in search of, self-
forgetfulness. Obeying an idle caprice, I urged my friend
to visit Saratoga for a few days, that I might study, without mixing in it, the wave of fashionists which ill health
and 'the mode' sent up from the metropolis.

"'The first time I saw Isolina Rienzi, she, in company
with some other young ladies, was on horseback; they advanced toward me like a whirlwind, passed, vanished, and
left me standing with my sketch-book in my hand, lost in
astonishment. An old groom, apparently their attendant,
limped after them on an old nag, which barely sufficed to
carry him half a mile behind them. As he passed me I
accosted him.

"'What ladies are those who have passed?'

"'They are Mrs. Cranstown's party,' he replied—'live
at the "Wood's Nest."'

"He rode away immediately; and I returned to the Con-
gress, where I had left Doctor Pemberton. He was preparing
for our departure.

"'Let us stay another week,' I cried with more animation than I had felt for years; 'I have seen a face.'

"'But, my dear boy,' exclaimed my friend; 'it was only
yesterday you were sighing for a change! We have been

here three days already. What kind of face was it, and whose property?'

"'It belonged to a lady who is of Mrs. Cranstown's party, and they live at the "Wood's Nest."'

"'So ho! a fair Republican has slain you with one of her eyes!' cried Pemberton. 'Bravo! and success to her!'

"But it was not exactly as the doctor imagined; I had been so deeply struck with the incomparable beauty of the lady's face that I felt almost faint for some time afterward, but I had no thought of wishing to claim it, I, the disgraced—the humiliated! Still, a desire seized me to transfer those lovely features to canvas, that I might have the never changing likeness to charm away my embittered thoughts by the dumb eloquence of its mild and innocent eyes.

"I think Doctor Pemberton toiled to bring about the consummation of my wishes. In a very short time he was able to tell me where the 'Wood's Nest' was, and the names of the five young ladies who formed Mrs. Cranstown's party. In two days he introduced me in triumph to the chaperon herself, who was visiting some friends at the hotel where we staid, and we received a friendly invitation to accompany her then and there to' the Wood's Nest, which was a cottage two miles out of the little town. I shall never, while this heart is fresh, forget the emotions which rushed over me when my unknown queen of all beauty was presented to me as 'Miss Isolina Rienzi,' and I held her small magnetic hand in mine. Something which had been lost for years came back to me; once more my heart, which had been frozen gall, melted to the sweetness of home. What I hoped, I could not tell. Her pure, modest eyes had revealed themselves to me, and I was happy. How swiftly the six weeks passed away! My faithful friend forbore to remind me in the slightest of the flight of time, but rather fostered my new-found interest by every act. He became an invaluable chaperon and confidant on all occasions to the merry girls, and I believe they scarcely cared to make up any little excursion or picnic without us.

"In this intercourse I rarely mingled, except on the outskirts, as it were. It was bliss enough for me to study the sweet, retiring loveliness of Isolina Rienzi, among the gay, sprightly, or sentimental dispositions of her companions.

I sketched them all in groups, which I allowed them to criticise and praise to their hearts' content; but I stole the lovely face of Isolina for my canvas, in all its moods and tenses, with a secrecy which puzzled myself. I never dreamed of addressing her alone; nay, more, I seldom ventured to speak to her at all, though I was on terms of playful intimacy with all the rest. Yet there was a silent sympathy between us which seemed to require no vehicle of speech, but throve on now and then a long, tender, yet proud gaze from her royal eyes, and sometimes the sudden touching of the hands.

" But my dream was rudely broken. Letters reached us from England, with the startling intelligence that my sister Alicia had been sent home from her studies in London, seriously ill, and her medical attendant apprehended the worst results; if I would see her alive, I must hasten home. When I received this letter, a storm of mixed griefs assailed me; all at once I felt the depth—the strength—the sweetness of my love for the 'Beautiful Rienzi.' I must leave her, and turn to my despair again. My gentle sister, whose affection might have saved me, was dying; the last scion of my blood was about to be snatched away. Ivanilla, you can appreciate the sorrows of my position.

" In the midst of my despair, Doctor Pemberton came to me, and his advice showed how his heart was interested in my happiness.

" 'Don't sit there with your head down, man,' he cried; 'throw trouble to the dogs. Go to your lovely lady—I'll warrant there's one in the case, that makes you grip to America like this—and tell her right square up what you want. I don't think she's the girl to send you home to poor Allie uncomforted.'

" I was almost in a frenzy.

" 'I have been in a dream!' I exclaimed. 'I forgot my tainted name and my doubtful honor when I dared to look upon Isolina Rienzi. She would turn with loathing from the son of an actress, whose dishonor has swallowed up in its blackness her miserable children!'

" 'She'll forgive all but faults in you. Go and try her,' urged Pemberton, warmly. 'Oh, man, what do you know about woman?'

" I had to leave Saratoga that evening, so there was no time for reflection. I went straight to the cottage, my mind in a whirl of re-awakened humiliation and grief. My sense of honor was so inflamed that I felt it to be ungenerous—nay, dastardly—to seek to sully her by asking her to share my degradation.

"I determined to bid them all farewell and go with my passion unspoken. But fortune had another course open for me. The ladies were all gone to some picnic or flower party, all but my treasure; and so I trod the well-known path by the brook-side, which was shut in by alders and wild wreaths of honeysuckle. There—just on the spot where once she and I had stood hand in hand for one sweet moment, while the other ladies flitted gayly up to the cottage from their flower-gardening—there stood my darling, weeping.

"With one spring I was by her side; her sweet hands were in mine; my new-formed resolutions were flying to the four winds—my mind rudderless. I was blind with the rush of passion; but I managed to be gentle.

"'What was the matter?'

"'She was tired, lonely—had been shedding a few foolish tears—forget them.'

"I could wait to hear no more; a swift foreknowledge quivered through me with a joy which was so intense that darts of delicious agony shot through my heart. I clasped her in my arms.

"'Tell me that you were lonely for me,' I whispered, hoarsely.

"Her lovely head drooped to my breast; she trembled, and with scarcely conscious hands clung to me.

"'Oh, Love! are you mine?' I breathed again; 'have I your heart?'

"She shuddered yet more; suddenly she drew from my arms and stood a moment motionless, with drooping, pallid face; then she flew to me and flung her arms about me, and that averted countenance was raised, with modest, burning cheeks and staring eyes, which poured one of those strange looks, solemn and tender, into mine. Oh, the joy of that moment! Heaven seemed faint in comparison. She was mine—this peerless Isolina Rienzi, whom I had not dared to woo—this was she, embracing me! I pressed my burning kisses upon the thrilling lips, upon the meek and loving eyes which had answered me so generously, upon the pale brow and scarlet, tingling cheeks.

"You smile, Ivanilla. Ah, Heaven bless you for these glittering tears—thank you, my little sister.

"But earth surged in at last. We had met but to part; oceans must roll between us; I must leave this pure, heavenly being, who had crowned me with her love. And I, what was *I?*

This last thought stung me from my mad joy like an adder. I put her from me and leaned against the tree, ghastly with the rush of horror. Wretch that I was to forget my degradation!

"'What has grieved you? Tell *me*,' murmured my gentle companion, tremulously; 'you know I have a right to comfort you now.'

"Oh, sweet consoler! how strong in her love, and yet how feeble she was—standing there, offering comfort to *me!*

"'You are *my* Victor now,' she whispered, with a shy and quivering smile; 'lay half your grief on me. Ah, can you not trust Isolina?'

"I know not how, she slid within my arms again, and was pressed fiercely to my dark heart, which leaped at the sweet touch, and conquered once more the honor I should have had. I should have kept my guilty secret and given her back the liberty I had stolen from her: it was selfish in me, when I was sure of her woman's love for me, to blast her sweet trust with such an ordeal. But when all was told—when she knew that the house of Joselyn had an ever-present skeleton in its chair of state—that the stain upon its escutcheon was whispered of and pitied by baser-born churls of yesterday's making; that, I, the heir of Joselyn, might be confronted at any moment by her who was once my mother, and hissed from my patrimony with the stigma which leaves its victim nameless—when this story of polluting darkness had been poured into the ears of the innocent lady upon whom I had set my degrading seal, once more she took my hand in hers and looked bravely in my face.

"'What shall I do to prove that all this makes no difference in my love for you?' she cried, ardently.

"'What? Would you still share the fortunes of such a wretch?' I exclaimed, incredulously.

"'How can I prove that a woman's heart is deeper than your fears would imply,' she said again.

"And now, Ivanilla, I committed a cruel wrong against the woman whom I loved, in taking advantage of the utter self-abnegation of her love to bind her indissolubly to my-self.

"You will scorn me, as I scorn myself, when you hear how I repaid her generosity.

"'You see me now, perhaps at my best,' I replied, gloomily; 'perhaps you would loathe me at my worst—a homeless, defamed, nameless outcast.'

"'Never—never,' she returned, clasping her hands.

"'Prove it then, by binding yourself to me by a tie which no man can break,' I uttered, in a low, husky voice.

"She started, and became a little paler.

"'I will give you my vow to be constancy itself,' she murmured.

"'Vows are idle words, when remorse and contempt come between,' I returned, impulsively. 'Nay, my Iso-lina; put yourself beyond the power of friends who would preach down your heart; be my wife this night, that I may claim you when I return.'

She flushed to the brow, and stood away from me.

"'Without father or mother to say, "Heaven bless you both!" without friends of either to approve? No, Victor.'

"Then I flung myself on the ground at her feet, with the despair at my heart painting dark assurances. I en-treated and urged, remembering only my selfish fears, until she came to me and raised me from my abject frenzy.

"'Never plead so to me, my Victor,' she said, leaning against me with a low sob; 'I will marry you, as you wish, and glory in my chains. The marriage vow can take the place of the customary engagement; each is sacred to me.'

"I caught her rapturously in my arms and whispered rapid directions, to which she listened with a hidden face.

"'Do not let it be known,' she whispered, 'it would be called so very, very imprudent of me—and I do not think it is, for I do love and trust but one, and should never marry another. Victor, this is only a solemn betrothal.'

"I read her sweet, girlish fears, and reassured her. The marriage should only be a betrothal, which bound us in-dissolubly, and no one should know of it except my friend Pemberton whom I could trust, and perhaps some one in the cottage whose reserve could be relied upon. When I could return from England we should be married publicly.

"'Yes, yes;' said my treasure, who was now quite radiant, 'and we shall tell papa and mamma and little Ivanilla all about our foolish former marriage. But Victor, there's no one in the cottage can be a witness; Miss Cranstown's old groom would run for a policeman, and the lady's maid is not to be thought of, and our old housekeeper would tell all about it to Louisa, and Belle, and Blanche, and Eleanor, and think she is recounting a love-match of twenty years back; oh, no, love, not Mrs. Halcombe.'

" 'We can easily get a second witness,' I exclaimed. 'But come, darling and get your hat, we have not long.'

" ' What? this very minute?' she said turning pale and carnation by turns.

" ' I'll tell you,' I cried, heart-smitten at the sacrifice I demanded, 'you shall not have to leave the cottage. I will bring a clergyman, and my friend, and be here in an hour. Mrs. Halcombe shall receive our adieus for the ladies who are absent, and no gossip can be raised.'

" When I was twenty rods away, down the brook path, I turned back with a new fear.

" ' How old are you?' I gasped. 'Are you under age?'

" She crimsoned between surprise and amazement.

" ' How fortunate that you did not ask me ten days ago,' she said. 'I was twenty-one on the fifth day of July. Four years younger than my inquisitive Victor.'

" This afforded me another sweet reason for clasping her in my arms. How did she know my age—witch?

" She had heard Dr. Pemberton mention the date of my coming of age; could she ever forget anything that referred to me? No! nothing—nothing, since she first met my eyes.

" I tore myself from her a second time, buoyant and triumphant. As soon as I presented myself to Pemberton, he shook hands with me furiously.

" ' It was yes,' he cried, 'let me congratulate you.'

" He stared at me when I told him all.

" ' Very imprudent, very!' he said; 'I wouldn't advise you to do the poor young thing such an injustice—if only for the sake of her name. I once had a dear friend of that name—he's dead long years ago, poor fellow; but this girl, Isolina, I've loved strangely, just because of her name. Don't, my dear Victor, if you can't trust to her heart, you needn't trust to the wedding-ring either.'

" 'It's no sacrifice for her,' I cried, radiantly, 'she's willing and what difference can it make? Only that imperti-

nent suitors cannot be pawned upon her, should her friends
choose to frown npon me.'

"I believe this last argument vanquished him; the idea
of any one looking down the claims of a Joselyn, roused his
instant antagonism; he was not enthusiastic like me, but he
came, determined to prevent my new-found happiness from
being dashed from my lips.

"We went to the Rev. Willard Melville, whose church
we had attended during our two months' stay, and laid the
facts of the case before him, He got us a license without
difficulty, and prepared to accompany us. His wife, woman-
like, sympathized with the lonely young bride and begged
to be allowed to go with us, and be her friend on the occasion.
So we returned in a cab, to the cottage, with the necessary
documents and the two witnesses.

"The cottage parlor was empty, a Bible on the table,
flowers on every stand. Mrs. Melville went up stairs and
tapped at the closed door which shut in my darling. In a
few minutes they came down, my love trembling and clinging wistfully to her one female friend.

"Oh! how lovely she was! The simplest of white robes
clad her bewitching form; a single white rose, like curdled
pearls, nestled in her bosom, a meet emblem of her girlish
purity of heart.

"In ten minutes she was bound to me, by the forms of the
Presbyterian Church, in a tie which no man could break.
My friend Pemberton and Mrs. Melville signed their names
as witnesses; they all wished the new-made bride joy and
prosperity, and my friend told her to write to him if any
service could be given at his hands. Then they all drove
away, and left me one hour to spend with Isolina.

"'Do you repent?' I whispered, proudly.

"'No—oh, no,' she answered, while her timid heart flew
into her eyes; 'not if you are satisfied.'"

"I sat down, but not alone; my wife was clasped in my
arms; those lovely, tremulous lips would never be another's;
the heart beating so wildly, so timidly, was mine forever.
What joy—and yet what cruel agony to recall the vanished
sweetness now.

"And yet I had to put aside these raptures, and make my
hurried plans to render our enforced separation less painful.
I made her promise to write me constantly, addressing her
letters to Dr. Pemberton. Our little secret should be kept

until I could return and openly claim her. If unforeseen trouble arose she was instantly to summon me, and I would assume my proper place as her husband.

"All this I proposed, to soothe the trembling misgivings of my dear girl; the moment of our parting was drawing near and grief was swelling in her lovely bosom. She feared some dark misfortune—we should never meet again—something would come between us.

"'Nothing can, my own wife, but death!' I whispered.

"We both live, Ivanilla, but her foreboding has come to pass.

"At last I had to go. I gazed once more into those lovesome eyes, which beamed as if Heaven's constancy dwelt within them; I pressed in my arms a form which clung to me with throbbing heart, and fond, murmured words; I breathed for the last time the dear farewell to my wife. My good friend Pemberton rushed out at the last moment for me, and our parting was mercifully brief. Still I remembered my beautiful bride, standing in the door of the little cottage, pale, tearful, yet striving to smile lest my heart should break—her last word a heroic one.

"'There is nothing to fear—I do not regret.'

"In a few minutes we were far apart, and I was steaming toward New York. When I reached the city I purchased the wedding-ring, and had my wife's initials engraved inside, with the date on which the ring should reach her—'July 16th.' I had an old family ring of the Joselyns, a curious piece of workmanship intended to conceal a ring inside; this I slipped the ring into, and sent with my first letter to my wife. It was during my passage home to England that I soothed my bereaved heart, by painting that picture of our love-scene behind the cottage, and which afterward in playful sport I sent to Isolina.

"I arrived home to find my sister in a decline, and rapidly failing. The joy which she felt at my return produced for a time a favorable effect; she rallied and seemed to throw off the disease. I was like my old self; and she clung to me with the most touching affection. I told her the secret source of my happiness; with what sympathy and wondering interest she listened; then when my darling's letters began to arrive, breathings of the purest and most exalted constancy, how my gentle sister's tears of love fell as I would read to her passages which she might share.

" 'Oh, if I might live to welcome home your noble Isolina!' she used to sigh. But it was not to be.

" The disease returned with fell power, and almost without warning she passed away. On the 5th of November I buried her beside my father in the Joselyn vault.

"I was now alone; the last of my blood was beneath a marble slab; nothing bound me to my echoing halls but the grief which for a time prostrated me.

" Dr. Pemberton, ever faithful, reminded me that happiness awaited me across the ocean; that my noble-hearted young bride would console me; and that it was my duty to go at once and claim her.

" The thought of her devotion, which had expressed itself in every letter, fired me with new hope. I would take her to my arms and reward her by a life of love for the noble sacrifice which she had made for me. I quietly got ready and prepared to embark by the first steamer. The carriage was at the door which was to convey me to the railway station, when a packet arrived by the Liverpool mail. It was from my wife, inclosing the six letters which I had written her, and demanding in the most imploring language a divorce, assigning no reason, but on the contrary forbidding me to make any inquiries into reasons which were strong and fatal as death.

" Such was the letter which came to me on the 14th of November."

CHAPTER XXIX.

VICTOR JOSELYN'S STORY—CONTINUED.

"O, she is fallen
Into a pit of ink! that the wild sea
Hath drops too few to wash her clean again,
And salt too little which may season give
To her foul tarnished flesh!"

MUCH ADO ABOUT NOTHING.

" I remained so long shut up with my wife's letter, that at last Dr. Pemberton came to the door.

" 'We shall be late for the cars,' he cried, ' what has come over you, my dear boy?'

" I opened the door, and with ghastly composure, waved him in. I felt as if I should never speak again. I pointed to the letter, and dropped, like a lump of lifeless clay, upon my chair again. The contents had simply stunned me; as yet I was insensible to wrath or grief. The doctor read it and folded it up carefully.

"'It's some infernal conspiracy!' he exclaimed, 'and I am not going to believe she ever penned this letter until she says so with her own lips. She's not the girl to throw you over treacherously. We'll see her face to face, and clear this up.'

"The passage from England, was like a heavy dream; it passed me and left me in the same condition in which I had left my home. On the 29th of November, I, with my friend, arrived in New York.

"We had not left the steamer, when a young man whose acquaintance I had made in Saratoga a few days before I left, accosted me, and desired to speak with me. I told him to call at —— Hotel in an hour, where I would be located. He would not leave me but accompanied me to the hotel in a carriage. When we were alone, the young man whose manner was very mysterious, locked the door, and slowly advanced, until he was close before me.

"'Victor Joselyn, you have come to this city for one who will send you back alone;' he said in a low, concentrated voice; 'her heart has changed to you, and she sighs to be free.'

"'Who are you sir, that knows my private movements and intentions so well?' I demanded; 'who has commissioned Cecil Beaumont to pronounce my destiny?'

"'I am Victor Joselyn's successor to the hand of Isolina Rienzi!' he answered, fixing his burning eyes on mine.

"'Wretch!' I cried, striking him; 'take that for slander!'

"He stood motionless, though his face had withered to colorless marble.

"'Do you wish a proof of what I say?' he whispered. 'See, then. She has promised to be mine to-night; there will be a concert; I am to fly with her from the concert. You shall go there; you will see her enter the hall leaning upon my arm; this will be proof that she has cast you off. Are you satisfied?'

"'No!' I shrieked; 'not until I see her face to face!'

"'You will request an interview, then, to-day; she shall

refuse it; you may persecute her if you are unmanly enough, she will fly from you, she loathes—fears Victor Joselyn.'

"'Demon!' I shouted and felled him to the floor.

"He slowly rose, and stood once more before me, and gazed at me with folded arms.

"'You have struck me twice; you have called me slanderer,' he uttered, in the same fiercely repressed voice, 'and yet this hand remains passive. Know you whom you have felled at your feet, Victor Joselyn? Your younger brother!'

"I turned from him in contempt.

"'I would stab you to the heart for the insolence you have given me,' he continued, bitterly; 'but the same blood flows in our veins—the blood of the actress, Victor Joselyn—the false wife—the false mother, who forsook her children to enslave anew other men, and degrade other children—the woman who lives this day, and if I choose to whisper the word, will confront you and claim the homage of her first born. Ha ha! brother—let me shake your hand.'

"I waved him from me, and groaned and fell.

"When I recovered, the mocking vision had disappeared, and Dr. Pemberton was holding me in his arms.

"I poured the sinister story into his ears, and for the first time his faith was shaken in Isolina.

"'Put her from you, boy!' he exclaimed, 'her heart has deceived you and her; she is perfidious, or that young man would not have been sent to you.'

"'I will not believe Isolina false without sure proof!' I said.

"We agreed that I should send a note to my wife, demanding an interview; that I should describe the contents of the letter that I had received in England, and ask if she had written it; that I should demand the reasons of her desire for a separation, if such was the case.

"A messenger was sent with the letter, and ordered to deliver it into the hand of Miss Rienzi herself, and to wait for an answer. He returned in an hour with a note, written, beyond all doubt, by the hand of my wife, and it said:

"'Despise me if you must; loathe me if it will assist you to forget me. The fault does not lie with you; *I* renounce our sacred vows; I demand liberty, and *oblivion* of the 15th of July. I have my reasons in my own bosom; attempt not to unvail my secret. If there is one spark of mercy left in your heart for such a worm as her you once loved, forbear to see her; return to England and live again.   I. R.'

"Every word of this unnatural letter was damnatory evidence of the truth of Cecil Beaumont's boast; she was inconstant; her very initials, which were no longer those of her husband, proved that she wished to be free.

"'Let us try one more chance,' said Pemberton; 'and if she's as false as I begin to think her, we'll off this very night from cursed New York, and leave mother and wife to follow their own devices. We'll go to the concert-room —she can't forbid you a public hall, and we'll judge for ourselves.'

"We drove at the hour appointed to the Cybelle Concert-room, and quietly took our places behind a pillar where we could see without being seen. I was watching the grand entrance, expecting to see my wife enter as one of the audience, when my friend violently plucked my sleeve. I looked upon the platform and beheld her whom I had come to claim as wife, enter, leaning on Cecil Beaumont's arm, a flush of pleasure on her face; magnificently dressed, my double ring discarded, though she had fondly written to me once that it should never leave her hand until her heart was cold in death.

"Stunned and maddened, I sat and watched; her treachery seemed complete. When she came forward to sing with you a duet, Beaumont crept near, and methought his mocking, triumphant glance swept round the hall to find the man whom he had supplanted; those lurid eyes—so like the haunting eyes which sometimes pursued me from my childhood, and which were indeed the eyes of my wretched mother—seemed to sneer and laugh at my calamity, and crazed me with sudden frenzy. Heedless of my friend's restraining hand, I leaped from behind the pillar and stood quivering with fury before my faithless wife.

"She saw me, and with an affrighted shriek fell back and fainted, while you, her small, foreign-looking companion, gazed wildly from face to face for the cause of her terror.

"The sight of the miserable girl lying senseless at your feet, tore my heart with remorse. With a heart turned to steel I walked out of the house, and my anxious friend kept close to my heels.

"He was afraid I would do something desperate; he was mistaken. I was never more calm; my ideas ranged themselves with precision; I felt composed as a frozen sea.

"We entered our cab; at the moment a small Canadian sleigh passed by us and dashed furiously on; it contained Cecil Beaumont and my wife; her head was upon his shoulder, his arm was passed round her, exultation flashed over his face.

"'This is the last act of the drama!' I said, pointing to them; 'there goes my wife and my successor to her vows!'

"'Pursue them!' shouted Pemberton; 'horsewhip the fellow!'

"'No,' I answered; 'that man is beyond my vengeance; a wrathful Heaven has decreed that he should be my brother.'

"There was a steamer about to leave for Boston that same night, and in it I determined to take passage, and leave the city of my humiliation. I no longer desired to confront my wife; I washed my hands of her, and resolved henceforth to leave her free.

"The pang which rankled longest was the discovery that she was not the pure, high-souled being I had worshiped; that the transcendent virtues and the nobility of her morals had not been genuine; that the Isolina of my love was a heavenly creation that had never existed.

"I wished to procure some sort of divorce, in order to leave her the more completely free, but Pemberton sternly opposed the measure, on account of the publicity which would ensue.

"'She has not waited for a divorce,' he said, bitterly; 'and you are not bound to drag your horses into deeper mire, until you have a handle to go by. When she has publicly betrayed her marriage vows, then you shall sue for a divorce, and when free, unite yourself to a worthy lady of your own land, and perpetuate the name of your house.'

"'The name shall die with me!' I exclaimed, firmly; 'I have wedded for the last time!'

"In due time we returned to Joselyn Wold, but I only staid until my affairs were all wound up. I appointed Pemberton guardian of my estate; made my will, leaving the whole of the immense wealth which had made the Joselyns so haughty, to endow medical colleges; named Pemberton as sole executor and manager.

Having thus deliberately cut myself adrift from my native land, I wandered about, sometimes the guest of an Arab shiek, sometimes a dweller in the palace of the grand vizier.

" My life was imperiled a hundred times, by the sandstorm of the desert; by hunger, thirst, sun-stroke, or the sword of the fierce native.

" Sometimes my thoughts lingered sadly about my forsaken land—my desolate Wold; if I had had a little sister waiting for my return, what strange treasures would I have gathered from the land of thirst and sunshine.

" At length I went to Astrabad, hearing that the plague was raging through it, and as I had some knowledge of the treatment of the disease, I hoped to benefit some one of the devoted people who were dying by hundreds. For the next two months I was occupied happily in alleviating the sufferings of my fellow-creatures, and I succeeded in checking the progress of the plague, six weeks earlier than had happened in twenty years.

" The plague was quelled at Astrabad, but it broke out with fury at Saree, to which I immediately repaired.

" I had not been at Saree more than a fortnight, when a caravan came into the city from Astrabad with a Mahommedan boy who carried an English letter for me.

" Here it is, covered with grease and postmarks, with not a little Zend scrawling—to send it to Saree by a sure hand. And these are the contents:

"'My Dear Victor:—Return immediately. I have reason to believe that a member of your family has been separated from you by fraud—you know who I mean. I am about to return to America to find the truth of the suspicion. Shape your course directly to New York. You will find a letter waiting for you in box ——, P. O. No more explanations in this, as it may not reach you. God speed my boy.
"Yours,   Alphonse Pemberton.'

" This letter startled me out of my apathy. It broke, like the peal which rends the thunder-cloud, my false resignation, and brought back to me the wild sweetness of the life which was forever gone.

" That same night I left Saree with a company of silk merchants, and journeyed to the Caspian Sea. I have not rested night or day for the last four weeks; even on board

the steamer which brought me to Boston, I was like a restless spirit unshriven. When I reached New York I found
a latter at the post-office from my friend, telling me to come
to a place called Ranelagh and inquire for the family of my
wife. I am to stay at Ranelagh until Doctor Pemberton
can join me, and tell me the secret conspiracy that has been
made against my happiness.

"I asked at the village for the family of Rienzi, and was
directed to Silverlea.

"I am here, blindly obeying the directions of my mentor;
he has brought me from the ends of the earth; from forgetfulness and resignation under my lonely lot, to Silverlea.
What is to be the result?"

CHAPTER XXX.

A SHADOW UNDER MY STAR.

"You ask what is to be the result," I said, speaking for
the first time since my friend began his story; "and it is a
great riddle to me. Your history has filled me with astonishment. God seems to have brought us very near together,
under one trial. I am bewildered. Can it be possible that
the woman who has attempted our ruin so persistently is
also the curse of the House of Joselyn? Let me ask you one
question, Victor. What was 'Stella's' maiden name?"

"Gemma Lancinetto, of the House of Lancinetto, in
Florence; a haughty family, indeed."

I clasped my hands in superstitious awe.

"She it is who has twice attempted my life, once attempted the life of my mother, by a poisoned ring, and
cast her mysterious coils so thickly round our hapless
Isolina that she has fled from our arms and gone, no one
knows whither."

"You amaze me, Ivanilla! Can this be what Doctor
Pemberton means? Can my wretched mother be the cause
of the separation of my wife from me? But alas! I can never
forget that Cecil Beaumont supplanted me."

"Isolina has not been false," I replied, in a trembling
voice; "whatever cause has led her to act so, I believe she
loves you still. Oh, Victor! when you hear the true story
of poor Cecil Beaumont you will not deem my sister in-

consistent for love of him! My brother, I welcome you to the bosom of a family which has been sorely tried; your affliction shall but cement the bond of love between us. I kiss you on the brow, my long-loved Victor Joselyn. Now I shall tell you my story. Where it touches on yours I know not; I shall tell you all, and may God comfort you."

*　　*　　*　　*　　*　　*　　*

Again the sun rose over Silverlea.

I was up first and paced the upper balcony, in the light of the rising sun, to commune with the God I felt to be my friend.

Victor Joselyn was beneath our roof; he slept sweetly after his long travel—slept peacefully among his friends. How lovely—how lovely was this Silverlea when bathed by morning's rosiest light! Creator of this matchless beauty, come down and fill this heart with patience, and teach it how to hope!

Something struck me lightly on the breast, and fell on the balcony floor. A ball of crumpled paper.

I gazed eagerly about, and down to the pillars beneath, but saw no one. I lifted the ball of paper and opened it. "*Isolina!*" I muttered with a swoop of hope at my heart. It was in my sister's writing, and began with my sister's name. I turned it to the orient clouds and read:

"Isolina prays Ivanilla Rienzi to have no fear, but to follow the messenger, that she may hear from her she loves faithfully what has torn her from her family. Come alone, and privately, if you would see for the last time your everloving—ever-remembering Isolina."

And she had appealed to me; she would see me once more, and then we must meet no more on earth.

Where was the messenger? I was all impatience to obey the call. *Fear?* I forgot the caution; wherever my lost sister was, it would be safe for me.

I leaned on the leafy parapets, and gazed abroad with eager, brightening eyes.

"Come—I am ready," I murmured, kissing the fluttering note.

Still I saw nothing but the snowy shafts of trees and dark waving branches; how should I conjure this messenger into visibility? A thought struck me; I must go now, and alone, or the messenger would not discover himself.

I stepped into the upper hall from the balcony. No one had risen; it was not four o'clock; I might be far away before they would miss me. I must not attempt to take any one with me; she had said, "Come alone, and privately." I prepared myself hurriedly, and supplied myself with some money; there might be need; she might be induced to fly with me; I must be able to command resources. When I was ready I found a pencil and tore the fly-leaf out of Dante's Inferno; my fingers trembled, but I wrote some lines to those who would miss me:

"DEAR MOTHER—DEAR VICTOR:—Isolina has sent for me. I must go secretly or not see her at all. I am going with the messenger, who came to me as I was on the balcony at sunrise. I trust in God, and am afraid of nothing. I will bring her back if this hand ever touches hers again. Pray for us both—and do not——"

I could not finish; agitation and anxiety made the words illegible. I inclosed my sister's note inside, and left them on my dressing-table. I flung myself upon my knees and prayed for wisdom and guidance.

I was calm when I stepped upon the balcony.

"Come now," I breathed, audibly.

"Are you alone?" replied a voice beneath me.

"Yes, I am alone."

I strained my eyes at every mass of foliage, but saw nothing.

"Go down to the beach behind the house, and if no one follows you I will meet you there."

Step by step I stole down the balcony stairs, and looked within the piazza for the owner of the voice.

"Let me see you," I said, softly.

There was no reply. I waited a long time. I began to feel a little afraid.

Then a man appeared from behind a rock and stood before me. I shrank back in dismay.

"Ralph Morecombe!"

"There is no time to lose. Come away."

"Are you my sister's messenger?"

"Yes, yes. Are you parleying here until some one comes?"

"I have given you my word that I am alone. Can you

expect me to trust to you, whom I know to be a bitter ene-my, without any proof of your good faith?"

"I have no proof, if the letter I brought was none. I told her that you would not trust yourself with me, and she said the letter I was the bearer of would be sufficient. Miss Ivanilla, I have delivered my message, and I have been re-fused. I will go back to her and say so."

"No, you shall not!" I exclaimed. "Her letter shall be sufficient. I will go."

"Why did Miss Rienzi hesitate so long?" returned the man, fixing his wild Bohemian eyes searchingly on my face. "Was she waiting for the eyes to come which would spy? How many legs has she employed to give chase?"

"I employed none but the eyes of God to watch us. Evade them if you can, Ralph Morecombe."

"Ah! I was hoping that villain, Nelson, would lurk within reach of my hand," said the old Italian, clenching his fist and shaking it at Silverlea in a sudden paroxysm of fury. "How I would have gripped his varlet throat. How I would have hustled him over the rock into the last trough he'd ever wallow in. He to smite me—the dog!"

"I am ready to follow you," I said, in a mild voice.

He glanced at me less fiercely, then started at a rapid pace along the beach toward the village, I following close behind.

Presently we struck the road which leads to Ranelagh, and there, tied to a tree, I saw the brown horse and carriage whose acquaintance my readers have made before.

I came to a determined stand.

"Before I proceed farther, I must demand some proof that this is not a conspiracy to put me in the power of Mrs. Ringwood!" I exclaimed.

"Your sister wrote that letter. Would she have told you to rush into danger? I have no proof, madam; I do not wish you to come. If you are still afraid, I will go without you."

He deliberately climbed into the carriage, took up the reins, and turned into the high-road. He seemed quite ready to drive off without me.

I allowed him to proceed until I was quite sure he would leave me, then I called to him:

"Come back."

"Are you coming, then?"

"Yes."

"Without any proof that I do not intend to murder you, and put your body into the first well?"

"Yes."

He took my hand and assisted me to the seat at his side. Instantly we dashed off at a rapid rate; through the dusty lane behind the village, and away into the country beyond, where fresh scenes gyrated in rapid succession before my watchful eyes.

"When shall we reach my sister?" I asked.

"Madam will be able to ·tell to a minute, when she is there," responded the man in his pure, cutting diction.

"What do you mean, sir, by such discourtesy?" I retorted, with some indignation. "Answer me."

"To oblige Miss Rienzi, I'll not quarrel with her, but to oblige myself, I'll not answer her."

"Your reasons, sir; I must have them."

"Very good; very well. The reason is that you and I may disagree any moment after you find out exactly where you are going; and in your anger you may post back to Ranelagh by the cars at Crookle-Back, and set the village on our track, which you know would neither be keeping to your lady sister's injunctions nor endangering yourself."

"Your caution is admirable, sir. If I should never return to my parents, they will be unable to trace my fate. Be assured, however, that I will not be betrayed into danger without a struggle. I am not a coward."

"I think you are not a coward," said the wild being at my side, flickering a sudden glance at me; "and I see you are a regular mastiff for those you love."

"Tell me—tell me," I exclaimed, encouraged by the kindly glance which the coal-black eyes had given; "is my sister well? is she happy?"

"Ask the lady when you meet."

After two hours' drive, we entered a small and smoky settlement, where a ruinous wooden bridge spanned a muddy inlet of the sea. This was Crookle-Back Bridge.

A train had just stopped, and we were only in time to procure tickets and secure our places, when we were clattering noisily toward New York.

Morecombe, through his gipsy eyes, watched my every movement with the vigilance of a lynx; neither approached nor addressed me during the two hours we were tossed together. We stopped at station after station, and More-combe was always peering watchfully about, but did not move. At last the guard shouted Greely's Mills."

Morecombe rose. We were ten miles from the city, at the very spot where Mrs. Beaumont had lived; where Cecil had tried to destroy himself, where young Rosecraft was buried. Was this Isolina's retreat?

I followed my companion out; he led me away from the crowd on the platform, to the wide dusty place, near the mills, where I could speak to no one without being seen. Then he went and got his horse and carriage out of the van; reharnessed the animal and drove up to where I was standing.

"Get in," he said, holding the step.

I silently mounted, and we proceeded as before. I knew nothing of the locality; I was only conscious of ever increasing wildness of scenery, and that we seemed to be cutting across the country. Soon all signs of civilization were left behind us; woods and rocks succeeded to cultivated fields and homesteads; the sun rose high in the heavens, and the busy air which was alive with the buzzing of insects became close and stifling, and brooded thick under the moveless branches.

All at once my nostrils hailed the welcome odor of wood smoke. I looked eagerly over the wastes of fir forest for the chimney of a house. I saw a light vapor rising blue at a distance; we soon reached the clearing and I beheld three small conical huts formed of bark.

We were in a gipsy camp.

"Madam is white as a swamp-lily," said Ralph More-combe, looking at me; "we shall stop here."

I allowed myself to be assisted to the ground; I was faint with hunger and heat, but I would willingly have traveled twenty miles farther rather than stop here.

A crowd of tawny-faced children surrounded us; some men and women, with long, black hair, and flashing eyes, rushed out from the tents, and reconnoitered us. More-combe coolly beckoned to one, and ordered him to unharness the horse, and give him oats and water.

"Come here," he shouted to the group of women, "this lady is your guest. Where is the queen?"

A tall young woman came forward; she had aquiline features, melting black eyes, olive skin, and a dazzling smile; a curious scarlet cloth cap was on her head; her hair hung straight and jetty down to the hem of her short blue cloth skirt, which was fancifully decorated with the wings of thousands of small rare birds; her feet were brown and bare and exquisitely delicate, yet sinewy, her bosom was covered by a scarlet jacket, covered with blue embroidery; strings of silver coins were on her neck and arms. This gay personage took me by the hand and pulled me out of the hustling, whispering children.

"Welcome to Adynma's camp," she said, with great dignity.

I turned a look of agony on my escort.

"Is this the end of my journey?" I gasped; "have you given me to a gang of gipsies?"

"No," said Morecombe, with an involuntary softening; "you were tired, and I stopped to give you rest. We have yet farther to go. By the blessed Saint Magdalen, that is true."

I suffered the woman to lead me into the largest camp of the three. There I was waved gracefully to a seat; then, as the queen retired, a beautiful child, clad in green silk, danced lightly toward me, and fanned me with a broad swamp leaf.

Presently the woman returned with a bowl in her hand which steamed with some savory stew which revived my sense of hunger most keenly.

Sinking on one knee before me, she offered me a heavy silver spoon, and murmured with her dazzling smile:

"Eat from Adynma's hand."

I gratefully accepted the invitation, and began to eat some curious mixture of different kinds of flesh, garlic almonds, and pistachio nuts, highly flavored and not unpleasant. Had my appetite been less keen, I should probably have turned from it in dismay.

"What place is this?" I asked, when my appetite was somewhat appeased.

"I do not know, lady," answered Adynma.

"Do you not live here?"

"Oh, no, lady. We are strangers; we have crossed the great river. We are wandering."

"The great river? Niagara? You have come from Canada?"

"Gentle lady, yes."

" How far are we from New York?"

The woman showed her glittering teeth.

" I am a child. I have yet to learn."

It was useless to attempt extracting any information from the gipsy queen. I began to ask her about things she was more conversant with.

" Sweet lady, your brow bears a message which I cannot read," said Adynma; "let me read your destiny."

She took my hand in hers, but I fell asleep under the royal gaze. I must have slept an hour.

When I awoke, the woman was murmuring in my ear:

" Lady—lady, the messenger awaits you."

I opened my eyes and raised myself; through the open door of the tent I could see Morecombe harnessing his horse, the time had come to resume our journey.

"Drink," said the gipsy, presenting me with a richly chased silver goblet of wine; ' the Circassian blood is faint without the blood of the grape; noon's sun is heavy when the tongue is parched."

With a low bow I quaffed the wine, and rose from my crimson couch.

"Lady, your destiny weeps," said the woman, mournfully. "I have been reading it; my soul is troubled; a shadow sits under your star; lady—you will lose a friend!"

"Come, madam," said Morecombe, appearing at the door.

I followed the gipsy out; my heart was chilled—vague awe and half belief followed her words. "I would lose a friend." Perhaps my sister. Heaven forbid!

Scores of children ran round me with outstretched hands, and shouted the only English word they seemed to know.

" Money! money! money!"

" Away!" cried Adynma, with a royal gesture of command; "the guest of your queen is sacred."

Nevertheless, I turned and gave them a few coins.

I expressed my gratitude to my kind hostess for her generous treatment, and seated myself in the carriage.

I was so deeply immersed in my speculations that I no longer watched the scenes through which we passed. I was aroused by Morecombe.

" We are almost there."

" What! at last?" I was thoughtfully recalled now.

"We have gone four miles since we left the gipsy camp. One mile more."

At last Morecombe stopped unexpectedly and alighted to drag aside a fir-tree which appeared to have been uprooted, but which in reality covered the entrance of a narrow path which meandered through the dense foliage. After replacing the tree, he led the horse up cautiously for some ten minutes, and finally stopped before what appeared to be a dismantled cottage.

There was an air of dissolution over the whole place.

The gipsy-camp was light and beauty and joy compared to this.

Morecombe silently lifted me to the ground, and turned away. At the same moment the cottage door opened with an agonized creak.

A figure stood trembling on the door-sill, a figure that could come no farther, though its eager arms were outstretched, and its lovely, passionate face was bathed with the tears of joyful welcome.

"Come, come, come!" cried my darling. "I cannot move for gratitude. Oh, friend, faithful and true!"

And I bounded into my sister's arms.

CHAPTER XXXI.

THE TIES OF BLOOD.

"God's mercy, maiden! Does it curd thy blood
To say I am thy mother! What's the matter,
That the distempered messenger of wet,
The many-colored iris, rounds thine eye?
Why? That you are my daughter."
ALL'S WELL THAT ENDS WELL.

I strained her to my heart; at first I could not speak. My arms wound themselves round her as if they would never loosen.

"What can tear us apart now?" I thought.

"Calm yourself," murmured my sister. "Be brave, my darling, and make the most of this merciful opportunity."

"Only tell me what to do?" I whispered. "I will be brave and patient, but I will never leave this place without you."

"Alas!"

Her beautiful face grew pale and despairing. She took my hand and suddenly led me in.

We were in a low, darkened room, in which at first I could distinguish nothing. Gradually the different objects grew beneath my gaze. Two windows were covered with a heavy curtain, which effectually shut out the light. A thick heavy Persian carpet was spread on the surging and decayed floor; a long, black couch extended at one end of the narrow chamber. There was no other furniture.

The figure, substance, or shadow—I scarce at first could tell, was gliding back and forward along the white wall, with a step as soundless as the cloud which sweeps between the sun and the furrowing grain. The hands are interwoven, and the pensile fingers clasp each other like slender silver serpents; the face no more is shrouded, no more is false, it hides beneath no cunning disguise. The eyes flash in the dark, and show their splendor, and their dread prophecy of ruin; the face is small and deadly, with pride unconquerable in the dominant brow and quivering nostril. Oh, a beautiful face, all marred by the sparks of hell! The fair, round throat swells and heaves like the gorge of a serpent, with the dumb fury that seems to possess the heart.

She passes to and fro with quick and desperate energy, heedless of those who look upon her.

"This," said my sister, turning her calm, angelic face to me—"this is the secret cord that draws me from you. This is my mother—my true mother; and she is sick, and insane, and in danger for past crimes; and a daughter's duty is to fly to her and guard her."

"Ah, me! what dreary deceit is this?"

"It is a dreary truth, my own Ivanilla. For this I have sent for you, that you might understand the might of the duty that God has given me. I feared that I must go away with what I longed to say unspoken; but, when I came here, I found her in this state, from past excitement. I dared to run all risks, and induce her servant to go and fetch you. I might have written, but I have been weak; I could not live without a farewell; and you, my darling, I knew you would rather come than read the outpourings of a heart of sorrow by the cold medium of paper. And that which I have to say—ah! how could I whisper it without your hand clasped in mine?"

I listened in passive and icy silence; I could not take in her words. That woman—that *murderess* her mother? Who, then, was I? Who, then, was Victor Joselyn?

Great Heaven! did she say *her mother?*

The maniac brought her walk to a sudden close by crouching on the floor and beginning to wail and wring her hands.

"Lost! lost! lost!" she murmured, hiding her face. "Oh, lost, and alone, and unrevenged!"

"Hush!" said Isolina, flying to her side, and bending over, "not alone, mother—your child is here. Take comfort, mother; I am here—I will not leave you!"

The woman rose, and laid herself upon the couch, and dragged my sister by the hands to sit beside her.

"Keep me, then," she muttered, "and don't lose me; and avenge me on Guiseppe—cruel, false, Guiseppe Rienzi!"

"Hush!" breathed my sister again; "I am going to sing. Listen."

Was there ever a stranger sight than this? My sister lulling by tender love our murderess to sleep?

Silence came, but I marked it not. The low breathing of the sleeping woman deepened, and at last my sister's light hand clasped mine.

"Come now," she whispered, "and I will tell you all, while she sleeps. Poor darling, you are very patient with me."

She sat at the foot of the couch; I knelt on the mildewed carpet at her feet, with my back to the woman whom yet I fiercely loathed; my eyes wistfully raised to the woman who was about to disclaim the tie of blood between us."

"My life was perfectly happy, and smooth, and natural, until last summer. I regarded myself as other girls regard themselves who have beloved parents and a happy home. I knew of no hidden destiny or plot. I felt myself what I seemed to be; the love of kindred knit me to those whom I believed my kindred. There was never an emotion of my heart which I hid from them until I went with Mrs. Cranstown last summer to Saratoga. There I sinned for the first time against my filial duty."

She paused; a slow flush rose to her pallid face; the tears in silent agony stole down her cheeks.

"I know all," I whispered, bending my face to her lap; "do not tear your heart by this retrospection. Victor is at

Silverlea; he has told me; he waits there for his beloved bride."

"Ah, me! say no more," she exclaimed, wildly, " he has no bride—no love. Yes, yes—I do love him— I ever will, in spite of all, though I may never meet him on earth."

"Be calm, dearest, be calm, God is merciful."

"Sweet girl, you comfort me. All is not ruin while there is a God. Yes, I will be calm. Let us not speak of Victor Joselyn; it is torture that I cannot endure. When you know all, your heart will bleed for me.

" When I returned from Saratoga, my heart tinged every thought with joy, and I looked forward to every succeeding week, almost, for my husband to come and claim me. I had no thought that the secret marriage would not be known for more than a month or two. Alicia Joselyn was thought to be recovering, and I expected Victor by each steamer.

" But you came home, and the secret was still unrevealed. How often I longed to confide to you the hidden sweetness of my life; but for the sake of my husband I resolved to guard the secret, lest it might be misunderstood.

" Do you remember the first day you ever saw Cecil Beaumont? That day brought the burden of my life.

"I told you before that he had made my acquaintance at Saratoga; he had paid me attentions since then which I, as the wife of Victor Joselyn, could not receive; I had already dismissed him, and reminded him of his betrothed whom he was wronging. He was furiously jealous of Mr. Joselyn, until I had told him what I had told Miss Cranstown once, that Mr. Joselyn was already married; I feared the consequences of his mad jealousy. I thought he had returned to Miss Meredith, until the evening in which he once more presented himself in the drawing-room.

"When you retired I asked him gently to explain his presence.

"'You deceived me,' he burst out; 'you informed me that the English lover was married. I have made inquiries, and find you have deceived me!'

"I was both affrighted and indignant.

"'How dare you question my word?' I asked. 'I again repeat that Victor Joselyn is married. Be that as it may, he is not to be mentioned again. As for you, I demand by what right you again return to me. I cannot, and will not love you.'

"He cast himself at my feet with such passionate sorrow that I was forced to weep. I tried to soothe him, but he was firm.

"At last he rose and expressed himself satisfied, and left me. The next morning some letters came to us both; among them was a note for me which overwhelmed me with consternation. It ran thus:

"'Isolina Rienzi will not refuse to meet at —— Hotel, this evening, at five o'clock, a lady, who holds her past history in her hands, and to save her from further grief, would warn her of a danger which threatens her.'

"This could only refer to my secret marriage with Victor Joselyn; what lady was this who seemed to know of it so well? And she had some danger that she would warn me of. I was terribly alarmed.

"You remember the wild storm that day? At the hour appointed I stole out, hoping to escape detection, thoroughly frightened at the consequences of my imprudent secret, and determined to confide to my father and seek his protection as soon as I returned, if danger indeed threatened my husband.

"It was a furious night, but I had not far to go; there was a cab drawn up on the other side of the street, and when I had fought my way against the storm for some rods, it followed me and stopped. The driver asked me if I was Miss Rienzi, and if I was going to the —— Hotel. When I said yes, he said he had been sent for me, and opened the cab door. I entered, and was driven rapidly to the place. I was instantly conducted into a private room, when a lady, whom I had never seen before, rose at my entrance, and flung her arms round me.

"'I have got you at last,' she cried, exultantly; 'do you know that you are my child? Did you ever hear of Gemma Lancinetto? I am she, and I am going to claim you from the wretched Guiseppe Rienzi! *His* child is in her grave long ago!'

"I dropped upon a couch when she released me, sick with terror and amazement.

"'Lady, I do not understand,' I cried. 'Who are you? did you not send for me, on some business connected with

my history?' Then she eagerly poured into my ears a tale
which slowly froze me into despair. Oh, Iva, what anguish
that was for the bride of Victor Joselyn and the happy child
of the Rienzis! She had been a young lady of high birth
in Florence, and was betrothed to my father. I blame him
not to you, his real daughter; but he was false, cruel, heartless to the one who trusted him. He left her to her remorse.
She fled from her friends, and in mad recklessness went on
the stage. Her genius and beauty captivated an English
gentleman of fortune, who married her. This was Victor
Joselyn's sire. She lived in England five years with her
husband, during which time she gave birth to three children.

"She was intensely wretched; the quiet English life did
not suit her ardent temperament; her husband did not understand her. She had never risen above the injury she
had received from Guiseppe Rienzi; she brooded on revenge,
and only lived to execute it. She became unsettled; she
must find her enemy, or she would die.

"On flying from her friends in Florence, she had lost
sight of him; now she determined to find him out if he
still lived. She began to travel about in her husband's absence, with this one idea; she visited Florence in vain; no
one could tell where Guiseppe Rienzi had gone; she visited
Padua, Rome, Naples, but without success. At last some
one who had been traveling through the United States
mentioned a famous architect that he had met in Washington. This was Guiseppe Rienzi. She watched her opportunity and went alone to Washington, firmly intending to
revenge herself now. She soon found her victim; he was
just married to a beautiful American lady, and she saw them
come out of their handsome house, and proceed to enter the
carriage which was to bear them away on their wedding
tour. This sight maddened the wretched conspirator; she
dragged the bridegroom back from the carriage door, and
aimed at him a frantic blow on the breast with a poisoned
dagger. It quivered to pieces, leaving the hilt in her hand,
and her intended victim seized her hands, and looked
fixedly at her.

"'Is this Gemma Lancinetto?' cried the cruel man who
had wrecked her happiness; 'do I see the beauteous Gemma
in this guise? What if I were to deliver you to that constable that I see watching us?'

"Defeated and despairing, she writhed from his grasp.

"'I will give you cause to remember Gemma to the day of your death!' she exclaimed in her native language, and fled.

"He made no attempt to pursue her; probably he did not care to confront her with his pale and innocent bride.

"As she hurried wildly through the streets, she suddenly encountered her husband, who was on his way home from a tour; he asked her no questions; his lymphatic temperament being disturbed by no pangs of jealousy, and she returned home with him, broken in spirit, and doubly humiliated by her failure.

"She lived at Joselyn Wold a year, and bore the third child; when it was three weeks old, an irresistible temptation seized her to forsake her wretched home and appease her craving for revenge by another attempt on her enemy.

"In an evil hour she fled with the hapless infant, and arrived in Washington for the second time. Guiseppe Rienzi was a father by this time; daily a beautiful child was carried in the arms of the nurse from out of the stately mansion; poor Gemma's heart turned with jealous hatred. She determined on a strange, half-insane revenge; the infants were about the same age; she would steal the child of Guiseppe Rienzi and put her own in its place. He should cherish a viper, which at the last, would sting him to the core; the infants were not dissimilar; their complexion and eyes were the same; they were both girls. The parents were absent on a journey. She succeeded in her purpose; she stole in at midnight, drugged the nurse, stole the daughter of the Rienzis and put her own in its place. She crept back to the hiding-place, and she says—ah, me! she says the child she brought away died in her arms. But, alas! I fear the hand that sped the poisoned dagger, sped the infant life on its dark journey!

"Iva, you know now who Isolina is!"

Once more she paused; the wild tale died to silence; but it danced in my brain with feet of fire.

"An infamous fantasy! I will not believe it!" I muttered, huskily. "Unnatural—foul attempt to tear you from us!"

"Do not struggle with the agonizing truth," said Isolina, bending with unutterable love over me; "I have struggled

long, but I had to take it to me at last. See how the
struggle told on me. Ah, it was bitter!"

"It cannot be true!" I cried, with sudden exultation.
"You have our mother's eyes—you are her child!"

"Alicia Joselyn had blue eyes and golden hair," replied
Isolina, mournfully. "Victor has described her to me;
and his father and mine," she added in a strong voice, as if
forcing her mind to grasp the truth, "had blue eyes and
fair complexion."

"But your expression—your smile is the mother's very
own."

"By sympathy and unconscious imitation. I have lived
a life-time as a Rienzi, you know. Alas! there is no room
for doubt. She showed me the 'Bloody Spear' of the
Lancinettos on her signet-ring. She says the same crest is in
my flesh behind my right ear. You see it?"

I lifted the lustrous band of hair, and looked. *I saw it.*

"She described most minutely the mode by which I had
been substituted for the true child; I could not but believe
her. After this she instantly fled from Washington for fear
of detection, and soon found herself in North Carolina, as
the principal singer of an opera troupe. She engaged the
attention of a Virginia planter, Ringwood Beaumont, who,
unaware that she was already a wife, proposed to her. Alas!
she married him.

"She says that she was happy—that the craving for revenge had been satisfied—that her high position, as the
mistress of a thousand slaves, suited her. Mr. Beaumont
was gay, unscrupulous, and proud of her beauty. She became the queen of fashion. Cecil was the only offspring,
and she centered all her affections upon him. Sometimes
she delighted herself by planning how she would reclaim the
child which the Rienzis believed their own, and thus stab
them through the heart; but she was too well satisfied with
her lot as yet to disturb it by such revenge.

"Twenty years passed away, and the war devastated the
vast plantation, killed Colonel Beaumont, and rendered her
homeless. She and her son fled with others to the swamps,
and strove to form a guerrilla party, but were speedily captured, and taken North to a Washington prison. After a
time they were liberated, and Cecil quietly settled himself
as an author, and lived with his mother in lodgings.

"He was in a profound melancholy when he returned to

Washington, but he did not confide anything to his mother. She meantime having searched vainly through Washington for her ancient foes, and failed to find them, began to fear that she should never be able to reclaim her child. Then it was that Cecil, becoming more and more unhappy, at last besought his mother to accompany him on some pretext to New York, as he did not wish to leave her alone.

He was determined to try his chance with me again, and, perhaps, having flattered himself with false hopes, he at length told his mother that a lady had been the cause of his melancholy, but he hoped to win her. He came to me, and you know the result; when he returned to his mother he was in such a state of mad grief that he raved of his sorrow. What was her horror, her consternation, at hearing that the lady was the eldest daughter of Guiseppe Rienzi, the architect!

" The mother was stunned; a grim fate seemed to have brought about the most awful results of her early unscrupulousness. Here was Cecil, the only human being who bore her love, almost insane over the rejection of her own daughter. She could not bear to tell him the facts of the case. She resolved to summon the daughter whom she had forsaken so long, to tell her of the story of her true parentage, that she might avoid these two men, Victor Joselyn and Cecil Beaumont, who were bound to her by the ties of blood. Alas! she had little mercy when she made me the wretched repository of her secret.

" In my anguish I betrayed the real state of the case between Victor Joselyn and myself. I told her that she was too late; that he was my husband, wedded to me in all sacredness.

" With a frantic effort at calmness, I besought her to spare Victor the knowledge that she had given to me, and I swore to devote my life to her, if she would hide her existence from him.

" 'That is good!' she replied. 'When illness overtakes me, as it often does, I should like my daughter to attend me. I accept your terms; but I must ask another promise from you; bury the events of this night in your bosom; return to the house of the Rienzis, and feign still to be their daughter until I send for you. I am not ready for you yet.'

"Stunned and bewildered, I promised all she demanded.

'And when I summon you, you promise to come, whatever the difficulties?' she asked.

"I agreed to almost everything, and she expressed high satisfaction with the interview. I saw that she trusted me; that I would be prudent and docile.

"She embraced me at parting with warmth. I returned home in a cab. Heaven alone can tell the inward despair of my soul; but I was able to keep calm, and guard my secret even from you.

"Next day I made a packet of all Victor Joselyn's letters and burned his photograph, and everything which reminded me of him, except a painting which he had made of the happiest moment of our lives, and the white rose which I had worn in my bosom on my wedding-day.

"Then I wrote to Victor demanding a divorce, and returned his letters. I hoped that he would not insist on a reason, but consider me inconstant or fickle; and my one prayer to Heaven was that we should never meet face to face.

"The day that should reveal me to him as *his sister* would have stretched me helpless at his feet. Oh! I am still wild enough, mad enough to pray that Victor Joselyn may never know that Isolina is his sister. Let him revile me, despise me—cease to love me, and throw my memory to the winds; but, oh! this last hopeless, infamous blow may he be spared!"

CHAPTER XXXII.

THE CROSS.

"For my heart was hot and restless,
    And my life was full of care,
    And the burden that was laid upon me
    Seemed greater than I could bear."—LONGFELLOW.

The door was opened gently, and Ralph Morecombe came in; he wore a look of apprehension, and a sealed packet was in his hand.

"Madam," he said, bowing low to Isolina, "the shadows are long on the grass; already the sun is low, and there are long miles between the Black Forest and my habitation."

"Do you mean that my sister, that Miss Rienzi, is to leave this to-night?" exclaimed Isolina. "Did you not promise me that she should stay until to-morrow? Remember the fatigue she has suffered. She is hungry, exhausted."

"Madam is in danger," he said, glancing significantly at the figure sleeping on the couch.

"What is the packet—who brought it?"

"It is for Mrs. Beaumont; a gipsy brought it. Miss Isolina Joselyn, I must insist! Miss Rienzi, the carriage will be ready in half an hour."

He pushed the packet under his mistress' pillow, and stood imploringly waiting some reply.

"She shall go in half an hour," said my sister, in a tone of agony.

He bowed, and instantly retired.

"I will not leave you!" I exclaimed, wildly, throwing my arms round her; "I shall stay until the danger comes; that danger is my father and Dr. Pemberton. I know well."

"What madness," muttered the poor girl, trembling; "my word is pledged to this woman; I must fly from them; I must, I must!"

"And can you send your poor Ivanilla away so coldly?"

"Alas! my heart will break! Sweet child—sweet, sweet friend, do not tempt me; comfort me; sustain my weak, bleeding spirit, or it will sink beneath its burdens. Pity this torture between love and duty, and end it for me!"

"True—you are no longer ours; you have chosen your mother; your choice is at least a contrast to the mother you forsake."

"Cruel, cruel! I lose the last boon—your love."

"Never!" I exclaimed, with passionate remorse; "go to your duty, saintly, noble Isolina. May I be worthy to love so pure a being, and may our Heaven of mercy support you. I will not torture you with my selfish affection; I will go away."

"I have yet more to tell," she murmured, restraining the outpouring emotions of her heart, and regaining her calm and sad exterior. "I should like you to know the whole of this dreary history, that you may comfort in part, that beloved mother, whom also, I am obliged to forsake; I should like you all to understand fully the motives of this last step."

"Dear sister, I am listening."

"And you do truly love the unhappy sister of your sympathy? Thanks, sweet, generous girl; I could not lose your affection."

"After that first interview with my mother, she held no communication with me whatever, though, for what purpose I could not divine, she had hired lodgings at Greely's Mills, ten miles from the city, and lived there with her son. Each day I expected to be summoned from my beloved ones; I was like the prisoner condemned to death, who thinks each step on the flags is that of the messenger who comes to lead him to the scaffold; the frightful pressure of anxiety, terror and helpless grief was more than I could bear; no wonder I plunged madly into distracting employments. You remember the 29th of November? Ah! well may your cheek blanch, fateful, wretched day!

"Miss Meredith and you were in your room, I alone in mine, when a boy was brought up stairs to me with a note. He stood by while I read it. Victor Joselyn and Dr. Pemberton had arrived in New York, and demanded an interview. The firmament seemed falling to crush me; rather than meet them I would die. I sent back the boy with an answer, reiterating my desire for a separation, and absolutely refusing an interview. The afternoon was spent in a prostration of grief.

"At last my heart betrayed me; I resolved to tell the whole of the fearful tale to my friend Dr. Pemberton, and entreat him to interpose between me and the man who thought he was my husband. I felt that I was not able to fight my battle alone. I wrote the letter and sealed it with many prayers and blistering tears. You know what became of the letter I intrusted to you; Cecil Beaumont, still hoping, still ignorant of the impassable tie of blood, snatched it from you and it was consumed. Then I went down to him, full of desperate courage, though the mother's promise bound me hand and foot.

"'You say you have a secret power over me, which will make me glad to accept you,' I said. 'What is that power?'

"'I have learned, by hints which my mother has let fall, that she knows more about your position in this house than the world knows,' he answered, significantly.

"'Indeed! And has Mrs. Beaumont not explained what she refers to?' I returned, quietly. 'I wish she had, and saved me the humiliation of listening to your unwelcome protestations.'

" 'She has explained nothing!' he cried; 'she would hide all from me, but I am too madly in love to let slip any stone by which I may build up my cause. If indeed you are a nameless child, wearing the honors of a true daughter, a whisper would drag you down from your high estate. That whisper shall never pass my lips if you put your hand in mine and say, "I am thine." '

" 'Alas, Cecil, you have heard enough to blast your happiness,' I sighed; "it is not I who am nameless—but I will say nothing. Take me to your mother's to-night, and you shall hear the other half of this story. I can keep silence no longer!' I muttered, clasping my hands and almost tearing them.

" The poor, hapless boy's sanguine nature instantly rose at this; he thought he saw signs of yielding.

" 'You will come to Greely's Mills to-night?" he said.

" 'Yes—to-night,' I returned, firmly.

" 'And this family?'

" 'I may never return to them. Hush! it is not to *you* I would fly; I am done forever with love. Now, be wise, Cecil, and return to the lady who holds your troth; believe me, there is no hope of me.'

" At first he would not listen, but after some time his elation was such that he declared he would do anything to please me to-night, with the proviso that he should please himself after he heard the story which I declared to be so fatal to his hopes.

" 'If, after I hear the story, I still ask you to be mine, will you consent?' he cried.

" 'I will consent.'

" 'Then my Beautiful is won!' he said, with a brilliant laugh. 'Send me the little *fiancee*—I will overwhelm her with kindness—I will convey her to the concert, and be the most devoted of slaves—*anything* you say is my law to-night.'

" When I was able to present my wretched face to my family, I left him playing jauntily at the piano, and joined you.

" What happened at the concert I can scarcely tell. I was condemned to watch the terrible elation of a lover who was under a fatal misconception. I knew nothing of any other face there until, while I was singing, I saw like a phantom before me the countenance of my husband, white, angry, accusing—and I fainted.

"I recovered to find myself in Cecil's arms, far away on a moonlit road, in a sleigh, which was dashing onward.

"My strength was all gone; I could no longer bear his embraces and words of burning love and triumph, with fortitude, and yet I had no strength to repel him.

"I wept in silence and misery, until he, jealous madman! began to rail at Victor Joselyn, and accuse me of still loving him.

"Then the infatuated boy recounted an interview which he had with Victor Joselyn, in which he boasted of my inconstancy; how he found that Victor had come to New York, I do not know. He told me what struck the last blow to my endurance.

"I poured forth, with the insulted, indignant imprudence of a woman, the whole of the bitter story.

"The last word was reached. We were crossing a bridge. He stood up and grasped my hand. Until then, blinding tears had hidden his face from me. It was disturbed, and chiseled into a convulsed stare of horror.

"'That ends all, then!' he muttered; 'good-by.'

"Instantly he sprang from the sleigh to the frail bridge rail, for a moment he waved his arms wildly, and then leaped down, with a frantic laugh, into the shallow, rocky stream.

"Almost at the same instant, as if earth was convulsed with the horror which I felt, a dull, tremulous explosion filled the air, and the crashing of rocks smote a thousand echoes; the horse, affrighted and unrestrained, leaped madly on, and I sank shrieking to the bottom of the sleigh. I was whirled impetuously on, until the horse fell down exhausted, and covered with foam, and I was dashed with great violence out on the ground, the sleigh overturning, and scarcely bruising me.

"At first I was stunned, but soon rallied and rose. I could not tell where I was, the road was not in sight, and the wild, snow-covered heath stretched round me.

"By the full light of the moon, I ran feebly back on the track which the sleigh had cut, to find the bridge. I wandered on and on, staggering blindly, and shouting for help, until my own voice sounded vague like the voice in a dream. I think I lay down and slept.

"I awoke to find myself in a bed; my mother's terrible face bending over me. My head was bandaged; I was so weak that I could scarcely speak. The daylight was streaming in.

"'The bridge!' I moaned. "Did you find him at the bridge?"

"'Hush!' she said. 'You are mad. You have killed your brother, and you are insane. I must send you to an asylum!'

"My will was quite passive. I believed that I must be insane; to be shut up and treated like an irrational being was an idea which rather pleased me; I was dead to life now.

"Before the evening of that day I was an innate of Doctor Oaks' private asylum, and calmly awaited the development of the madness which I felt stealing over me. All these weeks of imprisonment I was almost as imbecile as any of my companions; my intellect was dwarfed and petrified. Memory was mercifully erased from my catalogue of torments."

"But when I suddenly saw the face of my sister, gazing at me through the bars, so full of love—so full of sorrow, my heart awoke with a fearful bound. The old, blessed life rushed back to me in a blinding flash of recollection; joy sent the phantom of madness thrilling from my brain: I rushed to embrace my long-lost Ivanilla.

"These first days with you were very strange and sweet; my mind was yet weak, and I could not grasp at the sorrows of my lot. Your love was enough to engage my attention.

"But little by little I awoke from my long trance; I realized that I should never have returned to Guiseppe Rienzi's roof again; that I did dishonor to my mother and insult to my sweet foster-mother, by remaining; that, possibly, I might bring danger on your heads by returning, to you.

"You remember the trial? I dared throw no light upon it; I almost hoped that I would be condemned, that the curse of my life might end. What was my astonishment to hear that Cecil Beaumont was not dead! that my mother had deceived me.

"You remember we went to Silverlea; and that you ceased to wish any explanation from me?

"Ah, how thankful I was to rest awhile in peace! each day added was a boon that I thanked Heaven humbly for; I only prayed that God would let me stay a month with you, but He left me nearly three.

"Then the day long dreaded came. My mother found me out and came to claim her promise.

"'You promised to come and do a daughter's duty when I came to you,' she said; 'now is the time; bid the Rienzis farewell for life and join your fortunes to mine. I claim my own child.'

"'Give me a week—three days!' I cried, frantically. "Do not tear me away at a moment's warning.'

"'You love them!' she exclaimed, fiercely; 'you despise your poor, ill-fated mother, whose life is hunted for by these Rienzis. Then I will go to Victor Joselyn, and claim my place in Joselyn Wold; he will not turn his mother adrift.'

"'Spare him,' I gasped; 'let me take his place. I will go where you please, only do not go to him.'

"'You will come to-day, then?' she replied; 'they have put detectives on my track, and they are going to accuse me of attempting to poison Ivanilla Rienzi—an infamous lie, my child; and my life will be sworn away to the very death if they can find me. A malady is approaching me; I have had it twice; once when my perjured lover forsook me— twice when the dead body of Rienzi's child lay in my arms. I have heard that when this malady visits one the third time it becomes incurable. It is coming! In twenty-four hours I will be hopelessly mad! Look at my eyes—my throat; touch my temples and my pulse. See if it is not so?'

"She dashed off her blue spectacles. I saw with horror the wild glare of incipient madness in her eyes, and in the quick throbbing of her throat and temples. Infinite compassion filled my heart. I could scarcely forbear weeping.

"'Mother, is it hereditary?' I asked; 'I also was mad, you know.'

"'Yes,' she whispered; 'a Lancinetto has been shut up for the last three centuries; there is always a Lancinetto shut up.'

"'If this overtakes you, tell me what to do.'

"She then described exactly where we were to fly, and what duties I was to perform. These details took a long time.

"'I have one question to ask,' I said, when she was finished. 'Why did you make me believe that my half-brother, Cecil, was dead?'

"She laughed a short, exultant laugh.

"'Yes, recall it!' exclaimed the unhappy woman. Oh, it was sweet, and good to see. How it wrung Guiseppe's heart. How it whitened his hair. How it broke his stately presence. Oh, it was good.'

"'Come away, and let us never see him more,' I murmured, terrified at her vehemence and weeping with horror.

"'No, I would like to see Mrs. Rienzi, and her daughter first,' she answered, with an instant return of her quiet, natural manner. 'I have a small debt to pay them.'

"She spoke so mildly that I was deceived, and gladly consented to stay, that I might behold you for the last time, though I dared not bid you an open farewell.

"She told me exactly the moment in which I was to slip from the room and steal down to wait on the road for her.

"When she would say, 'I have spent a very pleasant forenoon with Miss Rienzi,' I was to rise and go out.

"We were to fly immediately to this place, which, being in the very heart of the forest, she said would defy detection.

"After waiting until the first vigilance of the pursuit should be over we were to leave the country.

"She was still in the midst of her plans when you arrived. I was suddenly made aware of some concealed motive for all these plans of immediate flight, when I saw my mother rapidly slip a ring on her finger, just as you entered. My foster-mother only bowed at the door, and did not shake hands; you, coming in after her, put your hand in the extended hand of the pretended Mrs. Ringwood; it darted through me like a knife that the ring was poisoned when I marked the prolonged pressure. How relieved I was to find no mark on your hand, my poor darling. Your glove saved you.

"Every movement of my mother inspired me with terror. I resolved not to leave her with you, for I saw she was already unsafe. When she said the words which were the signal for me to go, I dared to disobey, but her vengeful looks almost petrified me. At last, by intense watchfulness, I saw her shake some white powders into two of the glasses of wine, and she dared to designate with a threatening expression which glass I was to take.

"It was too much; even the dreadful spell which bound me silent broke when you lifted the poisoned glass to your lips. I dashed it to atoms, and saved you.

"When I recovered from my long swoon I found Dr. Pemberton with me; he soothed and quieted me, and said he would soon see me all right and happy, and joined to Victor again.

I can tell you little more.

"Weak and outraged at heart, and hopeless, I took the cars to Greely's Mills, and hired a horse and carriage to take me as far as a gipsy camp, when I paid the boy and got the gipsy chief to take me on his best horse to this miserable den.

"Here I found my poor mother in the first paroxysms of the disease, with no attendant but her faithful servant Morecombe, whose proper name is Rinaldo Moresco, a servitor of the Lancinetto family all his life, and devotedly attached to its interests.

"Now, my darling, I have told you all plainly and carefully what power moves me from all I love to an exile terrible as death; much I dared to see you once more and tell you what would set your gnawing hopes at rest. The time has come that we must part.

"You weep, my sister—ah, hush, my sister! Comfort yourself. Never weep that your power was overruled by Heaven.

"And now, receive my last charges.

"I give this withered rose into your hands for Victor Joselyn; tell him it is the marriage rose that nestled in the bosom of a wife who was never a wife, and whose right to his name has wrecked her happiness.

"I will be humble, and sue even for a brother's tenderness, since nature has denied me more; in heaven our love will be pure enough even for this restless and weak heart.

"Give the last of my love to your sweet mother; she was too pure to retain the offspring of Gemma Lancinetto. Ask her to meet poor Isolina up yonder, where the blessed never weep, and where the broken heart may ache no more.

"Tell him whom I have revered and loved as sire that I forgive him for the wrong he did my mother, and seek to be forgiven for the anguish his child has brought him.

"To you, beloved, faithful one, I leave a heart with love which only flows unchecked to you. And because I prize you dearly, deathlessly, oh, my little one, comfort Victor Joselyn if you can. I shall not live long; thank Heaven, the earthly struggle will end at last, and I will be in bliss, watching for you first.

"And remember—remember, Ivanilla, to you I say it, I will be at the pearly gates watching, praying for your entrance. All of you—oh, tell them, *all of them!*"

CHAPTER XXXIII.

TOO LATE.

"But, no, that look is not the last;
　We yet may meet where seraphs dwell.
Where love no more deplores the past,
　Nor breathes that withering word—farewell!"
　　　　　　　　　　　LONGFELLOW.

"The half-hour is past, madam," said Morecombe, opening the door.

My sister turned as pale as death; unconsciously her hands clasped round me and held me fast.

"I cannot—will not leave you," I whispered, desperately. "Let him drag us apart, if he dares."

"Farewell, Ivanilla," she cried, lifting her countenance now with a smile of seraphic purity. "I will meet you in heaven."

The small carriage was standing close to the door, with a fresh horse in harness; the sun was, indeed, low behind the trees, and rough were the miles that stretched between home and me.

In stupefied silence I took my seat, and dared but one backward glance at my beloved, standing on the threshold of the mildewed, crumbling dwelling. Her gentle lips tried to quiver into a smile of comfort, but they failed; and the holy eyes were raised to heaven, as if they would carry my hopes up there.

"I will leave you at the gipsy camp," said Morecombe,

grimly; "and you can rest there all night in Adynma's
tent, or let her husband drive you through to Greely's
Mills; it's fifteen miles from the camp."

We had not gone two miles when a shout greeted our ears,
and a large carriage, drawn by a pair of blooded horses,
came between us and the blinding sun. Morecombe drew
up stock-still.

A man, without a hat, sprang out of the carriage, and
ran to meet us; another vaulted from the box, and was
beside us.

"Now Heaven be praised!" I cried with joy, and gazed
in wonder and hope unspeakable on my father and Cecil
Beaumont.

"What is Ivanilla doing here?" gasped my father.

"I have been with Isolina. Oh, father, save her!"

"Where is your mistress?" demanded Cecil Beaumont.

Morecombe sat upright, looking straight before him—
silent, immovable as a Sphinx.

"Fellow, I shall not speak again."

Ralph's hand secretly jerked the reins; like lightning
the horse rose on his haunches and beat the air with his
fore-hoofs, then came down with a sidelong spring to the
ground; round came the carriage on one wheel, and
away we dashed, the infuriated animal galloping wickedly and champing his sawed mouth. Down in the
dust I had left my father's gray head, with helpless, outspread arms.

"Stop, stop!" I screamed, frantically.

On we sped past the trees, which seemed to dance past
us lonely and still; the branches hung above us and shut in
the hollow beat of the horse's hoofs.

"Now I will stop," said Ralph, turning his dark, merciless face to me, "and if you show these people where my
mistress is, I will shoot you in cold blood. Do you hear?"

He caught me round the waist, and whirled me out on
the bank, and the wheels rolled over my outspread dress,
and the carriage vanished like a dream.

I got up and looked vaguely about; in truth terror had
bewildered me; my limbs trembled—my head swam dizzily;
I fell against the hoary trees, and I ran unsteadily back by
the darksome way I had left my father.

Twenty minutes must have passed, and I heard the heavy
rumble of the carriage approaching. They stopped when

they came upon the pale little figure standing in the road, without a hat; and again Cecil vaulted off the box.

"My friend, have you escaped from that rascal?" he ejaculated, seizing my hand; "can you show us the way to the house?"

"My father!" was all I could say.

The carriage door opened, and Dr. Pemberton put out his hand.

"He's here, and safe. In, Ivanilla, and let us drive on."

I was dragged in, and the carriage moved off with a rapid motion.

My father was sitting on the back seat with his head against the cushion, looking very pale.

"Oh, papa!" I murmured, throwing my arm around him; "are you hurt, papa? oh, papa, tell me!"

"No; a little stunned, that is all. Sit here, Iva. Where were you?"

"Isolina sent for me this morning to come to her; she is in a cottage along here, with—with that person, and that person is insane; they are going somewhere out of the country, unless you are in time to force them to stay. Isolina has been made to believe she is her daughter."

"Cecil Beaumont has told us the story," broke in Dr. Pemberton; "she will have to prove that before we give the girl up."

They talked eagerly for some minutes, while I watched intently from the window; I was looking anxiously for some landmark to remind me how near we were to the fallen tree.

To my confusion, the place looked quite strange; I did not think I could ever have seen these crooked beeches before. I made them stop the carriage, and got out.

"We must find a fallen tree; which has been flung on the entrance of the lane which leads to the cottage," I said; "I fear we must have passed it.

Beaumont and the driver walked on, scanning carefully the tracks and woodpaths. Dr. Pemberton and I walked back.

I was right; we had passed it some two hundred rods; ten minutes was spent in finding it.

We shouted for the others, and dragged the branches away, they had been so cunningly placed that the foliage presented no contrast to the rest of the thickly matted undergrowth.

The carriage came up, and we took our places; the path was so narrow that the driver had to lead the horses by the heads; sometimes the wheels could with difficulty jam past the close-advancing trees. But we came at last to the hovel, and poured out of the carriage, silent and eager.

But I stood silently without, gazing at one object which told me all that need be told.

I knew that *that* sweet face would shine no more out of the lifeless silence; that we had been too late, and God had seen fit to snatch our girl from us after all.

My sister's black silk scarf was trailed across the threshold to where the deep wheel-marks had cut circles in the marshy sward. The cottage was empty.

"Iva, child, no one is there," said my father, coming out to me, and laying his hand heavily on my shoulder; "they're gone!"

And then he reeled, and was caught in the arms of his early friend, Doctor Pemberton.

"Look for what tracks you can," said the doctor, laying his patient on the grass, and anxiously bending over him; "never mind me, but see about pursuing them."

Young Beaumont was coming out of the cottage last; his lips curved into a line of bitter agony; his eyes all light and luminous fire, fixed eagerly on the ground.

"There!" he said, pointing, "they have taken that direction, and have fled over the mountains."

There was a faint track of wheels cutting the heath at the back of the house, and following it a few paces, a horse's foot-print became discernible, though the ground got more flinty and the trees gradually opened; a few paces more, and Cecil Beaumont stooped and picked up a lady's glove, and strode back to us.

"Lend me a horse!" he said, passionately, "and I will overtake them; they have taken a mountain track, which if they can pass alive, doubtless leads into some road not far off."

Almost before he had done speaking, the driver was divesting one of the horses of its harness, and fastening a saddle, which he dragged from the carriage box, upon its back! In unutterable excitement, the young man bounded into his seat, and sprang off, to be speedily lost sight of, among the trees.

I was trembling mutely, with my father's head in my lap,

while Doctor Pemberton strove to restore animation. How pale he was! how old and feeble-looking! alas! my father!

"Guiseppe! nonsense, man, look up! all's not lost yet—they've only a few minutes start; fie, man!"

With a faint groan, my father raised himself, and looked up. The amber clouds were drifting overhead; the faint, milk-white stars of September were peeping down wanly in the sunset glare. How serenely nature ever smiles when the heart is bleeding most!

"Poor Ivanilla!" he murmured, meeting my wistful eyes; "lost her mate! poor little birdling."

The doctor peremptorily insisted on my father entering the dismal cottage, and resting on the miserable couch where last I had seen our enemy reclining.

The curtains were torn down from the windows to admit the straggling rays of light, and some refreshments were brought in from the carriage, which Doctor Pemberton saw that we partook of; indeed, I was too weak and exhausted not to obey him gladly.

And here we resolved to wait until the driver could be dispatched to the nearest inn, which was at least ten miles off, for another horse.

While my thoughts were absorbed, the doctor called upon me to explain all that had occurred since his departure from Silverlea. Amid intense attention, I told them all.

"And so you know now, that poor Isolina had been married to luckless young Joselyn for more than a year! I had hoped, when I posted on here from the old country, to be able to ferret out the cursed spell that kept them apart; alas! we found what it was too late, Guiseppe!"

"Too late!" groaned my father.

"And do *you* believe that our Isolina is not ours?" I gasped, looking from one to the other.

"I believe it," answered my father, covering his face with his hands.

"And I believe it!" echoed the doctor; "she is strikingly like what Alicia Joselyn, her elder sister, was; the likeness is there."

"Papa," I murmured, "why do you believe it? Have you——"

"Was I what, my child?"

"Have you any reason to think that there could have been an exchange?" I said.

" Yes; a strange phenomenon is explained, which puzzled your mother and me all our lives, since Isolina was an infant. Oh, if we could have arrested the guilty wretch who has claimed her, I should have wrenched the truth from her!"

" Beaumont will overtake them yet; don't despair," said the doctor, trying to speak hopefully.

Then he began to tell me what had first induced him to interest himself in our cause.

" I received, three months ago, an anonymous letter in England, which stated that a lady named Isolina Joselyn had been injured by my misrepresentations, and if I would fulfill my promise of assisting her when in trouble, I would at once proceed to New York, where he, the writer, pledged himself to meet me, and put the facts of the case in my hands.

" Upon my arrival at New York, I found a letter at the post-office for me, directing me to Wrexville, a small village in Maryland.

" Implicity following my directions, I traveled South, and at the only inn of the place in question found myself expected.

" In two hours a young man entered my presence, in whom I recognized with consternation Cecil Beaumont who had carried off Mrs. Joselyn, and declared himself to be Victor's brother. He soon disarmed me, however, when he informed me of Isolina's true fate. He had been taking her that fatal night to the house of his mother, in the hope of inducing her to marry him there, when she informed him that she was his half-sister, and already the wife of Victor Joselyn.

" He allowed her to explain all the circumstances, then, fired by sudden despair, he attempted to put an end to himself by leaping over a bridge. He was only stunned, however, and much broken, and when he recovered he was in his mother's house. For six long weeks he lay at the brink of death with brain fever, and when he recovered he was lying at Silverlea, attended by his mother. When he regained his senses, she told him that Isolina was in a madhouse, incurably insane, and that the Rienzis had given up when they found she was not their daugher.

" It was well on in spring before he was able to rise from his bed. As soon as he was convalescent he left his mother, determined to join the army, and lose his life as his father had done.

"He passed through New York on his way South, and beheld Ivanilla Rienzi on the wharf of a European steamer. As he was unaware of the rumor which was circulated of his death, he merely gazed at her sadly, not daring to speak, after the misery his family had been to her.

"The same night he set off secretly to the seat of war, and obtained command of a regiment. A few days afterward he was astounded, on reading the New York papers, to see an account of the approaching trial of Miss Rienzi, with ample details of the story. He instantly wrote a note to the presiding judge, vindicating the young lady, and offering to appear, if such a course was necessary. But she was acquitted without such measures being required.

"Putting his narrative and my own experience of the character of Gemma Lancinetto together, I determined to acquaint myself with her past history and plots. Before long I found that it was the family of my own old friend, Guiseppe, who was being victimized, and I came to Ranelagh just in time to save Mrs. Rienzi's life from the machinations of the fair enemy who was presuming to claim poor Isolina as her daughter.

"Mad, is she? Then Heaven has sent upon her the just vengeance which He withheld from our too eager hands. But that poor girl! Oh, why were we half an hour too late?"

*   *   *   *   *   *

At midnight Cecil Beaumont galloped in, waking me up from a fitful slumber, my head on my father's pillow. The rider strode in to the dreary cottage, and one glance at his cold, haggard face, told that he had failed.

"They have escaped," he said, with almost the tone of a fatalist; "it was not for this wretched hand to bring restitution; the debt must stand, and Isolina must be the victim. Alas! why was I born to curse those whom I loved too well? Ivanilla, I have lost you your sister."

"You, Cecil? Oh, do not blame yourself," I sobbed, pressing his hand kindly. But the desperate look still lurked in his eyes, his thin, hollow cheek, and brow of passionate disappointment haunted me for years afterward.

Our journey home through the night passed like a distempered dream; my brain was thick—the wheels of thought so clogged that I seemed to lack the strength to wield such unwieldy machinery; fatigue, past excitement, and premonitory symptoms of disease were weighing heavily on me, and everything was vague and dim around me. But still I was sensible of one interruption to our homeward course, which often occurred to me afterward with vivid distinctness.

As we passed the camp of the gipsies I saw lights moving hither and thither through the trees, while shrill cries resounded eerily from near and far.

"What is the matter? Are they calling us?" exclaimed Pemberton.

The carriage stopped, and he thrust his head out of the window.

"What's the commotion about?" he asked of a young gipsy who ran up to the side of the coach.

"Baree, Baree!" came shrilly to my ears from the heights beyond.

"Did you meet an old woman in a scarlet cloak and black silk kerchief on her head?" asked the young man, eagerly.

"A gipsy? No!" cried the driver from the box; "not one."

"Baree is lost, then," said the fellow, moving away. And again came the piercing cries from sear and rocky cliff:

"Baree! Baree! Baree!"

We drove on after this interruption, and reached Silverlea at six o'clock in the morning.

There was woe to the hopeful mother and anxious young husband. Ah, what a cup of anguish was that to place to their craving lips.

And yet, in my dull, half-stunned condition, I could only watch sadly, and wipe my mother's woeful tears with mute pity. Words were of no avail, and I did not try them.

And to the stricken husband what comfort dared I whisper? Gone, gone, gone were his flowery hopes. Oh, bury them deep—stifle them for evermore.

Yet it was he who first took Cecil Beaumont's hand, and looked into his burning eyes with the glance of heavenly sympathy.

"Bear it bravely, Brother Cecil," he murmured, softly.

"Let us do our duty to God and man, and trust to meet our hapless sister in heaven."

And then his hand leaned kindly on Cecil's shoulder, and the brothers clung together heart and heart at last.

"I have wasted your life and hers," moaned the younger; "and restitution has been denied to my unworthy hands. Oh, Victor Joselyn, can you look on wretched Cecil so kindly?"

"The wrong is forgotten, Cecil, and forgiven."

"I will never find rest this side of the grave. Remorse shall haunt me night and day. I shall throw my life on my country's battle-field, and die in the midst of duty."

And, plead as we might, Cecil Beaumont went away, and the hollow, burning eyes, and the spirit which had broken beneath the heat of wild youth's fire vexed us no more in our desolate moaning.

CHAPTER XXXIV.

THE HAND WHICH LIFTED THE CURTAIN.

" Love took up the glass of Time, and turned it in its glowing
hands;
Every moment, lightly shaken, ran itself in golden sands."
TENNYSON.

Link by link the chain of Time is woven, and it comes at last that the fever dream is spoken of as a thing of the past, and ended forever.

Victor Joselyn lives in his desolate Joselyn Wold, not aimless and desperate now, they say, though the great sorrow of his life has left its everlasting mark; he toils among the down-trodden poor of his country, to win for them a more human life from their oppressors.

Cecil Beaumont has won a name among his father's countrymen for courage and intrepid zeal, which resounds from every lip; and the young general has made glory his bride, and fights with reckless bravery for his father's cause, and to avenge his father's death.

The woman with her secret vendetta is heard of no more, and two years have passed since Isolina trod the golden sands by the opal waters of sweet Silverlea with me.

But there came a day in the balmy month of September,

that the postman knocked at a certain door, not quite within the city noise, but just upon the flowery outer rim, and in due course of time two letters were carried in to the mistress of the pretty establishment, whose name, as read on the backs of the letters, which she wonderingly scanned, was: "Mrs. Ernest Lindhurst."

"What can they be," I ejaculated, glancing across at a gentleman, who was busied in the leading article of the *Times.* "Both in ladies' handwriting, and one so strangely alike. Oh, Ernest!"

The opened sheet fell from my hand, the quick blood fled to my heart, and surged there in a flood which almost burst it. My husband sprang to my side, and put his arm round me, and I leaned against him with closed eyes.

"Let me wait," I murmured. "I dare not read it yet. You read it Ernest, and tell me."

He caught up the letter and perused it at arms length. I still leaned against him, but I become calmer; for I was praying; I was saying, over and over again, in my soul:

"Thou God in heaven, prepare me for this joy!"

My husband finished the letter and clasped me close.

"Look up, my darling," he said, gently; "there is good news. You must take it bravely, dear, and don't get excited."

"Tell me—tell me! Isolina——"

"Isolina is free to come home. She is coming, dear; she will soon be with us. Can you listen to what she says?"

"Wait a while," I whispered again. And I felt that I could not bear it until I wept once more to Heaven for strength.

"Ever Merciful Father," I prayed, "crush me not with joy and gratitude! Put Thy hand on my eyes, that I may not be blinded with excess of happiness!

"Now, Ernest, I am calm."

"My Beloved Ivanilla—I am now alone in the world, and at liberty to come from my exile. My poor mother died yesterday, after a short illness of three weeks, which finally turned to disease of the heart, and carried her off almost in a moment.

"I have found a small packet addressed to your father; perhaps the contents may be some sort of confession. I know that the guilt on the unhappy soul of the corpse which lies so cold and forlornly calm before me now weighed it down into the hopeless melancholy which has oppressed us since we fled from America. She is gone now—oh, I weep when I dare to ask whither? A desire to reveal something tortured her during the last hours of her life, but she could not speak. Will this attempt at the eleventh hour to render perhaps restitution weigh against her mountain of crimes?

"My life has been sorely tried. I thank the Lord that I found comfort from heaven; and I tried to do my duty as a daughter. Shall I return to the only home I ever loved? Shall I be the bearer of the packet for Guiseppe Rienzi? Are the hearts of my dear ones still as warm and kind as when they had an Isolina?

"And when I dare to think freely of you all my heart cries yes, a thousand times. I will fly to you from my loneliness and sorrow; if my poor changed face can bring you sunshine, you shall have it; if Gemma Lancinetto's child can be nothing to you—but I have no fears, no doubts of your generous love. It will be sweet to depend on those whom I love and trust boundlessly. I will fold my weary wings in my childhood's home, and never leave it more. Peace at last, after long pain. Heaven bless my little foster-sister, and her true-hearted Ernest. I have not lost sight of you, though cruelly hidden myself.

"Farewell until a speedy meeting. As soon as the remains of this poor mother is buried, look for ISOLINA."

We did not express our emotions in very eloquent language, my husband and I, but we knelt down side by side, and though our tongues were mute, our hearts were translatable to One who now had deigned to answer many tearful prayers. And after this the great wave of joy swept more gently over us.

But it was hours after that we bethought ourselves of the second letter which had come for Mrs. Ernest Lindhurst, and which lay neglected among the tray of newspapers and periodicals.

I opened it with reluctance, loth to abstract myself from the new-come joy; and when I surveyed the long, closely written sheets, and read the first sentence, I turned to the signature with incredulous surprise.

"Lillia Meredith," I ejaculated; "what can she have to say?"

"Read it and see," was Ernest's suggestion.

And this was the letter of Isolina's enemy:

"MRS. LINDHURST:—I should not presume to address you if it were not with the hope of rendering tardy restitution. How hard I have been—what wrong I have done those whom you loved, no one has known but Heaven and myself. I do not write to plead forgiveness. When you read what I have got to say you will spurn me almost from your standard of womanhood—but if even at this late hour I can do you justice, I will carry a less remorseful heart in my bosom. Read, then, and judge of my merciless cruelty.

"It is more than two years since you lost your sister. I knew of your calamity, and had in my possession then facts which might have saved you all the anguish which has come upon you since, but in the wicked fury which I felt against Isolina Rienzi, I resolved to avenge myself by keeping silence.

"When the trial was over I returned home to Washington, filled with rage and disappointment that it had not succeeded. For some time I resolved in vain a scheme by which to punish Isolina for her unavoidable share in causing Beaumont to desert me.

"About a fortnight after my return an old woman in gipsy costume came to the door one day and craved to see me. I went at first to order her off the door step as she refused to go for the servants, but I soon found that she had something of importance to communicate, and only feigned to be a chiromancer. So I conveyed her to my private chamber and drank in eagerly all she had to say.

"She said that she knew something that Mr. Rienzi, whose daughter was acquitted of murder, ought to know, but she was afraid to go to him in case he might take her up for something she took away long ago. I was an acquaintance of the family; had been Miss Isolina's closest friend, she heard; would I write down what she was going to divulge and send it to Guiseppe Rienzi? She had traveled a long way, forty miles and more, on her old tottering feet, to tell me this for the love of justice, and to keep harm from being done. Would I see that Mr. Rienzi wasn't cheated out of his own?

"I soothed her fears and said I was ready to listen to all she could tell me, as indeed I was, but only from motives of the darkest vengeance—if I could get Isolina Rienzi in my power I was happy. This is the story as I dashed it down.

"The woman before me had been a child's nurse of respectable character apparently, and as such was employed by Mrs. Rienzi to attend her first child; the family were then living in this city, Washington, and it was twenty-two years from the time she was speaking.

"The woman, who was known by the name of Mrs. Cartier had fallen into bad ways, she said, and her recommendations were from some people who only knew the best side of her character; in reality, she belonged to a gang of thieves, and had only entered the house of Mr. Rienzi in order to pilfer what she could. When the baby was a few weeks old, Mr. and Mrs. Rienzi were sent for in haste to see Mrs. Rienzi's mother, who lived at some distance, and was dangerously ill. Consequently the child was left in the care of Mrs. Cartier and an old faithful housekeeper took charge the house. During the absence of her master and mistress, the nurse made her way into a cabinet and stole a large amount of gold plate and some costly jewels, which she carried off to the haunts of her gang, and the articles were instantly smelted in fear of recognition. This system of robbery went on with impunity for some time, until Mrs. Cartier received a sudden check.

"The baby was about a month old, and an uncommonly healthy, active, little creature, when one night, the 3rd of August, the nurse thought she would secure two or three silk dresses which were hanging in Mrs. Rienzi's wardrobe, in a room, just adjoining the nursery, as she had found a key which fitted it. The servants were all in bed, and the baby was quiet in the crib, so Mrs. Cartier hoped to slip out with her bundle, and dispose of it without detection. As she was folding up the dresses in the wardrobe, a shadow came between her and a candle which she left on the nursery table, and peering through the crack of the half closed door, she saw, to her horror, a person in the room, bending over the child's crib. This person was a very handsome young lady, with a long black cloak reaching from her head to her feet, its black hood framing in a very white face with large black eyes. This lady presently stood straight up, and the nurse saw that she carried something 'in her arms, under her cloak. She gazed fixedly at the wardrobe door, and suddenly made a step toward it.

"In an ungovernable fit of fear lest she should be caught in the midst of her theft, the nurse darted out by another door into the corridor, and sped into her own room, which also opened into the hall and nursery. She had no doubt that the visitor was some relative of the family who had arrived late, and came straight to the nursery to see the baby; and in the hope that the garments half folded up on the wardrobe floor might escape the lady's eyes, she flung herself upon her bed, determined to feign sleep should she be called.

"Scarcely had she placed her head upon the pillow than she became conscious of a very strong odor, which at once attacked her senses with benumbing effect. With great presence of mind she tore the pillow from beneath her head and dropped it between her bed and the wall, with a thrilling realization of some foul play being attempted, and lay intently listening for sounds. In a few minutes the nursery door of her room was softly opened, and the lady came in with the shaded candle in her hand. The nurse's back was to the front of the bed, and she simulated a heavy slumber, to which the lady listened for some time, then glided out with a scarcely perceptible laugh, muttering some strange foreign words.

"As soon as she was gone, the nurse sprang up in affected fright, and ran into the nursery, hoping to confront her. But she was gone, and the baby was wailing in its crib in a very unusual manner. She knelt down to hush it, and found to her astonishment that the child which she had left a few minutes before perfectly healthy, was cold as ice, and so dwindled and small that she did not recognize her. At the same moment she heard the well-known scream of Baby Isolina away down in the lower hall, a scream which was not repeated. Instantly divining that the babe had been stolen and another had been put in its place, she snatched the wailing infant up, wrapped a shawl around her shoulders, and ran steadily down into the street, determined to recover her charge, lest she should be blamed for its abduction; and in the investigation which would be made, she knew sufficient would be brought up against her to condemn her to penal servitude.

"Filled with this idea she ran rapidly after the lady, who was far down the street and as she ran, concocted a scheme for recovering the child without implicating herself if possible. She hoped to overtake the lady, and threaten to summon a constable if she did not exchange the child-

ren, but before long she began to be afraid of adopting so
open a course, lest the lady might know of her past mis-
deeds and assume a power over her in consequence. So she
thought she would try what stratagem would do.

"They had plunged into an obscure, though perfectly
quiet street, the nurse always keeping in the darkest
shadows, and at last the lady stopped at the door of a small
brick two-story house and rang a bell. A slatternly girl
appeared with a candle and let her in. To Cartier's delight
she recognized a face which she had seen before. She managed to attract the girl's attention, and beckoned to her.
In a few minutes she reappeared at the door.

"'What do you want?' she whispered, gruffly; 'I'm a respectable girl, earning a character, and don't want to see
one of ye.'

"'You're the girl that cleaned out young Walsingham of
five hundred dollars,' whispered Mrs. Cartier, 'aren't ye,
now?'

"'What's that to you? I've give it up now, and am airn-
ing my character. Go away, Cartier, that's a good un, and
don't spile my chance.'

"'You're quite happy here, then, and have all ye want,
same as if ye was a lady born, as that face o' yours would
make one think?' asked the nurse, insidiously.

"'Quite happy?' echoed the girl, bitterly; 'yes, if slavin'
from gray morning till this hour of night, with a mis'able
ten dollars a month and no soul to speak to, is happiness.'

"'Is that all ye get?' exclaimed the nurse. 'Come, now,
I'm not here for nothing. Somebody has had an eye on ye,
if ye *are* hid in this out-o'-the-way hole. Would ye like to
hear how ye could airn not ten but fifty dollars a month—
work jist mere play?'

"'To be sure I would.'

"'Well, then, let me in somewheres easy, where your
mistress won't find me. Hush! don't waken this baby!'

"The girl eagerly led her up stairs to her own bedroom,
locked the door and lit a candle.

"Having gained admittance to the house, Cartier was
clever enough to avail herself of her advantage. She first
of all applied herself to raising the girl's cupidity by promising liberal 'pickings' if she would return to the gang which
she had left some time previously, in a faint attack of contrition for her crimes. Having overcome all her scruples,

she then proposed that she should leave the house at once, carrying whatever she could find with her. After winning a complete ascendency over her, Cartier asked a few careless questions about the lady whom she had let in.

"Her name was Mrs. Joselyn; she had come from England and taken apartments in this house four days ago. She went out every day, and seemed sometimes to have an awful temper. All the boarders were afraid of her, and she spoke to none of them. She had a baby, pretty young and rather sickly, and it was her idea (the girl's) that Mrs. Joselyn, maybe, was on the hunt for her husband, who seemed to have deserted her.

" 'What do you think of this baby?' said the nurse, throwing off her shawl and displaying the face of the sleeping child.

"The girl stared in surprise, then looked behind its ear, and uttered an exclamation.

" 'Sure as death, it's Mrs. Joselyn's baby! I know her by the bit of a cross behind the ear! Gracious! woman, how came you by her? You aren't a witch, sure?'

" 'Mrs. Joselyn made a mistake, and grabbed the wrong baby in a hurry,' said Cartier, significantly. 'Now I'll put you in the way of getting your fortune made, if ye help me to get back the child I was appointed nurse for. I don't want no fuss made about anything I'm concerned in, as you may easily suppose from the number of prisons I've cheated; so if we can get the exchange made privately and then be off —the better for you and me. How came that mark there? It's not a cross, it's a lance.'

" 'Lance, cross, poker, or shovel, all's one to me, so's you put me in the way to make my fortune. She drew it with a sharp needle yesterday, and when the blood filled the scratch she rubbed black powder on it. I held the baby while she did it.'

" 'Lord, now!' ejaculated the other woman, in a tone of awe. 'What do you think it was for?'

" 'Dunno. Maybe to keep the devil off. Wish she'd warn him of her temper, for it's a "stunner," I can tell ye. But look here, now, it's not for nothing that there thing was scratched into the poor brat's flesh. She said to me when the black powder was all rubbed on. "Now, my girl, look at it well—look at it to remember it. The 'Bloody Spear;' imprint it on your heart; for I may die, and this child may fall into strange hands, and perhaps you of all on earth will be the only witness that this child is a Joselyn." Mad thing! I half believe she's *queer!* But do tell, for gracious sake, how came you by the child? I saw her carry it in past my very eyes.'

"Mrs. Cartier gave some half explanation, all the time carefully perusing the mark on the child's flesh. She resolved to make a duplicate mark on her little charge, if she recovered it, in order to mislead the strange lady should she return to Mr. Rienzi's house. She was strongly superstitious, and perhaps the belief that this mark imparted a peculiar virtue to the wearer helped to influence her impulse.

"'Has Mrs. Joselyn any plunder, worth?" she asked, cunningly.

"'Lots o' jewels, cash, dresses, rare ones,' whispered the girl.

"'Well, you look here now. I'll take all the risk of this lark. You make up your bundle and be ready, or stay here another day, just to shift the blame off yourself, and leave all your things open for to be searched. And if ye show me Mrs. Joselyn's rooms, I'll slip in and take what I can find, and leave this here baby to its owner, and all you'll have to do is just to keep watch and give me a safe passage out. Then give warning, and jine us to-morrow night. The old place, you know.'

"'All right, I'll not be in this mess there, but mind, I must have my share of the plunder.'

"'Half, as sure as I'm an honest woman.'

"'Surer than that ma'am, it must be.'

"'Little Toad! Well, then, sure as you're a born beauty.'

"'Humph! I'm spoilt in the breeding then! Well, I'll trust ye.'

"The two women stole down to Mrs. Joselyn's room,. and the nurse made her way safely in. The heavy breathing of the lady showed that she was asleep, and the room was very dark. The nurse coolly struck a match, and discovered by its aid where the bed was. The infant which had been stolen, was lying just asleep in a cradle alongside, and holding the lighted match in its face its nurse made out beyond a doubt that it was Mrs. Rienzi's child.

"Hastily she lifted, without awakening it, and put the other child in its place, who began to wail piteously. The sleeper only breathed the more heavily, and muttered a few words. Mrs. Cartier took courage and struck another match. By the light of this, she found an open box on the dressing-table containing black powder which she slipped in her pocket, then she secured the casket of jewels which was carelessly displayed on the table, and looked about for the cash which had been mentioned.

"At this moment Baby Isolina began to struggle preparatory to giving one of her imperative screams, and the nurse darted out, and flying past her accomplice stifled the child's cries until she reached the street. She ran every step of the way back to Mr. Rienzi's house, and reached it perfectly undiscovered. She did not dare to lay the child down until she had scratched with a needle the identical spear she had seen in the other, and rubbed in the black powder, at which the child screamed so violently that the housekeeper came rushing in full of alarm. But Mrs. Cartier allowed her to suspect nothing, and soon had the babe to sleep again.

"Mrs. Cartier had received such a fright from this midnight episode that she resolved to leave her situation, before her employers came home, which she did a few days subsequently, only waiting for another woman to take her place.

"She carried the box of jewels to the chief of her gang, retaining, however, the largest diamond necklace, upon every gold medallion of which was engraved the arms of some house. The diamond and a medallion linked to it, were all that remained of the necklace, and the old woman gave them to me as proofs of the truth of her story. The arms are those of the Joselyns.

"Mrs. Cartier saw the girl two days after her adventure, and heard from her that Mrs. Joselyn's child had been found dead in its cradle next morning—'With a face as black as if it was in a convulsion-fit, and a blue ring round its neck!' she declared, and Mrs. Joselyn was crazy-like and didn't seem to grieve a bit, and hung over the little body for hours wondering how it was so like her baby, and when Cartier ventured back to the boarding-house on some pretext, she heard that Mrs. Joselyn was stark mad, and they did not know what to do with her.

"The whole of this business caused Cartier considerable uneasiness lest she might be implicated and drawn into trouble.   She left Washington as soon as possible, and plunged into evil ways in New York.

"She sank very low, until her crimes had made her so well known to the authorities that she fled from the States, and joined a gipsy gang with whom she had lived for the last ten years, and gained some little tact in telling fortunes.

"During their wanderings in New York State she had become acquainted with some of the facts of Isolina Rienzi's trial.   Miss Rienzi was about to be torn from her friends under a false plea; she managed to obtain a sight of Mrs. Beaumont at Greely's Mills, and instantly recognized her, despite the change in her appearance.

"For the sake of the beautiful babe whom she had dandled in her arms, and nursed like a mother, she had taken a long and perilous journey to Washington to put the facts of that long committed transaction in my hands, who she said was a close friend, and would be glad to save Miss Rienzi from trouble.

"With earnest and repeated injunctions that I should at once lay this story before Mr. Rienzi, the old woman received a small piece of money from me and went away. And I—wicked—revengeful—could not bring myself to serve my poor friend so far, but waited seemingly to see what would happen.

"Some three months afterward, the same old gipsy woman sought my presence again.   She was double with rheumatism, foot-sore, famished, and distressed in mind.

"She said she had been traveling night and day for four weeks; that Miss Isolina Rienzi had been claimed by Mrs. Beaumont and was going to be taken away to Canada.   She had got hold of the information from the chief gipsy of the camp, who was bribed by Ralph Morecombe to assist them to escape.   She had seen the young Miss Rienzi going to bid her sister good-by, and she knew exactly how Miss Ivanilla would be hoodwinked, and she had come here to implore me in the name of justice to do something to restore the young lady to her family.   Surely I had not obeyed her former injunctions—Heaven's curses on me if I had not; the secret which for her own safety she had kept so long, was burning her heart up with remorse.

"I reassured her once more with fair promises, but what she had told me filled me with vengeful exultation. Isolina should be consigned to the companionship of such a woman as Mrs. Beaumont; yes, that should be her punishment.

"The old woman went away, and was found in a field some miles out of town, dead by a brook-side, her blistered feet in the water, her old scarlet cloak drawn over her face, dead from hunger and exhaustion.

"I knew that I alone could right Isolina Rienzi, and yet I hardened my heart and did nothing. I have kept this secret, well-knowing the terrible wrong I was doing Victor Joselyn. I have kept it until it was criminal to keep it, until anguish had crept deep into your hapless family, and you mourned not only a sister lost, but a sister who was nothing to you. One word of mine would have served you long ago. I might have said 'Canada,' when your wild surmises pointed to every country beyond this hemisphere, but I triumphed in the sorrow of those who had witnessed my humiliation. I gloried in having Cecil Beaumont recklessly fighting off the sorrow which his mad passion had brought him, and—I did nothing.

"This has been the revenge I swore to you on my carriage step, and it has been a bitter one; my head is in the dust with remorse; I can never, never face you, nor smile again, while conscience holds up this foul wrong before me.

"It is Miss Belle Cranstown who reached my strong heart and awakened my conscience; for months she has been a persevering, brave friend, drawing me nearer and nearer to repentance, in spite of my struggles. The link is broken at last. I have poured my guilty confessions at her feet; this is the course she encouraged me to take. She says to fear nothing, that you would forgive. I do not ask it or expect it. I am not worthy to utter one word in your presence. I have wronged you beyond forgiveness, and shall mourn it to the day of my death. Heaven keep you from all evil. Your repentant,

"LILLIA MEREDITH."

CHAPTER XXXV.

DONNA BELLA.

"She is coming, my own, my sweet;
　　Were it ever so airy a tread,
　My heart would hear her and beat,
　　Were it earth in an earthy bed."—TENNYSON.

The September sun was dipping into the rosy waters of ocean; he had left a throne of " turquois and almondine," upon which one tiny star was sitting, looking down to the lowly and lovely earth.

A little family were gathered on the southern veranda, where the ardent light came round in shafts and refractions softer than aught out of heaven, and touched the dangling creepers with fringes of gold and nestled among a bed of hoar petronias, gilding all their velvet and diaphanous petals into rarest fairy-cups, and seeking out the dusky King of the Blacks as it swung incense from its tiny censer.

My father sat in his bamboo chair and broad panama, with perhaps as bright a smile as that of other days, though softened now into a more beaming humility, as he passed one hand over the other in dreaming mood.

My mother stood by his side, her fair and gentle hands clasped contentedly on his shoulder, her face so mild, so exceedingly sweet and pale, raised slightly to the painted vault of heaven—the dear mother who had loved more than us all, and borne most meekly.

My husband—kind, steadfast, worthy of his name— paced before them, pouring some of the ever-present sunshine of his own heart into theirs; and apart at the western side, where the moan of the ocean smote our ears, stood Victor Joselyn and I—the only sister this world held for him.

The Atlantic cable had done its work—a message had flashed from our joyful hearts to that lonely Joselyn Wold, which caused the master to leave his throngs of grateful people and schemes of noble philanthropy to fly over thousands of watery miles to meet the long-mourned Rose of his faithful heart.

We were all gathered into Silverlea, which was the parent nest every summer, and the sweetest nest ever brood came home to; we were all gathered in, waiting for the long lost one, to tie Love's knot, and make the rosy band complete.

But day after day had passed; friends had poured in and gone away again; Victor had arrived, feverish and incredulous, to watch once more with spirit-sickening eagerness; hearts were sinking, low prayers were stealing up to heaven —yet she was not here.

Three weeks since that day of joyful tidings—and she could have been here a fortnight ago—vague fears were whispering in every heart: why did she tarry?

The eyes of love had stolen so often down these gravel walks, that they were dim and wavering, and hidden in a patient hand, the eyes of hope took up the watch, and were blinded and dazzled all at once.

Yet it was only a simple garden-hat, bound with black ribbon, just such as had shone between these rows of fir-trees two years ago, one still summer morn. It came steadily on, now disappearing behind the aspen shades, now gleaming nearer, a speck of white in a mass of dark green —no, it has stopped—where has it gone? Not back?

Poor soul! she is tired; she leans upon our iron gate; she bends her face on her crossed arms. If she were not so poor-looking—so lagging and foot-sore, I would say—Ah! heart of mine, leap not so tumultuously! *Can* it be—oh! can it be *my sister?*

One wild, glad cry! I am flying down to the dusty traveler. I cannot wait to speak my joy; I am going to clasp my darling close, close, close! I am going to drag her in from the flinty road, and bring her home, and lay her in the arms of him whose wife Heaven gave her to be. Oh, my heart, break not with joy!

She lifted her pale, tearful face. Her celestial eyes fell upon me, bright, tender, brave as the dauntless Minerva's who leans upon a spear; a slow, sweet smile broke over her lips.

"Come in!" I exclaimed, pushing open the gate to get at her; "don't stand out here."

"Is this my welcome? my faithful sister," she breathed softy.

And that reminded me of another's right.

"Come!" I cried, with hysterical vehemence, "Victor is

here, not your brother—that has been proved—not your brother, dear Isolina!"

"What! and I have given him such sorrow! Does he care to meet me now?"

White she grew as a Syrian lily. She drew back and hid her face in her trembling hands.

For he was coming, her lord, her life, her fate. He was coming, and her heart was failing her, with overwhelming love. She would sink beneath this fierce delight; she would drink one glance from his shining eyes—one glance, and die!

But he took her sweet hands kindly, gently; he spared her rushing agitation, and denied himself for her sake. He vailed these passionate heart-throbs behind a calm voice, and bent a gentle, reassuring gaze upon her.

"Do not fear me," he murmured; "I am your friend or your brother—until you wish to change the title."

"My husband!" she breathed, relinquishing herself to him, "since you love me still—yours till I die!"

Reverently he took her to his breast; he did not even now overwhelm her with the passion which filled him; this frail, trembling form must be guarded kindly; it must be cherished for a while ere it could bear its burden of happiness.

We led her up between us to to the vine-wreathed veranda, where her own true, dear parents were standing, hand in hand, rooted with joy, only able to cling together and gaze, and gaze, and gaze upon their Isolina.

Ah! life is like a lattice window in the sunlight; light and shade—light and shade; bars of gold and bars of gloom, until the frail lattice is shattered, and the light flows in with no more shadows.

But hush these haunting whispers! What might not restored love do? What might not peace and rest do?

Little by little we gained from her the story of her last two years of exile; she told it once and never reverted to it again; her gentle spirit held aloof forever after from the dark and painful memory of another's crimes. She had found, in gathering together Mrs. Beaumont's few effects, after her death, an open packet addressed to the deceased, which she had recognized as that which Ralph Morecombe had given to Mrs. Beaumont in the cottage in the forest. It was written by Barbara Cartier, the gipsy woman, and was a full account of Isolina Rienzi's real parentage, and

an entreaty that the Italian lady would return Miss Rienzi
to her friends, for if she did not Cartier would inform
Guiseppe Rienzi herself of the attempted abduction which
had taken place so long ago.

The explanations were ended at last; she was fully en-
throned in her rightful place, and could look from face to
face of her kindred with thankful eyes; she had a claim
upon us all—even upon Ernest, who waited upon her with
such brotherly assiduity. But best gift of all, the priceless
love of that true heaven-chastened heart, which was hers in
holy purity and rightfulness!

Ah! hold her in your arms—this wasted, ethereal form;
fling chains and chains of love around her, to bind her
from the spirit-land; come between her and these amaran-
thine wreaths, which wait her in the skies. You have loved
her fondly; you have mourned her long; oh, keep her angel
wings close pinioned —woo her back to earth!

CHAPTER XXXVI.

THE STORY OF THE VOW.

"But she, with sick and scornful looks, arose
To her full height, her stately stature drawn.
'My youth,' she said, 'was blasted with a curse.' "
TENNYSON.

My dear sister's little history, when from time to time
she had been torn from us, was a very mournful one.
Ralph Morecombe had come, like a rushing wind, into
the cottage, flung the few articles of clothing and valu-
ables together, and carried the fugitives off without a moment's warning. They escaped through a road but little
known across the hills to the nearest railway station, took
cars for Philadelphia, and proceeded by uninterrupted travel
to Canada, where they buried themselves in a remote French
Canadian village, to which there was little possibility of
tracing them. Mrs. Beaumont had seemed satisfied, and
signified her intention of remaining with only her daughter
and Morecombe to attend her.

Morecombe was a trusty protector, laboring faithfully for
their comfort, and becoming more and more attached to the
hapless young lady whom he had helped to bring into such
slavery. With daily increasing remorse he saw her bearing

unrepiningly a burden that was far too crushing for her slender frame, and when she would have failed through weakness and discouragement, he studied her wants, and guarded her from many a needless vigil with the capricious and exacting lunatic.

In a few months the very slender stock which Mrs. Beaumont possessed was swallowed up, and in order to gratify the extravagant whims of her who was formerly a woman of luxury, Isolina opened a small school. The gentle fortitude of my nobler sister shone out.

The pale and tender face grew daily sweeter; her very presence seemed to calm the troubled air; the American school-mistress came to be spoken of as a saint uncanonized, and the children all thought that the Madonna must be like Mlle. Lucille, as she was called, who was so good to her poor, afflicted mother, and so sweet to everybody.

And a day came when her cross was lifted at last. The wild, gloomy eyes had appealed to her for the last time, and the murmuring lips were still, and the word of confession which had tortured that trembling soul too late, was unspoken forever, and the worn child was free.

Ah! free to nestle home to hearts, which would close round her, and warm her chill life into fresh hopes—free to love unchecked, to taste the gifts whick God intended for her. She had expended the last of her scanty means in burying Mrs. Beaumont, and had but a few shillings to take her the long journey overland to New York. And now the old Italian, Moresco, signified that he would take her safely home to her friends; he would not have her without a protector, if she would take him to be her servant, as her mother had done before her.

But Ralph was claimed by another Master. On the day following the funeral Isolina found the nurse Cartier's letter to Mrs. Beaumont carefully concealed in her dressing-case, which, in the first astonishment of reading, she brought to Ralph. He recognized it as the packet which a gipsy boy from the camp had brought while Isolina was relating the circumstances which separated her from her family. The boy had been sent by Baree with injunctions to deliver it into Morecombe's hands for Mrs. Beaumont.

Such is the outline of Rienzi's experiences. We never heard the full weight of that trial which had rested upon her from her own lips; another, after this meeting, when our dear girl was far away in her husband's stately Wold, a good old priest, who was getting up a university for pious nuns, came all the way from the distant Canadian valley in which the French village nestled to relieve good Catholic purses of their superfluity, and from him we heard how truly heroic, patient, and self-suffering our Isolina had been to her reputed mother, whose terrible temper and daring infidelity had struck awe through the villagers.

And here is the strange letter which Isolina found, sealed and addressed to my father, and which began with the words:

"MY VENDETTA."

" You, Guiseppe Rienzi, first woke my heart to the bitter sensation of passion. I was beautiful and proud, of noble family, and an heiress. I might have wed a marquis, but I loved you. What were you? Bah! A student—an artist, with his bread to win—a sculptor without a chisel—a visionary, with a *respectable* name (bah, again!), and a slender patrimony when your elder brother, Andrea, should be served.

"If I had put my foot upon your hands for stepping-stones across the mire, I should have honored you above your position; but I flung my wealth, and my beauty, and my heart at your feet, and prayed you to deign to wear the trifles in your bosom. Who could withstand Gemma Lancinetto? You were dazzled, and I thought you loved me. I loaded you with chains of passion-flowers, and thought you were my captive; but it was *I* who wore the chains of iron, and not the flowers. I was the prisoner.

"You came to me one day; your eyes were flashing like the sun in his angry strength, and I trembled.

" 'They say Guiseppe, the poor student, schemes for Donna Gemma's gold,' you said, 'and if you love me, as you say you do, you will grant me a favor.'

" 'And what is that?'

" 'Publicly give your wealth to endow some church, and come to me a penniless bride. If you love me, you will love my honor.'

" 'And what an inconsistency that would be!' I jibed. 'I, who scoff at their temples, to endow one! I only glory in my wealth, and in showering it upon you, to throw it away!'

" I had unlocked the magic-box, and the gem rose up from its lurking-place which was to destroy me.

" 'You scoff at their temples, signora. What does that mean?' demanded my master.

" I laughed scornfully.

" 'It means that there is no God on my earth!' I said. 'God? Who is he? An essence—a myth? You are my God! I bow to but one divinity!'

" You went away, and I laughed until my maid knelt at my feet, and implored me to be calm. I pictured how my passionate love would craze your young heart with joy when alone.

" The next day a letter from you was brought to my silken pillow. It was not a lover's frenzied prayer for pardon for your harshness; it was a demand to know what creed I professed.

" My creed was the shortest on earth; I was an infidel. I had always been one. I believe I was born without a soul. Gayly I told you so, but added that my heart was more to you than a thousand souls. What calmness—what lack of worldly wisdom you displayed! You came to me loaded with the gifts I had lavished on you—the love-tokens, the honors—and flung them back to me.

" 'Henceforth, Guiseppe is bound no more to a woman without a God,' you said.

" My passion rose. I demanded—threatened. You showed no fear, but sternly silenced me. *I* to be threatened thus!

" ' I rose humiliated, overcome, terrified, and begged forgiveness, and you left me with my tears undried. Gemma Lancinetto was forsaken by the obscure stripling whom she had proudly worn next her heart. I met the curled lip, the vailed eye, the cynical smile when I ventured forth from my angry solitude. Those who before had worshiped my shadow shrugged their shoulders and crossed themselves. I was branded as 'the woman without a soul,' and was fabled a Xantippe. All shunned me, but the lowest and most sordid of my once countless throng of lovers. I found at the age of twenty-one that my life was blasted. I stood, as it were, unvailed before a hissing world, and it execrated me.

" Then in my heart of hearts, I made my vendetta against Guiseppe Rienzi. Oh, it was bitter, deep, lasting!

" Shall I detail my reckless life to you? No! You shall

know it if ever we meet at that Bar where you say God is—
'*if ever.*' My life shall be an eternal secret until then.

"Go to your grave with the pangs Gemma Lancinetto has
given you, and say, haughty ingrate, have I not promised
you life? If you had never seen Donna Gemma in her
beauty, would your hair have been so gray, your step as lagging on life's thorny way?

"Yes, I have sped my vendetta—my sweet, sweet vengeance!

"Guiseppe, these lines are for you, when your victorious
enemy sleeps in her bed of earth.   GEMMA."

Such was the singular letter which came to my father
from the dead woman, and it cleared him forever from all
blame but such as gilded his character with new laurels,
while it threw into the blackest shades the unholy passions which had wagered a life-long war in that poor heart
of dust.

CHAPTER XXXVII.

A BRIDE WITH ANGEL'S WINGS.

"From belt to belt of crimson seas
  Our leagues of color streaming far
  To where in yonder orient star
A hundred spirits whisper 'Peace.'"—TENNYSON.

For the last time I open these pages, and inscribe the
closing scenes of my beloved memories.

I would not have that Secret Vendetta unsped, for a
blessing was hidden in the hand of hate.

Come and look with me once more on "The Beautiful
Rienzi"—a last look, reader.

She is a bride for the second time. This is the evening
of her second wedding-day. You see the golden circlet
gleaming on the silver-pale hand. It catches the eye of
some one near—her husband. He takes her hand—'twill
never vanish from his heart until the cold hand of death
clasps it. He holds it in his close, close clasp, and lifts it
to his lips.

"You will stay with me a little while—my wife?"

Her pure face flushed deeply. Her eyes dwelt on his
wistfully.

" If God will spare me," is the meek reply; " and I think He will. I ought to comfort you before I go."

Then we gather closer, and the summer sea booms in with a louder swell.

There is Doctor Pemberton watching the bride's face with the constancy of a lover, and making private notes of approval or dissatisfaction. Until she need have no more watching, this faithful friend will guard her from every chilling wind with a tender solicitude only second to her husband.

There sits our father, and the gentle companion of his life, calm, smiling, thoughtful, after their long struggle; clinging the more closely to the Great Hand, which helped them since the Secret Vendetta was sped; trusting their loved ones all to Heaven, and fearing not much for future sorrows.

And here, with her bright face all sunny with the joy which others' joy ever brought to her, kneels sweet Belle Cranstown at my feet—the cherished friend, adviser, and comforter of my Ernest and me.

The musk-laden flowers flaunt in the shifting air; a thicket of yellow roses scatter their petals before the feet of the passers-by.

Softly they walk—warily after life's fevered battle. The Star of Hope is shining on them with a silver promise of days to come. They are looking into life's cup of sweetness, and, lo! it is not drained yet. They look into each other's saddened eyes, and find that love can have a resurrection; and so she gazes upon the thin, grave face with a gush of womanly tenderness and regret. She cannot speak for that past shame and sorrow, but she draws his head to her swelling bosom, and weeps upon it. God bless Cecil and Lillia—they may be happy yet.

And I am happy to sink into a cipher when my brother Victor is by. It is joy for me to see them joined at last. There will be paradise below when thus are united the noble and the good.

Come away. The shadows leave them, and the moon gleams in. Let us, too, leave them in their heaven of restored love.

*   *   *   *   *   *

She sleeps beneath the daisies of her English home. A

marble monument holds her name and her grave; fond hearts hold her saintly memory; God holds the chastened soul.

Let us not weep. She has done her work. Her gentle hands have scattered roses long enough for others—may they not hold the palm in heaven now?

God gave her the one wish of her sweet and humble spirit—He lent her for a season to bless the home of him she loved, and he is grateful, and repines not that his treasure went away to rest in heaven.

She has vanished from his stately halls, and her serene brows are crowned with bliss unspeakable, and his heart has followed her through these gates of glittering pearl, and the poor, and the needy, and the oppressed enshrine the lonely Joselyn in their grateful hearts, and call him a true nobleman.

We do not mourn her dead. We know that she sits by the gates of heaven waiting for us. Perchance she holds them ajar to watch over us, and shed her overbrimming bliss upon us. And we see this infant angel which she left to comfort us—the orphan boy—the heir of Joselyn Wold. He nestles smiling in my arms, and lifts his mother's blue, seraphic eyes to me. I weep, but I am filled with joy. I clasp him closer, and pray that he may also have her beautiful spirit.

Brave, patient, meek *carissima mia*, we shall not part in heaven.

Close the curtains on memory's cell; shut the blinds; I have recorded the end of THE SECRET VENDETTA.

[THE END.]

"A DEBT OF VENGEANCE," by Mrs. E. BURKE COLLINS, will be published in the next number (42) of THE SELECT SERIES.

DENMAN THOMPSON'S OLD HOMESTEAD.

STREET & SMITH'S SELECT SERIES No. 23.

Price, 25 Cents.

Some Opinions of the Press.

" As the probabilities are remote of the play 'The Old Homestead' being seen anywhere but in large cities it is only fair that the story of the piece should be printed. Like most stories written from plays it contains a great deal which is not said or done on the boards, yet it is no more verbose than such a story should be, and it gives some good pictures of the scenes and people who for a year or more have been delighting thousands nightly. Uncle Josh, Aunt Tildy, Old Cy Prime, Reuben, the mythical Bill Jones, the sheriff and all the other characters are here, beside some new ones. It is to be hoped that the book will make a large sale, not only on its merits, but that other play owners may feel encouraged to let their works be read by the many thousands who cannot hope to see them on the stage."—*N. Y. Herald*, June 2d.

" Denman Thompson's 'The Old Homestead' is a story of clouds and sunshine alternating over a venerated home; of a grand old man, honest and blunt, who loves his honor as he loves his life, yet suffers the agony of the condemned in learning of the deplorable conduct of a wayward son; a story of country life, love and jealousy, without an impure thought, and with the healthy flavor of the fields in every chapter. It is founded on Denman Thompson's drama of 'The Old Homestead.' "—*N. Y. Press*, May 26th.

" Messrs. Street & Smith, publishers of the *New York Weekly*, have brought out in book-form the story of ' The Old Homestead,' the play which, as produced by Mr. Denman Thompson, has met with uch wondrous success. It will probably have a great sale, thus justifying the foresight of the publishers in giving the drama this permanent fiction form."—*N. Y. Morning Journal*, June 2d.

" The popularity of Denman Thompson's play of ' The Old Homestead' has encouraged Street & Smith, evidently with his permission, to publish a good-sized novel with the same title, set in the same scenes and including the same characters and more too. The book is a fair match for the play in the simple good taste and real ability with which it is written. The publishers are Street & Smith, and they have gotten the volume up in cheap popular form."—*N. Y. Graphic*, May 29.

"Denman Thompson's play, 'The Old Homestead,' is familiar, at least by reputation, to every play-goer in the country. Its truth to nature and its simple pathos have been admirably preserved in this story, which is founded upon it and follows its incidents closely. The requirements of the stage make the action a little hurried at times, but the scenes described are brought before the mind's eye with remarkable vividness, and the portrayal of life in the little New England town is almost perfect. Those who have never seen the play can get an excellent idea of what it is like from the book. Both are free from sentimentality and sensation, and are remarkably healthy in tone."—*Albany Express*.

"Denman Thompson's 'Old Homestead' has been put into story-form and is issued by Street & Smith. The story will somewhat explain to those who have not seen it the great popularity of the play."—*Brooklyn Times*, June 8th.

"The fame of Denman Thompson's play, 'Old Homestead,' is world-wide. Tens of thousands have enjoyed it, and frequently recall the pure, lively pleasure they took in its representation. This is the story told in narrative form as well as it was told on the stage, and will be a treat to all, whether they have seen the play or not."—*National Tribune*, Washington, D. C.

"Here we have the shaded lanes, the dusty roads, the hilly pastures, the peaked roofs, the school-house, and the familiar faces of dear old Swanzey, and the story which, dramatized, has packed the largest theater in New York, and has been a success everywhere because of its true and sympathetic touches of nature. All the incidents which have held audiences spell-bound are here recorded—the accusation of robbery directed against the innocent boy, his shame, and leaving home; the dear old Aunt Tilda, who has been courted for thirty years by the mendacious Cy Prime, who has never had the courage to propose; the fall of the country boy into the temptations of city life, and his recovery by the good old man who braves the metropolis to find him. The story embodies all that the play tells, and all that it suggests as well."—*Kansas City Journal*, May 27th.

THE COUNTY FAIR.
By NEIL BURGESS.

Written from the celebrated play now running its second continuous season in New York, and booked to run a third season in the same theater.

The scenes are among the New Hampshire hills, and picture the bright side of country life. The story is full of amusing events and happy incidents, something after the style of our "Old Homestead," which is having such an enormous sale.

"THE COUNTY FAIR" will be one of the great hits of the season, and should you fail to secure a copy you will miss a literary treat. It is a spirited romance of town and country, and a faithful reproduction of the drama, with the same unique characters, the same graphic scenes, but with the narrative more artistically rounded, and completed than was possible in the brief limits of a dramatic representation. This touching story effectively demonstrates that it is possible to produce a novel which is at once wholesome and interesting in every part, without the introduction of an impure thought or suggestion. Read the following

OPINIONS OF THE PRESS:

Mr. Neil Burgess has rewritten his play, "The County Fair," in story form. It rounds out a narrative which is comparatively but sketched in the play. It only needs the first sentence to set going the memory and imagination of those who have seen the latter and whet the appetite for the rest of this lively conception of a live dramatist.—*Brooklyn Daily Eagle.*

As "The County Fair" threatens to remain in New York for a long time the general public out of town may be glad to learn that the playwright has put the piece into print in the form of a story. A tale based upon a play may sometimes lack certain literary qualities, but it never is the sort of thing over which any one can fall asleep. Fortunately, "The County Fair" on the stage and in print is by the same author, so there can be no reason for fearing that the book misses any of the points of the drama which has been so successful.—*N. Y. Herald.*

The idea of turning successful plays into novels seems to be getting popular. The latest book of this description is a story reproducing the action and incidents of Neil Burgess' play, "The County Fair." The tale, which is a romance based on scenes of home life and domestic joys and sorrows, follows closely the lines of the drama in story and plot.—*Chicago Daily News.*

Mr. Burgess' amusing play, "The County Fair." has been received with such favor that he has worked it over and expanded it into a novel of more than 200 pages. It will be enjoyed even by those who have never heard the play and still more by those who have.—*Cincinnati Times-Star.*

This touching story effectively demonstrates that it is possible to produce a novel which is at once wholesome and interesting in every part, without the introduction of an impure thought or suggestion.—*Albany Press.*

Street & Smith have issued "The County Fair." This is a faithful reproduction of the drama of that name and is an affecting and vivid story of domestic life, joy and sorrow, and rural scenes.—*San Francisco Call.*

This romance is written from the play of this name and is full of touching incidents.—*Evansville Journal.*

It is founded on the popular play of the same name, in which Neil Burgess, who is also the author of the story, has achieved the dramatic success of the season.—*Fall River Herald.*

The County Fair is No. 33 of "The Select Series," for sale by all Newsdealers, or will be sent, on receipt of price, 25 cents, to any address, postpaid, by **STREET & SMITH, Publishers, 25-31 Rose st., New York.**